# Confessions of a Nervous Shiksa

## Tracy McArdle

**In this clever debut novel, a film studio executive can't help wondering why her life can't be like th movies—or, at the very least, less like harsh realit**

Alexis Manning is a Los Angeles studio publicity V.P. wi a sick cat, a broken heart, professional frustrations, and sneaking suspicion she should have been a veterinarian. Whe her fiancé tells her she has to convert to Judaism or say goodbye, Alexis's well-scripted life hits the cutting room flo

Naturally, it's time for her to rework the plot line. Secure only in the knowledge that everything would be much easier she were starring in a movie, Alexis replays poignant scenes from favorite films as she breaks her own story down into dramatic clips in search of a tidy ending. The celluloid trials and triumphs of Russell Crowe, Melanie Griffith, Robert DeNiro, and Diane Keaton end up blending with Alexis's ov frustrations and yearnings, from temperamental actors and astronomical vet bills to the sweet memories of a simple childhood in Vermont. The result is cinema verite turned ins out, a homage to Tinseltown luminaries as seen through the lens of an endearing heroine's struggle to find herself.

**Tracy McArdle** lives in Boston, Massachusetts.

*Fiction*
Downtown Press Trade Paperback Original
August 2005
$13.00 U.S./$17.95 Can.
1-4165-0321-8 • 978-1-4165-0321-7
320 pages • 5 $\frac{5}{16}$ x 8 $\frac{1}{4}$

"Alexis—?" Dr. Kreezak said encouragingly. . . .

"I just don't understand why we can't have both traditions," I wailed into an oversized tissue. "Lots of families do that."

It wasn't that I wanted to deny our nonexistent, unborn children their Jewishness—I just didn't want to have to fake my own.

"You don't have to *believe* it!" snapped David.

"Then what's the *point?!*" I demanded.

After an hour, Dr. Kreezak pretty much told us what we already knew—that we seemed to be at an impasse and that there was nowhere to go but apart. What more could she say? "I commend you both for being so honest," she offered. "Would one or both of you like to come back next week? No, I'm sorry I don't accept credit cards. No, I don't validate parking."

Then David and I argued about that, me allowing that it was permissible for her not to validate, him snorting that for $125 an hour, covering our parking was the *least* she could do. No, our differences weren't just religious. In hindsight, the Christmas Eve Conversion Ultimatum was basically the straw that broke the shiksa's back.

# Confessions of a Nervous Shiksa

## Tracy McArdle

doWn
tOwn
press

New York   London   Toronto   Sydney

An *Original* Publication of POCKET BOOKS

 DOWNTOWN PRESS, published by Pocket Books
1230 Avenue of the Americas
New York, NY 10020

ISBN-13: 978-1-4165-0321-7
ISBN-10:    1-4165-0321-8

First Downtown Press trade paperback edition August 2005

10   9   8   7   6   5   4   3   2   1

DOWNTOWN PRESS and colophon are trademarks of Simon & Schuster, Inc.

Manufactured in the United States of America

For information regarding special discounts for bulk purchases, please contact Simon & Schuster Special Sales at 1-800-456-6798 or business@simonandschuster.com.

Designed by Jaime Putorti

*for my parents*

# acknowledgments

This story would not have been possible without the love, support, wit, wine, tolerance, music and humor of Samantha Glynne, Kimberly Jones, Val Van Galder, Robin Jonas, Christina Lynch, David Grabias, Anne Edgar, Daniel Mackenzie (listen to his music), Scott and Wendy McArdle, Marcos and Lisa Siega and Nick and Clarke Osborne. Thank you to Suzanne Pelletier and Nicole Rothrock for reading everything over the years. A special shout out to all the talented, ink-stained wretches of the Naushon Writers Workshop. My profound gratitude to the three superheroes of publishing: Sally Brady, my gifted teacher and cherished friend; Lauren McKenna, my deeply passionate and highly overworked editor; and Paula Balzer, the world's most honest agent. Thank you to my family for entertaining my literary ambitions over three decades, especially Mom and Dad for making every living relative and most of Cape Cod read my work. Much love and thanks to Nathaniel Francis Ryder Brady for teaching me presence, balance, and the finer nuances of the Sea Devil. And of course, my beloved sister Robin—you did it, didn't you, Cat?

Every so often somebody feels the need to list The Top 100 Films of All Time. There are two films that inevitably make the top ten and often the top three. They are, of course, *Citizen Kane* and *Casablanca*. The profound lesson of *Citizen Kane* is not that Orson Welles was a genius at 25, or that its flawless structure has yet to be matched. It is the knowable solace that no matter how accomplished, powerful or rich you are; that even if you've conquered and devoured everything out of life, nothing matters if you're alone at the end, mourning the loss of your childhood, the only time you were ever truly happy. *Casablanca* makes the cut not due to beloved Bogart and witty one-liners but because of one dirty, universal secret: Every woman in the world knows what it feels like to choose the wrong man for the right reasons.

And so do I. It happened in the year 2000, the turn of the new millennium, in a sunny land far, far away. And if it weren't for the hundreds of movies catalogued lovingly in my brain, I never would have gotten through it . . .

# One

| DATE/TIME | CONTACT | NUMBER | MESSAGE |
|---|---|---|---|
| 12/28/99 9:02 a.m. | Viv | Home | She'll be back in the office tomorrow—Call when you get in—how was your Xmas? |
| 12/28/99 9:05 a.m. | Donna/ Accounting | x145 | Why did we pay director's friend Roberta (can't read last name) $10k on *Late Nights*—we can pay her; just need to know what she did on film? |
| 12/28/99 9:09 a.m. | Billy | 323-555-7639 | What is David's cell #? Needs to talk to him about music for the play—how was Xmas in Vermont? |

| DATE/TIME | CONTACT | NUMBER | MESSAGE |
|---|---|---|---|
| 12/28/99 9:15 a.m. | Gail M./ MPAA Ratings Board | 310-238-0039 | *Late Nights* clip of D.H. is disapproved—cannot say "fag" or "candy-ass" on broadcast; re-edit and re-submit. Call if ??'s |
| 12/28/99 9:23 a.m. | Your sister Molly | Home | Checking on you . . . Misses you and hopes you're ok after what happened at Xmas. |
| 12/28/99 9:37 a.m. | Gary/Good Fun Promotions | You have # He's in St. Bart's til Jan. 3 | How many *Late Nights* hats do you want for Sundance? *Late Nights* condoms or thongs for cocktail party? |
| 12/28/99 9:40 a.m. | Sara-Anne | Home | How was Xmas? Call me! Hasa Littorai Pinot Noir-Theriot vineyard |
| 12/28/99 9:49 a.m. | Babette (D.H.'s agent) | Cell: 323-399-3947 | Needs 6 tickets to opening night parties at Sundance & schedule of what/ where they are/who'll be there; plse fax to her home; 310-299-3987; will studio provide a car? |

| DATE/TIME | CONTACT | NUMBER | MESSAGE |
|---|---|---|---|
| 12/28/99 9:50 a.m. | Dr. Niblack | VCA Animal Clinic | "Little" is due for her shots. |
| 12/28/99 9:55 a.m. | Eugene R. (think it was Eugene, director of *Shades of Gray*, but he wouldn't say) | No # (called from pay phone in Central Park?) | Why aren't we listed in *N.Y. Times* "Movies to See in 2000?" "Porky's 5 in 3D" is listed and we're not? "What the F*@!" (left on voice mail) |
| 12/28/99 9:59 a.m. | Tracie Mansfield | The *Tonight Show* | Has a hole in sched. this week for 2nd guest—who do you have in town (No to Eugene R; she already knows he's available— he called her). P.S. how was your Xmas? |

And this was all before ten.

Returning to your call sheet after Christmas is never fun, but this particular year was profoundly un-fun. Adriane, my turbo-charged assistant, was a machine. Like any seasoned Hollywood assistant, she knew how to get to the point of each call quickly and efficiently. Normally she'd e-mail or fax me the call sheet each day I was out of town, but not during the Christmas break. How *was* Christmas 1999? The worst in thirty years (the title previously held by 1970, when, to my horror, my older brother gobbled up the prearranged cookies and milk before my eyes while wickedly proclaiming there was no Santa Claus and, adding insult to injury, refusing to share the cookies).

Christmas 1999 was markedly worse, because from its start, from the cheek-kissed drop off at LAX by the trusty Adriane, I knew, I *knew* something was not right between David and me, even before I saw him lolling impatiently at the Delta Skycab podium wearing the same tolerant expression he developed whenever we flew back East. I knew it was going to be a bad Christmas. But I pretended I didn't know, because pretending is fun, even if you're not an actress. Besides, the capacity for make-believe is an elementary survival tool. It's the very essence of an alternative reality, which later will be achieved through drugs and alcohol, and later, by work and television, then still later, by therapy of course, and when that doesn't work, meditation or yoga, and then finally at the end of life, through religion or bingo—depending on what kind of person you are. Pretending is as essential to human beings as food, water and credit. That is why, while driving my parents' car on Vermont's windy, frozen road, Rural Route 114, on Christmas Eve of 1999, in the face of the new millennium, I was *pretending* that nothing was really wrong.

David, my fiancé, was sullen, silent, uncomfortable. He had repeatedly deflected my questions, my attempts to root out the truth, with the deftness of a skilled goalie slapping a determined puck out of net territory.

"What's wrong?" I asked again.

"Nothing."

"Come on, what's eating you? Tell me." He was as far away from me as the front seat of the Cadillac allowed.

"Nothing. I'm tired."

"David, you haven't said a word, you're tense, you're totally somewhere else, you didn't touch dinner, you couldn't leave my brother's house fast enough . . . please, tell me what is going on." I flicked on the wipers. It was snowing again.

"Alexis, I don't want to talk about it—okay?" Ah-ha. Always a determined girl, I gripped my crowbar and pried away until the top finally creaked open the slightest bit. A waft of foul air escaped, ugly, gaseous truths begging for release: "Do you *really* want me to tell you? Do you really *want* to know?" His face looked at once defensive and angry, like I'd walked in on him smelling his own underwear. I took my foot off the gas and let the car coast into the turn, a long, unpaved driveway flanked by huge evergreens heaving with snow, a scene that, at any other moment in my life, would be soothing and picturesque, like Maria's approach to the Von Trapps' household in winter.

"I didn't want to bring this up over Christmas . . . but if you want me to get into it, I'll get into it."

The pine trees may as well have sprouted fangs and ripped themselves out of the ground. What could have been more terrifyingly tempting? We were at the bed and breakfast now, the charming, snow-covered, quintessential New England Christmas bed and breakfast, with its quilts and doilies, hearty fireplaces and old brandy, new gay proprietors and organic bran muffins. We had the smallest room. It was ten below and snowing as we exited the car and headed for the wreath-covered front door in silence. I loved it here. David had been the picture of vomit-ready misery since we'd left L.A. three days earlier. We trudged up the tiny, ancient stairs to our room.

He took off his coat and hung it on a wooden peg. I waited. He looked briefly at the snow outside and spoke. "Alexis, I didn't want to ruin your Christmas . . ."

I closed the latch on the 200-year-old door to our room and tried to hold in the tears while blocking out the truth that was headed my way. "You're already ruining my Christmas. Everyone in my family has asked me what's wrong. You've brought everyone down, you're obviously not having fun, it's making me tense and unhappy, David, I wish you'd just be honest . . ." But he said nothing.

"What the hell's going on?" I demanded halfheartedly, because being a woman, of course I already knew. I started crying. Sometimes, this helps. David sat down hard in the Yankee-backed chair with the happy couple in the sleigh painted on the seat, brushed aside the antique rag doll and looked directly at me.

"I can't . . . I can't marry you." He looked at the ceiling, then back to me with icy eyes. "Unless you convert."

Had this been a movie and not number two on the top ten list of horrible moments in my life, the music would have swelled, I would have backed slowly toward the door, then fled the inn wearing only a white cotton nightie as I ran wailing through the snow outside, and he would have followed, shouting my name desperately, and we would have collapsed together into a marshmallowy snowdrift, angry wrestling giving way to passionate lovemaking. . . . *Lex, I'm sorry, I didn't mean it,* he'd say. *I love you just the way you are.*

But it was not a movie, so David quietly removed his socks, and I stared at my engagement ring wondering if it would be the last one I ever wore.

This was the beginning of the end. The end was long, months really. Extracting myself intact from three years with the wrong man whom I'd wanted to be right required careful, structured planning, like removing that frozen woolly mammoth from its Siberian ice tomb. It took equipment, specialists, commitment, knowledge and dedication, but mostly the thing none of us have enough of and aren't willing to give: time.

The couples therapist we saw when we returned from Vermont was a waste of time, but at the beginning of the end you still have to try. When you're already engaged, you have to believe there's something worth saving. Otherwise what kind of person are you? It was odd meeting there in the middle of the day, in the Century City office building. We fell into each other's arms in Dr. Kreezak's waiting room, beside the watercooler and potted fronds, both sobbing frantically by the time she came to collect us.

"Well, I see you two have gotten a start," she said with a cautious sense of humor. She looked like Talia Shire after her *Rocky II* makeover. Black hair, wide dark eyes, plum lips always half open, expensive skin. As we explained our situation (he was from an Orthodox Jewish family, I was a fallen Catholic now sampling agnosticism; he was an actor, I wasn't; his parents were wealthy, mine weren't; I had a job in an office, he had one in a bar; he had a dog, I had a cat), I got the odd feeling that she didn't know what to say to us and possibly felt guilty for taking our money.

"I love Alexis, and I want to spend my life with her," began David. "But my heritage is bigger than me." He settled into his chair and crossed his arms. His tanned, strong, muscular arms that had held me so many times, in so many places . . .

Dr. Kreezak looked puzzled. "I have to have Jewish children," David explained patiently.

"Alexis?—" she'd probed.

I had prepared my statement, knowing I would unravel the minute I got here, and I did. "I don't see why I have to change who I am in order for the children to know how important their heritage is . . . I mean . . . what about me? What about my heritage?" I said cautiously in a small voice, knowing this was the button that released the warhead, erupted the volcano.

"See, that's just it," snipped David. *"Her religion isn't even important to her!"* This was true. But it had suddenly become more important than it had ever been, now that I wouldn't be allowed to have a Christmas tree or Easter basket or the occasional Mass for my unborn children. It was true I never went to Mass—but David never went to services either. I suddenly felt sadly alone, vaguely Bridget Jones-ish, and yet *true to my cause,* like some discriminated hero. Sally Field as Norma Rae, Mel Gibson as William Wallace,

Julia Roberts as Erin Brockovich. I wouldn't go back. I had nothing against Judaism. I loved the holidays, devoured the food, enjoyed the stories from the classes I'd made myself take. I sang the songs, wrote in Hebrew (badly, but with great effort). But I didn't want to convert. More than that, though I wouldn't admit it at the time, I didn't want to be with a man who would make me. A man who would probably struggle with his career his whole life. A man who wanted more than anything to be . . . famous. But even more than that, I didn't want to be alone.

"Alexis?—" Dr. Kreezak said encouragingly, scattering my thoughts.

I had a feeling she was on my side. "I just don't understand why we can't have both traditions, lots of families do that," I wailed into an oversized tissue. It wasn't that I wanted to deny the nonexistent, unborn children their Jewishness—I just didn't want to have to fake my own.

"You don't have to *believe* it!" snapped David.

"Then what's the *point?!*" I demanded.

After an hour Dr. Kreezak pretty much told us what we already knew—that we seemed to be at an impasse and that there seemed to be nowhere to go but apart. What more could she say? "I commend you both for being so honest . . . ," she said. "Would one or both of you like to come back next week? No, I'm sorry I don't accept credit cards. No, I don't validate parking."

Then David and I argued about that, me allowing that it was permissible for her not to validate, him snorting that for $125 an hour, covering our parking was the *least* she could do. No, our differences weren't just religious. In hindsight, the Christmas Eve Conversion Ultimatum was basically the straw that broke the shiksa's back. When you thought about it really, we had nothing in common except our devotion to each other. He was an actor. I worked in the publicity department for a movie studio and didn't have much free time or, as the case was, sympathy for actors. He loved L.A. I yearned for the wet leaves and private seashores of New England. He worked out daily and had a deep-rooted fear of cheese. I seasoned movie popcorn with M&M's and Junior Mints. He was deeply committed to political causes. My idea of activism was snubbing the Gap. But we were in love, or rather, as I suspect with most millennial couples in demise, in love with being in love. Who cares if the person is right or not? When you have someone to pick you up at the airport, all seems right with the world.

Among other disagreements (religion, finances, careers, children, politics, cuisine, location) was the argument over how much money and aggravation David, not just an actor but a struggling one, was willing to spend on his dog Harve's cancer treatment. David and Harve's relationship was one of those things that had seemed so fresh and endearing at the beginning of our dating and had become unbearably annoying—a potential deal breaker—at the end.

According to the vet, Harve's condition was severe enough to warrant $8,000 in treatment thus far but was not visible in the dog (except for the occasional dime-sized tumor that the vet was only too willing to carve out for a few hundred bucks). In my opinion, the dog had suffered enough and should have been free to live out his days naturally. In David's opinion, Harve was to ingest as many drugs as possible and be regularly operated on, while we remained unable to purchase a new living room set. Harve, once a handsome and noble-looking bloodhound, looked like a homemade patchwork quilt gone awry and suffered bouts of unpredictable aggression as a result of his steroid prescription. Twice already I'd caught him threatening the refrigerator.

About a year before the beginning of the end, my "issue" with David and Harve's relationship went like this: We had noticed that Harve's "dimples" had enlarged in the past few months and thought that since he was an L.A. dog, maybe it was melanoma. A quick, astronomically expensive trip to the vet and the resulting lab work confirmed David's worst fears—Harve had mass cell tumors, and they were malignant. The first surgeries involved removing a few of them, under local anaesthetic. Each one of these trips cost several hundred dollars. Still Harve showed no symptoms, but the clinic thought he should undergo chemo anyway. This meant additional expenses in pills and carpet cleaning services, for the pills not only made Harve sick to his stomach but also affected his bowel control and, consequently, his dignity and our ability to entertain at home. By the time Harve came home with half his ear removed, wearing a large, blood-soaked turban and stumbling into walls while wetting himself, I thought we'd all had enough.

I closed the door of our bedroom so Harve wouldn't overhear. "How much are you going to spend? Five thousand? Ten thousand?" I prodded, a little too irritably. "It's not like he's getting better . . . look at him!"

"I'll spend whatever I have to spend! I can't let him die!" David snapped, looking at me as though I had just sprouted horns.

I sighed irritably. "He's not dying. He just looks like he is because of the weekly torture sessions *you* put him through!"

"What do you care? It's not YOUR money!" And the games had began. I was jealous of the dog, that was clear. The Relationship Pet God took notice and scribbled something in His notebook.

From the beginning of the end both of the animals sensed something was wrong. Harve, the cancer-ridden purebred, was overly needy and underfoot, while Little, my runty but authoritative gray cat, began to heighten her patrol duties, storming from room to room as if to root out the bad vibe that had infested our sunny world. Little was a rescued orphan, and human tension brought out her fear of abandonment (though she'd never admit it). I noticed she was losing weight. Harve's condition basically dominated the animal health issues in our house, though, and Little had to be in pretty tough shape to warrant a vet trip.

Little had never fully developed to correct feline proportions, hence her name. I found her one summer day while jogging through West Hollywood. A bunch of neighborhood kids were standing in a circle, poking something with a stick. I loped over and saw a tiny heap of gray fur. The eyes were stuck shut, and ants were crawling all over it. It looked like a small, angry dust ball. *I can't get involved.* I thought, turning to continue my run. We already had an oversized dog with cancer, and David's anorexic, bleached-blonde, part-time scene study partner had two dogs (one was eighteen) that she brought over constantly. The landlord hated us and the yard smelled. I didn't have time. Cats weren't affectionate. Cats peed in shoes. I still had three miles to go. *I can't. I can't.*

I ran home to get a cardboard box and my car. As I hoisted the kitten into the box, it hissed and lashed out at me with its pathetic paws. Once at home I put it in the bathtub with some towels and heated up some nonfat soy milk. (It was all we had, unless you counted the scene study partner's staple of sugar-free, fat-free, Irish Cream–flavored nondairy Mocha Mix, which seemed inappropriate). I dug out an eyedropper and squeezed the milk, which she did not want, into her mouth. I soaked a washcloth in warm water and cleaned her face until the crust around her eyes loosened and she could open them and see her savior. I would be a great mother someday. The kitten took in the situation, mewed irritably, and bit me.

When David came home from costarring in a Jack-in-the-Box commercial, I said, "Don't be mad . . . I have to show you something!" and I think he must have been expecting me to produce the brochure for business school or an eight-hour class to be a computer technician, because when he saw Little in the tub he looked delighted.

"She's so cute! You rescued her! What am I going to do with

you, Florence Nightingale," he laughed, his lovely eyes settling on the new addition to the family. He grabbed me around the waist and planted a wet kiss on my head. "I love you, you know that?" he said.

Later, the vet informed me that Little weighed one pound and was lacking all the antibodies she would have gotten from her mother. This (I should have listened more closely here) would mean she would be highly susceptible to illness and infection for the rest of her life. She was presently filled with worms and ear mites, and she had an eye infection and a bad case of feline flatulence. But she was beautiful and she needed me. *I'll save her!* I thought jubilantly.

"She might be okay if you can get her to drink or eat, and keep her inside," warned Dr. Niblack, the vet at the VCA clinic on Melrose. He was a small, red-haired man with tiny spectacles, strange shoes and enough freckles for all of Ireland. Someone I probably teased in grade school. One way or another those people always get even. Kevin Bacon found this out the hard way in *Flatliners*. "Keep her inside," Dr. Niblack repeated ominously. "You need to limit her exposure—"

*Rowl!* said Little, with the feisty spirit of a bear cub. She seemed to have no idea she was a cat. Harve's presence eased Little's dominance issues a bit, but even Harve, a good-natured, stupid inbred, grew weary of Little's bossy antics and occasionally cuffed her or pinned her to the ground with a full nelson and houndy growl. When this happened, David would laugh and I would yell, "Get him off, he's going to kill her!" David was like the parent of the playground bully. "Aw, it's good for her! Little needs to be put in her place!"

"That's not fair—she's from the street, she has issues!" I said defensively. Harve was friendly, but Little was smart. Harve was fun while Little was complex. Little may have been emotionally odd, but Harve was just plain dumb. Still, we'd been a family. And now our tribe was dividing.

Fortunately, I couldn't dwell on it, because now I was back at the office, and I had a lot of calls to return. I was grateful that Viv, my boss, the executive vice president of marketing for our label, wasn't back yet from Aspen. I hadn't planned on dealing with a devastating breakup the minute I got back to work, and I wasn't prepared to plan for Sundance, deal with the egomaniacally crazy director Eugene R., or edit the movie clip reel so it wasn't morally offensive to the MPAA (Motion Picture Association of America, or, as we in the studio marketing department liked to call it, Mostly Prudish And Annoying).

Adriane stepped tentatively into my office with a stack of bills and a week's worth of *The Hollywood Reporter* and *Daily Variety,* avoiding a rotting holiday fruit basket that *Late Night with Conan O'Brien* had delivered the previous week, before everything decayed, when my marital future itself was shiny and ripe.

"Are you all right, Lex?" she asked gravely but politely. I hadn't moved. In fact, I hadn't taken my coat off. She waited for my answer, and a wrinkle of worry crossed her flawless forehead. She was vacationed-fresh, with a glow to her caramel cheeks and a sparkle to her hair that hadn't been there before the break. Half Black and half Asian, and five-foot-ten with long, soft black curls, Adriane was the poster child for multicultural superhuman beauty. As patient as she was gorgeous, she was also scarily good at her job.

"How was your Christmas?" she tried hopefully, setting the pile of mail next to the call sheet I was staring at. In the state I was in there was no avoiding it, so I just told her. Everything. At the studio, in the movie business, you are the immediate family of your coworkers, like it or not. You spend at least fifty hours a week with them, usually more. There is no escape from the world of your job; it stretches from days to nights and weekends and vacations and sick days, and relationships have no boundaries, because that is the price for getting to work in Hollywood.

"Oh God, I'm so sorry . . . ," she gasped, genuinely shocked. "Is there anything I can do? Do you need a place to stay or anything?" The phones were chirping wildly, but her eyes were unwavering. Having a loyal assistant who is also smart and hardworking is like having the number one movie every weekend.

"No . . . thanks, though," I managed. "It's not violent or anything, we're both still in the apartment for a while, just to figure things out." Adriane nodded understandingly and silently, a move she had down pat from being a publicity assistant. "I'm just going to roll a few calls, check e-mail and probably take off," I said.

"OK, could you—sorry—these invoices need to be signed . . . today. If you can . . . ," she trailed off apologetically. Like I said, Adriane was a machine.

When I got home, David went straight to work and I went right back into therapy—at the Music Hall Cinema on Wilshire. I had to exit the freeway of my head for at least ninety minutes, and that's where I always went to do it, ever since I'd moved to L.A. five years earlier. I never minded going to the movies alone—in fact, I preferred it. Most people don't take movies seriously enough, don't understand the importance of the right seat, the power of timing the parking and popcorn purchase. The foreplay of trailers and previews, the sweet anticipation of the animated dancing candy, the honeyed tease of the dimming lights and that tender, infinite pause between the crowd's hush and the emergence of the studio logo that leaves you breathless with the potential of the imagined. If that seems a bit much, well, you don't love movies like I do. That moment is as close to perfect happiness as I've ever been.

You'd think that was something David and I had in common— the movies. In actuality what we shared was an innate inability to live in reality. I preferred to dwell in the world of celluloid heroes;

David's mental distraction of choice, like that of many struggling actors, was denial. When we first met, at least I *admitted* my problem when he asked me on our first date what I considered my "biggest flaw."

"Well . . ." I liked him, so I told him the truth. "My friends say I've seen too many movies." He laughed, because he could not know then how serious a problem it really was. We used to go to the movies, David and me, and suddenly I was sad with detail, the details of all the things we did together and all the things we would never do. We'd never have a fight where he dropped me on the side of the freeway, yelling, "So then *walk* home! *Fine!*" We'd never get drunk at Oktoberfest. We'd never go to Montana and worry about grizzlies. We'd never watch another movie and talk about how much better he would have been in the role, or how I could have improved the publicity campaign. My best friend was about to become a stranger. You'd think that wouldn't matter, since I hated him. The whole thing was very complicated.

While I was lost in *Being John Malkovich*. Little waited loyally in the car outside the Music Hall. A strange cat with peculiar preferences, Little loved the car. Meanwhile Harve was at home, busy taking David's side. Because David was still living in the apartment. It was still the beginning of the end, that terribly bleak period after Christmas, before I grew the balls to actually answer David's ultimatum, give the ring back or ask him to move out, when I pretended that our differences were manageable, that everything would be okay, that we'd wake up the next morning and he wouldn't be a Jewish actor, or I would be. Because it was safer this way, endless limbo, surreal nothingness on Planet Indecision. It was like the moment before you look at the pregnancy stick to see if it's blue, or that pause of eternity before you break the news about someone having leukemia. Before you fish or cut bait and you're just sitting in the boat, praying someone will tip it over or tell you what the fuck to do.

# Two

In *Splash,* a young Tom Hanks falls in love with Daryl Hannah, who happens to be a mermaid. They stroll romantically about Manhattan and have fantastic sex in his apartment. He names her Madison, and she gets him a fountain. When he discovers her terrible secret, he is angry, hurt, betrayed. But John Candy, his brother, sets him straight. "So she's a fish! So what! You found true love, and that's more than most people get in a lifetime!" What had seemed an insurmountable difference was reduced to a technicality in the face of true love. Tom Hanks was willing to convert to a merman for her. He was willing to give up everything—his friends, his job, opposable limbs—to be with the woman he loved. I could boast no such selflessness. I couldn't even be persuaded to give up cheeseburgers or elevators on Saturday.

Fittingly, it was New Year's Day that I finally knew for sure that my interfaith relationship of three years had to end. After the train wreck that was Christmas Eve and the awkward attempts at sifting through the wreckage (him waiting for my Decision and me not making It), we spent New Year's Eve at Mammoth Mountain, where we feigned a Happy Couple Holiday with our friends. The night before, as I was anticipating the end of the first millennium, my engagement and the world, I tried every distraction imaginable to distance myself from the crater of pain that had been growing since Christmas. As the hours til midnight ticked away I moved from one drug to the next and, when that failed, resorted to my menstrual migraine medication, a strong B-level narcotic to be used only in times of severe feminine helplessness. Oddly, nothing worked, and I felt more sober and in touch with myself than ever. A twisted irony, I thought, as I chewed up another Imitrex.

"Alexis, are you coming to bed?" David asked, removing his green HAPPY NEW YEAR! hat with the red sparkles and pausing at the bottom of the rented condo's staircase. Our language was different now, since Christmas Eve, inflected with a tense, suspicious formality disguised as respect. *Lex, c'mon* had become *Alexis, are you coming to bed?* Like we were in *Dynasty.* He had transferred the terrible burden of the Christmas Eve ultimatum from his own conscience to mine. Now that he had come clean he felt better, was confident things would work out once I wrestled with the impending Decision and made It. I could tell he thought I would give in, that everything would be fine once I got over the shock of converting and realizing I would have to wash two sets of dishes. But how could I tell him what I could not admit myself? I didn't want to marry someone who wanted to change me. Lies begin within. And grow, and cause pain, until finally no one can ignore them. Like pimples.

He waited for me to answer. In his weariness and resignation he was still, like the first night I laid eyes on him, shockingly handsome. Chiseled features, almond eyes filled with melted milk chocolate, a jaw you could slice a melon with, shoulders you could sleep on, his light brown hair an inviting forest your fingers could get deliciously lost in. And his wonderful nose, how the gentle slope of it fit perfectly in the crook of my neck, as if a bed had been carved there for it long ago. . . .

I didn't match him in the looks department, but I wasn't half bad. I was neither fat nor thin (which, in L.A., actually meant fat). I wasn't tall, but I wasn't short. My shoulder-length brown hair stubbornly refused to grow any longer and was neither curly nor straight. It had been every shade of brown, auburn, chestnut, mahogany (there are many on the market), but I had never, ever dyed it blonde, a point of personal pride. But my best feature had always been my electric blue eyes. When you looked at David, his striking feature was the entire package. Like a movie star. When you noticed me, the blueberry Big Gulp of my eyes (perhaps a little too big, a little too blue) didn't let you go. For better or worse, they betrayed how I felt every second of every day. It was hard to lie. Except to myself, of course.

"No," I finally answered him. I wasn't coming to bed. "I'm going to stay up with these guys until the mushrooms kick in." Midnight had come and gone, Times Square was still there. Marcos and Lisa were on the couch roaring at the DVD of *American Pie*. Frank and Sue were getting high on the deck. My Decision and I stayed up all night. I was not visited by any ghosts of New Year's past, present or future, nor did I have any clarifying dreams involving old boyfriends that made my situation easier in the morning. When I woke up, instead of a dramatic note of closure pinned to the pillow next to me, David was there. There was that nanosecond of unfiltered normalcy, like Anne Parillaud in *La Femme Nikita,* when she wakes up and, for a fraction of an instant, doesn't remember the horror of her life: that she's supposed to be dead. The agony of my situation came flooding back, and the first day of 2000 began.

We all stopped for lunch in a bar on the way back to L.A. I was nursing a cocaine/vodka/mushroom/champagne/pot/estrogen withdrawal migraine with a Killian's Red and our friend Marcos, his girlfriend Lisa, Frank and Sue and other assorted happy New Year's couples. Our friends were all blissfully unaware of the marathon mindfuck that was going on between us. Endless talking throughout the previous night, nothing resolved. Why is it always a snowy mountain condo or tropical resort, why always so picturesque, these palaces of relationship doom? Why does no one ever break up in a Motel 6 on a Wednesday or in an office after the Monday marketing meeting? You spend all night not sleeping, going from one end of the emotional rainbow to the other without arriving at a conclusion. Sometimes there is sex, muted and joyless, leaving you emptier than when you began. New emotions fill the hole eaten away by love gone wrong . . . paranoia, devastation, delusion, euphoria, hatred and forgiveness. You hate him, you love him. You wish he'd never been born, you can't imagine life without him. You already bought a wedding dress, you never wanted to marry him anyway. In the beginning of the end it didn't really matter why we were breaking up, only that it was his fault.

When we returned from Mammoth, David went to work and I went to the movies with Marcos. Betraying David, I told Marcos the whole story, from Christmas Eve onward. We sat drinking more Killian's Red in a bar outside the Music Hall after seeing *Magnolia*, the dark yet uplifting film with the oddly inspiring message that the one true thing connecting us all is loneliness. I had to stop going to weird movies. This one was too long, more than a little depressing and a tad self-indulgent (who really needed the flying frogs), and I loved it. Especially the sound track, which I'd purchased on the way to the movie in order to be fully prepared for its emotional tone. Marcos was more critical. I loved movies and I loved Marcos, an aspiring director who'd been a friend since we'd both lived in New York, because he never minced words and he worked hard. He had that worried look that guys have when they're hoping you won't cry but recognize that soon, you will.

"Lex, you know what all those people had in common?" he asked, paying for our beers.

"They were losers?" I offered, wanting desperately to be better than someone.

"No," Marcos said slowly. "They all ended up miserable because at some point in their lives, they weren't honest." Marcos, like most people from Brooklyn, had a gift for being painfully direct.

"You didn't really want to marry an *actor*, did you?" he asked me, smiling. "Be honest." Honesty was what had cemented David's and my differences, or had at least yanked the curtains of codependency aside to reveal them. We had completed a couples worksheet. It had been my idea. Something to do on the five-hour drive to Mammoth Mountain for the doomed New Year's weekend. Dr. Kreezak, the couples therapist, had recommended it as a way to work through our issues and see what was really a priority, what could be resolved and what was just someone being a selfish dick. There were various issues and numbers designating levels of importance (a #1 meant *I'm not budging* and #5 basically said *you win*). By the time we hit the 101 in Bakersfield, ours looked like this:

|  | **ALEXIS** |
| --- | --- |
| **What I need** | To know you will not spend our lives as a struggling actor 1 |
| **What I want** | Christmas, Easter, Labor Day & occasional non-depressing Jewish holidays 2 |
|  | To not give up who I am 1 |
| **What is a non-negotiable** | Not spending our lives struggling so you can be an actor 1 |
|  | Bacon 1 |
| **I wish you would . . .** | Not make me convert 1 |
|  | See that struggling to be an actor is no way to spend life 1 |

| | |
|---|---|
| **I want to work on . . .** | Your alternative career choices 2 |
| | Meeting halfway 2 |
| **I'm willing to compromise on . . .** | children 2 |
| | The color scheme of our future living room 5 |

**DAVID**

| | |
|---|---|
| **What I need** | Your unconditional love and support 1 |
| | A Jewish wife 1 |
| **What I want** | To be an actor 1 |
| | To be a father 1 |
| | A Jewish wife 1 |
| **What is a non-negotiable** | My children being the Jewish children of an actor with unconditional love + support from his Jewish wife 1 |
| **I wish you would . . .** | Convert and let me pursue my dreams 1 |
| | Have more faith in me 1 |
| **I want to work on . . .** | Being a better actor 2 |
| | Forgiving myself more [?] 2 |
| **I'm willing to compromise on . . .** | Your Hebrew (it's wanting) 3 |
| | Fasting all day on Yom Kippur 3 |
| | Excessive davening 1 |

I was actually encouraged when we exchanged charts—at least we were being honest with each other, which meant we would end up happily ever after, nestled securely in our historical Craftsman in Pasadena on one coast and the Nantucket beach cottage on the other. We'd be bicoastal, him taking off from his latest movie to make appearances at charity events in Hyannis, and me taking the kids to visit him on set when I wasn't working from home on something fabulous and lucrative part time. It was all going to work out. Just like it always does in the last two minutes before the title track comes up and the credits roll.

After the New Year's weekend and the worksheet revelations and *Magnolia,* I was intensely anxious and depressed, but still I weighed the same. Apparently there was no upside. On Saturday David got up early and left for play rehearsal without saying anything. Is there any feeling more hideous than sharing a bed with someone you can't look in the eye?

I thought about going to work. There was loads to do to prepare for Sundance, and a weekend day at the office would be productive. The party invites still had to be printed and laminated, I had to get some kind of Park City security guard for our party, score a free liquor sponsor, rent a four-wheel-drive vehicle, book some interviews for Viv with the trades . . . plus the press kit for *Shades of Gray* had to be edited, I still had to sufficiently befriend all of the actors' publicists and managers, and there were about twelve messages from the insane director Eugene R. that had to be dealt with, sooner or later. I loved the little details of work but hated them too. It wasn't brain surgery, it was movie publicity, but accomplishing small tasks and outwitting demanding talent representatives at a rapid speed was distracting and rewarding in a way that made life go by less painfully. And of course, I was constantly surrounded by movies and the people who made them. But today I didn't feel like going to work or being around anyone. As if on cue, the phone exploded. I let the machine pick up.

"Hey Lex, it's Frank and Sue, and we're just checking in. . . ." Frank and Sue, my favorite perfectly-happy-couple-to-both-adore-and-resent, since I'd been responsible for setting them up. They knew me well enough to detect something rotten in Denmark over New Year's. Sue's sleepy, sexy voice chimed in. "It's 2000 and we're still your best friends and we want to know if something's wrong in Shiksa paradise . . . you and David seemed sort of down at Mammoth." Frank finished for her. "Give us a call, sweets, there's a Chaplin marathon at the Sunset 5 tonight. And mojitos, as always, before that. Cheers."

What would Charlie Chaplin do in my shoes, I wondered, wandering into the living room, trying not to see any of the photos of David and me on the walls—not easy, since there were a dozen or so. I picked up Little and looked in her green eyes. "Would you convert for the right man?" Little stared at me indignantly. "How about the wrong man?" I asked her, noticing that she didn't look good. She looked how I felt. She'd never been very big; she'd always been simply a runty gray cat, but now she was positively thin and wispy looking, a graying Lauren Hutton. She'll be fine, I told myself. Cats always are.

I spent the hours while David was at rehearsal reminding myself of all the things that were wrong. He was argumentative, he was confrontational, didn't believe in karma, couldn't under any circumstances see the point of traveling to Cuba, wouldn't order pizza, threatened pedestrians. (One time he almost flattened the revelers at the West Hollywood Halloween parade? And when I told him how ridiculous that was, he chided me for *not being loyal*). Please. Oh yes, and he didn't say please and thank you, thought his dog was better than my cat, believed that he was destined to be famous and that fate would strike him randomly one night behind the bar. Harsh, but I needed cruelty to get through the morning.

It hurt too much to think about all the things that were right. How incredibly well he treated me, how thoughtful and generous, loyal, reliable, devoted, sweet he was, how far he'd come in so many ways, how well I had him trained. How I'd come home to the laundry folded, the seat down and the bed made. How I'd be picked up at the airport with flowers (dyed carnations with baby's breath, but he was getting there). How he'd draw me a hot bath and bring me chicken soup when I was sick, how he'd let me drag him to Orange County with a deathly flu because he knew how important it was for me to see my uncle before Christmas. How he sat through *It's a Wonderful Life* even though *Fiddler on the Roof* was on at the same time. How he not only offered to get a Christmas tree with me but bought it as well. How he cried tears of pride when I got 100% on my Judaism test. Pain, like joy, is in the details.

"*Rrroowwwwwl,*" said Little. She'd been holed up in a corner of the couch for days, losing weight and sleeping too much. I scratched her under the chin, but she turned away with an *Orrrwrlll.* Like a Katharine Hepburn character, she remained haughty and unsatisfied. My only thought as I pondered what might be wrong with Little was that I wished *I* could lose weight while sleeping fifteen hours a day. As it was I could do neither.

# *Three*

| DATE/TIME | CONTACT | NUMBER | MESSAGE |
|---|---|---|---|
| 1/5/00 9:29 a.m. | Your Mom | Home | Just checking in. |
| 1/5/00 9:40 a.m. | Director Eugene R. | @ Bev. Hills Hotel 310-276-2251 (under the name Rosebud) | Need to discuss *Shades of Gray* premiere plans and his friend who writes for *N.Y. Times*. |
| 1/5/00 9:47 a.m. | Babette (agent for actor D.H. from *Late Nights*) CAA | 310-288-4545 | D.H. MUST have his groomer at Sundance. Also what about her party tix? Plse call. |
| 1/5/00 10:04 a.m. | Frank & Sue (on conference) | Sue's office #—you have | Why haven't you called us back—are u ok? |

| DATE/TIME | CONTACT | NUMBER | MESSAGE |
|---|---|---|---|
| 1/5/00 10:16 a.m. | Viv | | Why is D.H.'s agent Babette calling her? |
| 1/5/00 10:43 a.m. | Jen/Travel | x488 | Confirming Sundance travel; you must go standby on return—only Sr. VP's get car service; take a cab. |
| 1/5/00 10:49 a.m. | Meredith/ Jewish By Choice | 213-355-9378 | Got your message; wld love to talk; call anytime. |
| 1/5/00 11:10 a.m. | Dr. Kreezak | 310-238-3847 | Re: schedule another appointment? |
| 1/5/00 11:13 a.m. | Bridget/ *Entertainment Tonight* | 323-956-2000 (Main #) | Do you have any parties at Sundance we should be covering? Only have one crew so it has to be A-list. Plse call. |
| 1/5/00 11:20 a.m. | Dr. Niblack/ VCA Animal Hosp. | Same # he left before | Re: Little's shots? |
| 1/5/00 11:59 a.m. | *Bitsie/ Richard Weinstein's office/ICM *rude—watch out | 310-550-4000 | We have not rec'd tickets to your Sundance parties. Call me ASAP. |

For a Hollywood publicist, phone calls are like parking ticket fines. When you ignore them, they usually multiply and increase in severity. The last call was the easiest one to return, easier than, say, updating my friends Frank and Sue on the breakup or hearing my mom's voice without crying (or the director Eugene R.'s, for that matter), or annoying Viv by forcing her to run interference for me with demanding talent agents who thought male actors needed $2,500 worth of "grooming" while skiing, so I dialed Bitsie and prepared for battle.

"He's only the biggest agent at the biggest agency in town," warned Bitsie, the first assistant to the biggest agent at the biggest agency in town.

"Exactly," I concurred, "so why would he waste his time coming to our little film's party?" We were the smaller, independent division of the big studio, and for some reason that made us hipper when it came to festival parties. The smaller the party, the more important you had to be to get on the list. My list was a random collection of press, talent, Viv's rolodex, filmmakers, trendy people we called tastemakers and buzz-builders, and anyone who was nice. This agent was none of the above.

"How about the fact that we have a CLIENT in your film?" she hissed.

"How about the fact that your CLIENT is in JAIL?" I shot back, because he was. Having a "client in your film," she felt, was reason enough for the entire agency's administrative staff—a viciously ambitious lot of some 100 people, most of whom had never met said client—to be invited to our one party at Sundance, which was not, by the way, for the film her jailed client was even in. I hoped briefly she wouldn't tell her boss how I berated her; he would then immediately call Viv and berate *her*. Hollywood logic follows one path—the one that leads to the biggest dick.

I was never so happy to return to work after the holidays. Sundance was looming, and there were parties to plan, hotels to book, journalists to cajole, actors to make famous. Everyone from *The Hollywood Reporter* to *Vanity Fair* would be there, without the protection of voice mail or assistants. And my expense account was always bigger than theirs. Journalists were easy prey at film festivals, and publicists would feast upon them like packs of fun-loving, slickly dressed wolves—who held tickets to every party. But this year, the real reason I wanted to go was that I was hoping that time away from David would provide some sort of epiphany about why we were breaking up, or at least the certainty that it was the right thing to do. I reluctantly added Robert Downey Jr.'s agent's name to our party list. The phone rang again. "Hello?" I said in the Wounded Voice. In the middle of the beginning of the end, you never knew who would call. It could be his mother.

"How are you?" my sister Molly's voice said, but it sounded like "How. Arrrre yoooooou."

Molly and her fiancé, Jack, were having problems and had been since about a year ago. Like mine, their issues escalated around Christmas, and like many people, they thought the answer would present itself or the problem would vanish once they got engaged. Neither happened, and the wedding plans were full steam ahead until the date for the hall deposit reared its ugly head and my father demanded to be part of the emotional loop. The wedding was postponed, then called off altogether, and Molly took a drive up the coast by herself to sort things out. Jack refused to go to couples therapy, and now they were in the netherworld of figuring out how to permanently cancel everything without losing anything. Worse, their CDs were still combined, and they had invested jointly in furniture. Truly, the only thing really keeping them together at this point was the dining room table and the cost of a single apartment in San Francisco. They were still living in the same Berkeley apartment together, albeit in separate rooms, still sharing meals, halfheartedly looking for separate apartments. She never had to ask him to water the plants; he just did it. He was a graphic designer.

She was a teacher. The spark was gone, that was all. A sensitive, anxious person to begin with, Molly had been constipated since Christmas Day.

"I'm okay," I told her. "Work's busy. I think David's going to stay with his friend Victor for a while, thank God."

"You believe in God now, huh?" she joked weakly.

"Hah. What's new with you and Jack?" I asked, hoping vaguely they were either getting married or not speaking.

"I don't know," she quavered. "Just that it's over and I don't know what to do. The weird thing is, it's not hostile or tense—like you and David—"

"Oh," I managed, wondering who had the better breakup going. Hers was more civilized, that was obvious. Mine had more potential for a dramatic weight loss, however.

"But it's still hard, and school sucks right now," Molly continued. "I had to buy my own scissors and thumbtacks again for a project. The school doesn't have scissors, Lex."

"Wow," I heaved guiltily, glancing at my own supply cabinet in the corner, which could have provided materials for ten classrooms. Molly had helped start a charter school and was exhausted every day. She had a master's in education from Harvard and made less than my assistant before overtime.

"Are you sleeping?" I asked her, knowing what the answer was. Molly was like the princess with the proverbial pea. She could only sleep well under the absolutely perfect climactic conditions, in her own bed, with no less than eight hours, four pillows, an eye mask, and one vanilla candle going.

"About two hours a night," she admitted. Molly, the youngest and, though she'd die before admitting it, the neediest, could imagine life on her own about as well as I could imagine life without the Music Hall Cinema on Wilshire. "As if that weren't bad enough, I can't shit, and I can't eat either," she continued. "I think I have an ulcer, my skin's breaking out, I look like a corpse—"

"You *don't* look like a corpse," I replied automatically. Molly and I looked nothing alike. She had luscious, full curls of honey brown silk hair that she cursed and I envied every day of our childhood, flawless olive skin and toffee brown eyes. She looked like Natalie Portman with curves and a worried expression. My one comfort in standing next to her was that people always assumed I was the younger one. I tried to be helpful. "You know what Tyler Durden said in *Fight Club?*"

"No."

"It's only after you've lost everything that you're free to do anything."

"That's not really helpful, Lex," she said dismally. "I wish we had a fight, or someone cheated on someone. This is so much harder. It's so hard to actually *decide* to end it."

"You'll figure it out . . . ," I lied, because for the first time in my life I did not have any fail-safe older sister advice. We were going through this milestone together. There was no clear path forged ahead for her, as with losing her virginity or buying a new car or cooking potatoes. I could not tell her to do what I was doing because I wasn't even sure it was right. In fact, I wasn't even sure what I was doing. We were calling it a Trial Separation, or Giving It Time. This is what people who prefer delusion do—the same people who insist that the dry cleaner shrunk their pants or that they enjoy shopping for food alone. Pretending.

Adriane appeared in the doorway, her headset dangling from an ear. "D.H.'s agent wants to know if we're flying his groomer to Sundance first class? And that his day rate is $2,500 plus a day of travel . . ."

"What the hell's a 'groomer'?" asked Molly, overhearing.

"Mol. I gotta go, hang in there. Don't be scared," I said into the phone, but she had hung up. I looked toward Adriane, who somehow managed to be cheerful and beautiful no matter who was demanding a private screening, an extra plane ticket, or macrobiotic meals in the middle of Utah. "No," I said to her out of habit, going back to my *Late Nights* party list.

She was so patient. Sometimes I suspected she was an android. "No, to which part?" she smiled carefully.

"No to first class, because there *is* no first class to Park City, and no to his day rate, because we aren't flying him there at all," I explained. "D.H. is going to be wearing a ski hat and a beard in all his interviews, so there's no need for a groomer, but please thank him for offering anyway. In the politest way possible, of course," I finished.

"But—," she smiled, getting ready to explain her latest terrifying conversations with D.H.'s publicist and hairstylist assistant. In Hollywood there is a hierarchal, trickle-up effect of ego, supply and demand. Adriane's job was to see that this problem never reached me. My job was to see that this problem never reached Viv. D.H.'s representatives' job was to see that his requests were never a problem. Hence, everyone is always very busy making or avoiding phone calls.

I looked up. "In the politest way possible," I repeated and hit the remote control for my door. It slammed on her question. At the movie studio where I worked, VP level and above got a remote control for their door. I still had to take a cab to the airport, but I did enjoy the drama of a remotely controlled slammed door. My cell phone screeched, and I dug it out of my filthy 1998 RED CARPET MAGAZINE'S YOUNG AND HOT! AWARDS promotional tote bag. I glanced at its screen: SARA-ANNE. I took a breath and pressed the green phone symbol.

I spent my twenties thinking I was abnormal because I never had that lifelong group of friends that everyone talks about—I'd never stayed in one place long enough to cement a clique. I had people from high school I kept in touch with (but let's be honest, they had spouses, houses and kids, and I had therapy, air miles and pets) and one stellar friend from college who continued to make it in every time I changed address books. I'd collected people along the way—from Paris, New York and London—from time abroad, friends with geographically diverse ambitions and stops along the career path. Having friends all over the world sounds a lot more glamorous than it really is. You miss them, you don't have time to talk to them enough and you can't see them because you're all busy chasing your futures. Welcome to the new millennium—many miles, many private treadmills. In L.A. there was Sara-Anne. Or she called herself *Sayerann. From Little Rock.*

Sara-Anne and I met five years ago when I first moved to L.A. and thought everyone's hair was naturally sun streaked. She was tall, achingly thin, and her hair was razor straight and had never been colored. Her most outstanding feature was her feet; they were size ten and always sported cowboy boots. Her ghost-white toes had never seen a day of polish. Sara-Anne said "Y'all" and "I'm fixin' to" and had an IQ of 163. She inhaled chitterlings, fudge and foie gras and weighed 105 pounds. When she needed a shower she said, "Damn . . . I am gamey." She won a poetry fellowship to Oxford, made a hat out of python skin, cultivated her own vineyard up north, and had buried her two-year-old daughter four years ago after a horrible accident. Sara-Anne was proof that there was nothing as resilient as the female soul, and that life had the potential to be infinitely cruel and wildly interesting at the same time. People like Sara-Anne were reasons to stay in L.A. She was a soulful, oddly gorgeous creature. Like a true friend, I spared her no details and took forty minutes of her time to do so. She listened dutifully to every detail of Black Christmas and even pulled over while driving down Coldwater Canyon for the conversation.

"I just don't understand why I keep ending up with the wrong men," I wailed, exasperated with myself.

"Ain't that the ugly truth, baby," she drawled in her dripping Little Rock accent. "I can love anybody, and I end up spending months with these guys I *know* I can't be with—go *around* me, fucker!" Sara-Anne's driving commentary was always colorful. A wine distributor, she lived in her car and logged about 1,500 miles a month traveling from restaurant to restaurant, liquor store to wine boutique all over the entire southern half of the state. "Do you *know* how many damn useless boyfriends I've gone through, sugar?"

"That's a relief, I thought it was just me," I laughed weakly. She was going to break up with Richard, her William Morris Agency boyfriend who wouldn't eat cheese or drink coffee and spent all of their road trips to Napa talking on his cell phone.

"Hang in there, darlin', we'll go bird-doggin' next week." "Bird-doggin' " was Sara-Anne-speak for seeking male attention while wearing suggestive clothing in bars designed for this purpose. Something to look forward to. Only I didn't feel like going bird-doggin'. I felt like calling David and begging him to take me back to a world where weekends didn't loom like a Steven Segal marathon.

I finished the Sundance party list and closed the program. The screen saver photo of David and me at the Golden Globes party last year smiled at me sickly. I called Walter at the IT help desk, and he walked me though changing it to the default spinning studio logo. It was boring but safe.

"Alexis, when are you going to Sundance?" David asked me for the fourth time. We were still sharing a bed while he made plans to move into his friend Victor's house. While I was in Utah, David would stay in the apartment to take care of Harve and Little. I knew he was eager to have the place to himself, though secretly angry he couldn't ride on my ticket to the festival this year. All those talent agents in one place; his strange enthusiasm last year had annoyed me.

"Sunday," I finally answered him. "When are you going to Victor's?"

My forced casual tone made him whirl in horror. He stared through me with those eyes. Bittersweet chocolate. "You can't wait . . . for me to leave . . . ," he said in the voice of Dirty Harry.

I grew watery. "No . . . no . . . it's just . . . I don't think either one of us can make any decisions about anything while . . . we're living together. I need space, you need space . . ." *I need to admit you are the wrong man for me and I can't do it while you're in front of me . . . you need to find a nice Jewish girl who won't mind marrying a bartender who might never land that starring role, and you can't do it while sleeping in my bed . . .*

"This afternoon," he said coldly. "I'll bring my stuff over to Victor's after rehearsal. I'll come back to the house to take care of the animals after you leave for Sundance."

It had been decided that during the Trial Separation, David would stay with Victor, another struggling actor. He could have stayed with any number of his friends from The Actor's Refuge, his theater group, but I found it interesting that he chose to stay with Victor. Victor's father invented the Clapper hand-free lighting control, so Victor's struggle wasn't quite the same as the other Actor Refugees. His house was different from theirs, too. So was his area code—310. I was to keep Harve at our apartment—part of the You Move Out Negotiation, because Victor already had two dogs and it wouldn't be appropriate for David to impose on his Benedict Canyon home with an ill bloodhound and his various bodily fluids.

Victor was a nice guy but was searching for love in all the wrong places. Mostly he picked up David's Model-Actress-Wastress scraps—thin, gorgeous girls who'd discovered with chagrin that David had a girlfriend with a day job. It was true I wanted David to go to Victor's. I couldn't hear myself feel while he was still in the house. "I'm taking Harve to rehearsal," David said coldly and headed down the stairs, grabbing his cell phone and a Power Bar on the way. Harve followed him, lumbering down the stairs like an elephant. Little and I sat on the couch and listened to the truck pull away.

It's oddly tiring spending more of your waking hours crying than not. I was getting so good at it that it was hard to stop. I could sniffle in public. I could wail at home. I could sob in traffic, bawl in the bathroom, weep at the gym, blubber while dog walking, and no one ever knew. I could stop and start on a dime like a Border collie. It was my thing. I was the best. It felt good to be good at something. I would have preferred anorexia, but you play the hand you're dealt. I was a crying professional.

That was the third time that day. Once this morning in the backyard in front of Little and an unsuspecting toad, then at work when I answered Viv's "So, how was your Christmas!" for about forty-three minutes during what was supposed to be the budget meeting for *Shades of Gray,* and finally, at Trader Joe's. I stopped there on the way home to harmlessly get a few things because there was no food in the house. It hit me hard, in the bread aisle just past the bialys—shopping for *one.* Buying food just for me, me alone, and not to share with anyone. It was biblically horrible. All the food in all the aisles filled with shopping couples grew blurry. I got in line, and the guy in front of me had several bags of chips. Chips. How David loved chips, his one dietary weakness. He'd gotten me so in shape, and now I was going to get fat, eating all this food alone. I added another block of smoked gouda to the cart.

Finally I couldn't hold it in, and I saw the cashier out of the corner of my eye watching me. He saw me crying and wouldn't look away. Naturally, this made me cry harder. The guy in front of me finished loading his groceries and left the store to go home to his wife, and the cashier took my cart and began unloading it, item by item on the counter. Swiss. Brie. Imported Jarlsberg. Cat food, dog food, cat toys. English muffins, black beans, echinacea *(does it really work?).*

"How are you today?" the cashier asked politely, ringing each item as though it were just a product, as though each can and jar were not filled with a special new kind of loneliness that would overtake me once I opened it. I tried to rein in my pathetic sobs, heaving with the difficulty. He didn't pretend the uncomfortable thing wasn't happening. He was a Hispanic guy with luscious toffee skin, a kind face and soft eyes like liquid liquorice and just the hint of a goatee. He looked right at me and asked, "Why are you crying?" as the Tuna for Cats can paused at the lip of the bag. Direct pity from a stranger in a red apron. Of course this made the tears cascade down my face like blood from a head wound.

"A long day? Tiring?" he offered, placing the numerous cat food cans into the bags. *I am a lonely woman with a cat, and that is how the world sees me,* I thought. He was making conversation, being nice to me. And the nicer he was, the more I lost it. It's odd the way genuine compassion weakens us, rocks our souls and empties our defense arsenals. I had nothing left.

When I arrived home it was time to unravel again, eating my microwaved burrito and cheese. Alone. I was home alone with my cat and my fabulous career and my ex-fiancé's cancer-ridden dog, eating microwaved food, while all over this bizarre, endless city people were out together, eating, drinking, talking, fucking, living, dying. God, I hated myself for being pathetic and weak and crying all the time. I hated myself so much that it made me cry.

That night Mom called again, and, finally getting me in person, accidentally told me the truth about her feelings on David. She was trying to reassure me that now I was ready to meet someone *who was right for me.* I, this time using the squeezed-voice, high pitched snuffle cry reserved strictly for one's mother, didn't quite grasp what she meant. "Well," she began in that tentative tone that is inevitably the overture to a disturbing revelation you're the last one to know, "you've never wanted to date *successful* men," she explained. Meaning, *men who have jobs that aren't minimum wage or involve name tags.* A defeaning pause filled the transcontinental wire before she added, "I don't mean that, I mean . . . you know what I mean."

Yes. I did. Oh, how to cope when your mother's right *again.* She tried to recover. "Well, how are you feeling today?" *Like my arm has been ripped off and you are now beating me with it,* I didn't say. The thing was, she was right. Why was she always right? It went back to high school when I chose Benny Sampson (class-cutting, leather-jacketed tough guy) over Thomas Bishop (honor studying, choir singing class president). It was just more fun to date someone different, someone whose goals were unlike mine—Benny's was to be the understudy for Motley Crüe's drummer—and who would find me fascinatingly ambitious and admirable. Someone with whom I could call the shots. Someone who made me feel . . . free.

"I THINK," Benny Sampson is yelling, "THAT WAS YOUR PARENTS!"

"WHAT?!" I yell back, for we are on his Harley '79 soft-tail, going about 75 down the main strip in the town where I am a teenager, and it's hard to hear. Benny, a five-and-a-half-year veteran of our high school, had come to pick me up for our date on the soft-tail.

"Alexis is not going anywhere on that," my mother said pointedly with all the authority her five-foot frame could muster when Benny showed up on my doorstep, the waiting Harley in our driveway. My father appeared, reeking of Brut and toothpaste and swearing because his top button wouldn't close. They were going out tonight too, to someone's anniversary party. This was back when people stayed married for years and had parties about it.

"What the hell is that?" he barks at Benny. The rule is no motorcycles. Period. Benny is told to come back with a car or not at all. Incredibly, he returns with a '69 Dodge Dart belonging to Billy

Nickerson, the pot dealer from up the street, who has a broken leg from a motorcycle accident and, lucky for us, can't drive his car. My parents leave for their party, and we drive the Dart directly to Billy's house to retrieve the bike.

"Why don't we just keep the car?" I ask reasonably.

"I don't have a license to drive a car," said Benny obviously. "Come on, what's the big deal!" The big deal is revealed when my parents, returning home to retrieve the forgotten gift they left on the kitchen table, pass us doing about 75 traveling in the opposite direction on our town's main drag. My mother has a very good memory, and my father, a very bad temper, and their Buick Regal whips into the McDonald's parking lot, does a 180 and gives chase. To my horror, Benny accelerates and slices into a side street, trying to lose them.

"STOP! YOU HAVE TO STOP! THEY SAW US!" I scream, but Benny is resolute. "NO FUCKING WAY! YOUR FATHER IS GOING TO KILL ME!"

Somehow, the '81 Buick Regal containing my parents is gaining ground. Fast. I briefly and absurdly think, *Piece of shit bike can't even outrun the Public Beagle* (as my brother and I, unbeknownst to our parents, had affectionately dubbed the family vehicle). Finally, Benny pulls over. I feel him shaking through his leather as the Public Beagle screeches to a blistering stop behind us. My father exits the car angrily, and he is a shade of crimson I have never seen. *You,* he says to me. *Get in the car. And you,* he says to Benny. Benny, one of the tougher residents of our high school and a feared presence in after-school detention, looks as though he may throw up or cry. Instead, he wets himself. We all pretend not to see.

*I don't want you. To see my daughter. Again. Ever.*

I didn't get engaged to Benny Sampson, which was fortunate, as he ended up in prison and addicted to steroids that made him pee orange, but I dated guys like him for a long time. The Harley David-son/Pubic Beagle road-race notwithstanding, I felt in control with guys like that. When you are in control you don't have to feel vulnerable, and then it doesn't matter when you get dumped. You can laugh, toss your hair and move on to the next sexy, tattooed, motorcycle-driving, Bud-can-drinking, pot-smoking, long-haired underachiever. It was fun. It was a habit. But David was no Benny Sampson. I wasn't in control, wasn't calling the shots and was feeling more vulnerable and alone than I ever had in my entire life. I hadn't won. There was no hair tossing.

# *Four*

| DATE/TIME | CONTACT | NUMBER | MESSAGE |
|---|---|---|---|
| 1/8/00 9:09 a.m. | Your Mom | Home | Just checking in; also are you coming to the Cape for July 4? Also, *Annie Hall* is on TV tonight. |
| 1/8/00 9:29 a.m. | Director Eugene R. | @ Bev. Hills Hotel (still under the name 'Rosebud') | Need to discuss *Shades of Gray* poster ideas; his new friend Monique is an artist; thinks she should design the press kit in Chinese lettering (?) |
| 1/8/00 9:50 a.m. | Gary/ Good Fun Promotions | On his cell | Do you want custom thong or XX-large condom for your actors in *Late Nights*? Other exclusive novelty gift? Pls call. |

| DATE/TIME | CONTACT | NUMBER | MESSAGE |
|---|---|---|---|
| 1/8/00 10:08 a.m. | Agotha | (??) | Wouldn't say—sounded mad. Will call back. |
| 1/8/00 10:16 a.m. | Viv | On cell | Do you know about the 'Hot List' deadline for Red Carpet magazine? Plse. submit Shades of Gray & Late Nights. Are photos approved yet? Also—Annie Hall is on tonight. |
| 1/8/00 10:43 a.m. | Tom/Photo Dept. | x489 | Confirming MPAA disapprovals on Shades of Gray pics— you cannot have two women kissing w/ open mouths; plse reselect key art or he can photoshop their mouths closed; plse call. |
| 1/8/00 10:54 a.m. | Sara-Anne | @home | Will be at the studio for a catering meeting today; r u free for lunch? |
| 1/8/00 11:03 a.m. | Razor/Red Carpet mag | 213-887-0389 | Need your submissions for our "Hot List" issue— deadline is tomorrow; "no" to Eugene R.—too old, but what about D.H. from Late Nights? Plse. call asap. |

| DATE/TIME | CONTACT | NUMBER | MESSAGE |
|-----------|---------|--------|---------|
| 1/8/00 11:15 a.m. | Viv | office | Warning: Eugene R. is coming in today. Will want to see you re: publicity plan, press junket & premiere ideas! |
| 1/8/00 11:25 a.m. | Molly | At school | Just wanted to tell you *Annie Hall* is on tonight at 9 p.m. on AMC ☺ |
| 1/8/00 11:59 a.m. | Viv | From her cell phone in 3rd floor conference room | Eugene R. is headed your way with someone named Monique . . . ? ☹ |

In *Annie Hall,* the best romantic comedy ever made, Woody Allen falls for a shiksa. He and Diane Keaton play with lobsters, go to movies and have sex, and then they go to L.A. and fall apart. La di da. There's no all-out war, no huge, divisive issue, but there's lots of therapy, and as they are flying home coach she says, "Alvy, let's face it. Our relationship isn't going anywhere." And he says, "A relationship is like a shark; it has to move forward or it dies. What we have here is a dead shark." She didn't love him anymore, but it wasn't because he was Jewish and she wasn't.

I escaped to the studio commissary in time to meet Sara-Anne for lunch while dodging Eugene R. and his new "friend" Monique. Adriane had provided the distraction of her gorgeous 5-foot-ten frame while I snuck down the back stairs past the screening room and through the lot to the executive dining area. Sara-Anne was already there, charming Clint Eastwood and the maitre d'. True to form, she had on a $1,200 Gucci blouse (she paid $120 at the Barney's sale), her best Levi's and her cowboy boots. Her long brown hair was done up in an elegantly casual twist. Homemade copper earrings completed the wine-selling ensemble.

"Mmmm, I had a poncho exactly like that one, made special from a Native American healer I met in the Badlands," she drawled wistfully as Clint Eastwood and his agent took her in. "Hey, sugar! How are you, honey!?" She lunged for me, completely forgetting the movie star next to her as she dragged us to the table she'd already negotiated. This was why I loved her. She was real, she was capable, and she was never, under ANY circumstances, a starfucker.

"So he gave you the Yentl ultimatum, huh?" she asked quietly, inhaling a breadstick slathered in butter as the waiter poured our water and offered us the standard carb-free, fat-free, fun-free specials. I ordered the grilled cheese, and Sara-Anne sweetly demanded a cheeseburger. "I am famished," she gasped. "Seven calls before noon. I'm ready for a pedicure and a J.D. on the rocks." Then she ordered one. No one lunching at the studio commissary ever ordered Jack Daniels. Arnold Schwarzenegger peered over his orange juice at table ten and stared.

I studied the room for spies. David had a few friends at the studio and a few from the bar who made it a point to lunch at the commissary once a week. I glanced to the back. There was Michelle Pfeiffer, the president of CAA, the *Times* head film writer, Drew Barrymore's agent, Adam Sandler's assistant—the coast was clear. "I can't do it, Sara-Anne," I said dismally, looking at my plate. "I feel like I've compromised a lot already and I've accepted all his flaws . . ."

"What—besides having two names he has *other* flaws?" she smiled sympathetically. I knew she'd never thought David Rothstein, aka Deke Rothrock (his "stage" name), was right for me, and I'd fought her on it in the past. She'd always been suspicious of "anyone who doesn't think their God-given name is good enough."

Now I was grateful for her perspective. I went on, unable to get the words out fast enough. "I know, I know, and now it's like he wants to change who *I* am too, change MY name, like all along he just expected me to convert, to be something else . . ."

"Did he leave?" she asked abruptly.

I hesitated, not proud of the situation. "Well, not exactly." The arrangement we'd decided on—at least until I left for Sundance—was odd. David was at the house during the day (while I was at work) to look for an apartment, use the phone, do his laundry. I spent nights there with Harve and Little and he slept at Victor's, in Victor's huge guestroom, eating Victor's gourmet groceries from Gelson's. I worried that by day he was reading my e-mails and ransacking the apartment, searching for evidence of my anti-Semitism as he marked the days until he could have the apartment to himself. In reality, he was desperately searching the *L.A. Times* classifieds and *Back Stage West* auditions. Loser. How I missed him. Sara-Anne listened patiently, chewing her cheeseburger as the business of Hollywood went on around us.

"Honey, you need to ask yourself one question: Do you love him? Or do you love *having someone?*" She stared at me sternly but kindly and took my hand. Nothing like a true friend to root out the simple truth of the matter.

"You didn't tell me you went both ways, Alexis!" A creepy voice invaded the table, and I looked up to see the director Eugene R. and an angry but amused-looking Viv and a young girl who must have been Monique standing over us. The maitre d' hurriedly assembled more chairs for the table.

"Hey, Viv," I gulped, caught.

"I'm Sara-Anne, Lex's friend," Sara-Anne offered, standing and thrusting a knobby hand toward Monique and Eugene R., who studied her hungrily.

"Sorry we missed you for the meeting," Viv chimed sarcastically, suppressing an evil grin and taking a seat. "Eugene was just updating me on what movies we should buy at Sundance," she teased, knowing I would have wanted to hear that part of Eugene's contribution. He was perverted and weird, but he knew his stuff.

Mostly, I liked Eugene R. He was interesting and smart and a survivor. But sometimes he wasn't in your world. Mostly, he stayed on Planet Eugene R. Occasionally he was so self-absorbed and vain (especially for someone who was over-bearded, balding and overweight) that being around him made me feel completely irrelevant. For instance, if my head was to suddenly catch fire, Eugene R. might look at me quizzically and say, "I wonder what the critics would say if *my* head were to suddenly catch fire . . ." But most of the time he was fascinating. His reputation with nubile studio executives was dastardly.

When we met at the test screening for *Shades of Gray,* he'd said, as I'd climbed into the limo next to him, "Are you an athlete?"

"What?" I'd gripped my questionnaires and plastic name tags tightly to my chest. Luckily, Viv had warned me. On his last film he had offered her round-trip tickets to Paris for one night in his hotel room. She had declined and the following day had messengered him a jar of pickles. He was allergic.

"You look like an athlete, you have . . . body confidence . . . were you an athlete in high school?" He'd shuffled closer and gripped an unsuspecting bicep.

"Shut up, Eugene," I had said, and we'd understood each other instantly. Still, as a neurotic director it was his job to torture me daily over every detail of the film's PR campaign. Now he was crashing my lunch.

*"Portland Girls* is the one that has the festival buzz this year," he announced authoritatively, spreading a hunk of butter on a roll. "That and the documentary about female genital mutilation, which I'm dying to see . . ." I glanced apologetically at Viv, feeling

guilty for leaving her alone with Eugene R. and his new friend, who looked all of seventeen, for two hours of discussions on how best to sell his perverted, dark movie to audiences who were innocently searching for a little joy.

"For someone who *loves* movies, I don't see much of you in the meetings about how to make *my* movie a hit," he oozed, squeezing my arm. *I only love good movies,* I thought as he stuffed his mouth with my fries and asked, "Have you met my Monique?"

"Your niece?" I shot back mock-innocently, and Viv kicked me quietly under the table.

Monique peered from behind stringy bangs, gave a short little nod and set a portfolio on the table. "You don't mind if I show you Monique's ideas for the cover of the press kit, do you?" Eugene chirped, clearing a space on the table. "Oh hey, there's Tony . . . TONY!" he called hoarsely to Tony Danza, who was standing at the opposite end of the dining room with the studio's head of TV.

"Wow, he looks great," said Viv.

"Yah," I nodded, pushing my plate away.

"Wouldn't toss him outta a warm backseat," agreed Sara-Anne, downing her bourbon.

Suddenly Viv brightened. "Hey Lex, maybe he's single. And. I think he's Catholic. Isn't he friends with Mel Gibson?"

Eugene R. gave an interested arch of his eyebrow and leaned in toward me with the breath of a toad. "Viv told me about your breakup, terrible shame but you're probably better off being single in L.A.," he heaved into my earlobe, and I glared at Viv.

Just then Tony Danza reached our table. "Tony, these ladies here would like to have sex with you, if you're available. Especially this one," announced Eugene R., squeezing my bicep again. Tony Danza laughed nervously and glanced around the room. Sara-Anne's mouth dropped, Viv escaped to the ladies' room, and I vowed to attend all the meetings for *Shades of Gray* for the future. I wasn't saving lives, but at least my job was interesting.

\*    \*    \*

That night, amid thoughts of how Tony Danza might look naked, I took the engagement ring off for good and put it in its fancy navy-colored hinge box, which I knew was in the study. I had been avoiding the study, where David's computer and his "work" were. I glanced painfully around. There, waiting innocently in the fax machine, was the program copy for David's upcoming show. Another play, but this time I wouldn't be in the audience wishing that his undeniable talent lay elsewhere. In real estate or bonds, for example. I glanced at the program. Naturally I read the whole thing and placed it carefully back in the receive position so my eavesdropping would remain undetected. I reread his bio. *Deke Rothrock dedicates this performance to Harve.*

Loser. I told myself that I was stronger (true) but that he was more stubborn (also true). Plus I was convinced he was getting all kinds of powerful Jewish advice, mostly from his female relatives. *Forget about that ungrateful blue-eyed shiksa, you deserve better.* As you probably know, there is just no competing with this. I wondered if he too was busy building up a wall, brick by brick, like mine. I wondered what his bricks were made of. I wondered if he, too, was thinking about the night we met.

We were out in a trendy bôite in Santa Monica, where Matt LeBlanc of *Friends* was having his birthday party. My friend from New York was his publicist, and we were *on the list.* Frank was there, having just moved to L.A. too. So was Sue, who moved to L.A. from Cleveland to be a TV writer, and who would fall in love with Frank later that year at an Oscar party for people who didn't get invited to any real Oscar parties. We were eating Matt LeBlanc's cake and singing "Happy Birthday" while all around us skinny, hip-slung-jeaned girls tossed their hair and displayed brightly painted toenails. The bartender had warm chocolate eyes and a kind smile.

"That bartender is hot," I say to Sara-Anne. I've just moved to L.A. from New York, and I don't know yet that when people turn to look at me and what I'm wearing when I walk into a bar, it's not about me. "I'm going to say hi."

"Newsflash, sugar. He's a bartender," says Sara-Anne, who is dating an accomplished Best Boy.

"Snob," I accuse her and make my confident way over to the rows of Heinekens and trendy vodka bottles.

"Hi! Can I have an Amstel light?" and I flash him the Smile and the Blueberry Big Gulp Gaze, and he flashes his and we're off. His name is Deke, and he is so hot—and he likes me. This is so easy, I love L.A.! I bet he won't ask me what book I'm reading or what I think of the *Observer*'s new media page or Tina Brown's latest venture.

We chat about traffic, the difference between New York and L.A. (L.A. is New York lying down, according to Quentin Crisp) and who invited me to the party. The crowd swallows me and Deke pours drinks like there's no tomorrow. Alas, there is another party to go to. "I have to say good-bye to Deke," I slur to my friends and head back to the bar. Deke Rothrock. Loving the ring of that. Alexis Rothrock . . . Maybe I would become Lexi Rothrock. Like a wife on *Dallas*.

"That guy?" sniffs Frank, peering through his New York intellectual black-rimmed glasses. "He looks like a model or something. He *can't* like women."

Then the L.A. Almost Famous network kicks in: "Hold on—I *know* him!" screeches Sara-Anne. "His name's Day-vihdd," she twangs, much more Southern when she's tossed back a few.

"No, his name's *Deke*," I protest, having dated a Josh Weiner, an Upton, and even an Abe Pudd, but never a Shane, or a Cody, or Deke . . . names of cowboys and the dangerous guys on soap operas. I wanted this.

"Naw, that's David Something-Stein. We met at Carrot Top's

barbecue two summers ago," she insisted. "My friend Erin, that crazy waitress at Campanile, the one who eats only grilled cheese sandwiches, she introduced us . . ." Suddenly he is so much less sexy. Not because of Carrot Top or Erin and her grilled cheese, but because he has a regular guy name. The mystique is instantly gone. He is just a bartender named Dave.

"Well, maybe I misheard him. What do you know about him?" I say, giving the bar a good casual scan to see if—*YES!*—he's looking at me.

"He's a player, I think," she warns. "And . . . he has a really big . . . *dog.*" She gulps her Jack Daniels, smiling her crooked, serene smile. "And a big truck. That's all I remember. Oh, he's an *actor.* Or is tryin' to be."

Houston, we have a problem.

"So let me just ask you, is your name Deke or David?" I ask in the juiciest voice I could muster when he finally calls a few weeks later.

"Well, Deke is my acting name because David Rothstein isn't a very original name. Plus there already was one in SAG. 'Deke' was an easy change," he says, his voice like a comfortable pair of leather pants. Buttery and soft, sexy but solid, welcoming.

After a breakup, like when you get laid off, you can only wander from room to room for so long. As anyone who's gone through the end of an affair (and who hasn't?) will tell you, you find new things to fill up the time. Every new empty hour alone is like a test that must be passed, a battle hard won. I took to reading the paper and watching lots of TV. I stopped reading my horoscope one day when it said the following:

> **Your kind of day. Examine, explore, discover. Highlight versatility, awaken intellectual curiosity. Someone comments, "Watch your weight." You should, too.**

I read it twice, then cried. I drifted to the TV section and was inexplicably drawn to the following program description: *World's Most Amazing Videos—Stuntman rides through a cave of fire; dancer pulls a muscle; electrocution; race car hits walrus. (TV14-V).* Whose job was it to do this? Describe bizarre events with acute brevity and precision, narrowing life down to its most raw and honest messiness? I wanted that job.

Fearing a panic attack that an hour alone in a once-shared apartment might bring, I needed something to do. Quickly. Check on Molly. I dialed.

"Hi, pathetic self-absorbed spinster sister here. What's the latest in your breakup?" I asked her. She made a sound like a hungry walrus. A half sigh, half groan, half plea to be put out of her misery.

"Jack's going to move out and stay with a friend but pay rent through February," she managed. "How are you?"

"I'm OK . . . David's living at Victor's, I took the ring off and we aren't talking." It was all true. Three simple sentences filled with pain, anger and resentment.

"I can't imagine that. Jack and I talk a lot," she offered, trying to be helpful but instantly regretting it. She changed the subject. "I can't believe I'll probably have to move again . . ." I pictured her on a crowded, charming street in Berkeley, groovy, trust-fund stepchild city to San Francisco, her tiny frame wandering sadly through her room, packing up her things one by one. Her dolphin photo album, the blue macramé plant-holder Grandma made for her, a pale orange cylinder of Metamucil.

"Maybe we should be roommates . . . ," I thought out loud.

Molly hesitated, then sighed. "I guess it is kind of weird the way this is happening to both of us, at the same time, isn't it?"

"I don't know if it's weird or some perverse DNA thing . . . ," I wondered.

There was a pause. "What's that supposed to mean?" she demanded.

"I don't know, just that we're both always with the wrong guys," I countered. "We let them propose, we said yes and now I'm half living with David and taking care of his sick dog, and you're unable to go to the bathroom and need a new apartment. Maybe we deserve each other." I'd wanted it to be funny, but somehow it wasn't. It was pathetic and sad. The sound of a bad joke falling flat in a warehouse full of sick crickets.

"We're not always with the wrong guys. I thought Andrew was good for you," she said, and not for the first time. (Andrew Sullivan, my high school boyfriend, who held the distinction of being the first person to get me high, give me an orgasm and break my heart, was a sore subject.) I hadn't thought about Andrew since . . . since my engagement. Oddly, a vision of him had popped into my head the moment before I'd said yes.

Andrew and I had had several aborted attempts at a relationship, beginning when we were fourteen. He was a wild, roaming, restless soul, and while he was exciting and fun, his tendency to forget I was his girlfriend was not. We'd had another tryst in college, but when I'd moved to Paris for a semester he'd gone on tour with the Grateful Dead. After one letter confessing his undying love for me, his true soul-mate, he'd "forgotten" to write at all. In adulthood we'd kept in touch on and off, and I'd sleep with him or call his number and hang up at least once a year. There was something there, untamed and wonderful, but I could never allow myself to depend on someone who loved fun more than he loved me. We hadn't been in touch since I'd moved to L.A, although I still got the occasional postcard from his globetrotting expeditions, some remote village in Africa or a quaint pub in Budapest. He was hungry for the world in a way that was sexy and inviting, but there wasn't really room in his plan for two.

"I don't want to talk about Andrew, Mol," I said testily.

"Is David—"

"I don't want to talk about David, either."

"Well, at least you have your fun, glamorous job," she said in the small voice of a lost toddler.

"That's true," I said, thinking of Eugene R.'s preposterous lunch crash, the childish argument with Bitsie, the MPAA, Tony Danza, Viv's lecture on how to negotiate the cost of a promotional thong. Who knew you could get them for less than a dollar each?

"It'd be fun if you were here, you know," I said. "Then, everything that feels like it's supposed to be funny but isn't, would be." The words landed, and I felt her give real thought to my proposal. I decided to get out early before the thought could solidify and be dismissed as the crazy idea it was. "I have to go," I said quickly. "I love you. Hang in there. I'm going to Sundance next week, so I'll call you from there."

"OK," she said. Then, "Lex . . ."

"Yeah?"

"Maybe I *could* move down there . . . I mean, there's nothing keeping me here anymore. And you do need a roommate . . ."

"What about school?" I said. She poured herself into that school, those kids, every day. The thing about Molly's job was that she was *needed.* My job was like making donuts. If I didn't show up to do it, someone else always would, and they'd be just as good at it as I was. Sure it was glamorous and fun and I was overpaid. All true. But the horrible secret is that most people in Hollywood jobs have no actual skills. They have friends and rolodexes and, sometimes, charm or balls.

Molly made an exasperated snort. "I could make more money as a waitress working three nights a week in L.A.," she said bitterly.

"You're not going to be a waitress," I told her. "I'd love it if you moved here . . . but you'd need to really think about it. I mean, it's really different from up there—"

"I know, I watch *Access Hollywood!*"

"And *I* watch the Learning Channel—sometimes. Mol, I gotta go. Take care. I'll talk to you from the festival."

"Maybe it will be fun," she said brightly. Or maybe it would just be cold and full of Mormons (Park City is the Mormon capital of the U.S.). I hung up, and the house was instantly quiet, so quiet; the noise of one person and an unwell cat. I looked around the kitchen. I kept using the same dish and fork over and over, for breakfast and dinner, just washing them and using them again. That dish sitting in the drying rack all by itself was the saddest thing I had ever seen. It never even made it to the putting-away stage; it must have been wondering why it now lived in the dish rack. A constant state of limbo, neither here nor there. I hated to waste a good cry on a dish, but there was no one to stop me. It was like being on acid, the state I was in. I was on emotional steroids. The craziest, most irrelevant object could make me emote like a Judy Garland drag queen. Focus, focus, need something else to focus on. . . .

*Murl. Murrrrlllllllmmmmm!* Little was acting weird, sleeping for hours, then emerging to inhale a whole bowl of food. She had that dazed, rock star expression. She didn't drink or clean herself frequently enough, and sometimes she wore old cat food on her cheek. When I force-fed her water from her old eyedropper she barely resisted, and most of it dribbled down her dirty whiskers and landed on David's comforter. *That his mother bought him.* Good.

The last time that Little was sick, she had a hole in her tail, which David and I realized was an abscess only after a putrid odor began following her around the apartment and a closer look revealed a bullet-sized puncture halfway down. She'd been in a driveway ruckus with the neighborhood cats, some turf war, and had paid the price for being both the smallest and the boldest. "A cat's teeth are like needles injecting bacteria," Dr. Niblack had said as he'd wrapped her tail after shaving it and cleaning it to her accompanying howls for the third time that week. "You should keep her *inside,* and she won't get into trouble," he advised, also for the third time that week. I glanced up at the Cat Breeds from Around the World poster. I had almost the whole first row, American Shorthair to Himalyan, memorized by now.

"What kind of life is that for a cat?! I don't believe in *indoor* cats, it isn't natural," I argued.

"That will be $98.50, again," said Dr. Niblack. The Elizabethan Poet / Satellite Dish collar she had to wear was not included. It alone cost $6.90. Little, being little, had trouble with the Elizabethan Poet Satellite Collar. Unable to master the spatial geography involved, she cut corners and crashed into doorjambs. Terrified, she'd lunge for the safety under the bed but, of course, would ricochet backward off the bed frame. And watching her eat was a pitiful sight. Luckily Harve would come to the rescue and clean off whatever food became lodged between her face and the collar, and together they would scramble for the morsels that fell to the floor.

Changing her bandage proved to be less fun and interesting that I'd originally envisioned. At one point in my life I wanted to be a veterinarian, before I discovered as a college intern how much fun the green room at *Good Morning America* could be, or that people actually got paid to sift through thousands of photos taken from a movie set.

Now Little was thin, and her hair was dry—she looked like the wasting actress-model who was the hostess at the Sky Bar. And she got cranky when I tried to move her. "I'm sorry," I said to my cat. It was time to take her to Dr. Niblack. I decided to board her there while I was away, as I didn't trust David to take her if she got worse. She hated it there, but I knew she was too weak to do much protesting.

David's phone rang. Someone was calling him about play rehearsal. His answering machine was on, and I had to hear his voice every time someone called him. "Hi it's Deke Rothrock, and I'm not in. You can try me on my pager: 310-545-2390 or my cell phone, 310-545-DEKE, or call my agent Marilyn Shapiro at Artists & Others, at 213-765-0909. Or just leave a message. Thanks!"

It was the recording he made when he first got the machine, days after we moved in together, when our pets were healthy, our CDs were combined, but we still had separate phone lives, *for his career.* The voice had the easy confidence of the romantically secure and professionally hopeful. I couldn't wait for that voice to get out of the house. I remembered his voice in the beginning, the early-stage-of-the-relationship phone voice. Whenever the phone rang in the apartment Sara-Anne and I shared back then, I leaped with glee to answer it, to hear his voice, to marinate in the sound of a cute guy wanting me. The beginning was three long years ago.

"Wow, he's fixin' to go home with you for Christmas, already, after three months?" Sara-Anne asked, raising an eyebrow. Concerned or jealous? Girlfriends. Can't live without them; can't force them to grow penises and make the world an easier place for everyone.

David was coming home with me for Christmas, our first one together. To meet my family. I think it is cute that he's not too proud to let me use my frequent flyer miles to fly him to Vermont. And since the airline is so overbooked by the time he actually gets someone to cover his shifts at the bar, I have no choice but to fly him first class, using, hell, almost all of my accumulated frequent miles. But so what! Who cares? We're in love, and I can't wait for him to meet my family! We'll play Scrabble, go for walks in the woods, make hot chocolate. He'll politely decline the bacon at breakfast, and we'll jokingly celebrate the fact that with Deke— sorry, *David*—I can spend *every* Christmas with the family in New England because he doesn't celebrate Christmas! Until now, that is. And he seems very good at it—the first year.

"I wish I could stay longer," he says, hanging up my brother's phone after unsuccessfully trying to get someone at the bar to cover for him.

"I know you have to work," I assure him, hugging him through layers of flannel and differences.

He shivers. "I'm glad I came. It's really beautiful here. I mean, I couldn't *live* here or anything . . ."

"You'll miss the sleigh ride . . . ," I whisper, my voice lost in the thicket of his marvelous hair.

He glances outside. "How am I going to get to the airport?"

If we'd been in a movie, the phone would have rung at that moment, and on the other end would have been a casting agent telling Deke Rothrock that he'd just landed a major part in the latest Ridley Scott-Tom Cruise blockbuster. My parents would have broken out the champagne, and David Rothstein would have joyfully hit the redial button to quit his job at the bar. In real life, my father is not exactly excited that Deke/David has to borrow his Cadillac for the three-hour drive in a snowstorm to the airport so he can take an earlier flight to L.A. to make his shift at the bar. The bill for parking the Cadillac overnight is $57. David has left a twenty in the ashtray. As the laze of the holiday wears on, my parents don't understand my impatience to get back to L.A., don't understand that this is *it, he's the one,* and as I dash into the airport terminal without looking back I don't see them wearing that worried parents face, don't see them exchange glances of knowing doom, realizing—as usual, years before I do—that I have made the wrong choice. I make the plane.

# Five

In *Beaches,* Barbara Hershey's husband is cheating on her with a gorgeous blonde. Barbara doesn't know it because she's become a kept wife who's put off law school and left New York City and her fun life with Bette Midler to stay at home in her big house, trying to find new ways to fill each day. One morning at breakfast her husband asks her, "What are you going to do today?" She thinks a moment and replies, "I'm going to buy a wrench." He looks up from his paper with a little scowl and asks, "Why?" She stares at her expensive plate. "Because . . . we don't have one," she concludes, knowing that her life, her existence, is pathetic because she is living not for herself but for a man who doesn't even know what she needs.

I dropped Little off to spend the following week with creepy Dr. Niblack before my flight to Park City that evening. It was a fancy vet clinic on Melrose, so they were open Sundays, for an extra charge, of course. Even for cats, L.A. had its nuances. I rushed out of the waiting area after filling out the patient questionnaire: *Cat is sluggish, appetite low. No interest in catnip-filled mice, "Animal Planet" or other usual stimuli. Nose is dry.*

I had the whole afternoon to kill. During a breakup you don't so much kill time as murder it. You can strangle it, suffocate it, torture it, maim it, draw and quarter it, disembowel or starve it to death. Whatever your method, it's all slow and excruciating. Time passes like a kidney stone. It is more manageable however, if you are otherwise occupied. So I finally did what I'd promised myself (and David) I'd do. I went to services run by Jewish By Choice. I was supposed to be meeting one of the founders. Meredith, who had converted from Christianity. I wanted to know why she'd done it, if someone had made her. She'd been incredibly sympathetic and warm on the phone, and she had invited me to come to services, check out the group and at least talk to someone. Still blaming myself for everything, I figured I owed the relationship that much—at least a last-ditch effort. I had to know that I tried. I had to be able to say I gave it my best shot. I had to know—could I be a Jew or not?

Jewish By Choice was, ironically, held in the basement of a church—the Baptist Church of the Redeemer, to be exact. That made it a little easier, I thought, although in my book, Baptists were quite possibly scarier to Catholics than Jews were any day. I mean, did you *see* Robert Duvall in *The Apostle?* At least it was on Sunday—the day I was used to being religious. When I entered the church-cum-synagogue I realized the service was nearing the end. The one thing I had noticed about Jewish services was that people drifted in and out, came late, left early, did their own time, caught up with friends in the aisles. It wasn't like Catholic Mass, where it's about as loose and casual as 1950s NASA calisthenics. Not that I'd know anymore. I hadn't been to Mass in years.

By the time the nineties rolled around, our family had become Holiday Only Catholics. Not only that but we were also church hoppers. Too restless and unfaithful to stick with one congregation or service, we sampled various forms of Christmas Catholicism with the secular curiosity of someone trying all the good restaurants in town. Every year we had the midnight mass argument, which goes like this:

*Dad:* Well, I like midnight mass, and the carols are better then, anyway. I want to go.

*Mom:* But George. It's only 8:30 and we've all been drinking, and we're already exhausted.

*Younger Sister:* I haven't been drinking.

*Me:* Why don't we just go tomorrow?

*Mom:* We can go to the 9 a.m. at the other church. The one with the live animal nativity scene.

*Younger Sister (louder this time): I* haven't been drinking.

*Dad:* I don't want to go to the 9 a.m. I want to sleep in and open my stocking at 9 a.m.

*Younger Sister:* I said I can drive.

*Brother:* Why are we even going? It's so hypocritical, it's not like any of us are remotely religious anymore. We'll probably all burst into flames the minutes we set foot in St. Paul's.

*Laughter*

*Me:* Is Father Rick still in jail?

*Younger Sister:* Father Rick got married.

*Brother:* Father Ken's the one in jail.

*Dad:* Well, I'm going to midnight mass. I'd like my family to join me, but if they're too drunk, tired, or pagan, that's fine.

*All (exasperated): Dad . . .*

When my brother and his family moved to Vermont, we could experiment further with our choices. Vermont is like the Berkeley of the East Coast—just colder, whiter and with more shotguns. Fortunately there were enough little white churches in his neighborhood for us to argue over which one to go to. David, being game that first year, had bravely decided to attend his first Christmas Eve service, the night the annual midnight mass argument occurred. We finally decided on the "Traditional" Catholic Mass at the little church down the road, and I can safely say that even if David hadn't been the only Jew in the state of Vermont that night, he felt that way. He stared at the priest as though he'd been an alien. Meanwhile, my sister and brother and I ribbed each other at all the hilarious parts of the Apostles' prayer, as my niece colored the pew, and the solemn Yankee congregation recited the lines in a scary unified chant that sounded like the chorus from *The Omen*.

Our irreverent approach to religion both shocked and horrified David, I think. As a Jewish man whose grandparents were on the last boat out of Eastern Europe before the Holocaust, he was, to say the least, respectful of worship and its traditions. Getting drunk for midnight mass—albeit accidentally—was, I suspect, revolting to him. I actually envied his devotion to his religion. For I had none, and as such, found it difficult to have faith in anything. Except, of course, movies.

So I needed a little guidance here. I hoped Meredith was there, but I didn't recognize any of the women in the church as the featured congregants in the Jewish By Choice brochure. It was an interesting name for the group, certainly more appealing than, say, Jewish By Negotiation, or Jewish By Ultimatum, which was pretty much how I was feeling.

A well-dressed, attractive older woman was a few feet down the last pew. She raised her hand and said the name of her father for inclusion in the Mourner's Prayer. She bore a terrible sadness, which was as visible as the scarf she was wearing. She was innocently pretty, which somehow made her seem even sadder, like Emmanuelle Béart in *Manon des Sources* or *Uncoeur en niver*. Then it was the end, and a few songs were sung. During the last song everyone joined hands, and I scanned the room feverishly for Meredith. The sad woman looked at me and motioned for me to join her. So I did, awkwardly, stepping down the pew as though I were naked and not just Catholic. I clasped her small hand and mumbled the song in a hum (because I didn't know the words, which were in Hebrew, and I was scared she would find out that not only could I not speak Hebrew and didn't know the song but also I was here not by Choice but by Guilt and Confusion: I was not Jewish by Choice but a Nervous Shiksa and Potential Jew under Duress. I hummed as melodically as possible under the circumstances. One guy in a front-row pew had a tie-dyed yarmulke and prayer shawl, and another woman up front was wearing a yarmulke and holding a Yorkie. This must be Reform, I thought. At least it's oddly interesting. Maybe I did fit in here. Surely I belonged somewhere.

A few minutes later the congregation exited to the sunny courtyard for the Hamotzi and Kiddush. This I had done before—you get bread and wine. Since I was raised Catholic, this was very familiar to me. The difference is that Jews get real bread, not some pasty papier-mâché-like wafer that makes you yearn for more than the sip of wine you get from a cup that everyone else has drunk from. Here they passed out little plastic shot glasses of wine for everyone, and by this time I was feeling sort of comfortable and perhaps a little self-congratulatory on what a trouper I was being, so I took one, said thank you, looked around and gulped it down. A minute later the blessing actually began, and everyone raised their cups, drained them in unison, and said, "Ahh-mainn." God I was stupid. I held my empty cup up, pressed it against my moistened lips, and pretended to drink.

I went inside to buy a ticket for the luncheon held after the service. Members had pink tickets; guests' were blue. I bought my blue lunch ticket and asked the woman manning the table if Meredith was here. "Are you new?" she asked brightly. I might as well have had a sign around my neck: LAPSED BUT SEARCHING CHRISTIAN. I told the woman why I was there, sparing her no detail, really, and she looked worried. After about fifteen minutes into my story, she went to get someone. Two people appeared next to her, and she introduced me as "This is Alexis, she's just joined!" They were very welcoming and pleasant but not, I decided, un-cultish. The man, Sheldon, was especially nice and began telling me why he'd joined the group. Within minutes I learned he was twice divorced, twice from non-Jewish women. We chose a picnic table in a sunny area.

"The first one converted, but not"—he raised his eyebrow—"because I asked her to."

"And the second?" I asked, reaching sadly for some lox. I loved Jewish food. I would miss bagels and lox and pickled herring, matzo ball soup and challah, knishes and tuna with mustard.

"She didn't convert either, but that *wasn't* why it didn't work," said Sheldon bitterly, curling his lip. I waited. Most men, if you just let them, will talk. "She had a really intense postpartum thing." He looked into his coffee cup as if the answer might be in there somewhere.

"Oh," I managed. It was going to get weird, I could tell.

Sheldon dove into the awkward gap headfirst. "After the baby, she completely changed, it was like she was a totally different person. We fought, I left, it was hell. Finally, I couldn't take it anymore," he said, munching on his third pickle, and I knew instantly it had been all his fault.

Sheldon shadowed me for the entire lunch, introducing me to other members, all of whom were, it seemed, single. "It's just a beautiful thing to have somewhere you can belong," said a pale, frail woman named Mary Fitzgerald. Suddenly, a vague intuition crept into my tired mind. Like joining reading groups, chairing charity events and cruising movie premieres, this seemed like just another way for those unfortunate enough to be single in L.A. to meet someone. I tried to imagine myself coming here every week. I tried to imagine embracing this hybrid of worship, these strangers who seemed—maybe this was mean—lost. Hell, I was lost, but at least I knew it and admitted it. I fucking *embraced* it. Or, as we in L.A. thera-speak say, I was *owning* it.

Religion. It was just another way to fill up the hole. You know the one, that nagging emptiness and vast meaninglessness that creeps up on you every so often and threatens to swallow you whole, demands an answer to, What the hell are you doing taking up time and space on this planet? No? You must be really busy. I made a decision. I had God in my life. Somewhere. Didn't I? I didn't need to go somewhere and have strangers bring him to me, and pretend I wanted to be there. That made about as much sense as a race car hitting a walrus.

Besides, there was a digitally remastered print of *Blade Runner* playing at the NuWilshire Cinema at noon—and if I hurried, I could still make it.

# *Six*

| DATE/TIME | CONTACT | NUMBER | MESSAGE |
|---|---|---|---|
| 1/10/00 9:10 p.m. | David | Cell | Where is Harve's medicine; did you throw it out? |
| 1/11/00 9:29 a.m. | Gerry/MTV Cribs | Cell in UT: 801-289-2736 | Doing special *Cribs* at Sundance at Levi's house; what talent do you have? Will pay for grooming but talent must wear Levi's hats. Plse call. |
| 1/11/00 11:10 a.m. | Claude G./ *Variety* | Cell in UT: 801-283-3927 | Heard you bought *Portland Girls*? Call; on deadline. |
| 1/11/00 11:24 a.m. | Dana B./ *Hollywood Reporter* | Cell in UT: 801-283-3938 | Heard you bid on *Portland Girls*? Call; on deadline. |

| DATE/TIME | CONTACT | NUMBER | MESSAGE |
|---|---|---|---|
| 1/11/00 12:30 p.m. | Viv | At Condo: 802-656-4323 or cell | Call when u get this; have big news; when are you getting here? |
| 1/11/00 12:35 p.m. | Jeffrey/*The Advocate* | Cell in UT: 801-273-3847 | Heard lead in *Portland Girls* is gay? Plse call. |
| 1/11/00 2:08 p.m. | Eugene R. | Lodge in UT: 801-455-7800 | Staying at the Penthouse Lodge at Sundance; call him about potential *Penthouse* magazine piece; he knows editor p.s. put him on list for *Portland Girls* party. |
| 1/11/00 2:20 p.m. | Marcos | Home | Have fun at Sundance plse get me an XL T-shirt. |
| 1/11/00 2:30 | Sara-Anne | 213-879-0099/ cell | Have fun at Sundance; enjoy the clothes & don't forget to "bird-dog" (?) |
| 1/11/00 3:10 p.m. | David | Victor's: 310-789-0923 | Did you get my message about Harve's medicine? (Sounded mad) |

Adriane had faxed me my call sheet at home on Sunday. In Hollywood there is no real weekend because everyone knows you will check your voice mail and e-mail at least once, and everyone wants to know which box-office numbers are real and which are fudged. Every weekend is a number—five million, fifteen million, forty million, or, on Memorial Day, ninety-ish million or better. By Saturday afternoon you know, depending on who you are and what studio you work for, how good or bad your Monday will be.

The sight of David's name sent my stomach for a loop. He was even passive aggressive in print. And Eugene R.—somehow, I had to get the man off my call sheet. But first I had to call Viv. "Call when u get this" meant "We have Important Work to Do and You Are Going to Do Most Of It." I was rereading the list of messages on the way to the airport and decided the only person I really had to call back was my boss. I pushed V.

"We bought *Portland Girls.*" Viv said by way of answering, as my cab blew off yet another yellow light bombing down Jefferson Boulevard on the way to LAX.

"What?! The one everyone's talking about? That's amazing!" I cried, real enthusiasm trilling through my voice. A brand-new, Sundance-hot movie to work on was just what the doctor ordered.

"Get your ass up here, Lex, the press is going *mental* for them," Viv added, the line crackling. I could almost hear how cold it was through the phone.

"The talent?" I asked.

"Mostly the director. Alexis, wait til you see him. He's de-*lish*. And, in a surprising twist, he's actually talented!" I loved Viv's sardonic sense of Hollywood humor. She was breathless with cold and excitement, pounding up Main Street in Park City. "We're on the map now, and this campaign's going to be fun," she added joyfully and hung up.

Viv had been exemplary in demonstrating restraint when giving me breakup advice or listening to my wails of self-pity. The day I'd told her about David and me, I could see her fighting not to look relieved that I wasn't going to marry a struggling actor who wanted to convert me. Viv had lived in L.A. her whole life and had already learned many of the painful lessons that seemed to await me each day, the first being, of course, that you do not date actors—you handle them.

After years of battling acne, insecurity, a bad marriage and an oppressive older sister, Viv had it together. She was tall, yoga-fit and had ridiculously thick black hair, which she straightened expensively every month. She had her own style: half Hollywood executive, half expensively-turned-out hippie. She had remodeled herself from an awkward, skinny, shy teenager with glasses and braces from Tarzana to a sleek, chic Woman in Film. She was also Jewish. And like most of my Jewish friends, she didn't agree with or even understand David's position.

"It's the most embarrassing thing about being Jewish," she'd explained when I'd confessed the details of my Christmas unvacation. "Who do we think we are, telling people they're not good enough for us unless they convert, it drives me crazy!"

Oddly, I'd felt the need to defend David's viewpoint. "It's for family, for tradition, to ensure the kids are Jewish—"

She replied in severe italics. "But they *wouldn't* be Jewish, they'd be *half* Jewish because I didn't care *what* Jewish law says, you're *not* Jewish, and no classes or rabbis or pieces of paper can *MAKE* you Jewish, anymore than they could *make* you Chinese, or green, or . . . *left handed!!*" She'd sounded personally offended, and it was comforting to know that a friend, a Jewish colleague, could articulate what I couldn't. Or wouldn't.

The cab pulled into the terminal entrance, and I was filled with hope. There would be lots to do with a new film at Sundance; I could lose myself in work. But film festivals were chaotic, and there were endless opportunities for things to go wrong, come undone, run late, bruise egos, cause yelling. The print could be lost, the critics could detest the film, the promotional items could be stolen in customs and auctioned off the following day on eBay. . . .

At Sundance this year my job was to generate publicity for our movie, *Late Nights*, which was screening in a special section of the festival, the section that no one cared about competitively but that had to accommodate our film because Someone Important from the Studio made a Phone Call. My other job would be to meet the filmmakers and "talent" from *Portland Girls*. It was one of those cool, smart, independent movies about real people that had been made for no money. My task would be to make the real people famous, thinner, more beautiful and less real and to help the filmmakers adjust to a world where movies of lesser quality are made for a lot more money. But in the process I'd help expose a quality film to a broader audience, and that was the part I loved.

D.H. Sterritt, the star of *Late Nights*, was, despite his rude agent, a desperately handsome and talented actor who was genuinely polite and intelligent and . . . nice. When I arrived in our hospitality suite at the Park City Marriott and saw him again, I had to collect myself. I hadn't set eyes on him since the final days of shooting, months ago. He looked like the love child of Mel Gibson and John Kennedy Jr., with a perfect body that was just loose enough not to be gay. God, he was handsome. For the first time in years I suddenly felt a pang of desire for another man, and I realized it was so foreign a feeling that it made me sad. For three years I hadn't even glanced at other men that way. And this one was not only an actor but he was also married. I squashed my attraction into my feet.

"Hey Lex, great to see you!" D.H. lunged for me and gave me the Actor's Platonic Bear Hug. I was suddenly grateful for the stack of cool clothes Sara-Anne had dropped off yesterday. I'd come home from Jewish By Choice and *Blade Runner* to find a little duffel bag filled with Sundancing outfits: cool jeans too big for her, tight little fuzzy sweaters with fake fur trim, a new red thong (In Case, she'd scribbled on the tag), a sexy black wool cap, a scarlet-colored fitted down vest and a pair of snakeskin cowboy boots that were too small for her. There was a note on the bag: Bird-Doggin' ammunition—knock 'em dead, Lex. For Chrissakes, don't puke on anything!

"Hey there, handsome," I flushed at D.H., who was standing a little too close to my furry sweater. "You ready for your close-up? We have a lot of interviews set up, and tons of press are coming to the party . . ." It was habit that the first words out of my mouth to any actor were always the answer to the question, What have you done for me lately? This was how you got them to cooperate. It was like training wild animals. Except the rewards for obedience were magazine interviews and photo shoots instead of chunks of raw meat.

"Hey, I hope you brought some *warm* clothes," noted Viv, tossing me a huge folder marked Portland Girls/Sundance while Adriane handed me the first of what would be many hot chocolates. She was already wearing her cell headphone, poor girl.

"Who cares about warmth when there's style to think about," said D.H., just before his cell phone chirped and he headed for the door, waving us both a kiss.

"You know, it's actually possible to be warm AND stylish," I replied, twirling around in my snakeskin boots and furry sweater and tossing my puffy down vest on the couch.

"Don't forget about dinner tonight!" called Adriane to D.H. He gave the thumbs-up sign and disappeared.

"Lex, I did not just see you flirting with an *actor*, right? I thought you were still in Shiksa Recovery?" Viv asked coyly as she settled into the couch with the festival screening schedule. Her job was to find the Next Big Indie Hit—and snatch it for as little as possible before the competition discovered it. I tossed my hat at her, which she caught in midair and threw back at me. "You seem cheerful. Are you medicated?"

"Ha. No. Just high on my work, Boss. When do I get to meet the *Portland Girls* team?" I asked, scanning the pages in the folder.

I'd read most of the press about the film on the plane already, but there was no substitute for a one-on-one with a brand-new director.

Viv looked up. "That reminds me—can you get them invites to the *Late Nights* party? You can just drop them into their mailboxes when you pick up your registration. We have dinner at eight tonight for *Late Nights,* and we'll need to set up another one too, for *Portland Girls*—at the Elk Inn. That's where they're staying. And God, sorry, but you have to invite Eugene R. tonight and D.H.'s agent, Hideous Babette and—"

"Monique, I bet," I interrupted. "Just tell me how many, and I'll work my magic," I told her, surprised at my own patience. I was so grateful to be here, to be working, to be busy, to be needed, that I didn't mind handling all the festival tasks that normally drove me nuts. Comfort the actors. Meet the new director and make him feel comfortable. Go to registration and cajole my way into getting more tickets for our screenings—for emergency purposes that could involve anyone from Robert Redford's relatives to Eugene R.'s latest tryst. Somehow find a restaurant and book a reservation for eight that could end up being for thirty or possibly two depending on everyone's mood, and arrange the seating so as to seem organic yet strategic—without offending anyone. Get everyone to dinner and back using local taxi drivers who do not like to wait two hours past the scheduled pickup and drop-off times. Organize field trips to secure free, expensive stuff for all the actors—to the Levi's house, the Sony house, the Fred Segal boutique, MAC makeup—all the things they could easily get for free back home in L.A. by using their own personal publicists. Somehow it was more fun for them to be squired around for free shit in Park City, Utah. No matter. I would do it all.

I headed over to registration to pick up my badge, our tickets, and any messages. My mailbox was stuffed full—all requests for interviews with the cast of *Late Nights* and, now, *Portland Girls.* A few premiums—a hat, some CDs, seventeen different movie stickers, a thong advertising the documentary about female genital mutilation (apparently I wasn't the only promoter who thought it was a unique idea), and party invites from the usual suspects—*Entertainment Weekly, Premiere* and *Entertainment Tonight, Variety's* "Ten Directors to Watch" party, one of whom, I noticed, was Kirk Olmstead, the director of *Portland Girls.*

"My, aren't we popular!" I heard a familiar voice tease. I turned with my arms full to see Billy, my friend the musician, standing there looking as gorgeous and as calm as ever. Billy Brady was my age, a very cool guy, but we'd never dated. We met when he opened for one of the bands playing at one of our movie premieres. I hired him for gigs whenever I could, and that included our Sundance *Late Nights* party. He'd agreed to play for free as long as the studio covered his transportation. We had always been "just friends," as unbelievable as that sounds. I'd seen him through a few Model-Actress-Wastresses, and he'd seen me through three years with David. The problem was that, in the process, he and David had become friends.

"I called you a few days ago . . ." The Careful Voice. Our friends were now using the Careful Voice with me. Christ.

"Hi, Billy," I said in an exhale. The fresh strength that came from working and being away from home dissolved in the presence of one of David's and my mutual friends. "Meant to call you back—sorry, it's been a little crazy." He studied my face as people swarmed around me, yammering into cell phones, stuffing mailboxes, throwing stuff away, yelling to friends across the room. Outside it was snowing.

"Um . . . ," he began awkwardly. I knew then that David had told Billy the breakup story. His version of The Story. Billy was *my* friend first and by default *my* support link, and now he was still hanging out with David because they were connected by that unique L.A. virus—the contemptible desire to be discovered. Billy was actually quite talented and very sweet. He was also hot, in that upscale, sexy, bohemian kind of way. Tousled black hair, eyes like a coming storm, pale Irish skin . . .

"I'm fine, Bill, really I am," I said quickly, giving him a Friend Kiss. "Let's not talk about David, okay?"

"I wasn't sure if you knew I was still seeing him—I mean, God that sounds weird, doesn't it . . . ," he blathered. I gave him my best forgiving smile as he continued, "I'm doing the music for his play, and so—"

"Whatever," I said, a little impatiently. A cute director type looked up from his mailbox a few feet away, and I felt as though I'd been caught being rude. I gave him an apologetic look, and he smiled sympathetically and winked at me. He looked familiar, like someone I used to know . . .

". . . wanted to make sure you're OK. Lex?" said Billy.

"Sorry. It's just, look, Billy, I need to focus on work here, not David. And you need to be brilliant at our party. Lots of snow bunnies at Sundance who love a guy with a guitar, you know," I sang. I had a lot to do, and I had to get Billy's concern/guilt out of my way.

"Thanks, Lex. You'll always be first with me—you know that." He put on his hat, some earthy Tibetan thing, gave a killer smile on and shifted his guitar to his other shoulder. "Gotta go find my room. I'll see you at sound check." And he pecked my cheek and was gone. I turned toward the mailboxes. The cute director guy was gone too.

After registration and forcing the Festival press relations staff to give me more free tickets to our screenings (and a few other ones I wanted to see) I checked into my $350-per-night tiny snow motel and took a much-needed nap with the latest copy of *Salt Lake City News,* which featured an article on D.H. that I had nothing to do with but reminded myself to take credit for when I saw the producer at dinner. An intense, type-A gay man, I'd managed to avoid him at the airport at the abysmal crossroads of Coach and First. I read the whole article, fell asleep and descended into inappropriate dreams about D.H. that somehow involved Harve and Little waiting outside my motel room, which, due to unforeseen studio budget restrictions, I was sharing with D.H. I woke up at 7:20 p.m., horrified that I had exactly ten minutes to shower, dress, check on the taxis for everyone and confirm the restaurant reservation for dinner. So I did what I always did when I ran out of time and a million things needed to be done. I called Adriane, who had, of course, already taken care of everything.

"Just get yourself to the restaurant, I had to give your cab to Eugene R. and Monique," she apologized.

"You're a saint," I told her. Maybe if I just held on to a great assistant for the rest of my life, I'd never need a husband, I thought, stuffing myself into Sara-Anne's skintight, cleavage-exploding, violet, rabbit-fur-trimmed hoodie and bolting out the door into the cold. A whole day and I'd only been sad about David once. This was progress.

After my fourth Mormon Promise, some sort of gin concoction that D.H. had persuaded the Riverwind waitress to invent for our table, I was feeling better than ever. Viv was mercifully seated between Eugene R. and Gregory, the *Late Nights* producer; I was stationed between the adolescent Monique and D.H. Adriane and D.H.'s gorgeous wife, Alana, a taut, stay-at-home mom, completed the ensemble. Hideous Babette, D.H.'s rude agent, fortunately had a more important (higher-paid) client to dine with. Alana kept leaving the table to call their nanny and check on their baby back at the condo, which left D.H. and me plenty of time to debate what a Mormon Promise might really be.

"Maybe it's a code among the multiple wives—a Mormon

Promise means you're the wife who gets the master bedroom tonight," D.H. whispered, and I heaved with laughter. When was the last time I'd laughed? I couldn't remember. The restaurant was filled with The Industry and Those Who Wanted to Join It. It was loud, festive, and clogged with cell phones. The Park City staff was barely managing the obscene demands. No dressing, no bread, why isn't there more alcohol in this drink, we had a reservation for five minutes ago, why are there no vegan entrees, where is the manager, don't you know who *I am?*, etc.

"The Mormons—they don't really have more than one wife, do they?" asked a stunned Monique, sipping seltzer. Poor girl, I didn't know what Eugene was doing with her, but she looked exhausted. She was so young, so pretty, so innocent. D.H. moved in for the kill.

"Sure," he boasted. "They have ten or twenty wives. Why do you think there are so many kids in Park City." Monique glanced nervously around the restaurant. D.H. rubbed his sexy two-day stubble. "It's a sin for them *not* to have sex," he teased her, gulping his Promise. Why couldn't David be this fun and successful?

"Stop it!" I hissed at him, laughing, feeling light-headed and suddenly remembering the altitude rule. Two glasses of water for every alcoholic drink. Whoops. I giggled, and Viv kicked me under the table. Her eyes pleaded "help," because Gregory was in mid-ramble about how the marketing budget for *Late Nights* was far too small and if they hoped to reach any audience or make any money, the studio should damn well double it. After all, he'd given in to changing the name from *Hearts on Life Support*, it was his baby after all, and . . .

But I couldn't help Viv because the Mormon's Promise was going right to my head, and D.H. was going right to my gut.

"Another?" asked D.H. sexily, just as Alana made her excuses to the table about the baby crying and her needing to return to the condo. D.H. made a halfhearted offer to accompany her, but seeing how much fun he was having (or how much alcohol he'd had), she sweetly told him to stay put.

"Speaking of wives," D.H. said to me quietly, after Alana had departed, "what's up with . . ." He made a dramatic roll of his eyes toward Monique, who was delicately making her way through some mesclun greens.

"So, Monique," I whispered invitingly as Eugene R. joined the Viv attack, demanding a bigger budget for the *Shades of Gray* poster design. "What's your, um, connection to Eugene? How did you guys meet?"

She beamed proudly, then flushed. "He spoke at my school! About film theory. Then we had coffee afterwards and talked for hours, he really liked my artwork, and he took me to see the Jack Demmy film, that French one?"

"Errr, Jacques Demy, *peut-être?*" managed D.H. helpfully. He was drunk, but not as drunk as I was.

The waitress heaped more bread onto our table. I held fast onto my Promise. "So, how's it going?" I asked Monique girlishly and cruelly.

She chewed a tomato and thought of her lover. "Isn't he amazing?" she finally gushed.

"Isn't he . . . old enough to be your grandfather?" mumbled D.H., snorting into his roll. Now I kicked him under the table, and he grabbed my thigh and squeezed. Uh-oh. Monique blushed.

"It *is* a bit of a May-September romance," she admitted. I noticed she was wearing one of those sweaters like I had in eighth grade, with the collar print and the three buttons.

"So," I leaned into her young, dewy face, "what do you do about . . . his . . . wife?" There were relationships of all kinds out there in the world, and I wanted to understand them all. If someone as bizarre as Eugene R. could make a young girl love him, there was hope for me.

"What did you say?" she gulped, the color draining from her

face. The highly intuitive Viv sensed disaster and shot me a death glare. Adriane went to check on our cars. Monique looked at Eugene R. with horror.

"What *wife?*" she said a little loudly, and we all grabbed for our glasses.

"Are you feeling any better?" asked Billy with concern. We were at the Mountain Club, at the sound check for the *Late Nights* party, where I'd basically been hiding out all day with only my laptop and cell phone and a pounding headache to connect me to the rest of Sundance. Between D.H.'s thigh grab and being the one responsible for Monique's discovering that Eugene R. had a wife, I wanted to forget about last night and bury myself in work. I'd paid the Riverwind bill as our dinner party had awkwardly dispersed following Monique's outburst. Billy had found me hours later at midnight, in a screening of a Native American documentary about wedding traditions, crying into a very large bag of popcorn. Apparently I'd called him, told him where I was and that I needed help getting back to my room.

"She was bound to find out anyway," said Billy helpfully.

"Thanks," I told him gratefully, arranging *Late Nights* thongs and condoms around the club, "but I still feel like a moron." Not to mention the fact that I'd puked on Sara-Anne's sweater. I headed over to the screening and hoped tonight would go better.

*Late Nights,* the story of a gay New York bartender who makes it big in the nightclub business, earned a standing ovation. By 10 p.m. there was a line of 100 people to get into the party, where the waitstaff wore T-shirts that said Make It Big. *Late Nights.* Billy strummed his guitar to the rapt attention of several hot-looking, fashionably warm women. It was thirty degrees out and snowing, and the people outside waiting were not happy. I didn't notice who was on the list and who wasn't, or which agents were yelling at the poor polite Mormon volunteers working the door. Viv must have been somewhere trying to find me, but unable to. She was having a discussion with the fire marshal, who was politely explaining that we were over capacity. The last time I saw Viv she was offering him a martini and the hand of the *Late Nights* lead actress, Jenna Wilson, whom *It* magazine had just labeled Flavor of the Month. In the article, Jenna was a 28-year-old overnight sensation. In reality, I'd seen her at David's Actor's Refuge workshop three years ago as a last-chance thirty-four-year-old.

Instead of manning the door like a good VP of Publicity should have been, I was standing at the bar next to D.H., listening to him tell me what an amazing job I'd done with the film and how everyone from the cast really liked me. Of course, they were all gay, except for D.H. and Jenna. We were both pretending the thigh grab hadn't happened. Suddenly he said, "Hey . . . aren't you getting married soon?" My smile lost its firmness as the rest of me began to tense up. Still, I couldn't believe it—D.H. had actually remembered. During the production of the film several months ago I had gotten engaged, and he'd remembered. As a publicist I was used to the fact that actors remembered nothing but their lines and names of people who could help them. I had worn my ring to the wrap party. D.H. had noticed. "Well . . . things didn't really work out," I said evenly. What a grown-up I was being. Seconds later the Berlin wall of party composure came down and I blurted out the whole story, ending with Jewish By Choice which made D.H. laugh. Somewhere behind him, through a snowy, frost-encrusted window, I saw Claude G., my *Variety* reporter ("my" because he covered our studio and I had once leaked him a story about Owen Wilson's creative differences) angrily gesturing and trying to catch my eye. The window was a little taller than Claude was, and he was jumping up and down trying to see into the party. He was standing next to the cute guy from the registration mailboxes, who also looked annoyed to be standing outside. It was easy to pretend I didn't see them as I gazed into the eyes of my sympathetic leading man, catching my own reflection in his delicious iris. I looked fat. And sad.

"Wow," said D.H. "I had no idea . . . you seem to be doing really well under the circumstances." He glanced at my naked left finger, helpless and alone against the world.

"I was," I said sadly, "until you brought it up." He reached out his hand to comfort me protectively, I thought, but actually he was reaching over me for another free Absolut and tonic. Alana appeared and engulfed him in a tsunami of spousal pride.

"Congratulations, honey!" she beamed, and he held her tightly, their eyes locked in a shared secret, and for a moment it seemed they were the only two people in the room. How did they do it? He was an actor, she was not, and they were married, they were happy, they had a child. As incredible as it seemed, I think they were together because they really wanted to be. The thigh grab had meant nothing; a harmless flirtation. D.H. loved her. He needed me, but he loved her. They surfed the room, chalking up compliments and promises of work with every step.

"You look sad again, what happened?" asked Viv, scanning the room for more fire marshals. "The party's a hit, you should be glad—especially considering the disaster you made out of last night. Oy," she added.

"I'm sorry, I was hammered," I moped.

"No kidding. I had to add another ten TV spots to Eugene's goddamn campaign to keep you from being fired." But I could tell she thought it was funny.

"I feel horrible. Do you mind if I go?"

"Go ahead—but do me a favor and go to BED, Lex, not to some stupid Iranian film about romantic poets or something, okay?"

"Fine," I muttered, annoyed that I had planned to go to that exact screening. I headed for the door, pulling down my sexy cap so no one in the line outside could identify me.

"We need you fresh for the press day and the *Portland Girls* meeting tomorrow!" she called encouragingly after me, but I was out the door.

I trudged through the snow back to my Best Western. It was cold, and I'd forgotten the feel of real cold. In L.A. it could get chilly, nippy, or sometimes, like when you got caught in a tank top after dark on the beach, *freezing*. But the hard, raw, violating winter cold that penetrates your core with an icy tenacity, well, that was a feeling I hadn't experienced in years. There was so much snow. I used to ski a lot, back home in the rolling New England winters. I thought about the fact that I used to wear thermal underwear, skis and ski boots in the snow instead of a *Late Nights* plastic party badge and a sexy hat that did nothing to keep my ears warm. I hardly ever skied anymore. The last time I skied was New Year's, when this new, sickening part of my life started, when I . . . hope. I was not going to think about that right now. As Scarlett said, *I'll think about that tomorrow, tomorrow is another day.* The press day was tomorrow—lots to worry about and do.

It took twenty minutes to undress. I remembered this, dressing in layers. God, it was annoying. Once in my single bed I pulled up all the covers, then fetched the musty pink wool blanket from the closet, threw that on top with my parka, then removed all my clothes from my suitcase and dumped them on top of me and watched Utah public television for the next four hours. There was no remote. Neither D.H. nor any other tall, dark, handsome stranger knocked on my door the moment I fell asleep.

When I was a kid the whole family used to go on ski trips all the time, to Maine, Vermont, New Hampshire . . . though how my father managed to both afford it and get the time off seems a complete mystery. The only explanation I can think of is that it was the seventies, when nine-to-five jobs ended at five, a week off meant a week *off,* lift tickets were $15, there was no such thing as two-way pagers and time stood still for days on end. During one trip my sis-

ter and I, at age eleven and fourteen, made the mistake of tobog-
ganing down the mountain at midnight with a group of guys who
had a six-pack and inviting gazes. I'd ended up in the ER at 4 a.m.
with a plastic surgeon called in from Boston to put my face back
together after I'd collided unpleasantly with a chair lift support
pole. I'd been the only one on the giant, careening sled curious
enough about our speed to stick my head out on the way down to
see how far we were from the bottom.

My father arrived at the hospital just as a nurse was taping a
huge maxipad to my face. He blamed himself for not having been
there, just as he hadn't been there when my brother had tackled me
on a dirt road at age two, leaving the classic chin scar of the daring
toddler. He had the uneviable task of calling my mother, a nurse,
at home to tell her what had happened under his watch. What I
have never told him is that the occasional scar, broken finger or
concussion is the willing price I paid for being raised to be confident, adventurous and independent—and even now I wouldn't
trade that for the face of Halle Berry or the body of Alana Sterritt.

I slept hard and long, forgetting where I was when I awoke to
the local station interviewing the familiar cute guy from the mailboxes and the outdoor party line.

# Seven

For Russell Crowe in *Gladiator,* life was simple. He knew the point of his life. The point was to stay alive. To last another 24 hours, minute by grueling minute. After his family was snatched from him so violently, he had no purpose, no point in existing but to join them one day. Then, in the latter part of Act Two, the reason to stay alive becomes teaching the nasty little emperor (played by a squirrelly Joaquin Phoenix) a lesson about honor. For the course of the movie Russell endures one impossible battle after another, each one more ludicrously horrifying than the next, because that is the hand fate dealt him. As his ambivalent will to live triumphs again and again and he becomes a hero, he gets ever closer to the end of his journey, to the only thing that will give him peace—his own death.

At that point in 2000, the point of my life was to stay employed, since my job was the only thing giving structure, meaning, a vague sense of being needed, to my days. During Sundance it occured to me that the happiest people are probably those who don't think much about the point of life but just get on living it.

Press days are an odd series of exercises for a publicist: pick up the talent, greet the talent, hope that talent had a good flight, make the talent pose for pictures, remind the talent what to say, worry that the journalists might not show up, call the journalists to remind them to show up, decipher when the talent is getting cranky, order the talent lunch . . . The press day, once you've assembled the great schedule and everyone has his angle, is like the Act Three climax. Everything is done except for the unfolding of the events you've spent so much time planning. Then, like most things you worry about in life, it's soon over. True, none of these exercises were particularly challenging or interesting on their own, but together they provided a full day of not being able to think about either David, growing old alone or being Non-Jewish By Choice.

D.H. arrived at the Marriott for the *Late Nights* press day looking snowy and fabulous in his Gore-tex jacket and Sorel boots. Even more fabulous looking was the winter-outfitted Alana and their one-year-old daughter who came to keep him company while he talked to *Access Hollywood.* They were in love, they were affectionate, and when she left to go to a screening of Kevin Spacey's new movie, which I didn't have time to see, D.H. asked if I could help her find the theater. To my dismay, she was incredibly nice.

"Don't I need a groomer or some makeup?" asked D.H. as the *Access Hollywood* cameraman checked his lighting. Adriane clutched the schedule and looked nervous but said nothing. "Am I pale? My agent's always saying I'm pale," D.H. persisted.

"No, you're gorgeous," I said authoritatively. "Put this on," I added, handling him a *Late Nights* ski hat. He obeyed. The camera rolled, and the selling began.

"Where are his talking points?" asked Viv, appearing with a giant mug, five-hundred-dollar sunglasses and a new North Face Sundance parka.

"In his head. He memorized them," I said as D.H. laid on the charm.

"How'd you make that happen?" asked Viv, impressed.

"*Late Nights* is not a 'gay movie'—it's a romantic comedy with an appealing *twist*," D.H. politely corrected his interviewer.

"I told him he could have four extra premiere tickets if he memorized them," I whispered to Viv. Naturally, we didn't even have the budget for a premiere, but neither the uptight producer nor the gorgeous actor knew that.

"Well done," she whispered back gleefully. She checked her watch. "Hey, don't forget about your meeting. I'm gonna catch a screening."

I left Adriane in charge of the rest of D.H.'s interviews and went to meet the *Portland Girls* talent. Kirk Olmstead was a 29-year-old first-time director from Portland, Oregon, and his film starred his alleged girlfriend, Danni Jones, 20, who not only had never acted but had never finished high school or set foot in a restaurant before coming to Sundance. Staring at the press clippings as I headed over, it dawned on me that Kirk was the guy from the mailboxes. Oops—and the guy who hadn't been able to get into our party last night. I made my way across the street and headed into a series of condos, searching for the correct number as I passed each door. 521/PORTLAND GIRLS.

Danni Jones was talking to the *New York Times* in her room while Kirk sipped coffee in the sitting room of their publicity agency's condo, which looked like a command center of the press hotel in a war zone. Posters, photos, flyers, articles were all over the walls; screening schedules, business cards, press lists and re-re-re-revised interview schedules were taped or tacked onto every visible surface. Laptops and portable printers surrounded us. Cell phones chirped various tones; publicists, agents and managers and the occasional Mormon festival volunteer or cleaning person entered and exited the fray looking bewildered. The TV in the corner played *E!* Entertainment Television (who was covering the festival live) loudly. I poked through the chaos. "Hi. I'm Alexis Manning, from the studio publicity department . . ."

I sat down opposite Kirk, who had been outfitted gratis by the festival in North Face gear but still wore his own ski cap shouting Portland's Best Brews! I took him in: He was young and smart and talented and funny and rugged and just shy of cocky. He had an odd, appealing smile—half baked, up to something. He reminded me of someone . . . but it wasn't David . . . and then it hit me. It was Andrew Sullivan, high school heartache. My heart took a little sky dive into my groin, and for some odd reason I was fighting tears. *What the fuck, not now, not now goddammit!* I scolded them silently. What had happened to the fun, confident me?

"The first thing I should tell you," said Kirk Olmstead as he sucked urgently on a Marlboro Red, which was absurdly sexy even though it was gross, "is that I wrote and produced and directed this movie, and I paid for it . . ." He paused, as if considering something, then continued, ". . . well, my parents helped but I'm planning on paying them back. Anyway . . ." He hauled a drag, smiled crookedly but earnestly and rubbed his eyes. He'd definitely been celebrating being the toast of Sundance. "This movie is the most important thing in my life right now," he said decisively, looking me directly in the eye and holding my gaze for what seemed longer than necessary.

"Yes, I know," I told him, and Kirk looked doubtful. Viv had given me all the press coverage to date, and I'd devoured it. I'd downloaded everything there was to know about Kirk Olmstead: only child, blue-collar parents, always a creative streak, an impatient student, years toiling in public television and video stores and guiding fly-fishing trips for rich tourists to pay for his first film. I explained patiently, "I've read all the press."

"What I mean is"—he sounded like he was trying to be tactful but didn't know how—"I'm glad the studio bought the movie and uh, I'm grateful, you know?" How big of him. We'd shelled out $3 million for his gritty little slice of life shot on 16mm and would spend triple that to market it. "But I want to be involved every step of the way. This is our shot, mine and Danni's." He looked at me a little conspiratorially. He had no idea what he was in for. I scanned the photos on the wall for a glimpse of the Sundance It Girl of 2000—Danni Jones. The photos were gritty, amateur, the poster a sad montage of unprofessional artwork that smacked of reality. In a word, cheap. It would have to go. I looked at the close-up of Danni Jones and caught my breath. She was something else. Wild, exotic, raw. Picture Angelina Jolie very angry, unpolished, short and the leader of a gang. That was Danni.

"I should tell you that Danni is very—"

"Young," I said, unable to stop myself from putting words into his mouth, which I would be doing now from this point until we released his movie.

He smiled and gave me a quizzical look that I took to mean *Shut up and let me finish.* "Yes. And she isn't very . . . she's . . ." He searched. Gave up. Smiled. Inhaled. I waited. God, he looked like Andrew. Or his mouth did. He rubbed his eyes. They were a brackish gray-blue, like the wintertime Atlantic. For a full thirty seconds David "Deke" Rothstein ceased to exist. I wondered, what was Andrew Sullivan doing now?

"She's *what?* . . . " I urged, getting a little impatient. D.H. was doing his snowboarding piece at three o'clock with *Entertainment Tonight,* and that was something I did not want to miss. With that, a stunning brunette with sultry eyes, rosy lips and a very pleased expression toppled into the room wearing a sports bra and Versace Leather pants and boots. She crashed into the command center table, toppling laptops, scattering press schedules and shredding a poster on her way down. "Fuck! My Irish coffee!" and the mug full of Kahlúa and Nescafé collided with Kirk's North Face parka, forever staining it with the absurdity of the moment. The energy of the room swirled into the girl and surrounded her like a crazy, sexy vortex of possibility.

"Danni, this is Alexis, from the *studio,*" said Kirk pointedly.

Danni, her exquisite black eyes gleaming with shockingly alert and dangerous pleasure, blew a wisp of hair from her face and seized my hand.

"Hey, a chick, I like this already. Howyadoin'?" She wiped her mouth and licked her lips, and all of her youth, the throbbing force of her untapped potential and rabid appetite for the world went shooting out her eyes and mouth and hit me in the chest with the force of a small explosion. Or that's how it would have happened had we been in an animated film.

Kirk stood up and wiped Irish coffee off his parka. "Alexis, meet Danni." Danni was going to be a star. That was clear. She was so *alive* that it was hard to look at her. I felt like a withered prune standing next to her, all 31 years of me. She was hungry and wild. Like the T. rex in *Jurassic Park*. I thought absurdly. *She's going to eat me alive.*

It took several hours for me to recover from meeting Kirk and Danni, though I must admit the sheer drama of it all was a welcome distraction. I had a new movie to sell and two new stars to groom. I hadn't a clue how we were going to domesticate Danni, but if PR agencies could make people believe that Ben Affleck could act and that Meg Ryan was a sweetheart and Renée Zellweger had a healthy relationship with food, then I could make Danni a star and Kirk could learn how to talk to the press without being so . . . honest. Their evolution from nobodies to Hollywood Hipsters was going to be, without a doubt, *more* press-worthy than Kirk's movie, which was a coming-of-age story about two girlfriends growing up in Portland. *Portland Girls* won the top prize at the festival. *Portland Girls* was gritty and real and moving, and it made you connect to the world in a way that made you feel a little better about being human. More importantly, its creators were young, creative and good looking. Mental note to call the Gap Ad people when I got home.

At dinner that night, originally for eight but eventually threatening twenty-six, Viv made me sit between Robert Redford and Kirk, forcing me to control my drinking and, consequently, my mouth.

"That was some party you had last night for *Late Nights,*" Robert Redford said to Viv, who tried desperately to read his tone. Good luck, I wanted to say. He's not the Golden Boy of Acting for nothing. Star-proof as I was, I had to admit I was in awe sitting next to him. It was difficult being professional and remaining interested in our new director with Hubble at the table. I could tell that Kirk was also having a hard time being unimpressed. The whole table—from D.H., his agent, Adriane, Eugene R., Monique (they'd made up), to Gregory and all the hangers on—awkwardly tried to treat him like a real person. Only the tired waitress at the Riverwind seemed unfazed.

"We must have had five calls from the fire department between last night and this morning," mused Butch Cassidy with a twinkle and a grin. Viv paled.

"I'm sorry about that. We tried to keep it under control . . . ," she began, shooting me a look.

"And for some reason, all those thongs in the street. Damndest thing . . . ," he smiled into his salad. Now I felt my stomach tighten.

"Dude. That party fucking *rocked!*" It was Danni. As unedited as they come. We all chuckled. "I got ten of those thongs! I'm wearing one now, and *man* does it itch!"

"That's where you were?" accused Kirk. "I stood outside for an hour trying to get in!" Then a look crossed his face and he shot me a glance—apology? I avoided Viv's stare and excused myself to the bar, where, much to my surprise, Kirk Olmstead joined me a moment later.

"Sorry, didn't mean to bust you like that," he said, paying for the tequila shot I'd just ordered.

"You're not supposed to do that . . . ," I said slowly.

"Do what?" he asked, grinning and studying me. I could feel his warmth, his naked curiosity. There was an utter lack of pretension about him that was disconcerting. What was he doing with that animal, Danni? "I'm not supposed to do what?" he repeated.

"Pay for things," I explained. "That's my job now. Enjoy it. You've arrived, and you are now on the studio's dime." I was suddenly exhausted.

"Well, shucks, in that case, make it a double." He grinned again. I felt my cheeks redden. "I could use a shot of tequila," he confessed. "These froufrou drinks you people all drink—who started that annoying trend?" He made himself comfortable on the stool.

"What about the dinner party!" I cried. "You can't just leave Robert Redford alone at the table."

"Uh, he's not exactly alone. And. To be honest, Alexis Manning," he whispered, leaning in and reading my credential badge, so close I could almost feel his hair in my mouth, "I'm more comfortable around him when he's on the tube and I'm on the couch in my skivvies."

"Me too," I agreed, and we toasted.

"To new beginnings then," he said, smiling a crooked, inviting smile. "And to never again getting left out in the cold at the hot party."

Right.

Several days, calories, phone calls and Mormon Promises later, I got home from a three-hour journey that took fourteen hours due to snow, Southwest Airlines and D.H.'s screaming child. I entered the apartment and noticed that David had packed exactly one box, containing pictures of us and the poems I'd framed for him. He'd left this box out for me to see. Passive aggressive packing. Stupid, sentimental poetry that optimistic lovers give to each other while stationed on Planet Wonderful. "The Road Not Taken" sat at the top of the box like a spike of pain for me to impale myself on. I picked up the frame, recalling the exact moment I decided David should have this. It was after his spectacular performance in a showcase that should have ended with a casting director or producer acknowledging his talent and paving the road to a glorious future. Instead his night had concluded with yet another long, lonely shift slinging drinks for casting directors and producers who were too busy getting ahead with the right people to attend showcases featuring unknown actors. In Hollywood the world is not only unfair, it is cruelly ironic.

*Two roads diverged in a wood, and I—*
*I took the one less traveled by,*
*And that has made all the difference.*

Boy was that true. One path led to a stable, comfortable existence of being ordinary; the other promised a shot—just a shot—at an extraordinary life but usually ended up being a dead end at the latest hot spot where the best-looking people in L.A. slaved beautifully, waiting for destiny to strike. I put on the *Magnolia* sound track, proceeded through a bag of peanut-butter-filled pretzels, and dialed Molly's number.

"Hi, Lex," she breathed into the phone, her voice a mix of exhaustion and bewilderment. "How was Sundance? Did you throw up, cry or both?"

I ignored her question, both irritated and relieved that someone in the world knew me so well. "It was good to get away," I allowed. "We got the hot movie there, *Portland Girls,* by this really cute director. He looks like Andrew Sullivan. How's school?"

"I hate it," she said tiredly "I don't know why I ever wanted to be a teacher. What's *Portland Girls* about?" she asked, pots clamoring in the background.

"Girls from Portland," I said obviously with a mouthful of

pretzels, and she suddenly began to cry. "Sorry Mol, I didn't meant to be flip . . . ," I apologized. I heard her take a breath.

"No, it's just . . . it's (a loud crash in the background) . . . Jack's packing his stuff."

"Oh," I said and felt jealous. Then ashamed. It was a combination I was getting used to.

"Are you listening to the *Magnolia* sound track?" she asked through sniffles. She'd changed rooms.

"Yeah, d'you have it?"

"Have it? I don't think I've turned it off in a month," she laughed mildly. We were more alike than we thought. Molly had been my little sister my whole life, and if she was feeling lost and lonely, then it was my job to take care of her, just as I'd always done as her big sister. I had always taken care of her, since we were kids.

"Mol, why don't you come down here for a weekend?" I said now. "It's awards season and there's lots of parties. My friend Billy plays at this club, you can meet Sara-Anne and Frank and Sue, you can come and see the studio, we'll go out to screenings and have fun . . ."

"I don't know . . . ," she warbled.

"Come," I said softly. Sundance was over, and real life was back. I needed support, but it was easier pretending it was the other way around. "Just buy a shuttle ticket and come down for the weekend, Mol." Please.

# *Eight*

| DATE/TIME | CONTACT | NUMBER | MESSAGE |
|---|---|---|---|
| 1/28/00 6:01 a.m. | Eugene R. | Home | Heard about Letterman; call him, has an idea on how to get around it. |
| 1/28/00 6:10 a.m. | Eugene R. | Home | What if the talent visited Letterman in surgery, or we had a skit where Mike Tyson was going to do Dave's bypass; call him (machine ran out). |
| 1/28/00 6:30 a.m. | Eugene R. | Home | Why can't we get Leno instead? Why do we even need Letterman—fuck him, he's not even funny. |

| DATE/TIME | CONTACT | NUMBER | MESSAGE |
|---|---|---|---|
| 1/28/00 6:16 a.m. | Eugene R. | Home | New ideas about press kit. Thinks it should be black paper with invisible white type with a secret flashlight needed to read it. Has a friend who's a graphic designer, could get it done cheap in Seattle . . . first we mail the decoder flashlight, then a week later we mail the press kit . . . (tape ran out—I left on voice mail). |
| 1/28/00 9:03 a.m. | Gail / MPAA | 310-238-0039 | Re: Clips of *Portland Girls* airing on all the entertainment shows were never sent for approval. Specifically heroin overdose scene and violence toward cows. Plse. call. |
| 1/28/00 9:04 a.m. | Frank & Sue | Home | How are you? Haven't seen you since New Year's. Call us. |
| 1/28/00 9:10 a.m. | Kirk Olmstead | 406-344-0398 | Nice meeting you at the festival; hope to talk to you soon about the *Portland Girls* campaign. |

| DATE/TIME | CONTACT | NUMBER | MESSAGE |
|-----------|---------|--------|---------|
| 1/28/00 10:09 a.m. | VCA Animal Clinic | 310-288-3933 | When are you coming to pick up Little? |
| 1/28/00 10:34 a.m. | Bitsie / ICM | You have it | Hi! Remember me? How are you? Sorry we couldn't get together for a drink at Sundance. Give me a call Re: Danni Jones— who is her agent? |
| 1/28/00 11:03 a.m. | Misha / W magazine | 323-433-6754 | Re: Danni Jones |
| 1/28/00 12:09 p.m. | Lisa / In Style magazine | 310-268-0996 | Re: Danni Jones |
| 1/28/00 12:13 p.m. | Diane / EI | 310-234-4312 | Re: Danni Jones |
| 1/28/00 12:45 p.m. | Sharika / VIBE photo editor | 212-355-0998 | Re: Shades of Gray photo deadline is way gone—Plse call her NOW; she "isn't playing." (think she means she's mad but not sure) |

Back at work Viv managed to secure a week's worth of our *Shades of Gray* talent appearances on Letterman through her friend the talent booker, starting on a Monday with Robert Downey (if he got out of prison in time) and ending with the rappers from The N Word on the Friday of opening weekend. Within hours Dave underwent emergency quadruple bypass surgery, and we learned that the show would be in repeats for at least the next six weeks and we would get no bookings.

Work was hard. There were many details flying in and out of my brain, my telephone, my e-mail and assistant, and trying to keep track of them all was like catching fireflies while blinfolded and stoned. Viv was patient but needed me in top form, and lately I felt formless at best. An artist from the *Shades of Gray* sound track needed to fly back from Detroit in time for a BET (Black Entertainment Television) appearance but didn't want to take the only flight available because it left at 7:00 a.m. *Access Hollywood* needed a clip of *Late Nights* by yesterday but D.H.'s agent wouldn't approve any of the clips I'd selected because she was getting revenge on me for not getting D.H. a groomer and not getting her into any of the Sundance parties; I'd just discovered that the MPAA had never seen / approved any of the clips either, further complicating things; *VIBE* magazine was demanding exclusive photos of our *Shades of Gray* star, Powerful, but Powerful thought he looked too fat in all the selects I made (because I was honest and had accidentally commented that well, he did look sort of doughy in the topless shot), so we would have to pull additional art from the bowels of the photo gallery on the first floor.

The problem was that once we'd acquired *Portland Girls*, no one had time to go to the bathroom, never mind go downstairs for twenty minutes to find thin photos of Powerful (which probably were not approved by his managers anyway). *"Lex, this shit is fucked up—putting fat photos of me in national magazines, come on, that shit ain't right."*

He had a point. I certainly would not want fat photos of myself in *VIBE* or any other national publication, but what Powerful didn't know was that I had other *shit* on my mind. I apologized and headed downstairs to find better photos of him.

Adriane intercepted me on the way down. "Viv says if you don't call Eugene R. back in the next hour she's going to kill herself, and what time are you getting to the Independent Spirit Awards nominations tonight, and Donna from accounting wants you to see her about the Sundance expenses and Jon in the photo department says he's working on pulling *Shades of Gray* exclusives for *Entertainment Weekly* and who approves that, and does Danni have an agent yet, because—"

"Okay, got it!" I snapped on my way down to the photo room.

"There's Twinkies in the conference room!" she called after me sweetly, undeterred. I used to talk to David five times a day at work, and now I didn't talk to him at all, yet the extra time in the day didn't seem to bring me any more productivity. I missed the weird things, broken details—I missed the way he used to fluff the pillow when he got into bed, the way he put the mail into *his* and *her* piles, his glass of milk every night, the way he used to scold me for pulling out my gray hairs. I thought I didn't need him, I thought I didn't love him, but I missed him. The permanence was setting in. Songs, photos, certain smells; the faintest whiff of that era when I had someone to go to brunch with brought dismal waves of self-pity. I checked the messages at home from the photo room phone. There were two calls from him. The first one revealed that Harve and Little had gotten out and were running loose in the neighborhood because I'd left the back door open. In the second he asked where the ring was. He was taking it back. "Where did you put the ring, I need to know. Just leave me a message telling me where it is. And put it *back in the box.*" *Click.* This message was so upsetting that I decided to call him back right then and there, when I was filled with the strength that comes with the need to be understood. My fingers shaking, I dialed the familiar numbers with practiced speed.

"Hello?" Naturally I lost it the second I heard his voice, and the crusty scab that had hardened at Sundance was instantly ripped off, taking a significant piece of flesh with it.

"David . . ."

"I want to see you, I miss the hell out of you," he erupted in a voice very different from the one on the message. The sound of his live voice was punishing; it was clear that I was not over him, I was not smug, I was not proud . . . but why did I still not want to convert?

"Why can't we work this out? It seems so . . ." I couldn't finish. There was just no adjective. I closed the door. Powerful's *Shades of Gray* photo selects would have to wait.

"I told you, I want to, but we have to meet halfway—" David exhaled.

"I don't see how me abandoning my entire religion and converting to yours is halfway . . . ," I replied tightly, an edge creeping into my voice.

"Don't you see how important this is to me?" he said, matching my tone. And then we were in familiar territory. We both knew our next lines by heart, how I was selfish because I wouldn't convert and he was selfish because he wanted me to. How I should respect his choice to be an actor and he should figure out how to provide for me and our imaginary children who would never have Christmas or ham-and-cheese sandwiches. I thought suddenly of the elderly Japanese couple in my neighborhood, who walked together on my block every morning. I would see their backsides, shuffling together in a rhythm, step by step, not touching, not speaking, not looking at each other but just being . . . together, as they must have been for decades, I imagined. For all I knew they met last week at Pink's hotdog stand, but they seemed to have that distinct unspoken familiarity of a sealed partnership. I watched them with something like hopeful envy. I never saw where they went or where they lived. And I never saw them look at me. . . .

"Lex . . . ," growled David impatiently.

As I thought about the Japanese couple I realized that this was about more than Christmas trees and dietary rules: it was about our futures, his and mine, not matching. It was about years—centuries, in fact—of cultural, social, religious, financial, geographical and culinary differences between us. Differences that didn't matter when it was just dinner, drives up the coast and sex.

"We don't want the same things!" I wailed, realizing how much I missed dinner, drives up the coast and sex.

"Why won't you fight for us?" he asked accusingly.

"I'll be at the house at six. Please don't be there," I replied with one last pathetic whine. How could one person cry so much? Surely that point you read about in novels and poetry would come, when there were *no tears left to cry.* No. Like sweat and shit, there's always more. I called Dr. Kreezak's referral and made an emergency therapy appointment for the next hour. Everyone at work thought I was in the photo room all afternoon.

I picked Little up from the clinic on the way home. She looked worse, and somewhat miffed to see me. "This is mysterious," said Dr. Niblack before I even had a chance to defend the fact that Little was an outdoor cat again. I waited. "She has a fever, which indicates infection, but I find no signs of trauma or an abscess." He looked at me for the answer. Was I perhaps torturing her?

"Could it be . . . emotional?" I asked. "I mean, there's a lot of uh, disruption in the household right now, maybe she's upset . . ."

"That might cause a decline in appetite, but that wouldn't cause a fever," he said, without adding, *you stupid layperson.*

"I don't know, she used to love Cat Chow, she used to drink out of the toilet every day . . ."

"Unusual for a cat."

"Yes, well . . . ," I concluded, staring at the Cats Breeds from Around the World poster. *The Himalayan, a luxurious breed, is known for its silk-like fur.* Dr. Niblack gave me a bottle of appetite increasers. I couldn't pronounce the real name of the drug, so that's what I called them. "That will be $67.98," said the green-suited intern.

When I got her home I forced an appetite increaser down Little's throat, which she spit up four times before it turned into a messy paste that ended up everywhere except in her bloodstream. What was wrong with her? Sara-Anne and Frank and Sue came over to inspect her. Sara-Anne brought a new Riesling that she was selling, and Frank brought some herbal cat medicine. He and Sue were still in their first year of courtship and things were going sickeningly well. They were in that phase where you go to organic tea shops and play backgammon all afternoon, then go home and have lunch and sex.

"Darlin', I think she's depressed," concluded Sara-Anne as she put a squirming Little back on the couch and Harve wailed for attention. "I can't believe you're taking care of this bag o' bones, too." Harve cocked his head and lunged at Little. We all yelled at him, and he shrank to the laundry room.

"She looks really skinny," added Sue, pouring us all second glasses of Riesling. "It could be worms."

"Maybe she needs therapy," Frank deadpanned.

"Well, she is a California cat," I joked to an awkward pause in a room full of people who were in therapy, then fought back tears as I recalled my own therapy visit that morning. Therapy—I used to silently scoff at people, even my friends, who "needed" therapy. Therapy was for people who were insecure, confused, for people who were so spoiled that the only problem they had was wondering whether they were happy. Ha. How smug I was. Now I knew better. No one is happy. Maybe Oprah. Or the Australian Crocodile Hunter guy.

Dr. Kreezak's referral, Dr. Loren Fisk, was in a nondescript building in West L.A. I sat in the pleather chairs in her waiting room, surrounded by ferns and old copies of *People* and *Ladies Home Journal.* Halfway through the article about Demi Moore on her own, Dr. Fisk ("Call me Loren") appeared in the doorway, a large woman with friendly curls, tiny eyes and a crinkly smile. "Alexis?" she said in the Careful Voice, which caused me to break down instantly. She managed to corral me into her office. I sat down in a red papasan chair, and she lobbed the first question: "Tell me why you're here . . ." and I wondered if all sessions started this way. So I took a deep breath, stared at her fake Picasso and told her.

"I get into relationships with the wrong guy. I make compromises I shouldn't. I pretend things are OK when they're not. I see the good in a relationship, but I ignore the doom. I pretend it doesn't bother me that he's an actor . . . and it does . . . and that makes me feel awful, judgmental. . . ."

"I see," she said.

Why wasn't she writing anything down? I continued, apologetically. "I force myself into the relationship, I make it work, I fall in love even though I know from the start that our differences are huge . . . but it's better than being alone."

"Yes," she murmured.

Boy, was her job easy. I sunk deeper into the chair. "So, um, I stay in it until the guy asks me to marry him, and I can't really think of a reason to say no, even though there are many. . . ."

"Why," she asked tenderly, leaning forward, "do you think you do this?"

"You think I know? Why the fuck do you think I'm here!" Loren Fisk waited patiently. I grabbed a fresh tissue. "Sorry."

How could I tell a stranger that I was critical, judgmental, impatient, had ridiculously unreal expectations about love—and that it was the movies' fault? Worse, I had recently found *a gray pubic hair.* I lived in a dream world. I'd be alone forever waiting for that moment in my life that resembled the last ten minutes of a Renee Zelweger romantic comedy.

"What happened in your last relationship?" Loren Fisk asked, scattering my thoughts. She spoke softly, as though I might be spooked out of the room like a trapped and frightened animal if her voice got too loud.

"We don't want the same things . . . ," I heaved. It was so embarrassing making warped cry faces in front of someone you didn't even know.

"And what do you want?" she asked tenderly.

I was hit with a thunderbolt of certainty. "I don't know."

"You don't know what you want?" she repeated gently.

"I want . . . ," I gurgled and thought absurdly, *I am choking on my own self-pity.* The clouds lifted. A precise desire formed in my head, but one so elusive I could only imagine ever achieving it. "I want to know what I want," I said. And she suddenly looked very sorry for me. "And I need someone to help me get there."

A movie can't even begin until the main character knows what she wants. I thought of Dorothy in *The Wizard of Oz,* who knew right from the start what she wanted. She wanted to go home. That was it. Point A to B. But without those colorful munchkins she'd still be standing there trying to figure out how to start the journey. They showed her the way; she'd had it easy. Not only did I not know where A was I didn't know what B was. I only knew what I *didn't* want. But that was a start, wasn't it? It had been an exhausting session.

"Therapy always starts off shitty," said Sue comfortingly. Frank chimed in, "If it felt good, it wouldn't be therapy, sweetie."

"If it felt good, it'd be a movie," warned Sara-Anne.

"Duh," I said. I glanced at my watch. Time for the workday to start again. Evening events are as big a part of Hollywood as the 10 to 7 workday. Life? What other life could you possibly desire when every night of every week of every quarter there is endlessly, effortlessly *somewhere to be?* Some hot premiere, a vodka-sponsored launch event, a gift-bag-laden award show or excessive dinner that someone's company is paying for. "Who's coming to this thing with me tonight?" I said to my friends.

Frank and Sue clearly wanted to go have sex, so Sara-Anne and I gathered ourselves into the car and went to the Independent Spirit Awards nominations, for which I had secured a presenting slot for Brooke Shields. She was one of the actresses in *Shades of Gray,* and it was my job to make sure everyone knew that by parading her on stage at every possible televised event from now until the movie opened. Brooke looked great, and they managed to name our movie in introducing her *("And now, star of the upcoming,* Shades of Gray *Brooke Shields!"),* thereby justifying $4,800 we spent on hair and makeup costs for the evening. How many people actually put together the fact that Brooke was starring in our film and that they should go see it as a result of her appearance was unclear. Such is the art of publicity.

Sara-Anne headed for the bar to get us free Veuve Clicquot. I scanned the room for someone interesting. With people like Brooke Shields and Benicio Del Toro in the crowd, no one paid any attention to me. At least I wasn't home staring at a microwaved burrito.

"Hey there," said a familiar voice, and I turned to see Kirk, with an expensive new haircut and a journalist from *Details* in tow. I instantly put up a hand to adjust my hair, and in the moment of realizing what I was doing I saw Kirk notice that the gesture, however subconsciously, was done for him. He looked like an expensive version of Andrew Sullivan.

"Hi there yourself," I said, taking a white Cosmopolitan from a passing tray.

"I called you yesterday," he said accusingly. Amazing. He'd already learned the tone to use when someone lesser had yet to return a phone call.

"You did? Oh well, it's been crazy since we got back, you know, lots to do on the campaign. I see you're . . . talking to the press?" The *Details* hack, a small, wiry guy with a smart haircut and a dumb T-shirt, looked uncomfortable.

Kirk gave a friendly smile and an introductory wave. "This is Rick, we met at Sundance. He's thinking about doing a story on me and Danni." Rather than meet my eye, Rick searched the room for other famous people to watch.

"Well, these are the kinds of opportunities it would be a good thing to discuss with me before you, ah, agree to them. Kirk." It was difficult to communicate this as pointedly as I wanted to while the journalist was in front of us. Kirk was oblivious in his bubble of new-fame cheer and good-natured innocence.

"Exactly. Hence my call . . . since I'm the *director* of the movie," he said, in an indefinable tone that threw me. Was he mocking? Flirting? Testing?

I wouldn't bite and played it straight. "Well, Kirk, why don't you come in for a meeting next week and we can go over some publicity stuff," I said with no expression. Parker Posey was announcing the nominations for Best Debut Performance.

"I have some great ideas," he gushed like a little boy, the director façade momentarily lost. "Like in Portland, I think we should have a series of screenings and Q&A sessions at the local theaters, with me and Danni. . . ." He waited for my reaction, and it was clear I was expected to be spellbound by his brilliance in matters of local-event PR.

"Fascinating idea. We never would have thought of that. Portland screenings for *Portland Girls,* I better make sure that goes in the marketing plan right away," I said evenly, eyes on the stage. Rick watched Kirk for a reaction, pen in hand. Great. Kirk's face slowly morphed from satisfied to quizzical and, finally, embarrassed. A playful and astonished smile took root and began to grow, and it was very sexy, and I smiled back until—

"*There* you are! Dude, you fuckin' *left* me backstage!" It was Danni, wearing Jean Paul Gaultier and high-tops. Her skin was radiant, and her hair had recently known expensive product. She sensed the presence of a woman in a suit. She turned. "Hey, how you livin', woman?" she huffed and thrust out a ring-heavy hand. A giant silver bracelet with a skull on it caught the lights from above. Her eyes were deep and black. Every ounce of her looked plugged into the life force of the planet. She scared me.

"Hi, Danni. Nice to see you again. Listen, I have to get going." (A lie, as I had absolutely nowhere to be except perhaps confirm that Brooke Shields's car was still waiting outside.) "Kirk, give me a call and we can get together for that publicity meeting," I said quickly. I turned just as Danni waved with one hand and discreetly grabbed Kirk's crotch with the other, the skull-bracelet one. Rick from *Details* scribbled wildly in his notebook.

"Who in Sam Hell is that?" drawled Sara-Anne cattily when I reached her at the bar. I polished off the Cosmopolitan as she started in on a J.D. and Coke.

"That," I told her with a sigh, "is my new star."

"What, they made a mini-clone of Angelina Jolie?" I almost peed laughing. "Well *he's* sure a morsel," she declared in Kirk's direction. "Kind of a hometown-boy-of-the-month, mmmm." She sucked on her straw and smiled at Matt Dillon across the room.

"Yup, he is," I admitted, thinking of the change in Kirk already since Sundance.

I got home late. I cleaned up the wineglasses and noticed that Harve had peed on the floor. He looked at me stupidly. "You did that on purpose. Don't pretend you didn't." He sat and offered his paw. Little had not moved from the spot where she had recently projectiled her medication. Still in my heels and glitter, I rummaged in the pantry and got Little a Rite Bite Cat Treat. Harve watched in insulted bewilderment as Little instantly scarfed down the treat. A street rescue, she ate only by scarfing. It was quite a sight, watching her wolf the treat like that, like this might have been the last morsel of food she would ever see, grab it while you can, like she did not trust in the promised bounty of tomorrow. I gave her another one and stuck my tongue out at Harve, who said nothing but sighed heavily and looked away. Then it hit me: I knew what I wanted. Must be approaching the end of Act One. I wanted David and Harve to find their own apartment soon. And I wanted Molly to come and visit, and, perhaps, replace them.

# Nine

When Simon, an artist played by Greg Kinnear, returns from the hospital in *As Good As It Gets,* his friend and colleague Jackie, played by Yeardley Smith, tries to explain his situation as delicately as possible. After she gets him comfortably settled on the sofa in his apartment (he's been beaten by gay bashers), she sits across from him with a worried look on her face, tears loaded behind her eyelids, and a pile of index cards on her lap. It's her job to break the news to him that he has no money, his art isn't selling and he needs a plan to get a plan. Fast. "Frank said the cards would be a good idea," she explains, tearing up. Simon looks at her hopefully, his face a train wreck of bruises and scars. Jackie looks down. The first card reads, *Simon, you're broke.* The next one says, *Tell him to ask his parents for money.*

Note cards would be a great way to get through obligatory post-breakup meals. I could have used some on my last supper with David, his birthday, January 31. That morning, Molly called first thing.

"I'm coming," she said in a voice tinged with hope.

"Yay!" I erupted, startling Little, who was sharing my yogurt. "To visit or to stay?"

"To visit and maybe see if I want to stay . . . ," she said slowly.

"We'll have fun," I assured her, picturing the two of us spending the weekend crying and watching pathetic movies about movie boyfriends and movie relationships and movie love.

"I can't believe I'm actually considering moving to L.A. Who would've thought!" she sounded perversely thrilled.

"It's an idea you get used to, and then five years go by." I said absently, then added quickly, "anyway, I can't wait to see you."

"Me too. So . . . what are you doing about his birthday?" she asked carefully. I mashed one of Little's pills and shoved Harve away from the counter with one foot. He played dead weight just to annoy me.

"I have to take him to dinner," I said reluctantly.

"Really? Is that a good idea?" she asked cautiously, and I thought, *No, it probably isn't.*

I responded quickly and defensively. "It doesn't matter, I can't cancel now. I can't pretend we didn't go out for three years. I can't pretend it's not his birthday. Besides, maybe there's a chance, that . . . I don't know . . ." My voice trailed off like the trickle of a dead river in August.

"Lex." It was all she needed to say. I understood. It meant, *You're wrong and you know it.* I let the silence following hang until it became expensive, dead air. Molly jumped back in. "Be honest with yourself, Lex. Only you know what's right for you . . . anyway, good luck tonight."

"Thanks. You make it sound like a job exit interview."

"Well, in a way, it is," she laughed. "Oh, I'm sending you a book," she added mysteriously and hung up.

For David's birthday I wrapped the ski pants and left them on the counter without a card. What was there to say really, except *Despite Everything, Happy Birthday!* It had been hell shopping for them. Every place I went—REI, The Outdoor Store, Sport Mart—we had been together. We had been one of those lolling couples, sweetly killing a Saturday afternoon, holding hands, trying on clothes for each other, buying stuff we didn't need—one of those couples that now seemed to stalk me in every store I entered. After three years, you couldn't just go cold turkey, could you? How could you give someone a mountain bike for one birthday and nothing the next? I had to get him a gift. It was too terrible not to.

Work was hideous. All day long I publicized at a breakneck pace as the release date for *Shades of Gray* got closer and closer, only to realize at five o'clock that I forgot to tell Claudia Schiffer's publicist that the movie's release date had moved. I broke the news, and she said irritably, "Alexis, do you have any idea how long it takes me to clear Claudia's schedule? Do you know how many tens of thousands of dollars she loses each time I do?" Poor Claudia.

"I have groomers and stylists on hold! When were you planning to give me the new date?" This job had too many details. I couldn't do it. *I should be bagging groceries,* I thought. Instead I was being scolded by *handlers*. Of models! It was too much, really. Were there still Twinkies in the conference room? I went to check.

Later, disaster struck in the form of *Shades of Gray*'s conspicuous absence from the esteemed *Entertainment Weekly* 2000 Spring Preview issue, despite the exclusive photo I had provided of Mike Tyson punching Robert Downey Jr. with Claudia in the background. So far, I hated everything about 2000. Viv pointed out, as did Eugene, that we were the only movie from the studio to be left out. This was particularly insulting, considering the fact that our division only had this one movie to promote in the issue. In my job, this was basically akin to a heart surgeon performing a heart transplant and forgetting to put in the new heart where the old one was.

"Should have been more thorough," was the only excuse I could offer, and I loathed myself because this was in fact not heart surgery but PR, and I was supposed to be an intelligent person. Viv, as a boss-friend, was disappointed but mostly concerned. It wasn't like me to be so flaky.

"Are you sure you don't want my therapist's number?" she asked, leading me into her office and hitting her remote control door closer. *CLACK.* "She was amazing during my first divorce."

"No. Actually, I *have* a therapist . . ." Like admitting you're an addict or a Scientologist, it got easier each time I said it.

"Well, how's it going?" she asked over her giant desk overflowing with rolodexes and call sheets, poster comps and *Variety*'s.

"It isn't working. I hate myself." I felt my face getting hot, the first warning sign of female meltdown.

She glanced at her call sheet and frowned. "That means it's working," she said knowingly. "You'll get past that stage." I snorted. Then I started crying. "You know," she said, tossing the *Entertainment Weekly* onto the pile on her heaving coffee table, "after a breakup, it takes—"

"I know," I sighed impatiently and recited, "it takes a third of the time you were with the person to get over them."

"No," she said patiently, "that's not what I was going to say. 'It takes, my friend,' she said in her dramatic Antonio Banderas movie voice, 'meeting someone else.' "

"Hhhmmphh," was all I could manage.

Viv's office was a corner one. Spacious and windowed. Outside, the palm trees leaned toward the studio gates, as if to catch a glimpse of the magic inside. "I'm taking you off D.H.'s movie," Viv said casually.

"Why?" I cried. "What happened?" This wasn't fair.

"Nothing, you're doing a great job, but with Eugene on the warpath and *Portland Girls* posed to save our jobs when his movie bombs, your plate is full, Lex." Her tone was decisive. I moped. "It's not personal," she insisted. "You've got enough talent to worry about. Let the agency handle D.H." I had to admit she had a point. D.H.'s movie was opening in a couple of weeks anyway, the fun stuff was done. Let the agency publicist come in at 6 a.m. to clip the mediocre reviews. Viv threw a pile of Kirk's new headshots on her coffee table. They landed in front of me with the dead thud of an unspent grenade. "The release date is September. Plenty of time to be in every magazine. Would you mind going through these and pulling some key shots for retouching?"

I couldn't think of a better way to spend the afternoon.

I scrambled to be able to leave work early (at six-thirty, welcome to the new millennium) for the Dinner From Hell. Whenever I left work early I inevitably paid the price. This time Eugene R. caught me at 6:37 p.m. on my cell phone (CALLER ID UNKNOWN, so naturally I picked up) to tell me his film was also left out of the *New York Daily News* 2000 movie preview issue. *Completely left out!* he barked into the phone. I tried hard to care. The flicker of guilt for failing to be an uber-publicist vanished as quickly as it appeared.

"I mean, how can we compete when we're not even mentioned!" he asked in a frightening tone from his preferred pay phone in Central Park, the place from which he usually called me and, I assumed, the elfin Monique. Then he launched into his favorite story, about how Alvin Thompson, a respected San Francisco critic who happened to also write for the Sunday Arts & Leisure section of the *New York Times,* thought *Shades of Gray* was the most important movie he had seen this year. It was always hard not to remind Eugene that it was still only January, and that Alvin Thompson, like most of the critics, was terrified of him.

"I'm losing you, Eugene!" I yelled into the phone, holding it at arm's length out my window as I pulled into the restaurant parking lot and switched it off.

Dinner was at Chaya in Beverly Hills, the sight of many a happy meal between David, Deke and me over the years. He was waiting at the hostess stand. As I valet-ed I saw him before he saw me. I seized the moment to collect my loneliness, nostalgia and neediness and stuff them into the depths of my discount shoes from Loehmann's. The outfit was work-casual, and intentionally un-sexy.

"Hi," I said neutrally as I walked in. He looked calm but cold. My heart pounded as I waited for him to say something, anything, to give me something, a half smirk, a platonic gesture. But he just stared at me, wearing a look like I had slept with his brother. I crumbled inside, piece by piece, but kept standing, my heels so full of everything I didn't want to feel that they were a tremendous support. This was going to be hard. "David . . ." My voice quavered.

"Hey, you twooooooo!" the curvy blonde hostess in blue suede pants suddenly cooed. She recognized us but was unaware of our current status. "When's the wedding?" We squeezed out a collective, fake smile.

"Not for a while," I settled on, as she led us over to our regular table, by the fireplace and Mena Suvari's trainer. David walked and sat in silence but scanned the room for anyone important. I could tell he had something to say and was working up the courage to get it out. After spending three years together, I knew his tics. The way he chewed his lip when he was nervous, the way his eyes darted if he was lying, the way he stared that icy glare when he felt betrayed. But I couldn't quite read him now. Our ghosts had passed through voice mails and in the apartment, me there at night and him during the day, but in actuality I hadn't set eyes on him at all for weeks.

He peered over the huge, stiff menu and said all at once, "I still want to marry you, and I think we can work this out, I already feel less strongly about certain things than I did two weeks ago. We don't have to be kosher, you don't have to light the candles if you don't want to; I know it makes you uncomfortable—"

His words derailed me even though somehow a part of me had

been expecting this. "David . . . ," I began, trying to sound sympathetic yet firm. It was my father who'd actually predicted David would come back after the initial absence ready to bargain. There really is nothing quite as infuriating as your father being right, particularly once you're over thirty. I burst out that religion was not our only issue. I explained my feelings about his career choice, how different we were, how I wanted to raise our future children where I'd been raised, in New England, with parents who worked regular jobs and had health insurance and cars with good gas mileage. I couldn't stop myself. I was gushing torrents of cruel honesty now. The relationship would drown in this river of unfortunate truth.

"What are you saying, suddenly you don't *approve* of my lifestyle? It's not *good enough* for you?!" he spat incredulously.

"I can't marry someone who is doomed to spend every brunch, every dinner, every birthday party or barbecue we go to wondering who in the room can help him," I said tensely, staring into the basket full of breadsticks and flatbreads and fancy crackers but no real bread. Around us the clanking of dinner as usual by people who don't eat.

"Well, *I* can't become an uptight Catholic, move to New England, get a stupid, soulless job selling insurance and deny who I am—an actor," he said tightly.

"You're a bartender," I said and immediately regretted it. Two sides of me fought an ancient war. Here was a nice guy, who loved me, treasured me, and with him I would not be alone. Here was a guy who wanted me to be something I could not, who had the wrong ideas about the future and Hollywood and the nature of work itself.

"Is this about money?!" he demanded.

"No, it's about *values and priorities*," I countered evenly. *"Ours don't match, Deke."* I had decided to be honest, like Molly said.

David dropped his gaze, put his hands on the table, stared at me icily and said, "I can't believe you just said that. I don't even know you anymore. Where is the girl I met three years ago?" and I had to think about that.

It's three years earlier and we are driving to LAX, my mom, dad and me. They have finally met David. They came out West for two days and then rescheduled their flight to leave early. They don't understand the trees here, they resent the left-turn culture, and for them the idea of a drive on the Pacific Coast Highway is not relaxing. As usual I am taking it personally, making it about me when really they just want to go home and get their mail.

It is tense because my dad is asking the Questions, the questions Dads ask only on a ride to the 7-Eleven for milk on Thanksgiving or on the way to the airport in the Final Moments of a Visit. The kinds of questions I don't answer, so that Dad ends up having a one-way conversation with himself, with me as the audience. "David seems like a great guy . . ."

It always begins this way. *Yes, he's a great guy.* "Does he have a plan in case the acting thing doesn't pan out?" I turn the AC on high. *He's thinking about his options.*

"And what about the religion issue." I brake to avoid hitting the mango salesman. My mother inhales a gasp. *What about it?*

"I mean, you two have some pretty significant differences, don't you?" Dadspeak for "Have you thought about the consequences of your actions?" *Dad, we love each other. Duh.*

"I think you might be underestimating your differences." Amazingly, he has not even raised his voice. *You know, you could be happy for me!* I swerve resentfully toward Terminal 7.

"I just think you should have a plan, that's all. I don't want to see you get hurt." His words sit in the shallow of my eardrums, unprocessed, uncontemplated, unable to make the leap into my brain, the wise words of a good father meaning well. I stop the car in front of the terminal. "Do you have a plan, Lex?"

*No!* I pop the trunk. "Well . . . do you have a plan to get a plan?"

*   *   *

David and his celery bisque dove into my memory unpleasantly. He repeated, "I can't believe you."

"And *I,*" I inhaled fiercely, "can't grow old in this fucked-up city while I support you our entire lives."

"More wine?" smiled the waiter, before leaving quickly.

"You don't support me!" David hissed, furious now.

"Not *yet.*" I couldn't stop myself. Was I being a monster on purpose? Pushing him, testing him to see what it took to make him hate me? I stared into his eyes, now frozen solid, like hateful little nuggets of indigestible chocolate. He put down his glass and gripped the stem. His color rose slightly.

"Who do you think you are? I work hard at that bar—you think I *like* it?" His voice was like acid. "You think every second I don't wish and pray I could succeed doing what I love to do? You fucking *Spoiled princess . . .*" But I was undeterred, my mean streak on cruise control.

"It's time for another plan, David, you're thirty-five years old! You want to be slaving away behind a bar until three in the morning and sleeping until noon when we have kids? Do you?"

"Now we're having kids? I thought we were *breaking up,*" he said in a wretched voice that caught the busboy's attention. He picked up his steak knife, to stab me I thought, but mercifully the waiter appeared again. We retreated to our corners, removed our mouthpieces and sucked water.

"Save room, because we have a lovely lavender crème brûlée . . . ," said the waiter, clearing the first course. Then he glanced at us, lost his smile and moved away quietly while we both started crying, mostly, I think, from emotional exhaustion, which led to a perverse sort of relief laughter. David sighed hugely, gulped his water and looked at me fully.

"Lex, Lex, I'm sorry . . . I don't know what's happened to us," he said as he buried his face in his hands.

"I'm sorry too," I blurted. "I do love you, I love what we had, but"—I summoned all my strength—"in your heart you know how different we are, David. It would only get worse as we got older."

"This hasn't been the easiest two weeks for me," he said. "My mom's heart condition took a turn for the worse . . . ," he said, withering.

"Oh, God . . . ," I said instinctively. And now I felt responsible for this, too. His mother's condition was probably being worsened by the fact that David, her eldest son, was unhappy and stressed out and she knew it. A Jewish mother whose eldest son was dating a Catholic, and trying to be an actor two thousand miles from home in a city peppered by riots, earthquakes and Buddhists, she was a professional worrier.

"I'm worried about Molly," I admitted, seizing the common ground, even if it was just familial concerns. It felt comfortable to be sharing feelings with him again.

"What's wrong?" asked the old David.

"She hates her job, and she and Jack are done. They called off the wedding, he's moving out . . ." I trailed off, and now I was crying about something new. Yet the tears were the same. Felt the same, tasted the same, hurt the same.

He took my hand and seemed to be truly concerned. "Really? They're not getting married? What happened?" For the first time in our relationship he was interested in hearing about poor Molly, who was suffering her own identity crisis up in San Francisco, without the benefit of sunshine or movie stars to ease the pain. David seemed to be really worried for her. I felt genuine affection for him, as though I had overlooked some of his qualities . . . then I realized he was probing me for the reason Molly and Jack had split, searching for some parallel, eager to pinpoint a family pattern. The jerk.

"Maybe you both expect too much," he offered pseudohelpfully, then glanced around the room as the front door deposited Ray Romano and two network TV executives. Deke was back. This angered me and gave me strength to say what I wanted to say to him.

"Anyway, I think Molly might be coming down here. For a *while*," I said flatly, not looking at him. "I thought she could move into the apartment . . . with me," I added, staring at the pepper grinder. At Chaya, every table had its own unique one.

"So . . . that's it then," he said matter-of-factly. I looked up at him, the man I was once going to marry, the man who had come to this dinner ready to negotiate, the man who wanted to be an actor and wanted me to be Jewish more than anything else in the world. I was suddenly filled with a ridiculous, deep envy—at least he knew what he wanted. He was starring in the movie of his life and he was going to get to the third-act payoff if it killed him. Meanwhile, I was muddled in the expository first hour of an Eric Rohmer film without subtitles.

I thought briefly of the bittersweet moment, years ago, when David and I had confessed our favorite films. I had to know someone pretty well before I ever sacrificed that information. It revealed too much. David hadn't hesitated. *"Rocky, A Star Is Born* and *Wall Street,"* he'd said wistfully. The theme? The Underdog. Or, more cynically, Look Out for Number One.

"What about yours?" he'd asked casually, as if this hadn't been a test at best and a trap at worst.

I'd stalled, protesting, "I can never narrow it down to three . . ." But he'd probed, and I'd made the mistake of looking into his eyes. "Okay. Well, I've always loved *the Way We Were, Dr. Zhivago* and *Cinema Paradiso."* I'd said finally, knowing too well their common theme and certain he'd never guess it. Longing. Longing. Now in the restaurant, at The Last Supper, I stared into those eyes again.

"So that's it," David repeated, incredulous, his lip curling and his eyes locking on mine. I nodded, full of shame, confusion, self-pity and a million other hideous feelings.

The waiter appeared, joyful and good-looking as ever. "Are we all set here?"

David looked at me. "Yes. I think so," he said coldly.

This was the end of the beginning of the end.

# Ten

Meryl Streep and Robert DeNiro starred in *The Deer Hunter* back in the seventies. Then, movies meant something besides weekend box office numbers, stars wore gowns and not lingerie to premieres, and studio executives weren't allowed on sets. As Michael, DeNiro is on military leave, walking the mental tightrope between the steel mills of Pennsylvania and the jungles of Vietnam. He stops by the grocery store where Linda (Meryl) works, and she's sitting on the floor in an aisle stamping prices onto cans *(kaCHUNK, kaCHUNK)* while crying. He appears around a corner of kidney beans, sees her (he's always wanted her) and asks, "What's the matter, Linda, what's the matter?" Sobbing, she replies, "I don't know *(kaCHUNK, sniff)*, I don't know *(kaCHUNK, sniff)*," and he leaves, helpless. Hours later he returns to give her a ride home, and she climbs into the shark-shaped Pontiac, sighs, stares out the window and asks him, "Did you ever think life would turn out like this?" He puts the car into gear, looks at the road ahead and says, "No." And they drive out of frame.

I went to my preferred therapy on the way to work. The Music Hall Cinema was enjoying a Stanley Donen retrospective, and the press screening of the digitally restored print of *Seven Brides for Seven Brothers* was at 8:30 a.m., meaning, if I"d had a breakfast meeting at 9:00 I wouldn't have been in the office until at least 10:30 . . . This was the beauty of living and working in L.A. in entertainment. Who would know I didn't have an important breakfast meeting? Who would notice if I sauntered in at 11:00 instead of 9:30? Anyone who was up and somewhere this early was either at yoga, a twelve-step meeting or a power breakfast. I took quick steps across the worn scarlet carpet, toward the old concession stand and the vintage movie posters. They even had fresh popcorn. Marcos was joining me. An aspiring director, he was the only one of my friends who knew that Stanley Donen wasn't the latest twenty-year-old designer showing at Fred Segal. We settled into my favorite seats (fifteenth row, third and fourth chairs in) and munched quietly.

"How's it going with David?" he whispered as the lights dimmed, even though we were the only ones in the theater, except for one guy in front us in the seventh row, fourth chair.

"It's not. We kind of officially ended it on his birthday," I whispered back steadily.

Marcos sighed. "I'm sorry, Lex. That's tough." The original trailer for *Funny Girl* came on and my eyes filled with tears, but they were for Fanny Brice and not David.

"Don't be," I told him. "It's the right thing. It sucks, but deep down I know it's the right thing."

He turned to me, his chin greasy and covered with salt and popcorn fragments as Barbra Streisand and Omar Sharif twirled on the cobblestone streets of the Lower East Side. Marcos had the kindest eyes of anyone I knew. Liquorice-black, always watery, cloaked in long, dark lashes. "Lex, I have to tell you something." God, I hate when guy friends say that. Like he was about to confess what my secret nickname in the college football locker room was.

I waited. "We never liked—" He stopped and reconsidered. "We never thought David was . . . right for you."

"Oh," I said mildly, because deep down, I knew this. I knew that David had called Marcos on more than one occasion for a chance to audition for one of his music videos, and that when Marcos had finally given him a shot one day, he'd turned up late, stayed an hour, taken the complimentary Adidas sneakers and left, later telling me that "it was a waste of his time."

"Are you moving out?" Marcos asked, changing the subject.

I kept my eyes on the screen. "I don't think so. I'm going to stay at the apartment for a while and take care of Harve for him while he stays with Victor and finds a place."

Marcos scowled. "That sounds like a baaaaaaddd idea, Lex."

I knew this too, so I made an excuse. "I know, but my sister might be moving in and until that happens—"

"SHHHHHHH!!!!" said the guy in the seventh row, turning around angrily toward us. My heart stopped because it was—Andrew Sullivan? What was he doing here? "D'you *mind?!*" the voice hissed in the darkness, and it wasn't Andrew Sullivan, it was a cute guy wearing a Portland's Best Brews hat—it was Kirk Olmstead. But he couldn't see us. The hot new director had actually gotten up at 8:30 a.m. on a Tuesday to watch a Stanley Donen film by himself. No Danni in sight. I spent the next two hours watching Kirk Olmstead watch *Seven Brides for Seven Brothers* and secretly hoping he wasn't gay. Then I went to work.

| DATE/TIME | CONTACT | NUMBER | MESSAGE |
|-----------|---------|--------|---------|
| 2/2/00 9:01 a.m. | Kathy/ Finance | x8000 | Your Sundance expense report. Plse provide job number for dry cleaning bill and parking tickets. |

| DATE/TIME | CONTACT | NUMBER | MESSAGE |
| --- | --- | --- | --- |
| 2/2/00<br>9:15 a.m. | Molly | Home | Got my flight—can't wait. Plse call. |
| 2/2/00<br>9:17 a.m. | Tracie/<br>*Tonight Show* | 310-292-3847 | Let's talk about Danni Jones. Do you have tape? How does she clean up (ha ha)? |
| 2/2/00<br>9:37 a.m. | Beth Jones/<br>CAA | 310-288-4545 | Re: Danni—have an agent? Plse call. |
| 2/2/00<br>9:40 a.m. | Tim<br>Bernstein/UTA | 310-273-6700 | Re: Danni—have an agent? Plse call. |
| 2/2/00<br>9:55 a.m. | Tiffany for<br>Bruce<br>Weber | Images/<br>323-383-4857 | Re: Danni—wants to shoot her; has an alligator for one day in Baja in March; concept is "Wild Things," Tara Reid has committed; poss. Jaime Presley. Plse. call. |
| 2/2/00<br>10:01 a.m. | Viv | Office | Where are you? Call when you get in. |
| 2/2/00<br>10:20 a.m. | Jennifer/<br>MPAA Ratings<br>Board | 818-995-6600 | You cannot have the word "motherfucker" in a TV clip; disapproved. Also plse define "tight" in context. Also, "Geezer"? Only 1 "shit" per character per clip. Call if??'s. |

| DATE/TIME | CONTACT | NUMBER | MESSAGE |
|-----------|---------|--------|---------|
| 2/2/00 10:23 a.m. | Molly | Home | What should she bring to wear? Also Aunt Louise called—saw you on Access Hollywood in background of Sundance party. |
| 2/2/00 10:34 a.m. | Chuck Paterno/ WMA | 310-274-7451 | Re: Danni—have an agent? Plse call. |
| 2/2/00 11:01 a.m. | Billy | Home | Playing tonight at Largo; come if you can; Don't worry—David won't be there. |
| 2/2/00 3:29 a.m. | Powerful (?) and Herb? | Didn't lve. # | (It was on my voice mail when I came in.) Reach out to him. Wants to discuss "some tight shit" re: premiere guest list (?) |

The next morning I took Little to see Dr. Niblack again. He took us to the examining room, where he left us for twenty minutes to study the Cat Breeds from Around the World poster. *(The Manx cat hails from the Isle of Mann, its lack of a tail its most distinguishing feature.)* He took her blood and her temperature, and it was hard to say which pissed her off more.

"I can't find an abscess," he declared, sounding disappointed and feeling her abdomen. She growled, a monstrous, menacing sound like a Yanni tape played backwards. "It could be *internal,*" he said, emphasizing the word with medicinal doom. Then, "There's been no trauma?"

"Not to *her*, no."

"How long since she's eaten?" he asked. God, his shoes were weird, half hippy, half futuristic, athletic warlord Nike creations. Where had he gotten them? Berlin? Marrakesh? I bet they were comfy. . . .

"How long—"

"Oh. Sorry," I said, looking up. "About three weeks."

"She hasn't eaten in three weeks?" he asked, understandably surprised.

"I mean, uh, I've been, uh, sort of force-feeding her by smearing yogurt on her mouth," I explained quickly, looking away. *(The Persian is known for its extraordinary coat and its fierce loyalty.)*

Oh God, he was going to call the ASPCA. "It's probably not a good idea to, ah, smear yogurt on a cat. They are very fastidious creatures," he said. Smart-aleck vet, thought he knew everything. I really should have gone to veterinary school. This guy certainly knew his way around feline abscesses, but he could have used a lesson in bedside manners.

There was an awkward silence as Dr. Niblack looked into Little's ears. The answer wasn't there, it turned out. "We'll run the tests," he concluded. "I'm afraid we might be dealing with something a little grander than I'd hoped." Then, out of nowhere, Dr. Niblack lost his professional veneer. "Wow your eyes are blue! I've never seen that shade of blue before."

"So?" I said defensively, caught off guard. Dr. Niblack took a step backwards, this small man with odd footwear and one hand on my cat.

"So they're . . . nice, that's all. Sorry if I upset you." He reddened and stroked Little apologetically.

"Sorry, it's just . . . ," I said as I held in a sob. "I love this cat. I can't let anything happen to her. She's more than a cat, if you know what I mean . . ." I trailed off. *(The Blue Tabby is a rare and beautiful color variation of the American Tabby)*

"Try not to worry. Whatever it is, we'll figure it out," he said reassuringly. He scribbled in her chart, smiled nervously and was gone. And I suddenly wondered, could I have imagined this scenario when I was a little girl pretending to operate on my stuffed animals and telling everyone that I was going to be a veterinarian when I grew up? Was I being punished for not becoming a vet? Did vets need publicists? Dr. Niblack could certainly use some PR skills. At what point do our lives take on a direction of their own, willfully disobeying the neat and silent path we laid out for them on Career day in fifth grade? I tried to remember when I decided to come to L.A.

Four years ago I was sitting in the middle of my empty studio apartment in New York, dust bunnies, busted phone cords and used wire hangers littering the 15 x 20-foot floor. The movers packed up my life in less than two hours. All that remained was my one suitcase, my phone, the leather backpack Andrew Sullivan had bought for me in Chile and a futon. I'd be driving to Los Angeles with Andrew, who was going to "drop me off" before he flew off to Asia, where he'd be climbing, hiking, fishing, biking, trekking and being generally irresponsible and free for six months, while I continued my glamorous career path on the left coast. Andrew wouldn't write to me for three months, and I would be furious at first but would gradually forget him as I hiked, climbed and trekked my own way through the jungle that is Hollywood.

Sitting in my empty studio apartment on my last night in New York, I was missing it already but eager to leave, because what no one tells you is that what New York City does to your shoes, it also does to you. The phone rang.

"Hi, it's Dad." *Hi Dad.* "Are you all ready to go? You and Andrew have your route mapped out, you have a cell phone, you have triple A, a spare tire and condoms?"

*Dad.*

"Well, I'm excited for you, honey, the new job sounds great. I've never been a fan of L.A." *That's because you're from New England. You're allergic to warmth and optimism.* What I don't say is that this is why I love him.

"Listen, I want to tell you something." I knew his tired line was coming. Yeah, I know: California is the only state that is 800 miles long and half an inch deep. "No. Something else." *What. The pizza guy's here.*

"I'm proud of you." *Thanks.*

"One more thing." *God, Dad, what?*

"Don't forget," he paused for dramatic effect, "who you are." Right. He hung up before I thought to tell him that who I am is largely the result of what a great father he has been. He taught me how to throw like a boy, how to talk Mom into buying Apple Jacks instead of Bran Flakes, how to make cool Halloween costumes that don't cost money, how to tell the truth, how to change a flat tire without a man and how to do your job, even if Claudia Schiffer's publicist makes you cry and perverted, angry directors call you from pay phones in Central Park demanding to be in every spring preview. I remember who I am in Hollywood—and who I am not—only because of him. He would tell me, "It's OK to have dreams, Lex, but no one *succeeds* until he turns dreams into action."

*Montage: Fun-filled cross-country drive to Los Angeles with high school "friend" Andrew Sullivan. Drinking at Mardi Gras in New Orleans, fishing in the Mississippi, buying illegal fireworks in Alabama, eating chilidogs at a rodeo in Texas, sharing an intimate dinner at the Inn at Yellowstone, making out in front of the Grand Canyon, running out of gas just before Vegas, breaking a whiskey glass against a mirror in a Los Angeles hotel bar, a high school prom photo being ripped in two, a jet bound for Thailand. End montage.*

The book Molly had sent me, *Surviving the Loss of a Love*, seemed hopeful when it arrived. There were twenty chapters. Chapter 1 was "You will Survive." I turned the page. Chapter 20 was titled "Thoughts of Suicide." Somewhere in the middle was "Sundays Are the Worst." This turned out to be true, so it was best to over-book Sundays.

One Sunday it was Sara-Anne's birthday brunch and then a movie with Frank and Sue. Meals with Sara-Anne usually ended up being expensive; the skinny hillbilly bitch had an insatiable appetite for life and the taste buds to match. I could eat everything in sight yet taste nothing and derive no satisfaction from stuffing myself and gaining five pounds overnight. Sara-Anne was like a French woman—she ate everything, the richest, most disgusting, fattening things in the world, like blood sausage, head cheese, foie gras, caviar and stuffed tripe—and could distinguish the subtleties of every flavor. And naturally, she knew the perfect wine to go with each dish and usually had a bottle or two of it wrapped in burlap under her basement stairs.

The thought of spending too much money on anything made me nervous. I would be tackling rent on my own soon. I left the house an hour early to get Sara-Anne's present—Viv and I had decided on a silly spoiled-girl-gift-kit of body lotions, bath gel, candles, a nasty piece of underwear and a satirical advice-on-men book. Funny how those clever basket-type gifts comprised of a bunch of impractical stuff you think is cool wind up being three times the cost of a single thing the person might actually have wanted. For what I'd spent at Anthropologie I could've bought her an airline ticket to Italy or a stake in a new vineyard.

Of course, once I set foot in Anthropologie, the super cool and highly unique girls' paradise store where you can buy glitter lip gloss, jeweled picture frames, silk brassieres or a couch, I realized how inadequate my outfit was. A few minutes wandering through the racks, and my whole wardrobe seemed wanting and desperate, the clothes of a spinster in the making. Clothes that would make people say, *"It's such a shame . . . she's really let herself go since the breakup . . ."* Suddenly the impending brunch required a new, hip shirt that would be irrelevant in three weeks. I decided rather quickly that I deserved whatever I wanted and grabbed the nearest, most ludicrously overpriced tie-dyed cotton garment outfitted with sequins and the face of Brigitte Bardot in silhouette. It was orange and magenta, with sparkly beads, Janis Joplinesque.

"That is soooo darling on you!" squealed the salesgirl, a noodle of tan skin, magenta hair and bangles of silver. I never thought my life was going to turn out like this. Somewhere in New Hampshire, veterinary students were comforting colicky Holsteins.

Sara-Anne's other friends were all wildly successful, smart, interesting, nice women. This should have been comforting, but it wasn't, because they were all married with kids. In fact, two of them were lactating. Producers, TV writers, magazine editors, heads of marketing, web designers—it was a who's who of hip girl careers. I soon grew depressed and ordered the most fattening and cheapest thing on the menu. Poached eggs with cheese, hash browns, biscuits and hollandaise. Viv looked on in silent horror, and the carbohydrate-free women who didn't know me pretended not to see my plate. As all women inevitably do, we ended up swapping man stories. Apparently even after you're married they still fall asleep on special occasions and forget to tell you when you look nice. One of the women had a brother-in-law who was a veterinarian, and he was supposedly single and cute.

"You know, he's really grown up the past year, since he decided to give up river guiding and go to vet school," said Lynda, editor of

*In Style* and the sister-in-law of the man in question. I looked to Sara-Anne for confirmation.

"I don't know, sugar," she sighed. "Any man who's putting his first up a horse's tootsie could be trouble, if you ask me." She downed her mimosa.

"He's a canine specialist," protested Lynda dryly.

"Lex loves animals and the outdoors and all that shit," said Viv, painting her nails with Sara-Anne's new color, a whorish red titled I'm Not Really A Waitress. "A vet might be the perfect antidote for the Actor syndrome," she added, winking at me. I glared at her, knowing she'd had her own thespian affair years earlier with a former Brat Packer who had since fallen off the planet after becoming bloated, bald and Betty Forded.

Sara-Anne reached for another muffin. "Then again, the guy I'm dating gets fucking man-ee-cures," she mocked, and the table howled. She still had not eliminated Richard the caffeine-fearing, cheese-hating agent.

"I can introduce you if you like," whispered Lynda, smiling kindly across the table. "He's an atheist," she added, in a quieter whisper.

For part two of Sunday Alone, Frank, Sue and I had decided to see *All About My Mother*. *Late Nights* had opened that weekend, and as with every weekend when we had a movie opening, I dutifully bought tickets for our movie and went to see something else, in the same theater, that I actually wanted to see (having usually seen our movie no less than eleven times throughout the life of the marketing campaign).

Frank and Sue pulled into the driveway in an unfamiliar Land Rover. There was a third person with them. I realized that they had brought a "friend," Steven, who would be serving as my "not-a-date" without my consent. This is an annoying move that only your best friends will pull on you. Steven, I knew, had gone to college with Frank and had moved here from New York in search of sunshine, fame, fortune and an affordable apartment. Steven was cool. He was tall and reedy and wore loose jeans with vintage Pumas and had started his own record label—but I wanted nothing to do with him. And I was secretly irked at Frank and Sue for pulling the "blind-date-out-of-a-hat" trick on me. So, for the next two hours, in the belly of the Music Hall Cinema, I escaped to Spain.

Pedro Almodovar must be a woman. His film explored the power of estrogen in its many forms—gay, straight, mother, daughter, transvestite, drag queen, nun. Another movie I'd have to shield my parents from. But the story was so original and compelling that I literally disappeared for two hours. When it was over I was momentarily shocked that I couldn't speak Spanish, and sad that my new friends were gone forever. The lights came up, and with them, the unwelcome onslaught of Sunday evening and the sinking realization that you were another week closer to your last. Molly called it the "Sunday Night Yuckies."

Steven drove us all back to my apartment and shut off the engine. Uh-oh. I glanced at Frank and Sue in the rearview, but they were reading the Music Hall program for March. "I'm beat," I said cheerfully, meaning, *This is as far as this evening is going to go.* Steven walked me to the door. Oh, no. Why, oh why, couldn't he just be like my high school boyfriends and drop me off at the corner while the car engine was still running? I did not want to invite him in, so when we arrived at the door, I let Harve out as a distraction. Steven was a dog person, having fled the wrong woman in New York two years earlier taking only the alarm clock and the Doberman.

"Hey, cool, a bloodhound!" he said amicably as Harve exploded, yodeling, down the front walkway. Frank and Sue glanced up from the safety of the car. We all spent the next forty minutes searching for Harve up and down Wilshire.

"I can't believe you have to take care of Harve," mused Sue sleepily, when we finally captured Harve in front of In and Out Burger and dragged him back to Crestview.

"That's the price for keeping the apartment until David finds something," I admitted. Steven chivalrously hoisted Harve by his fat through the front door, but not before Harve slobbered on him and released a boisterous fart. "Seems like you got the bum deal there," noted Frank, pushing his glasses off his face and rubbing his eyes.

"Nice to have met you," Steven remarked. The universal language of a first and last date. My friends drove away and I headed inside. It was actually starting to feel like my own apartment. Except for Harve still being there, taking up space and doing nothing all day. Plus, I had to clean up after him. It was all too familiar. I tucked myself into bed with Little on the pillow beside me. It was so weird, David was in the house, but he wasn't. He was everywhere and nowhere at all. His presence was dissolving, and every day the memories hurt a little less and annoyed me a little more. And that night I loved Pedro Almodovar more than I ever loved him.

# Eleven

In *Singles,* a great early '90s movie featuring cameo appearances by members of Pearl Jam and Xavier McDaniel, Bridget Fonda and Matt Dillon play a young, on again/off again grunge couple who live in a Seattle apartment building where everyone is a friend. All the tenants are young, cool, good-looking twenty-somethings, and everyone knows everyone else's business, but they also take care of each other—emotionally, financially and sometimes sexually. It's a groovy, communal style of living where your landlord and neighbors are your pals or sometimes your bedmates, and most of them share your tastes in music, pets and clothing. Naturally, this kind of thing only happens in the movies and not in the real L.A., where your neighbors and landlords are to be feared and respected, but mostly, watched closely from afar.

"Who is *Agotha?* . . . " inquired Adriane politely as I scanned the list of numbers on my call sheet. The grosses for *Late Nights* had come in. As expected, the box office numbers were bloated in Los Angeles, New York, San Francisco and Provincetown. I wondered briefly what the weather was like today in Provincetown, if there was anyone strolling on the quaint seaside streets, holding hands, ignoring the cold, buying bad art. . . .

"She's called twice, whoever she is," continued Adriane, slipping the trades on my desk, along with an invoice for Brooke Shields's hair and makeup at the Independent Spirit Award nominations and a scrappy-looking VHS tape that contained, if my orders had been followed, Danni's audition tape for *Portland Girls.* *Entertainment Tonight* would give us two pieces and two days of "teasing" the pieces, for a total of four hits, if they found the tape "broadcast quality," a term which was debatable, depending on the level of the celebrity in the videotape. Of course, they'd deliver the *Danni Jones Becomes a Star* piece only if I could deliver compelling B-roll of either Brooke Shields or The N Word talking about their romantic scenes in *Shades of Gray.* And once I did my part and they did theirs, I'd use the *Entertainment Tonight* piece to get Danni on the *Tonight Show.* In Hollywood, nothing generates publicity like publicity.

"I left the message on your voice mail. And don't forget about the Cannes meeting." Adriane was a vat of pure, distilled patience. She was trying to determine, in the Hollywood Assistant kind of way, whether the unfamiliar name on my call sheet was a Call Back, Put Her Through Now, Ignore Forever or Take A Message. No learning curve is as painful for the Hollywood assistant as the Hierarchy of the Phone Sheet. Friends and one's mother are always to be put through; strangers, never; agents and personal publicists, never on the first call; journalists, it depends—do we need something from them or do they need something from us?

"What?" I said absently in Adriane's direction.

"It's on your voice mail," she repeated. I punched in my voice mail code, R-O-C-K-Y. *Rocky* had always been one of my favorites, not only because he lasts the distance but also because he gets the weird girl from the pet store. Sylvester Stallone had since disappointed me cinematically many times, but I still cherished him for screaming the name of the woman he loved after being beaten senseless by Apollo Creed, the Master of Disaster. The message played, and a familiar yet terrifying voice crackled to life. It was my cold Austrian landlord, Agotha, whom I couldn't help thinking of as Agotha the Hun.

"Ve have a problem," the voice coughed. "I am getting calls from ze neighbors, complaining about barking dogs, screaming cats and ze like (ze like?). And you cannot block ze gate! I am not happy about zis, Alexzis. Pleese call me."

It was true that Harve and Little were often cooped up in the house or yard, with David and me using it at different times. He left them there for hours on end when he couldn't bring Harve to an audition, and sometimes Harve escaped, hence me "blocking ze gate." But it wasn't just our gate, we lived in a duplex, which meant a shared yard and gate. Being the upstairs tenant, we weren't really supposed to have a dog, never mind a loud, abscess-ridden cat. You could say we had sort of dominated the shared yard. In fact, if you said the downstairs tenants never got to use the yard at all and were hissed at or peed on when they did, you would not be wrong. I hadn't noticed Little puking or Harve yowling in the yard, but the neighbors apparently had, and so had Agotha.

I knew the tenants below us, a French couple, were too good and silent to be true. Did they hear us fighting before David went to Victor's? The woman was an artist, and she worked from home; therefore she was always around to witness anything Harve and Little did (digging, puking, escaping) in the yard, and she had obviously complained to Agotha the Hun. I had lent them my brand-new *Star Wars Special Collector's Edition* DVD collection over the holidays, and now they had betrayed me. L.A. You can't trust anyone once they get what they want from you. The last thing I needed now was irritated neighbors and an angry landlord ordering me to get rid of my cat or move out.

I wanted to buy my own place, but I couldn't fathom coming

up with enough money. My bonus was coming in a few months, but I feared it would be spent on credit card bills, Little's health and taxes. How was it possible that I had a six-figure income and was nearly broke? More importantly, what would my grandfather say if he knew? Every time I paid money for something I knew I could do myself if only I put the effort in (like a car wash or a meal) I'd think of him and feel a tinge of guilt laced with sweet nostalgia. I spent summers with Grandma and Grandpa in New Hampshire when I was a kid. Even back then Grandpa was astounded that an ice cream cone cost one dollar, women were driving buses, there were black doctors and the word *gay* had a secret meaning. I loved him fiercely anyway. At moments like this I missed him terribly.

A loud chirp went off in my bag. I reached in for the phone and glanced at the screen. A foreign 323 number. To pick up or not to pick up, that is always the question. I pushed a button. "Alexis Manning."

"What did we do today to ensure *Portland Girls* wins the Oscar?" asked a sexy voice that sounded like it was underground and had been up for days.

"Hi, Kirk," I said, fighting a smile. "Is this one of those conversations I have to pull over for?"

"I thought you'd be happy to hear from me." He sounded oddly disappointed. Again that strange earnestness, so out of place.

"Always," I answered quickly. "How's Danni adjusting to stardom?"

"She's at her GAP photo shoot," he said, somewhat annoyed. "Her manager is getting her into a movie with Jude Law."

"You better get used to that," I told him. There was something about him that was . . . normal. He was vulnerable, motivated, optimistic in a way that was strangely soothing. It wouldn't last, I thought sadly.

"Every agent in town is fighting over her," he said proudly.

"Yes, I'm aware," I said, thinking of all the calls I hadn't returned.

"And . . . we're going to Cannes!" he crowed, sounding like a little kid.

"Yes, I'm aware of that too. Hey, that reminds me, I'm scheduling a photo shoot for the two of you. I need some stills. Your headshots"—they were amateur and bad—"don't do you justice," I told him diplomatically.

"OK, sounds good, boss. I'm your publicity slave. Tell me where and when to be and I'll be there." *In my bedroom, tonight, with a vat of popcorn, a bottle of tequila and a director's cut DVD of 9 1/2 Weeks,* I didn't say.

"Will do," I said, hanging up and storing his number, missing the R button, so it came out KIK.

That afternoon, in the middle of the Cannes strategy meeting, I realized I had to solve the apartment/Harve problem. I couldn't allow him to get loose, nor could I continue to blockade the gate with lawn chairs and the gas grill to keep him from escaping. I called Agotha to negotiate, but she chose not to lower my rent, despite my "situation" as she called it, when I explained my dilemma about David, Harve, Little, the possibility of Molly moving in, the difficulty of paying for the apartment on my own. . . . David was not going to pay rent for long when he could only use the apartment from nine to five. But when the end of the end finally arrived, would he try to claim the apartment I'd spent weeks searching for on my lunch hour while he was rehearsing for a Duracell commercial? Who would get custody of our common possessions? Our old roommates and shared friends? The gym membership, the Blockbuster account? I suddenly understood why celebrity divorces required teams of lawyers. It was over, but it was a long way from the end. I had to get him to move out.

"I don't understand why you don't just make him leave," said

Viv irritably, balancing Cannes folders and screening schedules as she pushed the elevator button.

"It's not that simple," I argued. "You know how hard it is to find an affordable apartment that takes pets. And I need a new roommate before I kick him out." She shrugged. As we rode the elevator to the third floor, I suddenly got an idea. A big idea.

"Heyyy . . . ," I said slowly, tasting the idea, "what if I asked my dad for my wedding money and used it to *buy* the apartment. Or *some* apartment?" I said.

Viv brightened. "There's the smart girl I hired! I knew she'd return eventually."

I chewed on the potential. The proverbial wedding stash, combined with what I had saved, might be enough for a down payment. My bonus would add a little. I talked myself into the truth of this. "My dad would go for that—he knows the value of owning real estate, and he probably can't imagine that money being used for a wedding any more than I can," I told Viv hurriedly.

"It's a plan," she agreed. Not totally. But it was a plan *to get a plan.*

Dr. Niblack called in the morning with Little's test results. Dogs barked in the background, echoing as if from a tunnel. "I'm afraid . . . Little has an internal infection. I think this is in her body cavity, some sort of reaction to an outside agent," he explained. Agent?

"I'm going to prescribe stronger antibiotics." I heard him shift in his ugly shoes. The antibiotics (have you ever administered large pills to an irritable cat?), he said, were $68.50. The Relationship Pet God was laughing somewhere. "We may need to do X-rays," he added, without expression or sympathy. "But first let's see if the new medication is effective."

I added *pick up Little's new medicine* to the mental list of things I had to do before work or during lunch hour, the time during which we live our lives. *Get David to move out* fell right beneath that. *Research real estate options* was there. *Tactfully ask Dad for my wedding money,* that had top priority. *Stop thinking about Kirk Olmstead* was also floating around the list, sometimes first. And sometimes last.

# Twelve

In *The War of the Roses,* Kathleen Turner as Barbara Rose loathes the man she once lusted after so heartily: her husband, Oliver Rose, played by Michael Douglas. After two children, the house of her dreams, a couple decades and a lot of dinner parties later, she's done. All she wants is the house. All *he* wants is her continued devotion *and the house.* He just doesn't get her anymore. Finally over dinner one night, he demands to know the real reason it's over. She leans in, looks him in the eye and says, "Sometimes, I just want to smash your face in." It goes downhill from there; he accidentally murders her cat, and she not-so-accidentally makes pâté from his dog, then they kill each other. Danny DeVito has to pick up the pieces.

I was just turning on *Jeopardy!* when David called. It started out harmlessly. He wanted me to fax him some audition sheet that he left sitting on the phone/fax/copier/scanner/printer. We actually had some pleasant chitchat about work, Harve, Little's mystery ailment, Sundance, but I couldn't leave it at that. I had to pick the scab. I decided to mention that I really hoped he got the part. I told him that maybe we could be . . . friends.

"You don't really believe that, *do you,* Alexis?" he said icily.

*I'll take Disasters for $600, Alex . . .*

"David, please . . . ," I said quietly.

"You're amazing," he said with disgust. "Suddenly you're rooting for my acting career? You know, I've realized that the fact that you have a problem with my career is really a vote of no confidence in me—and why should I want to be with someone who has no confidence in me?"

"That's not fair!" I protested. "You can't blame me for not wanting to spend my life married to someone who's desperate for stardom and angry about not getting it."

"I'm not angry anymore," he replied angrily. "You know what's weird?" he continued in a tone I'd heard him use on inefficient valet parkers. "Alan and Melissa—you thought they'd never even get married!" It was true. They were his friends. They'd gotten married, and now he was spending unhealthy amounts of time with them. "Melissa is *totally* supportive of Alan as an actor! She even rehearses with him!" he cried triumphantly.

"And she's totally supportive of his Texas-sized trust fund!" I yelled back.

Then, a powerful silence. "Ah-ha!" he finally said, and I knew what was coming. "So *that's* what this is about! *Money.*" The word slid from his mouth like rotting garbage. I'd never liked Alan and Melissa. David pounced on my gaping silence. "*Wow,* I didn't think *you* were like *that,* but I guess I was *wrong,*" he said in that calm, icky voice of mock disastrous revelation. The voice that unhinges the door of civility and leaves it swaying, broken and damned, in the wind.

If he was bringing out the big guns, then so was I. I removed my 13th-century saber out of its discretionary sheath and prepared to use it. "It's not about money, you *idiot!*" I fumed, in full lather now. "It's about living a certain lifestyle, sending your kids to a good school, taking trips to see our families, buying a decent house in a nice neighborhood, it's about having credit, retirement savings, working normal hours, driving a car instead of an oversized truck that makes your dick seem bigger, it's about being a *FUCKING GROWN-UP!*"

"I *am* a GROWN-UP!" he screamed. "I want those things too, but I'm not a *SELLOUT!*"

"I'm a SELLOUT *because I have a job with health insurance?!*" I shot back loudly. The French artist downstairs tapped on her ceiling (my floor) with what sounded like a broom handle. I asked David how he planned to have any of those things when his main concern was if he'd gone to the gym that day and whether the agents he was meeting really believed he was only thirty. It was then that he chose to hang up on me. I faxed him the audition page, for a character on *The Young and the Restless (Blair Whiting Thomas is tall, erect, and carries a deep, mysterious secret in his heart)* and went to bed.

I woke in a sweat, feeling cruel and judgmental. Shouldn't I respect him for not giving up on his dream? Why should I condemn him for caring about his religion just because I felt nothing for my own? I accused him of trying to change me—but that's exactly what I'd been doing to him. The truth had arrived at last, and, like an uninvited dinner guest, the truth wasn't always fair.

"Maybe it *is* fair . . . ," said my therapist, Loren Fisk, the next morning. "Maybe that's why it bothers you. You have to admit that you were wrong."

"I think we were both wrong," I replied. *Especially those of us who pursued the relationship knowing certain religious requirements might end it.* Duh. She should be paying *me*.

"That sounds petty, Alexis."

"Please don't call me petty," I said tightly. "I *really* hate that. Don't. Call me petty."

She looked up quickly, as though someone had thrown something at her, and said, "I'm sensing some resentment." *And I'm*

*sensing you're a hack and that I never want to come back here again.* I
didn't say. I sniffed noisily and swallowed some tears and mucus.
"OK, let's try this," she said, glancing at her watch. "What is it that
you really resent about him? What is the one thing that he didn't
do for you, that made him wrong for you? Let's identify it, and
then maybe you can let it go."

"Besides taking three years of my life, proposing, turning me
into a confused religious half-breed then deciding I had to be fully
Jewish or nothing?"

"Um, yes, the one thing besides religion," she said. "And this
time let's try it without the sarcasm." Now she was getting personal, confiscating my weapons. But I thought of something. I'd
thought about it before. It was a bizarre conclusion.

"He never took me fishing."

When I was a kid we had a cottage on a sleepy lake in Maine. It
was rustic and quiet and had a great old wooden dock. Molly and
our brother and I spent our days catching frogs, diving from the
dock and most of all, fishing for bass and pickerel in the lake with
our cheap plastic rods. This is where I learned to swim, to build
tree houses and catch twenty fish in a day, to be outside for eighteen hours straight, with no concept of what an hour even was.

One day Molly and I were fishing (or rather, I was fishing and
she was hurling her line repeatedly with great determination) and
she snagged her line in my hair. Again. It took a moment to discover with no small amount of horror, that the large rubber worm
lure was stuck not in my hair but my head. Before I could finish
screaming, my parents appeared on the dock, Mom with car keys
in hand and Dad looking like someone had just woken him up.

"What happened?" my mother asked wearily. I pointed to the
offending faux worm lodged in my scalp. My father sighed. This, I
could not know at the time, was his hard-earned vacation from a
job he did not love.

My mother has always been there to take me to the hospital.

She always got me put back together again, and because neither one of us ever enjoyed dolls, shopping or talking about our periods, rides to the hospital were our mother-daughter bonding moments that I would treasure forever. In fact, I like to think that my childhood was largely responsible for my mother deciding to become a nurse, which she managed to accomplish while working and raising three children before the age of thirty. I, on the other hand, could not seem to manage a two-bedroom apartment and a cat while earning a salary a nurse could never hope to reach.

Despite this traumatic event, what I could not explain to either David or Loren Fiske was that I loved fishing because it reminded me of childhood, a happy, confident time. I knew who I was, where I was going and what I wanted. Fishing on the lake for hours was one of those things that created that treasured nook in a day, the space that time forgot. Childhood is full of those things. You only had to worry about missing dinner, which was made for you. There was no schedule because tomorrow was years away and you were never going to grow old.

But I didn't tell Loren Fiske any of this. Instead I sat back, a heavy sigh deflating my chest, and listened to her standard eulogy about the dangers of living in the past. Loren Fiske had not understood the fishing narrative, or me, and an expression of weary distaste had settled on her face. I left therapy and drove to work, where, as usual, my call sheet was waiting.

| DATE/TIME | CONTACT | NUMBER | MESSAGE |
|---|---|---|---|
| 2/10/00 4:45 a.m. | Eugene R. | Not reachable | Ran into Farrah Fawcett (sp?) she wants to go to the NY premiere of *Shades of Gray*. Should we invite the Knicks? |

| DATE/TIME | CONTACT | NUMBER | MESSAGE |
|---|---|---|---|
| 2/10/00 9:01 a.m. | Jen/ Caroline Z's office/CHAT | 310-239-4855 | Has your tickets to the CHAT Golden Globes party; will be at Will Call. |
| 2/10/00 9:20 a.m. | Dr. Niblack/ VCA Animal Hosp. | 323-383-4848 | Needs to schedule X-rays for Little—recommending Dr. Salome for it. |
| 2/10/00 9:34 a.m. | Viv | Office | Where are you? See her when you get in. |
| 2/10/00 9:40 a.m. | Molly | On cell | Can't wait to see you. On United 12:30 shuttle. What should I bring to wear for the CHAT party? |
| 2/10/00 10:03 a.m. | Henrietta/ Playboy | 323-339-3211 | Re: Danni Jones—has she lost weight since the movie? |
| 2/10/00 10:13 a.m. | Mom | Home | Have fun with Molly this weekend. How is Little? Do you want to come to the Cape for July 4? How about for Presidents' Day weekend? |

| DATE/TIME | CONTACT | NUMBER | MESSAGE |
|-----------|---------|--------|---------|
| 2/10/00 10:23 a.m. | Becca/ *In Style* | 323-248-7200 | Very sorry; no tickets available for the GG party; Kirk and Danni are on the list; that's it. Plse make sure they know we will provide a car and need photos. |
| 2/10/00 10:32 a.m. | Sara-Anne | Cell | She's doing the wine for the *CHAT* party—are you going? Plse. call. |
| 2/10/00 10:36 a.m. | Kirk | Cell | Can you get me tix to the *CHAT* Golden Globes party? |
| 2/10/00 10:42 a.m. | Sally McNeil/ *People* | 310-248-7648 | Plse. Call. Vry Important. |

We'd hired another publicist to help with *Portland Girls,* and the day was mercifully busy. The phone hadn't stopped since we'd returned from Sundance. Viv wanted my opinion on the latest poster ideas for *Portland Girls,* and Adriane was scheduling the photo shoot for Kirk and Danni's new look.

"Do we want sushi or Mexican at the shoot?" she yelled from her cubicle.

"Macrobiotic," I yelled back. "For Danni." The girl who'd never been in a restaurant was now macrobiotic, having spent a week at We Care, a colonic cleansing spa in Palm Desert.

It was kind of scary, having a staff and praying every day that they wouldn't discover I was, as Ally Sheedy admitted in *The Anniversary Party*, a fragile, paranoid neurotic. I was getting more done, and my confidence as a manager seemed to be growing. The day was still filled with minor irritations, like Ben Stiller refusing to do the *Howard Stern Show* for *Shades of Gray* because, he argued, he was only in three scenes, and I couldn't get a ticket for the *In Style* Golden Globes party, and the sound editor for *Portland Girls* screwed up the TV clips so they wouldn't be ready in time for CNN's opening piece on Independent Films, and Eugene R. had inappropriately propositioned a female reporter from *People* magazine while her tape recorder was rolling secretly in her purse . . . heart surgery it was not. But at least I had a place in the world . . . and for this I was infinitely grateful.

Molly arrived on the 12:30 shuttle from Oakland. She was still hideously irregular. She'd been with Jack through five years, three cities, two cars and four apartments, and it wasn't easy to let go. I didn't know how she was coping, but I was thrilled we would be together for the weekend. Misery, as they say, loves company that's equally miserable.

I was excited to pick her up. I hadn't seen her since the disaster that was Christmas, and I really wanted to grocery shop and clean the apartment so it would feel comfy and homey for her when she arrived. But since she hadn't eaten or gone to the bathroom in a week, I was torn about what to buy—plus I was worried about facing that cashier in Trader Joe's again.

"You didn't go shopping?" she cried outside Terminal 4, her curls and freckles sinking in rain and disappointment. It was so good to see her. She had on her blue fleece, sandals with socks, and jeans. Her old teacher's bag heaved from her shoulder. We hugged, and someone's back cracked. "You're skinny," I said.

"I know you are, but what am I?" she mocked in her Pee Wee

Herman voice and climbed into the car, throwing her bags in the back. We pulled away from the curb, dividing a biblical puddle. "Since when does it rain in L.A.?" she asked.

"This year has been full of surprises. Actually, it's called El Nino and—"

"Lex, I teach science. I know what El Nino is."

"Sorry," I said hurriedly. It was so refreshing to have an outsider in L.A. Someone who had no agenda other than to escape her own. We stopped at Ralph's on the way home, loaded up on chips and bread, then settled into the carb central kitchen to make a huge salad garnished with cheese, chips and salsa. Molly retold the Jack saga, down to the day before, when she'd had a panic attack in the middle of the night and Jack had gotten up, said nothing, and started reading through the apartment listings in the *Guardian*.

"That doesn't sound like him," I offered.

She inhaled a forkful of cheese and croutons. "Well, neither of us is exactly ourselves right now, to say the least."

Little appeared, looking irritable and hungover. "What's wrong with her?" asked Molly.

"I think maybe she's upset by the tension in the house. She'll be fine," I said, knowing it was a lie. Molly tried to pick Little up, but Little was having none of it and gave a half-hearted chomp at Molly's hand before trotting snottily out of the room. *Mmmmm-rrrrlllll!*

"Hey! You brat," she said as Little disappeared. "Does she have another—hole? What do you call it?" She tossed her curls and let out a sigh. I was suddenly so grateful for her presence. Here was someone who knew me, loved me, understood me, no matter what was wrong or twisted or pathetic about me or my cat, and I felt the same way about her.

Keys. Molly and I froze. The doorknob downstairs turned, the familiar creak of the hinge. "Is that . . . him?" she asked, a salsa-laden chip pausing before her open lips.

"Yes," I mouthed, waiting for the grueling moment to pass.

"What's he . . . doing?" she managed, unhappily surprised that Deke's presence had slipped into our afternoon.

I took a breath. "He comes to pick up and drop off Harve. That's the deal. He's living at Victor's and I can stay here as long as Harve can. Until one of us moves out. Him, actually, I've decided."

David opened the door, deposited Harve inside without saying a word and left. The energy in the house completely shifted. We hadn't spoken since the phone battle, and I felt like the bad guy, guilt edging over me like the flu, gaining momentum. Was he going to end up a famous, secure and happy star, grab his Oscar, peer into the camera and say with glee, *"You* didn't believe in me— *Hey, how's your career promoting actors?"* Would I care? That day, yes. But if that happened, I planned to sell all the stuff he left in the apartment on eBay *(Deke Rothrock's old T-shirts—$1,000! His dog's pill bottles—$50! Deke Rothrock's half-used Speed Stick—$500!)* and use the profits to finance a beach house in Cape Cod.

"This isn't a good situation, Lex," Molly said evenly, looking me straight in the very blue of my eye, a tactic she knew made me uncomfortable. "Neither of you can move on this way."

"I know. He's supposedly looking for an apartment," I said. Nothing like your little sister acting like your mother. Being right, that is. God damn it.

"When?" she demanded.

"When he's not working out or auditioning for soap operas?" I replied as I stared into Paul Newman's salsa.

"Lex," said Molly sternly, but I didn't meet her gaze. "This isn't right. He has to move out of here, or you do. Now."

"I know, easier said than done," I sighed. She frowned, wrinkling her forehead in the most un-Botoxed display humanly possible. This was more comforting than anything she could have said. "I'm working on it," I told her, keeping my wedding money real estate plans to myself. "Let's talk about more important things," I cajoled. "Like . . . what are you going to wear to the Golden Globes party?"

"Where's your closet?" she asked without missing a beat.

# Thirteen

Andrew Sullivan's favorite movie had always been *A River Runs Through It*, which I also loved, but for different reasons than Andrew (Brad Pitt, of course, being one of them). Brad Pitt and Craig Sheffer are brothers, raised by a loving but strict father who believes in responsibility, God and fly-fishing. The story follows the boys as they grow up in early twentieth-century Montana and learn to be men. The brothers are close but very different. Brad is reckless and wild, seizing life and testing its boundaries daily, whereas Craig is more deliberate, serious. Craig goes away to college and marries while Brad stays local but dances to the beat of a different drum, becoming a saucy newspaperman and a supremely gifted fisherman. After seeing the world, Craig comes home again, but things are different. Brad is not only restless but also angry now; his world is too small. The only place that hasn't changed, and where the brothers find peace, is the river. In the end no one can steer Brad from his predestined path of violence and self-destruction, and only the river can offer any solace to his devastated brother. He grows to be very old, fishing alone in the waters of his memories with tears in his eyes and a piercing calm in his voice-over, by the time the credits roll.

When I watched it (at least twice a year), I always tried to imagine what it must have been like, living in the Montana frontier during that time, or someplace with miles of empty land, a river, endless sky, a place so real and hardy that sheer human survival— not your career, your love life, your movie campaign, yoga, therapy or anything else—was what you did every day.

Despite my longings to be a homesteader on the new frontier, the CHAT magazine Golden Globes party at the Sky Bar was somewhat what the doctor ordered. It was a veritable who's who of CHAT magazine flacks, fodder and filler. Best of all, Sara-Anne was doing the wine. When we arrived they only had my name on the list, without a *plus one.* For a brief, horrible moment I thought we wouldn't get in, and the glitter and control top pantyhose would be for naught. But then I conjured up a Stern Publicist voice, and a small girl with a timid expression and a headset rushed over.

"Alexis? Of course, come right in, I didn't recognize you," which was odd since I'd never met her. It was Jen, the assistant to Caroline, the West Coast CHAT editor, the woman who'd made Adriane cry on the phone. Like Lou Gossett, Jr., in *An Officer and a Gentleman,* Caroline was tough but fair.

"Are Kirk Olmstead and Danni Jones coming?" she asked breathlessly. "I don't know," I replied, since the only way to ensure a celebrity actually showed up anywhere was to drive them there yourself or pay them an obscene amount of money. "Adriane had me put them on the list," Nervous Jen persisted.

Molly stared around us silently as though she'd just been deposited on another planet. Everywhere beauty, fame, thinness, hipness, plastic surgery, designer clothes, top shelf liquor and free lobster. The intoxicating silliness of it all. "They're not going to In-

Style *instead of* our party, are they?" Jen asked in a voice of rising panic.

"Of course not," I lied effortlessly. We were ushered in, Molly in her new velvet skirt (the result of a reckless bender in Anthropologie) and me in my standby moonlight silver halter dress. We gawked at Hugh Grant and Uma Thurman and other impossibly good-looking, rich and famous people who were being watched. Luckily I knew a few industry types and Molly was impressed. She tried to be calm but kept running into the ladies room, where she would scribble on a napkin the names of stars she saw to tell the other teachers on Monday. "I don't want to leave anyone out," she explained. "Who's that?"

"Nick Nolte."

She thought a moment, twirling her curls around one finger. "Who's he?"

"Angry, drunken cop type," I laughed. We made our way over to the other bar, where Sara-Anne, in a green, skintight silk number, was busily pushing her wines to the stars. We strained to get a better look at Claudia Schiffer's outfit. Suddenly a familiar voice invaded our space. "Manning, is that Gucci on you?"

"Hi, Kirk. This is my sister Molly." Molly smiled her glorious freckly smile, a wholesome, real smile, a smile I had forgotten. It made its way onto Kirk's face and I felt left out. "So what are you doing here?" he asked. The standard Hollywood party line for *How did you get invited?* Kirk was wearing a blue silk shirt under a V-neck sweater. Cashmere. He was evolving but he looked like a Banana Republic Model and not a hot young director. "Who dressed you?" I found myself asking, and Molly looked horrified.

"Well, the check from the studio hasn't cleared yet," he began in a funny voice, looking at me with a hooded, downcast glance. He arched one eyebrow (exactly like Andrew Sullivan used to) and said, "As a result, I haven't been able to hire a personal stylist . . ."

Molly laughed warmly, looked at him wide-eyed and said, "It's weird, but you look exactly like—" until I stepped on her toe. She understood, and thankfully Kirk missed the whole thing. "Believe it or not I still dress myself," he said. "Though when it comes to Cannes, I'll need your help." He winked. Where was Danni?

"I'm not going to Cannes," I said. "You're on your own." I sucked more vodka through an expensive, scarlet straw. Vince Vaughn teetered by with a giant model. "Isn't it 'CAHN'?" corrected Molly, who had majored in French and lived in Aix-en-Provence.

"However you say it, we're going! *Portland Girls* on The Riviera . . . how cool is that?" said Kirk a little too eagerly, and was instantly embarrassed. Our eyes met for a split second and Molly said, "Isn't that Steve Martin!" and dashed off with her pen and napkin.

In this way, hours passed, and before long we were tired and sore-footed and ready for immediate pantyhose removal. It was also difficult not to feel poor, fat, ugly and untalented in this environment.

"Hey, Nathalie . . ." A young hipster was sizing Molly up in the valet line. She flushed crimson as he leaned into her space confidently. "Uhh, my name's Molly," she stammered, staring at his vintage adidas and backing into a heat lamp. "Ow, oops."

The hipster peered over his Prada sunglasses and stuffed a leathery hand into a ripped-just-right jeans pocket. "We're going to Chicken and Waffles if you ladies wanna join us," he slurred, handing Molly a business card that said *Zack Posh. L.A.* "I'm Zack. Meet us." Zack Posh disappeared into the waiting crowd as Molly asked, "Chicken and waffles?" The crowd squished us. "It's a late-night eating place where you get chicken and waffles," I explained.

"Weird. You know how long it's been since a guy like that hit on me?"

"A guy like what, like he walked out of *Swingers?*" I laughed. "Yeah, actually," she mused, "that's exactly what I mean." She looked boosted and I was grateful to Zack Posh, whoever he was. "Who's Nathalie, anyway?" she asked, rubbing her back where the heat lamp had burned her. "He thought you were Nathalie Portman, Mol," I said, scanning the line of cars for mine.

"Who's—"

"*Beautiful Girls, Where the Heart Is,* the new *Star Wars . . .*"

"Wow," she said again. "Maybe I *could* live here." Finally, my trusty VW Golf pulled up to the front and several famous people glanced at it with pity.

On Sunday Molly and I made popcorn and hot chocolate and settled in front of the TV with Harve and Little. We watched the preshow and then the Golden Globes, where all the beautiful, rich, famous people we saw at the party last night were now on TV, looking even better than they did last night and with completely new outfits and whiter teeth. We felt like little kids again, together, safe in front of the television with our favorite snacks, the only thing missing being footie pajamas.

It was hectic getting into work the next day; I hadn't checked my voice mails, and I had a morning marketing meeting. Super Shuttle was coming at ten for Molly, and as the hour neared, that tense, anxious look started gaining momentum on her sweet freckled face and I felt vaguely responsible. She sat in my office flipping through *Premiere.*

"I don't want to go back," she said in the voice of a scared little girl. "I can't face him. I hate my life there . . ." and she lost her slippery footing altogether and scrunched her face up, sucked air and finally let go. Her shoulders, covered in fleece, convulsed as if shivering from the cold.

"Mol, Mol . . . ," I said soothingly, but Adriane was buzzing me about the meeting. I remote controlled the door on her persistence. *Clack.* "Why don't you think about coming down here? For a while, I mean, until you figure stuff out—"

"Go to your meeting, I don't want you to be late," she qua-vered, wiping her face and recovering. I wanted her to be happy, I wanted her to figure out what she wanted and be OK. In a grotesquely selfish way, I thought, if she's OK, if she's not nuts, then I'm not either. Maybe there wasn't some weird genetic Man-ning female trait that rendered us so mired in nostalgia and long-ing that we couldn't function in the present, making us incapable of loving someone for who they were because we wanted them to be more like who *we were.* Our expectations weren't just high—they were intergalactic. We both knew this, but we were as power-less against the handicap as if we'd been born deaf.

"Think about it, OK?" I said softly, realizing again that it really was the perfect solution. Molly should be my new roommate.

"OK, I will," she mumbled, sniffling. She looked at me with those big brown eyes, and it was like she was three years old again.

"It's going to be OK," I told her, wondering if this was true. I hugged her hard, giving her the "Manning pat"—three short taps on the shoulder blade to let her know that the hug was meaningful but over. The hug my father gave me when he dropped me off at college, the hug Molly gave our next-door neighbor and prom date by default, the hug my brother gave us at his wedding. Molly tried to hold on longer, but I ended it. She thought I was giving her tough love. What I was really doing was trying to get away before she could see my tears. "Come on, I'll walk you to the shuttle," I said. I'd offered to get her a private car to the airport and sign the invoice as Danni Jones, but she'd declined, God bless her.

"I'll take Pathetic Breakdowns for 200, Alex . . . ," she grum-bled, wiping her fleece sleeve across her eyes.

"Stop," I told her. "You're entitled to a good cry. Don't worry about it. Do you have all your napkins?" Molly checked her back-pack for the scrawled list of A-level stars from the party.

"Yup. I'll rewrite it on the plane."

We walked to the elevator, went through the studio lobby and into the parking lot. Viv was getting out of her car with a bunch of new poster comps for *Portland Girls.* The top one had Danni in silhouette, complete with skull bracelet, staring into the mountains. The tagline said, *"Sometimes going home is the only way to leave it behind . . ."*

Molly climbed into the Super Shuttle blue van, pressed her face against its window and waved. Viv and I waved back from the marketing parking lot. "Has Molly been crying?" Viv asked as the van whisked Molly back to the land of fog, Teva sandals and the wrong guy.

"She's depressed. She hates her job, doesn't love her boyfriend and is questioning everything in her life right now," I summed up. I had learned some skills in PR, and getting to the point quickly or avoiding it altogether were two of them.

"Is her cat sick too?" said Viv without missing a beat.

"Ha, ha. Isn't Miss Vivian funny." Viv hated it when I called her the name of Julia Robert's whore in *Pretty Woman.*

"Isn't she twenty-eight? That's the turning point, I remember it well," she mused, always one to offer the been-there, done-that perspective. Viv had gotten divorced from her first husband and abandoned bulimia at 28. She sipped her Starbucks latte with her free hand. "We'll have to keep an eye on her. Monitor her movements and moods." She set the posters down. "I hereby proclaim MollyWatch 2000."

"It's not funny. This is my little sister," I snipped.

"I know it's not funny." She blew on the coffee. "I had a troubled sibling once, too. For a year he sold roses at LAX and lived on potatoes. That's why we're starting MollyWatch," she said earnestly.

"She's just lost. She's thinking of moving here," I said, helping her pick up one of the posters and absurdly resenting Danni for how heavy it was.

"Molly, here? Why?"

"Well, we're both starting over. I can't afford to live alone. We could start a new life . . . together." I grew misty.

"Now you sound weird," said Viv, and I teared up. "Just keep an eye on her. She's your sister, she looks up to you, she needs you. And stop crying, for fuck's sake! You're better off without that shmuck," she added.

Viv picked up the remainder of Danni's cardboard doubles and led me toward the door. "You'll be fine. She'll be fine. The cat will be fine. You'll get over this. In no time you'll be back, better than ever, a phoenix rising from the ashes," she said, licking the white foam off her top lip, still collagen free. Though sometimes harsh, Viv was one of the real people. She told the truth, and she was trying to help. *But I don't feel like a phoenix rising from the ashes.* I didn't say. I felt like one of those toeless urban pigeons, mired in the weight of my own droppings.

All day I kept thinking of the *Magnolia* sound track and those deathly depressing yet precisely accurate Aimee Mann songs. *"It's not what you thought/when you first began it/it's not going to stop/'til you wise up . . .*

The Amtel is a machine used a lot in Hollywood so assistants and executives can communicate silently while on separate phone calls. You can type a personalized message about who is on the phone **(Your mother is calling collect),** and the recipient can press a button that says **Take a message, I'll call back** or **I'm out of the country,** which sends an instant text reply to the sender's Amtel machine. I like the buttons that say **I'm in a meeting, You handle it** or **Under no circumstance.** The Amtel, though used in other businesses, is ideal for Hollywood, because there are really only these ten ways to answer a call:

1. Yes
2. No
3. I'm in a meeting
4. I'm out of the country
5. Have them hold
6. Have them hold and then disconnect
7. Voice mail
8. You handle it
9. You're sorry but you can't comment
10. Transfer to Accounting

There is also a button that says **I need to talk,** but I have never used it.

The next day was going OK, humming along to the joyful rain that was now a daily thing, when I got the call I knew was coming. Adriane Amtelled me: **Your Landlord.** My Austrian landlord. *The Hun,* I thought, as I pictured her unsmiling face, ever present unfiltered Kool and cruelly knobbed fingers stroking my rent check. "Alexzissssss," she hissed, "Vat are your plans?"

"I'm not sure . . . I need a little more time," I stammered. I was scared of her. She reminded me of some evil mastermind from a James Bond movie in the seventies, but they were mostly men. "David—I mean Deke—is moving out," I explained, trembling.

"Vhen?"

Hah. The million-dollar question. *When it's bloody well convenient for him,* I didn't say. "I don't know, but I'm staying, at least for a while." My voice had gained a little strength, as it always did from being irritated with David.

"You'll pay dis rent by your*self?*" she sounded skeptical. I heard her sucking violently on the Kool. If she were in a movie, Maggie Smith would play her. Or a drunken Vanessa Redgrave. Or Roddy McDowall.

"My sister may move in . . . ," I began, but my voice had lost its nerve again.

"Alexzisss, I came today to de house and found de front gate *tied up* and the vicious dog in dere!" To this I could say nothing, since it was indeed I who had piled the dirt up in front of the side gate to prevent Harve and Little's escape. *"It's a mess back there,"* she said in her gravelly cold war accent, and she was right. At least it was Harve, and not Little, who broke the gate, it was Harve who rooted under the fence, it was Harve whose medication made him unruly and prone to digging, it was Harve whom David would be spending his life with, not me.

"I'll definitely stay until May," I said forcefully, with newfound courage. It was only February. I loved that apartment, and I couldn't imagine giving it up. But then, I used to feel that way about David.

"And ze dog must go," she said thickly. I told her I agreed. The artsy fartsy neighbors had complained more than once. Not just about the noise from Harve but about Little sneaking into their apartment and vomiting up her pills. All over the woman's artwork, apparently. Why my cat didn't feel comfortable doing this in her own apartment. I don't know. She only did these things because she was alone all day. David often picked Harve up and took him on daily outings like the favored child, Little staying behind, staring forlornly out the window like young Ebeneezer Scrooge left alone at boarding school for the holidays in *A Christmas Carol.*

The next day I was greeted by a letter in the fax machine. It was composed on an old-fashioned typewriter, double-spaced, with the typos vigorously whited out and angrily typed over. It looked like something from the forties. I pictured its author in a dungeon of a basement, a single bulb swaying over the old Remington that she'd probably salvaged from the war. The letter was no-nonsense and made no attempt to conceal her disappointment in me as a tenant. It was also notarized, never a good sign.

DeaR Alexis;

This letter shall serve to reinforce our conversation held yesterday. Alexiss, you can not continue to block the gate with garbage cans or ropes or dirt as this creates fire hazard. Furthermore you have agreed to remain on the premises until May, and have agreed to solve the animal problem immediately.

Alexis, when you moved in you told me you had no pets. You did not tell me you had a rather large dog, which bleeds alot, and one cat who yells and vommits. I suspect the neighbors downstairs have said nothing to you because they did not want to make their living situation uncomfortable. but (sic) there have been several complaints about the noise and it must stop. Alexiss, I understand your situation but I will expect to be reimbursed for the cost of the gates repairs. The current tenants below will be moving in 30 days and I expect to have no trouble with you and the new tenants whom will move in at end of month.

Sincerely and respectively,

Agotha

At least I had bought myself some time with Agotha the Hun. I prayed to the God of Fallen Catholics Who Want Things: *Please God, give me friendly, cat-loving new neighbors downstairs, Please let Molly move in, please, please, please.* But I couldn't force it; it had to be her decision. I would not big-sister bully her; I would not spin, persuade, entice or cajole her. I would not call her.

She picked up on the first ring. We compared job stresses ("I can't be a teacher anymore," she said. Me: "Don't beat yourself up. Plenty of people are driven crazy by children." Her: "Is that what you think? That I'm crazy?" Me: "I didn't say that!" Her: "Did Mom?").

We talked about breakup etiquette and deduced that while she was more mature in hers, I was closer to a resolution. "Have you had the there's-a-chance-for-us-in-the-future talk?" I asked her. "Yeah, but Jack said he just didn't know and needed space," she sighed. "He was pretty open, and we've talked every day since he moved out." What was that like, I wondered, being able to converse with your future ex without screaming? Her sister radar acute, Molly sensed me feeling bad and jumped in.

"Lex . . . ," she said quietly, "David's a jerk." I didn't say anything. "Lex," Molly repeated, and I could feel her opening something, the lid of an idea that had been canned a while back.

"What Mol?" I sighed slowly, not daring to hope.

"I've decided to come to L.A." The words were like a big Up-With People song that drenched my heart with joy. I knew this was the right thing. Together we would repair each other and figure out how to be happy, since both of us seemed really good at being overly self-involved and pointlessly unhappy. Maybe I'd get this arrangement right. It was like I couldn't hold on to anything, like I couldn't commit to anything—an apartment, a therapist, a job, a motive or a fiancé.

I took a breath. "You mean it? Mol, that makes me so happy, it's gonna be great . . ."

"Is that from *Revenge of the Nerds?*" she asked. *'It's going to be a great year, Louis'?*

"What? Oh, uh, no, that was from me, actually," I laughed. Molly was always trying to beat me at the movie quote game. "I'm glad you're coming," I told her.

"I don't know for how long, or what the hell I'll do when I get there, and I have no car and no money and no job, but you've got yourself a new roommate. Stock up on Ex-lax."

This was the end of the middle of the end.

# Fourteen

| DATE/TIME | CONTACT | NUMBER | MESSAGE |
|---|---|---|---|
| 2/12/00 5:01 a.m. | Powerful & Herb | Powerful's cell: 917-366-3746 | "WHASSUP" Give a shout out. They loved the *ET* piece w/ Mike & Claudia, why can't they get some love (think he means publicity) . . . tape ran out. |
| 2/12/00 8:30 a.m. | Loren Fisk | Office | Re: Appointment this week; Plse call to schedule. |
| 2/12/00 8:37 a.m. | Aunt Kris | 714-384-5766 | Heard Molly is moving in w/ you! Call her. |
| 2/12/00 9:27 a.m. | Tracie/ *Tonight Show* | 818-840-2000 | Do you have any more tape on Danni; loved the *ET* piece. It's a def. "maybe." |

| DATE/TIME | CONTACT | NUMBER | MESSAGE |
|---|---|---|---|
| 2/12/00 9:32 a.m. | Viv | cell (back from Awards Strategy Meeting at 11) | Want to talk about Cannes when you're off the phone; also, DH's agent sent cake as 'thank you' for our work on *Late Nights*; plse come eat it. |
| 2/12/00 10:40 a.m. | Sassa (?)/ Club promoter, New York | 917-238-3939 | Re: *Shades of Gray* premiere; can do party; need to discuss fees, security and dressing the space; plse call, but not before noon. |
| 2/12/00 12:01 p.m. | Rashid/We Care spa | 559-318-0029 | Re: Bill for Danni Jones? Plse call. |
| 2/12/00 1:40 p.m. | Sue Simpson/ Nickelodeon Kids Awards Show | 310-282-3744 | Danni and Kirk as presenters for awards? Hair, makeup & car provided. Must be willing to be "green slimed" on camera. (Tom Cruise did) Rosie O' D. is host. |
| 2/12/00 1:47 p.m. | Dan/*Details* magazine | 212-288-3887 | Wants to do a piece on Kirk, profiling Danni; "From Nothing to Nirvana in One Sundance" (is doing it w/ or w/out studio's cooperation). Needs artwork. |

| DATE/TIME | CONTACT | NUMBER | MESSAGE |
|---|---|---|---|
| 2/12/00 1:55 p.m. | Mom | Home | Re: Coming to the Cape for Presidents' Day weekend? Maybe you can get a 7 day fare (check Travelocity). |
| 2/12/00 2:03 p.m. | Agotha? | Wouldn't leave number (became hostile when I asked) | Your rent check is due. Downstairs tenants are leaving, new tenants in a week or so. Gate is still broken and cat vomit was on driveway. |
| 2/12/00 3:20 p.m. | Eugene R. | Cell | Heard Jack Lemmon died. He worked with him and can offer interviews and soundbites to all TV shows. Plse pitch. |

More rain, the cold kind, even in L.A. It was the kind that keeps your shoulders scrunched all day. I left work early for a 5:30 meeting. What I did not say to Adriane as she was juggling the options for the *Portland Girls* promotional items (snow globes, baby-doll Ts or commemorative maps of Oregon?) was that the 5:30 meeting was with a Russian masseuse named Egda. The place was a cheap, out-of-the-way single room off Olympic in Koreatown and was utterly frill-free, but Egda held the power of the beyond in her fingers. Egda had hands that made you feel like no one had ever touched you in your life. She knew what she was doing, and better still, she was not in the process of trying to be something else (an actress or producer, for example), and she had never been featured in *In Style* or the "So Cal" section of the *Los Angeles Times.* She was Egda, masseuse (not *massage therapist*—Egda snorted at such a term). She kneaded my abdomen with great authority. "Ouch!" I whined with rapidly diminishing control, realizing that I'd gone from three years of daily physical human contact to none at all. For this reason, Egda's touch was a mixed blessing. When she released the tension in my lower back, I sobbed, but not from physical pain. Something in there, twisted, wretched, dense and wrong, was getting out at last. Lies I'd told myself, anger I'd embraced, promises that had come out of my mouth I'd never intended to keep. They must have all been in there, stored in the lower back, below my mouth, in the underneath regions of my heart but above my ass.

I got home to find the yard gate unlocked and the neighbors finishing their move out. The husband was moving stuff out of the garage, and he looked at me and explained, "We're moving." Like I thought he was stealing dog chews from my side of the garage or something. I said, "That was fast." Then there was the awkward moment of two people who distrust each other but know the games are over and both parties have, in their own ways, won.

"Yes. It was fast. Good luck." And he was gone, a piece of his wife's odd artwork under his arm. David and I had actually driven them to buy their own home, to flee loud neighbors and irksome pets and evil landlords forever. It was nice to know our relationship had at least done someone some good. "Good luck," he repeated, driving away in the rain with lampshades and broomsticks poking their necks out the side window of his Volvo.

I decided to go home for my mothers' birthday, which was, conveniently near Presidents' Day weekend. Molly wouldn't be arriving for several weeks. It seemed stupid to miss yet another of my parents' milestones because I was "busy at work." Or because it was originally the date of my engagement party. After Molly's postponed wedding plans went up in flames and my engagement party ceased to be, my entire extended family left a trail of broken bed and breakfast reservations across New England. There was much Colonial shame and damaged Yankee pride for which my sister and I were largely responsible, but it was my mother who'd soaked up the blame and weathered the biting comments. The least I could do was show up for her birthday. I already had a plane ticket. Why not? Birthdays should be more celebrated. When did they stop mattering? Someday in the new millennium, like unscheduled visits, busy signals and Sunday dinners, they will probably cease to exist altogether.

More often that not these days Birthdays were just a day. Maybe there's an office cake. Flowers possibly. E-cards, which really are not as satisfying as something you can hold in your hand. A few calls maybe, which are voice messages really, since no one is ever home or available to have a real conversation. Life moves too fast now. Imagine a calendar, any calendar, which just had boxes and numbers, with nothing ever written inside? No *Beach House Rental,* no *June and Bert's 50th,* not *Terry's Retirement,* no *Dentist, 3:30* . . . no hopeful little happy bridges to get us from one box to the next but just . . . boxes. Empty boxes that went on and on . . . like, well . . . like how life feels right after a breakup.

I left David a pleading message at 5:30 a.m. (on his "service" number) to either repair the gate or keep Harve with him. Predictably and disappointingly he did neither, instead choosing to loop more stereo wire (yes, stereo wire) around the latch to keep it shut, thus perpetuating the "fire hazard." How hard was it to just go buy a latch for the door? I dialed angrily, waited impatiently for the beep and said evenly, "Molly is moving into the apartment on March first. You need to make some plans." That was all.

He left me messages every day at around 4 p.m. on my machine at home, telling me what he was doing with Harve. "Hi. I'm taking Harve to his treatment. I'll drop him off around 5." "Hi. I've got an audition at Warner Brothers and I've left Harve in the house. Little's in the basement. She puked on the couch again . . ."

We communicated this way strictly via voice mail: other dimensions of our fractured selves existing somewhere in the electronic ether of impersonal telecommunication. Even they couldn't get along. I suddenly had this feeling that it was going to be ugly when we separated all the combined belongings *(That's my garlic press! You don't even like garlic! How would you know, you never cooked for me! Yeah? Where's my Led Zeppelin box set? Don't even try making off with The Juicer!" Who gives a shit about the juicer, you vain, self-denying freak!* And so on.)

"What are you talking about?" asked Molly worriedly. We were on the phone again, me staring at all the stuff I didn't feel like separating in preparation for her moving in. She was less sentimental than I, but had her own burdens. She carried the simultaneous weight of her failed relationship and career burnout like a depressed snail with a double mortgage. "Just stop worrying about the stuff already," Molly commanded. "You can always buy another garlic press. That's the least of your concerns, Lex. When is he moving out?"

"I don't know. I left him a message about you moving in," I said defensively, wondering if David would be taking the computer. She waited. "Well, is he . . . going to . . . leave?"

"I told him March 1," I said carefully. "That's three weeks notice."

"Are you going home for Mom's birthday?" she asked, changing the subject intentionally, and I could hear Alex Trebeck in the background. Molly was a *Jeopardy!* fiend. *I'll take Irrelevant Holidays for $200, Alex.*

"Yeah, she called," I said, rubbing Little's head. "It will be nice to get away. Can you go?"

"No, I can't afford a plane ticket right now. Who's watching Little?" she ventured accusingly.

"I haven't thought about it. David, I guess."

"You have plenty of other friends, Lex." Molly's tone was teacher-ish. Waiting for me to find the lesson in the conversation all by myself, rather than leading me to it. "You're right. I do. But I'm watching Harve when David goes on his family cruise." Patient disappointment filled the wireless technology between us. "He's going on a *cruise, now . . . ?* " Molly asked incredulously. I could hear the bell ring at her school. "Well, yeah," I said, feeling weirdly defensive. "It was already planned with his family . . ."

"Unbelievable . . ." she said in a contemptuous tone. "Mol," I sighed, "don't make it any more annoying that it already is, okay?"

*What is the St. Valentines' Day Massacre? That is correct.* I called Sara-Anne, who was more than happy to agree to force feed Little her yogurt and antibiotics. "I'll get that stupid feline bitch to eat, don't worry, darlin'," she drawled. "You goin' home for some northern comfort with your folks?" Indeed I was. The false embrace of L.A. was suddenly suffocating.

"How's Richard?" I asked her. "Still here, baby." She laughed her smoky, southern laugh. "Still here."

I woke up in the middle of the night from a dream about Andrew Sullivan, the boy I'd loved, who'd taken me fishing in his canoe, introduced me to the Grateful Dead and cheated on me with a cheerleader in my own car during Homecoming. Andrew. What was Andrew doing now? Probably married and still brewing his own beer and skiing untamed mountains and reading nonfiction history books about boats and building kites and breaking hearts with his rugged Yankee practicality and maddening sense of freedom. Not that I'd thought about him much in the past ten years. The jerk. Why had he never called?

In the dream, I was at the Cannes Film Festival and Andrew had directed something. I was running around trying to get tickets and seat people and procure swag bags for Kirk, and we kept missing each other. Andrew was too busy to stop to talk and so was I, but we each knew the other was there. There was just no time to figure out what to do about it. The dream ended with both of us on separate escalators on the way up somewhere, with no way to make either stop and no idea where each other's escalators went and no way, save an embarrassing abandonment of dignity, to leave my escalator and get on his. Maybe it was a sign. What could it mean? Maybe I should call him. Maybe he had been gravely injured . . . maybe he was single . . . no. I would just go back to bed.

On Saturday I was killing the day by pretending to fix the gate when that elderly Asian couple passed by the house in their elderly Asian couple shuffle. They glanced through the gates at the mess, looked at each other and shuffled on. They took each step together, slowly, as carefully as the one before and the ones to follow. I caught them on different blocks all the time. They wore comfortable shoes for old people, the kind with the horizontal tongues that are usually gray or beige. He wore a hat (I hesitate to say "rice paddy hat" but that's what it looked like) and she was rarely outside without her kerchief. They were always together and they never saw me. They were the neighborhood mascots for monogamy.

I left the house for a few designated hours because David had promised to get some of his things when he picked up Harve for the day (he was like a weekend father whom Harve couldn't wait to see). Harve would stand at the door with his ears cocked, waiting for the truck's engine. When it rounded the turn onto Crestview he would begin his serenade to his long lost hero, *Rrrooool, rooo rooohh.* Sometimes, he would pee himself.

When I came back David had strategically completed a tiny passive aggressive strategic maneuver again, a gift that kept on giving. He changed our computer screensaver from the spinning dragonflies we made using Photoshop on my birthday to one of the standard Microsoft defaults—a simple and endless maze of brick walls that kept multiplying and turning corners and leading into more brick walls. Constant, frantic movement—but never progress. It reminded me of his life. Maybe that's why when my phone rang later and David was leaving another dog custody arrangement message on my answering machine, I picked up. He was caught off guard. In the Act II of the breakup movie, it went like this:

> *Alexis* (irritably) The gate is really becoming a problem. Agotha was here again.
> *Deke/David* You're not the only one being inconvenienced—*I'm* the one living out of a suitcase!
> *Alexis* And *I'm not* the one who's too lazy to look for an apartment! Molly's moving in and you need to get your shit *out of here!*

"I was wrong about you," he hissed. I thought you were different but you're just like every other girl in this city!

"You think you're perfect? You're *not!* You think life is a fucking movie? You think Clark Gable or, or . . . (he searched for the name of a more current screen idol) *Viggo Mortensen* is going to sweep you off your fucking feet?! WAKE UP! In real life you have to stick with someone through the good and bad! But with you it's just what YOU want, what YOU need! YOU, YOU, YOU!"

"Fuck you, David."

He responded in a tone unlike anything his voice had ever produced in the years I'd known him. "Why don't you just find some rich guy with a Jaguar—that's what you really want *isn't it!*" Click, this accusation was, I knew, absurd and out of left field. What David didn't know was that before hooking up with him, I'd already done that. But the famous comedian who'd asked me out after seeing me in the green room of his show during my first week in L.A. turned out to be less than charming. In fact, after he'd inquired over dinner if my parents were still fucking and whether I minded driving myself home in his Jaguar because he couldn't risk getting another D.U.I., I decided that perhaps a rich famous boyfriend wasn't all it was cracked up to be. It was then my friend chose to reveal to me that he was rumored to masturbate into a towel everyday before the taping of his show. Two months later, I'd met David.

David called back to apologize for lashing out and to say that he did not hate me, and that he would get his things together and move out after the cruise but in the meantime we should be civil to one another. Civil. I was going to marry this guy. And now we would be civil. How had we reached this point? Then I remembered. His fault. My fault. I started being honest about what I wanted and everything unraveled, every last thread of the emperor's new clothes.

# Fifteen

In *Baby Boom,* Diane Keaton unexpectedly wakes up from a plumbing-estimate-induced hysteria episode in Sam Shepard's veterinary office. She's had trouble handling the adjustment of adopting a baby, losing her job and moving from Manhattan to Vermont. She doesn't want to admit it, but she belongs there, despite the picturesque snow and the downright friendliness of folks, particularly the local veterinarian. Sam is handsome and real, earthy and smart, and of course she initially hates him, only to fall hopelessly in love with him by the end, leaving her big-city advertising job behind forever to do her own thing in Vermont (becoming rich by selling natural baby food), experiencing true love for real this time. But she endured a very personal hell before she came to this realization, and she learned an important lesson—that wherever you go, you take yourself with you.

It rained biblically on the Sunday of Danni and Kirk's publicity photo shoot. Lynda, the *In Style* editor from brunch, would be there, to see if Danni warranted a story on *Portland Girls'* style. This would involve hiring a Hollywood stylist at about $1,200 a day to buy clothes and accessories and formulate a "concept" for the "style" of a Portland Girl, because not only was Danni not really from Portland but it was also unlikely her personal style was what *In Style* had in mind. I agreed to supervise the shoot, despite the fact that Lynda had not invited me to their Golden Globes party.

I didn't want to leave Harve alone in the house all day, and Little had to be monitored, so I packed them both into the back of the VW and took them to Smashbox Studios with me. Passing Shakey's Pizza on Olympic, my cell phone chirped insistently: VIV CELL.

"Hi, I'm on my way," I said instinctively.

"She's bringing the veterinarian brother-in-law," said Viv matter-of-factly.

"Who?" I asked.

Her voice filled with static. ". . . Lynda . . . birthday brunch . . . brother . . . when    we . . . talked    about . . . food . . . your plate!"

"You're breaking up." I inched past strip mall after strip mall, auto body shop after nail salon. Why were glamorous photo shoots always in the seediest parts of town? "Can you hear me? . . . how about now . . . what?"

"Sorry . . . canyon . . . coffee? . . . see you—" and the line disappeared. VIV CELL became ***. At the photo shoot, Lynda's brother-in-law, Ron the veterinarian, indeed appeared. He was short and mousy, the male version of Lynda without her height or looks. He had a mustache that was so wrong that at first I assumed he'd found it in the prop room and was just fooling around. But his it was. Lynda introduced us as Danni's hair got twisted into hot curlers by someone named Laser and Kirk played with the expensive espresso machine without noticing me.

"Hi," I said and held out my hand to the vet-in-training. "I used to want to be a vet."

Ron considered this and finally settled on, "Well. It's a lot of work, but it's rewarding."

"Yes." I felt the weight of my clothes on me. Nothing. It was painfully obvious that we'd both been told about each other. I tried but didn't find him attractive. Honestly, who sported a mustache without a goatee these days?

He didn't dig me either, but he was interested in Harve's mass cell lymphoma, and he was really intrigued about Little's ailments. "She's been sick for a month?" he asked as we helped ourselves to donuts. Danni was squishing into size zero outfits behind a curtain. Occasionally we'd hear a "This rocks!" or "No fuckin' way—get *this off!*" Was Kirk helping her get dressed? I tried to focus on the veterinarian.

". . . eating at all?" I heard Ron-the-Veterinarian-Related-to-Lynda of *In Style* say.

"Oh, um, she eats occasionally, yogurt sometimes," I sighed. "She's on medication for her appetite, and antibiotics for an infection, but we still don't know if it's another abscess—or what, exactly," I said quickly, wondering why Kirk wasn't talking to me.

"She's been checked for feline leukemia?" Ron asked clinically.

"She's been checked for everything. I think she's staying sick just to get attention," I joked.

Mr. Veterinarian Man didn't think this was funny. "I think she should be X-rayed," he said. We sat down together to watch Danni get famous.

Unless you're the one being photographed, or you're Annie Leibovitz, photo shoots are not much fun. They eat away hours of your life and are tedious and sound much more glamorous than they really are. Every shot has a setup, props to find, outfits to perfect, hair and makeup and constant lighting adjustments . . . and one frame out of every roll—maybe—is usable. It's a lot of work creating fantasy. During one of Danni's outfit changes, Veterinarian Man came out to the parking lot to meet the animals, who were lying happily in the back of the VW. It was pouring. Little immediately dove under the seat to hide while Harve yodeled and peed, smashing the window with his madly wagging tail. Stupid dog. Every time I went to the car to let him out to pee I got soaked, this time being no exception, and Mr. Veterinarian Man did not shield me protectively with his overcoat. For some reason I didn't own a proper raincoat. The car reeked of wet hound and skinny cat.

"It's funny, *he's* got tumors and *she's* got holes . . . she's a *holy* cat and he's a *lumpy* dog, heh, heh . . ." I announced for no reason. Ron looked at me as though I'd uttered some German and begun disrobing. The moment passed like a difficult birth.

"Hmmm. A shame," he said finally, shifting his glance to the pavement. The rain was cold, the sky the color of soaked smog. The official weather of Planet Dismal. We marinated in the awkward silence of people who are supposed to be interested in one another but are not. "Well, maybe I'll see you at the clinic sometime," Ron said to fill the gap. A shovelful of trite conversation tossed into the hole that we were never, ever going to fill.

We shook hands, and he left. I didn't know how to flirt anymore. I experienced an acute absence of feeling, like a sexless android, a squirming Lance Henriksen from *Alien,* who remains expressionless even as he is torn violently in half by the angry alien mother beast.

Inside the studio I watched Danni and Kirk conceal their relationship from everyone. I had known instantly they were "involved" even before he'd let it slip the moment we had gotten him drunk enough at the film festival. Kirk had neither confirmed nor denied it since, and I didn't want to know any more than I already did. They were supposedly in love, riding this new wave of fame and acclaim together, after struggling in the trenches of anonymous and thankless art for so long. They had no clue what they were in for, but I did. *It's going to end,* I wanted to tell them.

*Danni's going to be a star—because it's our job to make her one, to wreck your little world. You will cling to her as she grows, quickens, and finally rockets out of your orbit altogether, unless of course you upgrade first and immediately direct another, bigger movie, find another actress. There will be pain, loss, anger, denial, resentment! It will be ugly and you will suffer!* Our job was to drive a wedge called fame between them. When she dropped twenty pounds and missed airplanes and photo shoots regularly, and he was driven by a ruthless agent to accept his next directing gig on a script he hated for four times the money, we would have succeeded. Then, one or both of them would be seduced by someone like Eugene R. But before any of this happened, I had to seal Danni's *Tonight Show* booking.

I watched them. It would be harder on Kirk—he was complex, he felt pain and compassion, studied people and what motivated them, knew kindness. Danni was young, unfinished, and, like all actors and other people who refuse to grow up, staggeringly self-centered. The makeup and hair people, the stylist and photographer, the caterer and photographer's assistants all doted on her. She was like an exotic and feral animal that was unaccustomed to being cared for or touched, but the look in her eye said yes, yes she could get used to this, this was interesting and new and, quite possibly, a lot of fun. She also saw the odd look in Kirk's eye watching it all, and yes, that could be fun too. And the free food! Endless cappuccinos, seedless grapes and top-notch sushi that someone somewhere must be paying for.

Kirk looked on at the entire ceremony with a vaguely curious and nervous expression and once or twice reminded someone that he had discovered Danni, and that, well, he *had* directed the movie. . . . No one was listening, because Bjork was playing very loudly and the prop fan was blowing fake hundred-dollar bills and maps of Portland everywhere. I felt sorry for him. I felt that I knew him, could help him navigate this treacherous new terrain, could be his friend, even protect him. I had sensed something in return, but the tornado was coming for him, and I wasn't sure he had it in him to get out of its way.

"Stop staring at him, Lex, it's so obvious," whispered Viv from behind a giant cappuccino.

"I'm not!" I barked instinctively. I felt my cheeks get hot and my stomach sink.

"OK, you're not." She winked and leaned against the white wall of the studio as Danni grew increasingly joyful frolicking in the fake wind as Lenny Kravitz groaned. "He's totally into you. That, too, is obvious, my friend."

"Viv, that's ridiculous. I've just built up a good rapport with him, what I do with every director."

"Hmmm. Like with Eugene R., for example." She poked the foam with a long, bejeweled finger. I glared at her, irritated that she was always right. "Well. Why don't you work on your *rapport* with our new *star,*" she said, handing me a stack of Polaroids of Danni. "Send these to Tracie at the *Tonight Show.* We need that booking." And she tossed her hair and went about the business of diplomatically convincing Kirk's producer that ten minutes needed to be cut from his beloved movie.

After the fourth trip to the wet car to let Harve out, it was 6:30, and I grew irritated and decided to go home, reasoning that no one at the photo shoot—Viv, Lynda, Kirk, Danni or Lynda from in style—really needed me.

"Where you going, Manning?!" asked that voice, just as I had one foot on the wet pavement out the studio door. Why did I get a shiver when he said my name? It was annoying, especially since I couldn't control it.

"You guys don't need me here, you're dong great," I explained, smiling a publicist smile.

The rain pounded the parking lot in front of us. "This is getting boring," he said, shifting from one foot to the other.

"Well, get used to it, you're going to have a lot of photo shoots from now on . . . ," I began.

"I don't mean the photo shoot," he said evenly, staring into my eyes. I felt my face redden. "Whoah," he arched his eyebrow in that smirk. "They should invent a new name for that shade of blue . . . like, Liquid Sky . . ." He took a step closer.

"Do you need something, Kirk?" It was as polite a voice as I could manage.

"Midnight Mystery. Or Indigo Pool . . ."

"That's inventive, but I really have to get going—"

He put an arm in front of the doorway, ignoring or missing my rudeness. "How come you're always on your way somewhere in a hurry whenever I want to talk to you?" He smiled crookedly and leaned against the door. I could almost see the molecules of chemistry between us. No. No. No.

"I—I'm really busy. I don't mean to be unavailable to you, Kirk—"

"You don't? Or you do?"

"What?" Now I was confused. And—I have to admit—a little intrigued. The model behind the receptionist desk demanded we come in or go out. Kirk flashed her an electric smile, and she retreated. He turned back to me.

"OK, then. You get back in your hamster wheel, Manning. When you're ready to stop running and step out of the cage, let me know."

"If you have something to say to me, Kirk, I wish you'd just say it." I was getting wet now, as it was raining sideways and the studio awning wasn't much help. Harve was roo-ing in the background. Kirk opened his mouth in a half-amused, half-annoyed expression, and suddenly there was a burst of scarlet and black behind him.

"Dude, I need you in here! Should I wear the boa or the aluminum with these Diesel pants?" It was Danni, with hair, makeup, and ten years added to her face. In one hand she held a scarlet boa drape and in the other was a halter-top that looked as though it were made from sheet metal. Angelina Jolie as a midget prostitute in designer clothes. "Hey, Lex, man, you leavin'?" she barked. "Check you later, chick!" and she grabbed Kirk's arm and led him back to the studio.

"I guess we all have our hamster wheels, huh?" I said and Kirk turned briefly, smiling as he walked backwards.

"If you're going home, turn on AMC," he called. "They always have a good movie on Sunday afternoons!" And he slipped back into Fantasyland with his raven-haired nymph.

When I got home, I gave Little a pill and turned on the TV, my friendly safe deposit box of wasted time. How Kirk had guessed this I had no idea. I had watched more television in the last month than I had since the *Dukes of Hazzard/Laverne & Shirley* era. To my delight, *Ghost* was indeed on AMC, and Little, Harve and I caught the whole third act. I watched Demi Moore when she was still fleshy, Patrick Swayze when he was still chiseled, and Whoopi Goldberg when she was still funny and I cried at the end, because they were young and attractive and really loved each other. They were soul-mates, together for the right reasons—only he didn't really understand that until after he was dead. Men.

David came over the next night to drop off Harve, who'd been with him all day going to the gym and Starbucks and soap opera auditions (and not looking for an apartment). I heard him open the door, deposit Harve, and then I heard him climbing the stairs. My stomach knotted. I was in the study, busy late e-mailing the MPAA, the *Tonight Show* and everyone else on my call sheet from the previous day. Why was he coming in? Was he going to kill me? But he came in and just gave me a polite smile. Being human was just full of surprises. We sat down on the study futon. We talked about Harve's tumors and Little's mystery illness. We talked about

Sundance, and about the Golden Globes. He asked me about Kirk, Eugene R., and then he asked if I could introduce him to them. "David, I—," I began, not knowing what to say. Except that I felt desperately sorry for him.

"Well, you know, just thought I'd mention it . . ." He smiled, an earnest, sad, but optimistic reflection of his own opinion of himself. "I'll have to figure out a way to meet these people on my own now." I stared at the floor a moment, then changed the subject. "What are you doing about an apartment?"

"I'll try to find something by the fifteenth, that way Molly can move in even if my stuff is still here, I promise. After my parents' anniversary cruise it'll be easier."

"Thanks," I said gratefully, wondering if I could ever forgive him for going on a cruise *now*, when to me every day of his life seemed like one long vacation from reality.

He got up to leave and sighed, a deliberate, patient sound. "Lex, it's not easy finding an affordable single that will take a dog . . . a dog is a lot harder than a cat." He was right. It would be hard, but it could be done. Like most things, he just had to be a little more disciplined about it. "Hey, why don't you bring Little to the Pet Vet Clinic? They're really good there, they've been treating Harve for a year now," he said helpfully, looking at Little stretched out on a pile of his belongings. "I'll leave you the number," he added, and we looked at each other for a moment and realized there was nothing left to say. He smelled of vague spices and leather, his stubble just perfect for a Marlboro Man ad. "I'm going to go now," he finally declared.

"I . . . I went to services at that group, you know," I called as he headed for the door.

He stopped at the top of the stairs. "How was it?" he dared to ask, in a tight voice.

"It's . . . not for me." I saw his head drop an inch. "I just thought you should know," I added quietly.

He took a breath, stiffened, and our connection, three years in the making, was gone forever. "Take care, Lex," he said. He patted Harve good-bye and left. And the air in the apartment opened up like a cautious spring bloom.

David left the Pet Vet number on my office voice mail at 11:30 p.m. In Hollywood this is known as late-calling. No agents or managers or executives that had a name for themselves ever called back a publicist between 9 a.m. and 6:30 p.m. It was a wicked form of Powerful Phone Tag; this way they could never be accused of not returning calls, but they returned calls when they knew you wouldn't be there. Sometimes, they lunch-called you between 12:45 and 2:00, knowing you wouldn't be there. It's an art form, passed down generation to generation. I tried to one-up them by early-calling them, usually from home, say at 8:30 a.m., their poor assistants knowing that was one more return call they'd have to do that night when they were still at the office at 10 p.m. late-calling the insignificants of the 310 area code.

I decided to take Little to the Pet Vet before my trip to see my parents. Maybe Harve's doctors would see something that Dr. Niblack had missed. She protested wildly from the confines of her kitty carrier. "I was referred by David Rothstein," I said to the attendant, who was tiny, blonde and wearing bunny hospital scrubs.

"We love Deke!" she said brightly. *I used to,* I didn't say. "What seems to be the trouble?" Where to begin? I decided to stick with Little's symptoms. I told them about the internal and external holes in her history, the appetite increasers, the yogurt, Dr. Niblack's antibiotic cocktails, the smell of a sickly feline . . . "Hmmmm, this IS a mystery!" she chirped. What was she so cheerful about? Perhaps her nose job. "Has she been X-rayed?"

"Not really," I said irritably. She looked puzzled.

"Why don't you leave her overnight?"

"Actually, can I leave her for the weekend? You board here, right? I'm going away for a few days." Little would be better off here with professionals than rummaging through the empty wine bottles in Sara-Anne's apartment. Sara-Anne was a dear friend and wholly reliable, but she was not, like most firecracker women from the South, a cat person. I'd asked Billy too, but he had so many gigs and girls going on it wasn't a stretch to expect him to forget Little was there at all and have her starve or escape from his Hollywood studio apartment by the time I got home.

"*Rroowll,*" Little managed, while swiping my pinkie as I tried to pat her good-bye through the carrier. She was tough, but she didn't like being left alone any more than the rest of us do.

Sara-Anne drove me to the airport. She rapped on the front door with a cowboy-booted foot, two Styrofoam cups in her hands. "Sugar, hurry up, my seurrat is getting cold!" I opened the screen door, and she whooshed in with the energy of a beautiful, brief comet. "Try this, try this! I pulled a sample, this is the first tasting . . . I'm so excited, try!" She held out a cup.

"What is it?" I dropped the behemoth suitcase to the floor. She held an uncorked bottle in the crook of her elbow, her long brown hair trailing dangerously close to the edge of her Dixie.

"It's our seurrat, my first early harvest by the lunar cycle, try it! Try it!"

"You know I don't know anything about wine!" I pleaded. She had electric taste buds and a nose like a shark, sensual heights most people saw only on the Discovery Channel. She could tell the history of a place simply by inhaling its air. She had found her calling. She once introduced me to a thick, buttery Chardonnay by saying, "This, Lex, is Rita Hayworth. That's all y'all need to know." And somehow, it was.

She held out the cup. I hesitated. "The first time you got laid you didn't know anything about sex either!"

I drank it. It tasted like red wine. "Mmmmmm," I said, wishing I had a talent for this, for anything.

"What do you taste, come on, come on . . . ," she bubbled.

"Umm. Berries? Cinnamon?" I was useless.

"OK, what else?" she encouraged.

I drank again. "Fall," I concluded. "It tastes like a happy fall day from my childhood in Maine."

"Now you're talkin' like a winemaker!" and she kissed me. "Now take a bottle to your parents." Sara-Anne didn't just suck the marrow from the bones of life. She made soup out of it to share with everyone she met, and she ladled it out in generous helpings—but she still hadn't broken up with Richard.

On the flight to Boston via Pittsburgh the guy behind me requested black coffee with a swizzle stick. If it was black, why did he need a swizzle stick? Why would he request that? Everyone has different needs, and no one understands anyone else's. And why should they?

During the flight I sat staring out the window watching the country go by, while *The Story of Us* played on the screens. Michelle Pfeiffer and Bruce Willis were going to make it after all but probably only because of the kids. The movie ended, and as I glanced around at all the people flying East for a real reason I was stricken with the despair of having no goals. I felt cynical and oddly outdated, like everything I used to know and was good at was somehow irrelevant now, in the year 2000. I couldn't keep up, I couldn't slow down. I had no Internet stocks, and I didn't day-trade. I didn't have a palm pilot or Tivo or even a DVD player yet. I knew scads of people yet couldn't seem to really talk to anyone. I longed for the past and was terrified by the future. I missed my family but feared they no longer really knew me. And worse, I no longer really knew myself. I had friends, but none of us seemed to have enough time for each other. We were all too busy trying to win. I wondered if anyone else felt this way, or if perhaps I was just a fragile, self-pitying neurotic with a bunch of irrelevant, solipsistic, first world problems. Somewhere over Philadelphia, it passed.

In some strange way, being home with my parents turned out to be a setback to my emotional progress. I felt blank all day, wandering from room to room in their house, which seemed, with each visit, more and more like my grandparents' home. *Consumer Reports* on the coffee table, bifocals and coupons in the dish on the center island, notices about card games and white elephant sales from the Nautical Club, a few toys in the closet for the grandchildren. Even the faint smell of mothballs wafted out from somewhere. I was a child again.

My mother loved her birthday gifts—all the organic bath and beauty products I'd gotten at the farmer's market. My father marveled that we could muster such enthusiasm for "soap." Men. God, they were uncomplicated. It was useless teaching them, maddening trying to understand them. We drove through the rain to Chatham, the next quaint town up the tricep of Cape Cod, an area that increased in real estate value roughly $50,000 per mile. I bought flower prints from an old antique shop that would've cost three times as much at the Beverly Center and would have been chemically stained to look as authentic. I also found some handmade earrings for Adriane; when I called the office to check in, I discovered that Caroline from *CHAT* magazine had made her cry again, this time over her insistence at having Kirk and Danni's first interview together exclusive for a month, a request that, Caroline knew Adriane was powerless to confirm or deny. Adriane e-mailed me my call sheet.

| DATE/TIME | CONTACT | NUMBER | MESSAGE |
|---|---|---|---|
| 2/19/00 9:01 a.m. | Rhonda Wallace/ CAA | 310-255-3838 | Is Danni's new agent. Would like to discuss PR strategy for Danni. What about Media Training? Can we get the *Tonite Show*? Plse. call. |
| 2/19/00 9:14 a.m. | Tracie/ *Tonight Show* | 818-840-2000 | Polaroids are great, thanks. P.S. Who is Rhonda Wallace and why is she calling me? |
| 2/19/00 9:32 a.m. | Viv | Office | Call her re: Cannes planning for *Portland Girls*. We need to media train Danni before she talks to ANY press. |
| 2/19/00 10:43 a.m. | Jojo Free/ PETA | 310-266-7544 | Re: Cow tipping scene in *Portland Girls*; they are issuing a statement and need a studio comment by 2 pm (referred to Corporate Communications). |
| 2/19/00 10:56 a.m. | Marcos | Home | Buster Keaton retrospective at MOMA tonight; want to go? |

| DATE/TIME | CONTACT | NUMBER | MESSAGE |
|---|---|---|---|
| 2/19/00 11:32 a.m. | Caroline/ CHAT | 323-388-4756 | Kirk & Danni exclusive/CHAT must be first (heard *Details* is doing something?!) or we will kill the story (I said she had to talk to you). |
| 2/19/00 12:09 p.m. | Eugene R. | No # (sounded like a pay phone) | Wants to meet Danni Jones for his next movie; can you arrange? |
| 2/19/00 12:16 p.m. | Juan DeMarcos/ *TONGUE* magazine | 323-433-6655 | New magazine by Gene Simmons of KISS (the band); needs movies for Summer issue (I pitched Danni)— also who buys full-page ads at studio? |
| 2/19/00 1:43 p.m. | Beth/Corp. Communications | x4533 | Re: Cow tipping scene in *Portland Girls*? Also: meeting w/ MPAA this week; would like to review guidelines w/ you; plse call. |
| 2/19/00 2:10 p.m. | Dr. Niblack/ VCA | 310-243-5768 | Re: Little—do you want to schedule X-rays? |
| 2/19/00 2:28 p.m. | Missy/ Pet Vet | 310-273-4744 | Little is doing fine, but not eating much. |

| DATE/TIME | CONTACT | NUMBER | MESSAGE |
|---|---|---|---|
| 2/19/00 | Gary/ | Malibu Cell # | *Portland Girls* maps |
| 3:14 p.m. | Good Fun | | are 1.99 ea.; hats are |
| | Promotions | | $2.05; do you want |
| | | | him to price thongs? |

On the way back from Chatham my father pulled into a construction site for one of the "trophy homes" that was being built on the water. Someone had torn down a classic New England three-bedroom cape and leveled the property in order to install a thirteen-room "beach house" where no one would live for nine months out of the year. It was happening all over the Cape, and now that my parents were locals, they didn't like it one bit.

"Wait til you see this thing, it's a *McMansion*," complained Dad as he ambled the Caddy down a private dirt driveway as long as their road. The house eked into view. It was going to be one of those dwellings that resembled a wedding cake. Tarps and scaffolding lay about its skeleton, tools and boards scattered the yard. Deserted by the builders, it had been left for the weekend like a half-dressed mistress. We got out of the car and trudged through the damp sand of the front yard. If it was *your* home, it was, without a doubt, spectacular. If you were a neighbor of modest means and a penchant for the traditional, it was an atrocity. The winter sea wind was fierce, and I whipped my head around to keep the sand from shooting into my eyes. That's when I saw the sign.

## CONTRACTOR:
## ANDREW P. SULLIVAN / BOSTON, MA / 617-975-9400

It couldn't be, that was too weird. First the escalator dream and now . . . this? My high school boyfriend was building trophy homes blocks away from my parents? My mother, being a mother and never missing anything, saw me staring at the sign. "Hey," she said loudly over the wind and sea, her tiny frame bent against the elements. "Is that Andrew, *Andrew?* The Andrew Sullivan you went to high school with?"

"I don't know, maybe. I'm sure there are a lot of Andrew Sullivans in the Boston area, Mom."

"Didn't he drive you to California?" she asked, not innocently. Yes. He did. But that was a long time ago.

"Lexy, Lexy . . . come on, be realistic," Andrew is saying, sitting one stool from me at the Whisky Bar and an emotional distance several stools greater than that. Late twenty-something, rugged, handsome, salt-of-the-earth. He's a little out of place here, but not uncomfortable about it. In fact, his energy is calm and confident, appealing. He's perfect, except for that part about being unavailable. He is the only person who ever calls me Lexy, when he isn't calling me simply "Manning."

He is wearing a wrinkled gray polo shirt and hemp shorts long before anyone outside Woody Harrelson knows what hemp is. He smells of whiskey, dust, wind, grease, rose water (from the hotel's free toiletries) and good sex. His hair is windblown, and his smile is crooked. He is the man I want, but I want to have him and eat him too. And he has other plans. We have just driven across the country—3,000 miles and many American landmarks together. For me, each moment and mile drew us closer and made us richer in the experience that was life at twenty-something, a precious few ticks of freedom on the universal stopwatch, and I don't want it to end. We've picked up postcards in every state, and over the years Andrew will send them to me from other, more exotic locales, penned from his globe-trotting travels. I'll get a Graceland postcard from New Zealand, a Grand Canyon note via Indonesia, a Texas Longhorn sent from Russia. A talented fisherman and man of immeasurable patience, Andrew could do that, hold onto things for months or years before finding the perfect opportunity to release them into the world. Naturally, I sent all my postcards on the first day of our trip.

Once we descend into the Los Angeles basin, the director in me is hoping Andrew won't continue on his planned route to Alaska and the Canadian Rockies for the summer after dropping me in L.A., but rather will spin the Dodge Dart around in the middle of the 10 freeway, tires screeching and tears burning in his eyes, and hurtle back to me as Sophie B. Hawkins' "Damn, I Wish I Was Your Lover" blares from the sound track of our volatile union. This, however, is not Andrew's vision of the parting.

"What are you saying, Lexy, you want me to cancel my plans, move to L.A., drop my business in Boston and do what? Pump gas here? Come on, babe, you knew this trip was just a trip." His voice is full of laughter and affection, but I hear only the laughter. He reaches for me, but I turn away. Just a trip? Doesn't he know how road movies end? *Butch Cassidy and the Sundance Kid, True Romance, Thelma & Louise*—the travelers always end up together. Even if they have to die. He doesn't get it.

"But . . . we're amazing together . . . how can you just let it go . . . again?" I say stupidly, helplessly. He stares at me with gray eyes, calm and inviting, devilish and charming, wise and wild, eyes that are already on the door that leads to the next adventure. He holds my face in his rough hands.

"Manning. You've got plans. You're going to conquer the movie world. I've got stuff to do. We'll see each other again, I've got a feeling . . ." And the kiss is electrifying and pure but maddening in its brevity, infuriating in its elusiveness.

"But . . . ," I argue pointlessly. If I hadn't loved him so desperately, I would have bitten him. Instead I throw a whiskey glass Western style and order him out of the bar. He leaves without being asked twice.

*   *   *

Back in the year 2000 on the million-dollar lot in Chatham, I tried to keep the earth level beneath me. What if Andrew P. Sullivan, Contractor, builder of the house, pulled up any second? What if my high school boyfriend suddenly appeared and saw me and my parents marveling at his creation, I freshly disengaged, he probably married, successful, happy, building trophy homes with his trophy wife. We had to get out of there and fast.

"Was he the one on the motorcycle?" asked my dad.

"No. He was the one with the cheerleader," I said.

"Oh. I liked him." He gave a private little smile. "Is he building homes now?"

"I don't know, Dad, I haven't talked to him in years. Do you guys want lunch?" On the way to the Impudent Oyster I lay low in the seat, peering out the top of the window. What kind of freak was I, a Californian vacationing in Cape Cod in February? We had Bloody Marys and Oysters Rockefeller for lunch, then returned to the house and napped out the quiet, cold rain all afternoon. I loved Cape Cod in the winter. Depression here fit like a snug glove; it was the state emotion.

The weather and the oysters got me thinking. I loved New England but could not imagine what I would do here. What could I publicize in Cape Cod? I had a career in California but I had no roots, no connection anywhere, to anything, except, perhaps, my rolodex. I wondered, Did I even want to get married, settle down, slow down, stop eating Advil for breakfast, cereal for dinner and have a family? Maybe I just wasn't one of those people destined to do her own yard work and rave about the pediatrician. Perhaps it was my fate to forever be someone who spent $18 on a bar of fancily package body soap because it smelled good and I deserved it. Or maybe that's just the way I felt today. Vulnerable. Sad. Nostalgic. Not working.

This was not real depression, I told myself, this was merely

Extra Strength Self-Pity enhanced by bad weather. I knew people who had battled real sorrow. I thought of Sara-Anne, wearing all her prom gowns, one after the other, to meals at her parents' Southern plantation, where she returned to heal after her daughter's death. She would eat a breakfast of chocolate cake and champagne, and trek through the rest of the day into evening reading *Gone With the Wind* to her father on the porch. Word by word, sentence by sentence she devoured her grief, her dad silently stroking her hair, sipping iced tea as he listened. Sara-Anne muscled through her swamp of sadness one day, one dress, and one page of Margaret Mitchell at a time.

My parents seemed to be relieved that David and I were through. I wasn't sure; maybe they were just glad the hell of limbo was over. My dad liked to see a plan. They had been supportive of me making a decision, one way or another. I was grateful for them. I knew their greatest pain was to see me unhappy, but my deepest fear was to disappoint them.

"So Molly's moving in next month?" confirmed Dad from the den, the basketball game humming in front of him. He was wearing the tattered slippers I'd given him for Christmas ten years ago and a Land's End cardigan.

"Yup," I said, shelling walnuts with my mother in the kitchen. We spoke through French doors separating the two rooms.

"You and Molly and the cat?"

"Yup," I said. "I think it will be good for us. When did you start wearing *cardigans?*" Somebody scored something.

"I'm glad. We were worried about you both," said Dad. "And. You are too thin." At last some good news. In L.A. it was the ultimate compliment, but here it meant something was obviously wrong with you.

I wiped off my hands and wandered into the den. "Dad?"

"What?" he answered absently, his eyes glued to the television.

"I'm thinking about . . . getting into some real estate . . ." This was going to be harder than I thought. I sat down on the ottoman. On the TV men were running and sweating and earning millions of dollars.

Dad turned to me with a bright expression. "That's great, Lex. You have something in mind?" He grabbed a handful of Doritos.

"Well, sort of . . . but I. Don't have enough for the down payment. Yet. Exactly."

"Do you have a plan?"

"Well, I was wondering . . . um, actually, if you might . . . ," I mumbled.

He turned to me and exploded with a laugh. "You think *I* have extra money?" The orange crumbs stuck to his chin.

"No, Dad, I just—"

"Sweetheart, if your mother and I had that kind of investment cash around, with all due respect, we'd buy something for ourselves in South Carolina or Florida. I wish I could help you, but the stock market was a little rough on our portfolio last year, to say the least. Shoot, shoot, dammit!" He was back to the game.

"Well I'm not asking for *your* money, exactly, but . . ."

"What. You want an advance on your inheritance?" He laughed again, then he saw I wasn't laughing. We'd always been able to read each other pretty well. Over the years I realized that I was just a younger, more privileged, female version of him.

Now my mother was in the room. I groped for the words. "It's just, I'm not going to be needing, uh, the wedding support now, and . . . I just thought . . ."

My mother's face fell, and she got that worried look on her brow. "Lex, your father and I bought a boat." The words came out as if dumped hurriedly from a can. I stared at her. "We thought it would be a good investment for when you and Molly come down in the summer, we can all go fishing, and John and the kids aren't so far away now . . ." She trailed off, and my father silenced her with one of his looks.

"Oh." I said. My wedding and investment property were sitting in a harbor in Harwich port.

"Won't it be fun to have a boat again? Just like the cottage in Maine . . . ," coaxed my mother encouragingly. "Of course if you ever do decide to get married, we'll help you."

"We just thought it might be a while before that happens," said my father. "Again, I mean." Tact was never his strong point.

I felt like crying, but for some reason I started laughing. "Well," I said. "There goes that idea then."

My father gave a little frown. "I can help you work out some financing for a loan if you're interested. I have all the mortgage and monthly nut calculation websites saved upstairs."

"That sounds good, Dad. Thanks." I stood up from the ottoman and stretched. "Do you guys want to go to a movie tonight?"

Dad frowned again and turned back to the TV. "You know your mother can't stay awake past nine o'clock."

"Why don't you call Andrew Sullivan while you're home?" said my mother in the maternal haze of good intentions. "Seems he's in the area, and I bet he'd love to see you!"

"Yeah, why don't you," said my Dad. "*He* must be making an awfully nice living . . ."

"It might be nice to see your old friends . . . ," ventured my mother, as usual meaning more than she said.

I popped a Dorito in my mouth and settled into the couch with the whole bag and the latest *Consumer Reports*. "I don't really have time, Mom."

She looked perplexed and returned to her tomato sauce. It was true I was doing absolutely nothing except wandering from one meal to the next. I felt like a loser, nestled here in the spacious comfort of a nest I left long ago, eating solid carbohydrates dunked in my mother's homemade tomato sauce, going to the hardware store for caulking with my dad, wishing I could make a career of this lifestyle where I was cherished and safe and it was cold outside. But it was just a weekend, and I was only an extra, a witness to their 35-year bond that I could not even begin to understand.

Molly called during *Jeopardy!* after I had taken the mandatory walk to the beach to freeze my ass off and be grateful for the climate of L.A. She told me about her new antidepressant, and I told her about wanting to move back in with Mom and Dad. *I'll take Alternative Medicine for $400, Alex.*

"You might want to talk to your therapist about Zoloft," Molly said. I pictured us in an infomercial, two sisters, a split screen, cross-country conversation, me in the icy, gray February of Cape Cod and her in a shiny bluebird day on the Golden Gate Bridge. "It helped me!" she'd say, and my side of the screen would crackle, go static.

"Hey, I saw Kirk Olmstead on CNN last night," she said. "He was at some party with that Danni girl. And your friend Billy playing at some premiere. He's cute, but he looks fatter on TV." The *Magnolia* sound track was playing in her background.

"Everybody does," I said, thinking of Kirk and wondering weirdly if he was happy. "Andrew Sullivan is building a house right down the street," I told her.

"No way! Are you going to see him?" Molly had covered for me a few times when I had not returned from one of Andrew's parties.

"What would be the point?" I sighed dramatically. "I'm in no mood to confront people from high school."

"It's not like he's just a person from high school who you haven't *seen* since high school, Lex," she said, and then I could hear her wishing she hadn't said it. Alex Trebeck filled the moment. *"This 'holistic' Chinese practice uses needles to make tiny punctures in the skin so energy can flow."*

"Well, whatever. When I get back I'm going to try to start dating again," I told her.

"Me too. When I get to L.A. I'm going to look up Zac Posh," she said.

"Who?" I asked.

"You know, my admirer from the Sky Bar Golden Globes party." I laughed, picturing the hipster with the sunglasses and adidas and drunken sway, on his way to Chicken & Waffles. "Anyway," continued Molly, "dating's a good way to find out what you want."

What did I want? *I want to know who I am, and where I am going.* I knew I wanted to stop giving landlords my money, and I wanted David gone. I wanted to make *Portland Girls* a hit. I wanted Little to get better, and I wanted to live with my sister again. Maybe together we could create a home, get a new life. Maybe it would all be different now.

*Act III for $300, Alex.*

# Sixteen

In *Broadcast News*, Holly Hunter finds out just what kind of man William Hurt really is with the help of a videotape. Across every genre, in almost every movie, there is a device called "the McGuffin." This is the last-minute twist, that piece of information that enables the character to save the world, forgive his father, condemn his lover, solve the murder. In *Broadcast News*, for example, William Hurt has demonstrated emotional vulnerability by crying during an interview, but Holly, a smart news producer, knows he had only one camera for the shoot. How did they capture the spontaneous tears in a cutaway shot from the hardened news anchor? They didn't. He worked up the tears afterward, method style, and edited the tape accordingly. Holly's got the raw tape, and she knows he lied. He can't understand why this bothers her. She leaves him at the airport with a bikini on his head and seeks comfort from her loyal, honest friend, Albert Brooks, who isn't as handsome or as successful as William Hurt—but he's there for her, just as he's always been.

On the way back to L.A., I called everyone I knew during my layover in Pittsburgh. There really is nothing more depressing or

boring than traveling alone when you're alone. My parents had un-
ceremoniously dropped me off outside the terminal by the sky
cabs. When I turned for the Movie Moment Airport Wave, the car
was gone. I trudged through security alone, stood in line at the
gate alone, inched up the jetway with the happy couples and their
children and their prevailing germs alone. Depressed by the
pageantry of meaningless activity while waiting for airplanes, I
called all my friends, one by one.

"Lex, where've you been?" Billy asked in a scratchy voice.

"I was visiting my parents on the Cape," I told him.

"That would be why you're calling me at seven a.m. on a
holiday?"

"Whoops, sorry Bill."

He yawned. "I heard your sister Molly's moving to L.A."

"Yeah. We're starting our own sitcom, two recently unengaged
sisters," I told him.

"Is she cute, your sister?"

"She's hideous."

"Lighten up, Lex. Just cause you can't have me doesn't mean
your hot young sister won't be interested."

They called my flight, and I stuffed the remainder of a Cliff bar
into my mouth. "Billy, I gotta go. See you when I get back. And
don't get any ideas about Molly."

"Allrighty," he said in his charming voice, and I made a mental
note to protect Molly from him and all Artistic Types when she got
to L.A.

On the way home from the airport I picked up Little from the
Pet Vet Clinic and asked to speak to the doctor. Bunny Scrubs
(whose name was apparently Missy, but who cared) told me to
have a seat. In a few minutes, a young, handsome, Italian veterinarian holding X-rays burst out into the waiting area and said,
"Little, Manning?" I leaped to my feet. He looked like Andy
Garcia.

"Yes? . . ."

"I'm Doctor Salome. Follow me," he said. He led me to an examining room, where Little was waiting angrily in her carrier. He swept in, closed the door and tacked her X-rays onto the screen. On the opposite wall was the familiar Cat Breeds from Around the World poster. *The Chartreuse is known for its agility and grace . . .*

"I'm glad you brought her in," he said. He smelled like rubbing alcohol and puppies. His eyes were watery espresso cups. He opened her chart, and there it was on his left hand, a wedding band.

"Do you know what's wrong with her?" I asked him.

He hesitated a moment. "It looks like . . . some sort of mass, and it could be . . . a tumor. Luckily we have some of the best oncologists in the country here at Pet Vet . . ." and he launched into a pitch that involved, among other things, chemo, discounts on boarding and a monthly payment plan.

"But . . . you're not *sure* it's . . . cancer, yet, right?" I couldn't believe it. The Relationship Pet God was getting revenge at last.

"We won't know until we do some more tests, but there is definitely an unwelcome mass," he said with concern. An unwelcome mass. Like what David had endured on Christmas Eve.

"Not just an abscess?" I persisted.

"Alexis . . ." He spoke gently, and I wondered if he was going to ask me if I was all right. Put a hand on my shoulder, embrace me, ask me to go out for coffee, morph into Andy Garcia, tell me his wife didn't understand him, brush my hair from my face and—

"We need to open her up."

"What?!" I cried, immediately putting a protective arm around the kitty carrier.

He stiffened. "She's not getting better, and I can assure you she is going to get worse if we do nothing . . . there is also the possibility of an internal abscess."

"What?" *The Andalusian is a long-haired relative of the Persian . . .*

"A deep infection in her body cavity, like a hole that goes from the inside out, if that makes sense." He looked grave. "Exploratory surgery is the only way to be sure." I couldn't stand the thought of cutting her open, risking her life and not knowing if it would even help. Still, he was so handsome and nice, I didn't want to disappoint him.

"I need to think about it, OK?" I finally said. *Open her up,* Jesus Christ.

He put that left hand on my shoulder. "OK, but don't take too long, OK, Alexis?" I nodded. *"Roooollllll!"* growled Little.

When we got home from the clinic, there was a message from the cleaning service about rescheduling the weekly appointment. David had called to cancel it, since he had "a big audition tomorrow and needed quiet in the house." Apparently the cleaning people would interfere with his rehearsal (it was hard for him to recite his lines while the illegal Mexican family vacuumed around him).

He was close to landing that job on the new series *(Bristol Connors is rugged, tough—and accustomed to wearing the pants in the family . . . )* and would have to move to New York immediately if he did get it. Part of me wanted him to get the job. I even said a prayer. *Oh God of Nothing, give him a break, let him get the role so he can see what this business is really like.* In any event, the apartment needed cleaning. Being a man and having exactly one other thing to focus on, he couldn't possibly do it. Loser. So I decided to clean the apartment myself. Once I began I couldn't stop; Little and Harve scampered for safety as I went through every drawer, every closet, every dustball of the last three years. I ripped open the Everything Drawer in the kitchen, and the contents scattered on the floor with a bang. "Shit!"

Little hissed, and Harve charged over to see what in the pile might be edible. There it was, a crumpled ball of paper, with a few paper clips and a small tube of Aadvantage Anti-Flea System tangled in its folds. David's Christmas list. Yes, he who felt uncomfortable in Vermont, he who shunned our taste for eggnog-soaked midnight mass and Scrooge, he who dropped the atomic bomb of breakups in a Jim & Jim's Bed & Breakfast on Christmas Eve . . . *he* had a very detailed list of things *he* wanted for the holiday he did not believe in, would forbid me to celebrate with our unborn children and labeled trite and meaningless.

## DAVID'S LIST
(Cashmere) V-neck black sweater, size L (J. Crew)
Seat covers for 1990 Yukon truck, black
Basketball shoes, Nike Pro-Sport Gel size 10 in grey/sky blue
    (Sports Connection.com)
Calvin Klein white (L) T-shirts (V-neck)
Powder Gain Protein Shake Mix, 84-oz. tub (GNC Stores na-
    tionwide)
SAG Membership Dues (for one year)
Leather backpack (Cole-Haan)
Gift certificate to Niketown
Subscription to PREMIERE magazine

Reading this list made me mad. Was I wrong to be angry, resentful, to find something . . . creepy about it? Was I wrong to feel shame and pity for my family out shopping for these items, braving holiday crowds to purchase these gifts for someone who didn't even respect their traditions? I mean, it's not like he put that he needed some socks and a warm sweater. Was I anti-Semitic? Pro-Christian? Neo-atheist? I decided, finally, that David was a *hypocrite.* I let the word settle in and sign a long-term lease. If it had been a movie, I would have set fire to the crumpled list and watched it burn in my unused fireplace, but instead I simply tossed it with some old cat food and superglue into the kitchen bin.

While David was on his cruise, I spent my days worrying about Little, preparing for Molly's arrival, and, of course, working. The *Entertainment Tonight* piece and the Polaroids from the shoot, along with a phone call from Rhonda Wallace, Danni's new agent, had gotten us a meeting for Danni with Tracie, the *Tonight Show* booker, and her senior producer, Bruce Tuttle. Together they represented the last hurdle before Jay Leno himself. This was what was called a pre-pre interview. Or a "meeting." In Hollywood, when you don't know what the point of something is *(Does he want to get into my pants or my rolodex?)* or what to call it *(Am I going to be fired or invited to dinner for a promotion?),* it is a meeting. In this case, the meeting was an interview that determines whether the talent is really up to the witty banter and storytelling-while-looking-fabulous that a national late-night talk-show appearance demands. It was challenging enough pretending the actors in our movies were skilled raconteurs who could manage an unscripted conversation. But until the day before, Danni hadn't even known who Jay Leno was.

"Hey, woman, how you livin'?" she exhaled into my car as I picked up her and Kirk for the meeting at their rented house in Beachwood Canyon.

I pulled the cigarette out of her mouth. "Danni, where is the suit we bought you?" She was wearing a navy blue mesh football shirt (cut at the midriff) and white leather pants. And of course, her flame-emblazoned motorcycle boots completed the ensemble.

"I didn't want to get it dirty," she said in a mock corporate voice, before adding, "heh-heh-heh," bullet-riddled laughter at someone who didn't get her.

After some negotiation with Kirk's help, Danni was introduced to the Stella McCartney black pantsuit. Very Catherine-Zeta-Jones-at-the-SAG-Luncheon. She still looked wild, but at least the nose ring and skull bracelet were gone. Her huge backpack bounced on her tiny frame as we headed for the show entrance on the NBC lot after a thirty-minute drive and three security gates. "Ah, yes, Miss Jones, a pleasure," said the guard at the final booth at the soundstage, an older, heavyset woman with tight curls who clearly knew all the comings and goings of the *Tonight Show.*

"Hey dude, right on," huffed Danni, not breaking her stride as she offered the woman a high five. I shot a look at Kirk, who shrugged with an annoying aloofness. It was inconceivable to me that he was sleeping with her. Was he? We walked along a long green hallway that was so confined it could have been in a trailer. The funny thing about the *Tonight Show* (and the soundstages of all the talk shows) is that it feels very fake; it's a small set surrounded by compromised space. The dressing rooms are housed along a long, cramped corridor with a low ceiling, with the evening's guests' names typed up on pieces of paper that are fitted into metal slots on the face of the door. Richard Gere. Peter Gabriel. Tara Reid.

"What's she doing here?" said Kirk irritably.

"She has a movie to promote and hip bones to display," I whispered, and he smiled generously. A point for me. Meanwhile, Danni was going for Tara Reid's dressing room door. I grabbed her arm just in time.

"Dude, I know her, it's *cool.* We smoked a doobie at the *Urban Legend II* premiere," she huffed dismissively.

"Well, OK, but right now she's probably really nervous and doesn't want to be distracted," I said tightly. What was I, the crotchety old aunt? "We are not here to socialize," I added authoritatively.

"We're not?" said Danni directly, her eyes, black as caviar, searching me for an opening. "I thought we were."

The late-night talk shows are taped between five and six, and there is wine for those guests who may need it. There is a traveling cart, a sort of upscale version of the old-fashioned candy vendor, which rolls up and down the hallway between the dressing rooms. This is where the publicists are usually camped out, unless they actually have a real relationship with their client: In that case they are in the dressing room assessing the contents of the *Tonight Show* gift bag and using the land line to call their offices. The guy who pushes the cart offers guests a variety of distractions to calm their nerves and take their minds off the fact that they are about to go on national television—chocolate, gummy worms, a deck of cards, a glass of wine, cigarettes, a coffee mug with a picture of Jay Leno's chin on it. Everything short of Valium. Shortly after the cart arrives, Jay Leno knocks on the dressing room door to greet his guest and to review the general subject matter of the interview, which he is holding in his hands in the form of blue note cards. "So, wow, you're really learning how to tap dance?" or "So how is the Dali Lama these days?" are tidbits he might open with in Richard Gere's room. David Letterman, as a rule, does not break the ice this way with his guests, and its known among publicists that the weaker, unprepared ones sometimes cry when faced with his raw, sugar-free New York demeanor.

We passed the goodies cart, from which Danni grabbed a pack of cigarettes and a toothbrush, and headed for the greenroom, where the guests' guests (and managers, hairstylists, publicists and agents) hung out on cheap couches in front of a big television playing—what else—that day's taping of the *Tonight Show*. The greenroom at a talk show is never really green. It's gray, oddly shaped, and furnished with large couches and square coffee tables. On this day, Richard Gere, his publicist, wife and assistant, Tara Reid's publicist, and Peter Gabriel, his manager and brother were stationed comfortably on the black leather couches watching Jay's monologue. An NBC page in khakis and blue blazer stood guard over the bottled water. No one had touched the heaping mound of fresh fruit, cheeses, cookies and bagels, but everyone had been well hydrated with Evian. Danni looked around and froze in her black pantsuit.

"I gotta pee," she announced. It seemed urgent, so I directed her back down the hallway to the ladies' room. "I can find my way back, I'll just be a second," she said, turning quickly, a piece of long, straight hair trailing across her face into her mouth. She was practically shaking. I'd never seen her so . . . vulnerable?

"I'll wait for you here," I said firmly.

"Dude. Don't embarrass me. I'll be right back, I promise," and she flashed a wicked smile.

"Don't smoke in there!" I ordered as she slammed the door. I headed back down the hall to wait for my temperamental, utterly unpredictable star. What did Kirk see in this beast?

As promised, Danni did return to the greenroom just moments later—wearing her original outfit, complete with the ridiculous boots and the mesh jersey. It had been stuffed in her backpack the entire time. Everyone looked up as the greenroom door slammed behind her. Richard Gere spoke first.

"Hello," he said warmly, smiling, and I thought for a moment that Danni might throw up on him. "Congratulations. You are the actress from *Portland Girls.* right?" He strode across the worn carpet, past the promotional posters of Jay Leno and Branford Marsalis, past the heaping food. "We loved that film! The best one at the festival," he boomed. He was oozing silvery movie star handsomeness, and Kirk bristled visibly. Danni was simply staring, wide-eyed and terrified, so I swept in to prevent the moment from collapsing upon itself.

"Danni's a little new at all of this," I apologized to Richard Gere in my Publicist Voice. "This is Kirk Olmstead, the director of *Portland Girls.* and I swept a hand in Kirk's general direction, accidentally hitting him in the nostril. He took a step back, turned crimson and gave a short, stupid wave.

Richard extended his hand. "Well, you two must be on the top of the world! What's it feel like to be the stars of Sundance?" Tracie the booker and Bruce Tuttle the segment producer glided professionally into the room as Danni finally spoke.

"You know, dude, we all die, and everybody's dump smells the same."

Somehow Danni got the booking for the *Tonight Show.* I was spending the evening with a bag of chips and a gallon of Benjamin Moore Nantucket Linen, painting the study that would become Molly's bedroom, when Viv called to tell me the news.

Her appearance was scheduled for early summer, just before the movie opened. True, they would like to offer some suggestions for a designer to outfit her, but we got the booking. We were counterprogramming July 4 weekend with a limited release for *Portland Girls*—anyone who couldn't get into the latest *Star Wars* sequel and wanted a narrative arc and a script but no explosions or digital animation could go see our movie. It was a risky strategy, but Viv managed to convince everyone it was right. Kirk was less than thrilled that he had to wait another five months for his movie to come out.

I felt vaguely annoyed that Danni was going to be rich and famous and on the *Tonight Show* and I wasn't. This is the daily life of a publicist, fouled by self-pity and an irritating sense of false entitlement. This was offset by a gnawing guilt when I reminded myself that there were people in this world who had lost not one but two limbs to land mines. People who were literally dying of thirst, people who would never earn more than minimum wage, people who had to live in Chechnya or Ohio. And many, many people who would never work in the movie business.

I, on the other hand, had exciting first world problems. Why, for example, did Powerful and Eugene R. think that *Entertainment Weekly* should put them on the cover for *Shades of Gray?* Why was the budget for the movie's New York premiere party only

$29,000 when Sassa, the must-have party promoter, insisted it should be at least $100,000? Why was the divisive argument of our department currently maps or hats for *Portland Girls?* Maps or hats, maps or hats, we have to decide!! Why did Danni keep repeating to journalists that "we all die and everyone's dump smells the same," and how would I convince her not to say that to Jay Leno on national television?

The week passed. No postcard from David or anyone else on the cruise. I imagined him on the promenade deck, trading jokes with Isaac the bartender and sipping something stupid and pink. Meanwhile L.A. was drenched with rain. Dull, endless, cold and wet, it was no longer romantic or literary. When the weekend arrived I would be picking up Molly to start our new life together. I woke up early to cross another day off the calendar and saw that Harve had peed on the floor, in the shape of Italy. The phone rang. It was Mom.

"How are you, honey?"

"Fine," I said, grabbing a paper towel. "How's your new boat?"

"It's in storage until the spring, you know that," she said testily. "You're not really upset about that, are you?"

"No," I admitted. "But if might have been nice if you'd waited, even a little while. Christ, when did you buy it, the day I told you the news?" I wiped up the pee, and I heard my mother inhale sharply, a sign she felt guilty. "It was a great price. Opportunity favors the prepared, Lex." Right you are, Mom. "Besides, it's just as much your boat as it is ours."

"I'll remember that in July."

"Well, anyway, I think it's great that Molly's moving in with you," she said, remaining positive. "When is she coming?"

"I'm flying up to get her this weekend," I replied, suddenly remembering that it was really happening. "I think she's doing better," I added, knowing Mom was worried.

"Good. You know that house down the road?" she asked,

changing gears, and I did my best to feign ignorance, waiting for her to continue. "Well, it *is* Andrew Sullivan building it. We stopped in. He's quite successful, he's doing a lot of large-scale homes in this area." The sound of a mother meaning well. I said nothing as I finished wiping up the pee.

"He asked about you—"

"I hope you told him I was just fantastic," I said irritably and headed for the kitchen with the soiled paper towel, stepping on Little's tail on the way. *Rowrrr!*

"He's awfully cute," she trilled.

"Yes, I remember," I replied patiently. I opened a can of food for Harve and mashed his pills into the mush. He circled at my feet, tripping himself.

"He's not married."

"I have to go, Mom."

*Roooo!* said Harve.

# Seventeen

In *Falling Down,* an unrecognizably nerdy Michael Douglas becomes unglued, suffering a complete meltdown at the hands of
regular, everyday annoyances. One after the other, incompetent
people, infuriating inconveniences and maddening rules are rules-
type obstacles chip away at his practiced exterior until he is Every-
man with an Uzi. He embarks on a disturbing criminal odyssey,
which seems funny, at first but by the end you're not laughing.
You're thinking, *It could happen to anyone, really.* Because life isn't
fair, unless you're on Oprah or you're Charlie in *Willy Wonka and
the Chocolate Factory,* where good people who tell the truth do,
eventually, prevail.

Agotha the Hun called at the crack of 7:30 a.m. to remind me
that a plumber (i.e., member of her vast, underground organiza-
tion) would be coming to the house to install water-saving devices
on the toilet. She expected no problems wit gates, dog, cats or
*anytink elzz!* Hmmm. She was updating fixtures and appliances to
fit certain standards; she was trying to increase the value of the
property—why?

A luxurious growl in the driveway interrupted my thoughts—

Victor, picking up Harve in his Mercedes. I pretended to be in the shower as Victor discreetly collected Harve from the stairs. David had given him a key before leaving for the cruise. I didn't feel like discussing Harve's meds or what kind of a time David might be having on the cruise.

On my way to work I dropped Little off at Kikki the Cat Woman's house. I'd found the ad in *LA Weekly.* *(Loving day care for your pets while you're at work!)* Since Harve was with Victor, I didn't want to leave a rowling Little alone in the house all day, with Agotha lurking around with prospective new tenants. So I had arranged for her to spend the day with Kikki. Kitty Day Care—I'd become one of *those people.* Like a working divorcée, I'd pick her up for the weekend, in time to meet Mommy's new roommate—Molly.

Kikki lived in a small house in Venice and did not have a kennel license or any other kind of permit that legally allowed her to keep more than fifteen cats on the property, which was less than a quarter acre at most. So although she was clandestine about her services, she was cheap. She was also one of those freaky cat people who valued animals more than people (sleeping in bed with them, kissing them on the mouth and cooking eggs for them in the morning), which meant that she never turned you down when you needed to unload a pet in a pinch. When you approached her house the smell hit you a few feet from the front steps. Unmistakable. Cat(s). Then a chorus of mewling ensued for roughly twelve minutes before she would actually open the door, usually about only halfway, and greet you wearing a T-shirt and tights.

When I dropped off Little, Kikki was in black leotards, covered (and I mean *covered*) with cat hair and having an allergy attack. Last week she had just had a collagen injection in her lip, so when I called to make Little's arrangements it was difficult to understand her *(Hen ah you goee to dwop hewh off?")*. Today she was better and wanted to talk. It was like dropping my kid off at camp. Kikki told

me that she was planning on getting back into bed with the cats to
"watch Andy Griffith reruns." "Okay," I said, not really knowing
what else to say.

I got to work a little late, and Adriane handed me my call sheet:

| DATE/TIME | CONTACT | NUMBER | MESSAGE |
|---|---|---|---|
| 2/27/00 9:57 a.m. | Princess Cruise call service (?) | 800-MY-SHIP | Re; from passenger Deke Rothrock; want to make sure Harve is ok; plse call ref. number 345HARV |
| 2/27/00 10:23 a.m. | Molly | Home | What time are you coming on Sat.? Want to know what time to rent the van. Also plse bring your cell phone for the drive (she doesn't have one). |
| 2/27/00 11:05 a.m. | Kikki (?) made a meowing noise? | 310-239-4755 | (I left on machine) "Wittle ate all of her omwette!" (?) |
| 2/27/00 1 1:30 a.m. | Brucey / Dolce & Gabbana | 212-388-4500 | Re: Outfitting Danni for Cannes? Referred by "Cheryl." Need sizes and a credit card. |

| DATE/TIME | CONTACT | NUMBER | MESSAGE |
|---|---|---|---|
| 2/27/00 11:45 a.m. | Corey / PARADE mag | 310-248-7200 | Re: Danni; Fall cover story is 'Inspiring People;' Eugene R. suggested Danni. Has she lost weight or overcome anything personally horrible? (editorial requirement) |
| 2/27/00 12:30 p.m. | Beth / Corporate Communications | x4533 | Re: Cow tipping scene in *Portland Girls* is being cut. She is preparing a statement about cows not being harmed or run over in any way. Call if questions: refer press inquiries to her. |
| 2/27/00 1:14 p.m. | Dr. Salome / Pet Vet | 310-277-3736 | Re: Little—have you made a decision yet? Surgeries require a week's notice. |
| 2/27/00 1:45 p.m. | Claude G. / Variety | 323-556-2455 | Heard you are cutting *Portland Girls* and director is suing studio? Need quote, on deadline; has spoken to cow people (?) |

| DATE/TIME | CONTACT | NUMBER | MESSAGE |
|-----------|---------|--------|---------|
| 2/27/00 1:49 p.m. | Kirk | Cell or home | Call him. VERY Important. |
| 2/27/00 1:50 p.m. | Viv | Office | DON'T CALL KIRK until she talks to him. |
| 2/27/00 2:05 p.m. | Victor | 310-223-0098 | What time are you picking up Harve? |
| 2/27/00 2:30 p.m. | Marcos | Home | *Star Wars* movie marathon tonight on AMC; wanna come over? Frank & Sue are coming. |
| 2/27/00 4:01 p.m. | Rick / *Details* | 212-268-9811 | Re: Story about Kirk and Danni. Plse call. |
| 2/27/00 4:34 p.m. | Bridget / *Entertainment Tonight* | 323-456-8909 | Is Robert Downey being released from prison to attend the *Shades of Gray* premiere? Story airing . . . |

The cow tipping scene in *Portland Girls* had to be cut, it was that simple. It wasn't needed really, since all it did was (1) add ten minutes to the movie, (2) demonstrate that Danni's character lived in a rural town that was too small for her (a plot point easily accomplished in the heroin-snorting-with-best-friend scene) and (3) piss off PETA, something no studio needed on opening weekend.

I felt bad for Kirk; he thought he was being screwed over by the big bad Studio and that cutting a scene from his film was at best an insult and at worst, sacrilege. I wanted to call him, reassure him, help him navigate these new waters for which he was unprepared and underdressed, but Viv was the boss, and if she didn't want me talking to Kirk about the "issue," then I couldn't. We had to be a united front when dealing with the temperamental talent, so I ignored my call sheet except for one message.

"Hello?" said Molly in a voice more hopeful than I'd heard from her in a while.

"Hi," I said brightly. "Did you know there's a *Star Wars* marathon on tonight?"

"Know it I do, but watch it, I will not," she said in her Yoda imitation, followed by a withered sigh.

"Why not?"

"I have to finish packing," she said, suddenly tired. "They had a going-away party at the school for me today." Doubt and despair crept into the line.

"And let me guess, they were all really nice and now you love the school and Berkeley's a great city and now you don't want to leave, right?" I shot back, not giving in to sympathy.

"Yeah. Kind of like getting your hair cut on a good hair day. It's just, it's really happening now," she said, her voice cracking. "I can't pretend I'm in a holding pattern. I'm unemployed, unengaged, homeless and broke." She gave a little laugh of helplessness. "I have no life now . . ."

"You will," I said gently. "Listen, it's a big transition, and you have to take one step at a time." She sucked air through the line. The silence meant tears were flooding her vocal cords.

"How would you feel about staying with Aunt Kris next week, so you're not in the middle of me trying to get David out of the apartment?" I said boldly, the thought having just occurred to me. I had a feeling the leaving might get ugly, and Molly didn't need any more stress.

She took a breath. "He's never going to leave, is he?"

"He will, I promise. But you won't be able to get settled til he's gone anyway, so you might as well stay at a big house with a pool and a retired, doting, rich aunt." Spin, spin, step right up and buy my story.

"That does sound better than giving his stupid dog blood transfusions or whatever," she admitted. Suddenly Adriane AmΤelled me: **Kirk—again!**

"Mol, I'll see you Saturday at about nine, okay? Everything is going to be great, you'll see."

*"It's going to be a great year, Louis,"* she laughed weakly.

Adriane's five-foot-ten-inch frame was in my doorway. Kirk was not going to hang up. Viv had broken the news about cutting the film, in addition to the fact that he had to add a song to the end credits, and he was looking for an ally. "He's holding," Adriane said expectantly as soon as I met her eye.

"No," I said flatly.

"He says," she breathed slowly and patiently, twisting a curl around one slender finger, "that he'll wait."

I straightened dramatically in my ergonomic chair. Looked out the window to the blue sky and gray air. Pushed line one. "Hi, Kirk. What's up?" I chirped innocently.

"You mean besides the fucking fact that your fucking studio is planning on fucking hacking up my film? Nice of you to take my call, by the fucking way."

"I'm fine, Kirk, thanks for asking," I purred in a professional ass-kissing tone. "And how are you?"

"Don't bullshit me, Alexis," he growled. So I turned off the spin and told the truth. "Kirk, the movie's too long. It needs tightening, you even admitted that . . ." *And if it's only 90 minutes we'll get more theater playtimes and make more fucking money,* I did not tell him.

"What's this bullshit about adding a song at the end?" His voice oozed contempt. I'd never heard him like this before. It was true we wanted the new Aaliyah single for the closing credits. Otherwise the film wasn't uplifting, wouldn't reach the youth demo, and wouldn't garner word of mouth. The ending was too ambiguous, too contemplative, closing on Danni hitching a ride out of Portland at dusk to the sound of . . . *crickets.* It was art, for God's sake, and the studio needed to make back its investment by making it . . . marketable. This was the hardest part of the job.

"You know you have to talk to Viv about that. I'm just the publicity person, Kirk," I argued.

"You talk to her," he pleaded in a new voice laced with vulnerability, a lost kid asking someone to help him find his way. "She won't listen to me—the cow tipping scene took two weeks to shoot!"

"So what? You got paid, don't you get it? Viv knows what she's doing. And it's not *your movie* anymore!" I argued, frustrated. There was a silence, as though someone had just sliced his throat. I took a breath. "Kirk, almost every great movie is cut by someone in some way the director doesn't initially agree with."

"Oh yeah, like what?" he challenged.

"*Fatal Attraction*—the ending was changed—"

"That was *after* a test screening—not before the movie was even completely mixed!" he snapped. "And don't start with me about how the original *Pretty Woman* script was way darker than the film, or how they Disney-fied the literary version of *Breakfast at Tiffany's*—or didn't you know that was a *book* first?" So he knew his stuff. I inhaled deeply and tightened my Spokesperson for the Company belt another notch.

"Kirk, I think the film is more palatable to a wider audience if it has fewer quirky, *potentially alienating* details that—"

"OK Alexis Manning, Super Publicist, you're giving me your

best spin, fine, but I *know* you don't really think that! I *know* you!"
His voice was rising, cagey, risky, going someplace weird. What did
he mean, *he knew me?*

"What are you talking about?"

"You love movies! I saw you there!"

"What? Where?" Now I was alarmed.

"The Stanley Donen retrospective! I saw you crying at the
*Funny Girl* trailer at eight in the morning! Only a weird freak who
loves movies more than anything—someone like ME—would be
there!!"

"Kirk, I—"

"You can't stand up to anyone there, can you? You wimp. I
thought you had balls—"

"I'm sorry . . ." I searched my mental files for the right thing
to say as I struggled with the embarrassment and odd thrill of
his confession. "We all love the movie, but you have to understand—"

"I'll see you at the screening tomorrow, Alexis," he spat, then
hung up on me. Hung up! Now he was Hollywood. Adriane
Amtelled, **Little is on the phone.** I picked up the call in a mild
panic. It was Kikki. She told me Little was fine but that she looked
worried.

"She always looks worried. That's how she is," I sighed wearily.

"I know, but this is different," explained Kikki. "I think she
misses you. And I think," she paused, searching for the right tone,
then choosing badly, "that she's *worried* about you. She can stay
here an extra night. She knows how busy you are. She loves you
very much, Alexis." The Crazy Collagen Cat Woman shedding
prophetic light on my personal, ugly truths. Why had I taken the
call?

This call was interrupted by another Amtel from Adriane. Victor, who was "alarmed" because, according to the Amtel, **Harve is
not eating** I picked up line two. "Hi, Lex," Victor said, in that I'm-

not-judging-you voice reserved for David's friends when they addressed me now. "I'm alarmed because Harve is not eating."

We both agreed it was better to be safe than responsible for Harve's impromptu death, so Victor drove him to the Pet Vet Clinic on Overland, in the middle of the day in the pouring rain, a fifty-minute drive from Los Feliz. Just because he was independently wealthy and wanted to be an actor didn't mean he didn't have anything else to do. The vet did a blood test, then he prescribed more medication, then he actually told Victor to go home and prepare white rice and steamed chicken for Harve to encourage his appetite. Which Victor went home and did. He called me that night. "Hi, Alexis, it's Victor," he said in a voice that was clearly trying not to be annoyed.

"How is he?" I asked. I was watching *Jeopardy!* The category was Famous Ruins.

"He seems OK, at least he ate dinner," said Victor. "I made him steamed rice and chicken." I, meanwhile, was rolling up sliced turkey and dunking it into a jar of Grey Poupon. Cheese curls completed my meal. "Um, I thought I should let you know that David sent me an e-mail . . . ," Victor said carefully.

"Oh," I said, thinking *What is Stonehenge?* to Alex Trebek.

Victor continued, ". . . he said his phone seems not to be working." I waited. I could hear blame approaching. "I guess he tried to call in from the ship (it's very expensive, apparently) to check his messages, and the line didn't pick up and he thinks, that, uh, you must have accidentally unplugged it . . ."

"I haven't touched his phone," I said neutrally, willing Alex Trebek to say, *What is Pompeii?*

Then Victor, the ever supportive friend, said, "I really don't know why he's calling me about that, I guess he thinks I'm his own personal concierge." Was that sarcasm I heard? From Best Friend Victor?

"I'll check the line," I told Victor, "and I'll pick Harve up from your house tomorrow night." We hung up. One more day. Just get through one more day and then the ark would land, the cruise would be over and David would return to find Molly here. Every passing day he didn't move his shit was another pinprick in the thin skin of my patience. Like with Chinese water torture, bad perms or smoking, you could not easily undo the cumulative effects. No matter. I'd get a head start.

I turned off *Jeopardy!* and set to work separating the books, mine *(The Dalai Lama Explains Happiness, An Introduction to the Jewish People* and *Anna Karenina)* and all five of his *(The Way of the Audition, An Actor Prepares, 100 Great Monologues, The Big Book of Abs,* and *The Count of Monte Cristo).*

"This is my favorite book," he'd said more than once. I hadn't read it, but I was so curious that I seized it from the shelf the day we moved in together. Frustrated and annoyed, I bought the abridged version the next day. "Why is this your favorite book?" I asked, realizing now with some discomfort that I was partnered with someone who put a tremendous value on revenge. "I just love the way he pursues, finds and gets even with all the people who did him wrong."

Oh.

I didn't want to negotiate the division of the books; I didn't want to talk about who got what. I didn't want to argue anymore. I just wanted him to take what he wanted and leave forever.

The next day I woke up to find there was no hot water, which I instantly attributed to the installation of the new water-saving toilets, Agotha's latest plot against me. I called her to discover she was "having some tests done today at the hospital," part of the prep for her "surgery next week." *What, having a heart installed?* I didn't say. As a result of her medical complications, Agotha was not available to come to the apartment and wait for the plumber. So I—*resourceful!*—called the plumber myself and arranged to meet him at the house between noon and 2:00, knowing full well if he showed up at all he'd arrive at 2:05, which he did.

On the way to work, my right-side window got stuck halfway down and wouldn't budge no matter how hard I forced it or yelled. Then my cell phone car charger went dead and refused to fit into the cigarette lighter no matter how hard I forced it or yelled. I could not fly to and drive a van back from San Francisco without a working cell phone. I got to work knowing I'd have to leave again in two hours to meet the plumber.

Viv emerged from her office holding a life-size cardboard standee of Danni in *Portland Girls*. The tagline was now, *Sometimes, home is the last place you expect to find yourself.* She put Danni down and said, somewhat testily, "Lex, where are you going?"

"I have to meet the plumber," I said. "I'll be on my cell."

"We have the screening in an hour," she complained. We were reviewing *Portland Girls* for the first time without the now-famous cow tipping scene and, of course, to see where else it could be cut. Kirk was coming, and Viv needed reinforcements.

"I promise I'll be right back," I lied. It was exhausting being my own personal assistant, but I'd always vowed never to become one of those people who made my assistant pick up my dry cleaning, my cat or my coffee. Adriane had enough ridiculous details to monitor.

"I need you to sign Danni's We Care invoice!"Adriane called insistently, but I was out the door.

The plumber took all of eight minutes to wander into the basement and relight the pilot light in the hot water heater and charge me $40 to do it. I was very embarrassed. I'd never felt like such a . . . *broad* in my entire life. "Why didn't you relight it yourself?" he asked, scratching his greasy forehead.

"Because I don't know how!" Duh. Stupid plumber.

"Why didn't you read the instructions on the sticker here, on the heater, where it says 'Steps one to four to relight the pilot'?" he asked. I got back to the studio barely in time for the screening, diving into my seat just as "A film by Kirk Olmstead" appeared on the screen.

"Nice of you to show up," he growled, and I glared at him. He had a huge hickey on his neck.

"Nice bruise," I said nonchalantly, and he rolled his eyes and ignored me. What was he doing with her? What kind of self-denial factory was he working in? In truth, the hickey reminded me that I hadn't had sex in three months. But then that thing happened, that thing that always happens when I sit down in a dark theater. Everything—my anger, irritation, frustration, arrogance, impatience, rudeness, vanity—evaporated into the story as the film unspooled. The young girl goes home to take care of her sister after her mother's death, finally reconciling with her father, watching her best friend OD on heroin, finding love in the least likely place, and coming of age. It was a sweet, sad story, which I loved, despite the constant presence of Danni. Every time I watched it, it was like leaving the planet for 106 (now 96) minutes.

Viv took Kirk into her office after the screening and closed the door. I heard some yelling, then laughing, then the Aaliyah song being played very loudly. It seemed she had won, so I crept out of the office at 6:15, just enough time to get Little and make it back to the Sprint store to get a new charger. The whole time driving there I was nervous that it would start to rain again, because now my window was stuck open. I knocked and yelled at Kikki's door for fifteen minutes before she came to open it holding a plastic bag in one hand and a blue icepack on her lip with the other.

"Cowugen weaction," she mumbled. She handed me the plastic bag of "her cat food" which "Wittle wikes." Well no wonder, I thought, peering into the bag and seeing the crushed remains of stale Cat Treats. Kikki's Kitty Kibble. "You should market this," I said, because I didn't know what else to say. Freak.

I couldn't escape in under ten minutes of incomprehensible

chitchat, during which I learned about taking fat from one's ass and putting it in one's lip as an alternative to collagen (I mean, *you couldn't have a weaction to wour own fat, wight? It's alweady in yooh!*) but also during which Kikki offered to take Little for free one day next week—the *moving day.* It would be nice to have one less thing to worry about as David was extracting himself fully and finally from our lives. I accepted.

When I pulled out of Kikki's driveway, I immediately noticed that smell that Little . . . *emitted* . . . when she was nervous or downright terrified, which was often. Apparently there is something like a fear gland that all animals have, and the combination that came to mind when I noticed the putrid odor was sweat and shit on a hot, airless day. On top of this was the general feline aroma of Kikki's quarters. Kikki must have been aware of her home's odor, because with every overnight night stay each illegal boarder was bathed before being returned. Little was no exception. I looked into the backseat and, despite the fact that she had just had a bath, Little was shedding like crazy. Shaking, shedding and smelling. I opened all four windows a crack. The right rear one didn't open at all but instead made a loud vibrating, buzzing noise that hurled Little into the front seat and against the windshield with great force when I braked instinctively in alarm. *"Rroowwll!"*

And David was on a cruise and thought I unplugged his phone accidentally on purpose.

I got home and, needing strength, chugged a beer before climbing into David's truck (which, naturally, had a parking ticket and no gas) to go pick up Harve at Victor's house. It was still raining. Victor had left a note:

> Alexis:
> Thanks for coming to get Harve. He has had all of his medication. Could you give David this vet bill I put on my Visa ($846.90)? The vet said to call within 48 hrs

to check in. p.s. Harve ate a chicken and rice dinner
at 6:00.

*That will be his last,* I thought. There was no way I'd be making
that dog anything to eat but stirred Alpo with lukewarm tap water.
So I packed Harve and his paraphernalia (bed, leash, blanket, dish,
bandages, down pillow, six kinds of pills in a huge Ziploc baggie)
into the truck, where Little had just thrown up about a pound of
crushed Kitty Kibble, and drove home. In the rain. I arrived at
10:45, and the message light was blinking. I was afraid to listen
but finally pushed the button. Thank God, it was Viv.

"Hey, Lex, just letting you know we won." She sounded exhausted. "Kirk's OK about cutting the cow tipping, editing the last
scene and we're putting in the song . . . but I had to promise you'd
go to Cannes to get him a full interview schedule. He thinks that's
a favor, whatever that means. Anyway, make sure Adriane does
your travel soon," and the message ended. Suddenly I was going to
Cannes, to take care of Kirk. Was this his revenge, or a plan of
some other kind?

Little and I climbed into bed exhausted. I had a 7:30 a.m. flight
to San Francisco to pick up Molly, who would have to spend her
first week here with Aunt Kris in Orange County because David
had not moved out or even packed yet, because he was on a cruise.
And he thought I unplugged his phone.

This was the beginning of the end of the end.

# Eighteen

In *Georgia,* there are two sisters. Mare Winningham is the sensible, together, talented one—a popular folksinger. Jennifer Jason Leigh is the twisted, self-destructive, strung-out loser sister with no talent who's on a desperate quest to be not just a folksinger but also a clone of her perfect sister. Mare, a serene and compassionate woman, doesn't know how to deal with Jennifer as she slips ever deeper into a warped existence of booze and self-denial. In the end, she rescues her the only way she can, with compassion and singing. But Jennifer's so wrapped up in her own corrosive orbit she can't see the forest for the trees—that her sister only wants her to be happy, and that she really ought to pursue something else with her life.

The rainiest day of all time was the day I flew up to San Francisco to meet Molly, pick up the U-Haul and move all her stuff out of the apartment she shared with Jack. Their split had been gradual and painful, but they were still speaking, still feeling tender toward one another and were actually guiding each other through the emotional chaos and devastation of the breakup. He'd even made an Excel sheet for the division of the possessions. Since it was San

Francisco and not L.A., four of their friends had shown up to help us move. We all went out to lunch afterward, and the atmosphere was polite, kind, calm, rational—in a word, surreal. It was a macrobiotic Asian fusion café, and the food, although completely unrecognizable, was delicious. Molly and Jack sat opposite each other at the Formica table, his hand cradling over hers in a protective, reassuring way. Their friends asked polite questions.

"Are you going to look for a teaching job?"

"Do you think you'll buy a car?"

"Maybe you can get tan!"

Jack paid for the gas, carried all the heavy stuff, and made sure we knew how to drive the truck that was far too large for either of us to be driving, particularly on the interstate, in our conditions, for five hours. He behaved suspiciously like a decent boyfriend. He and Molly embraced for what they knew (but pretended they didn't) was the last time. They actually seemed very compatible and respectful during the whole ordeal, down to the dividing of the houseplants, and I found myself in the awkward and unfortunate position of being envious of my little sister's breakup.

"So we'll talk soon, OK?" Jack said, holding her. In northern California the sky was gray and pregnant with change. "Ymmpphh," Molly managed, holding her African violet close to her chest, so close that a few dirt crumbles stuck to her shirt on her right breast and stayed there. No one brushed them off.

As Molly and I lumbered up the ramp to Route 280 in the truck, we were both quietly sobbing, her for Jack, me for her. We spent a few careful moments in the aptly named breakdown lane before beginning the taxing process of navigating our way onto this new freeway together. The rain unloaded, drenching the truck, the breakdown lane, and any crusty remnants of joy left in our souls. The truck had no radio. Six hours to go until our new life. She thought it was a bad idea to stop at Burger King, but I needed fattening fast food to go on. The truck lumbered around

the sopping parking lot, and I finally managed, with great naviga-
tion, to park it. We made our way wordlessly into the haven of orange and red cheer. I got in line, and she went to the restroom. We
sat in a fluorescent tangerine booth. She contemplated the food on
the tray.

"I don't think," she said softly, "you should eat that."

"Don't judge my eating habits just because you can't get regular," I said, meaning to be funny, but she didn't laugh. As we approached Bakersfield, the combo cramps kicked in (*Mr. BK
Broiler, meet Miss Strawberry shake!*) and with some strange comfort I realized that once again, she'd been right. We arrived in L.A.
eight hours later, and it was not only raining, but it was also pouring and dark. We pulled into the Miracle Mile neighborhood and
turned onto Crestview, the enormous truck lumbering like a sad,
wet elephant down the street.

"This is it," I said, turning off the ignition and leaving a deaf-
ening silence where the noise of the engine had been. We sat in the
giant truck in the driveway, the rain dancing on the tin roof, the
green of the front yard glistening with rain. Molly began to sob,
slowly at first, then harder as each raindrop seemed to reinforce the
finality of her decision. Drip. She left him. Plink. She moved to
L.A. Patter. She was voluntarily unemployed. Toink. She knew absolutely no one here outside of me. Toc. She had no car. Poink.
And no money. Patter patter patter PATTER PATTER. . . .
WHAT HAD SHE DONE?

"Come on, it's not that bad!" I said. I couldn't stand to see her
so upset. "This is a nice neighborhood! This is Miracle Mile!" I was
trying to lighten the mood, to cheer her up, but it wasn't working.

"I'm exhausted," she sighed. "Can we unload the truck in the
morning, when it's not raining?" she asked. "Maybe your friends
can help us."

I didn't want to upset her further, so I didn't explain that she
was in L.A. now, where it rained once a year for three weeks and it

would not stop tomorrow. She was in L.A., where friends didn't let friends guilt them into helping you move, and you couldn't offer to buy them lunch to bribe them because nobody ate normal food. The rain insulted us in sheets as we dashed to the front door of the apartment—our apartment, the apartment where My Sister and I lived now. Harve and Little watched silently from the window, wondering if any good could come of this new development. Meanwhile, David's ship was docking somewhere.

Molly and I woke up early to the phone ringing. It was Billy, calling to welcome Molly to L.A. but not to help us unpack. "Why not?" I asked him irritably.

"It's Sunday. I'm working, Lex."

I snorted. "Who works on Sunday? You don't even have a job!"

"Are you kidding? I have to finish the music for this National Geographic special," he said groggily. "Anyway, I want to meet this sister of yours, but I can't today."

"Not that I want you ogling my sister, but I haven't seen you in ages, come on!" It was true. A visit would be good for Molly.

"No can do, luv. By tomorrow I have to have the snake theme music done—but my new CD is almost finished and I'm gonna have a big release party. Well, big for me anyway. You guys will have to come to that."

"All right, that sounds cool. We'll be there," I told him. It was hard to stay mad at him. Besides, Molly and I could both probably lift more than he could.

We slugged in the boxes together all morning, one by one. Molly quickly saw that David's things were still everywhere, soaking up the positive estrogen vibes we kept trying to distribute throughout the house. "How can I put my stuff away? His crap is everywhere! Has he packed *anything?*" she asked incredulously.

"Yes," I said matter-of-factly. "He packed a bag to take on the cruise." She rolled her eyes. In the end we simply piled all her things in the middle of the living room, the only spot there was, really. This was pure torture for Molly, who, like our mother, liked things neat, orderly, and not in a pile. Then she had to do something even more upsetting—subdivide her stuff and pack yet another bag to take with her to Aunt Kris's house, where she'd be fielding invasive questions and concerned looks for the next week, or until whenever David got around to actually moving.

"God, what a jerk," Molly commented as we hauled the last of her lamps in and shoved them in the last pocket of space left.

"I know," I said, kicking David's weights into the closet. "I painted the study for you, but there's no sense putting any of your things away until he takes out the desk and computer."

"He's so inconsiderate. He's like two different people," said Molly, who never judged anyone needlessly.

"Maybe that's why he couldn't seem to settle on one name," I quipped, opening the pickle jar. She tore open a bag of chips.

Harve appeared under the table. "And," she huffed, "I can't believe he's making you take care of Harve through all this!" She kneed Harve and his tumors away. Suddenly I felt guilty. After all, I was the one who'd let the relationship go on for so long, knowing deep in the recesses of my insecure heart that it would never survive in the long run.

"He wasn't always such a jerk, Mol . . . he changed," I admitted, and she didn't say anything, meaning that she was aware of this and had kept quiet, probably for a long time, while letting me figure it out myself.

"I just hate that he always acted like he was the center of the universe," she said, digging into her turkey sandwich.

"Is that a term you learned from the sixth-graders?" I asked her teasingly, and we both laughed.

Little materialized on the countertop. "Life would be so much easier as a cat," Molly sighed, patting her head.

"Maybe, but not that cat. She has more problems than you do, believe me." There was a long pause as Molly considered this. "What are you going to do first?" I finally asked her in a more serious tone, meeting her eyes.

"Look for a job, I guess," she said, sighing again and glancing out the window at the gray sunlight. "Think you could get me a job at the studio? Maybe I could give tours or something."

"You don't want to do that," I said quickly, picking up Little and depositing her on the floor. Molly looked at the newspaper spread out on the counter. "Aim higher, Mol."

"Maybe I'll take a course in real estate, seems like I could eventually make decent money doing that. And they get to make their own hours." She thumbed through the paper, wrapped up the chips, then reconsidered and opened them again. We were so much alike.

"Speaking of real estate, there are new tenants moving in downstairs here," I told her, quietly omitting the part about the angry landlord. Molly had enough to think about without fearing an impromptu run-in with Agotha the Hun.

"Well, I hope they're nice," she said absently. She put the paper down. "God, it would be so great to not have to rent and worry about that kind of stuff anymore, wouldn't it?" She looked around. It was a nice apartment, twice the size of anything either of us had inhabited in San Francisco or New York. "I mean, imagine if you owned this place, or any place—"

"I did imagine it, before Mom and Dad bought a boat with my wedding money," I huffed. She stared at me a moment, digesting what I'd said.

"They . . . what?!" She practically choked on a corn chip.

I nodded. "You heard me. It's sitting in the marina in Harwich port. Til spring, of course, when we'll all go fishing together, apparently. It even has a *name.*" She waited patiently, knowing I would answer her unasked question. "The *Sea Devil,*" I finally said, trying and failing to conceal my bitter tone.

"Oh my God, Lex. I'm sorry. That's kind of . . . horrible, I think. Isn't it?" Then a thought occurred to her, and her face regrouped in sadness, the memory of the past few weeks outlined in four wrinkles on her forehead. "What did they do with *my* wedding money?" she asked slowly in a tight voice.

"I didn't ask. Maybe they bought an engine." This was cruel of me, but I was trying to make her laugh. Instead, of course, she began to cry.

"I'll never get married," she whimpered, "even Mom and Dad don't think I will!" and she stared quietly into the bag of chips before hurling it across the room. Little and Harve scampered after the crumbs.

There was a giant, still moment that enveloped the kitchen, and I touched Molly's shoulder. "Molly . . ."

"How am I ever going to get through this?" she cried in a muffled wail. "I just walked out on my whole life. I miss him, Lex . . ."

"You have to give it time," I said softly, thinking of how irritated I was at David, which beat the hell out of longing for him. "And therapy . . . ," I added, opening the Sunday *Times* movie page. She glanced up, miserable and helpless, struggling through tears and snot. "Look, Mol, a John Hughes double feature at the American Cinematheque—this afternoon. Anthony Michael Hall and John Cusack are doing a Q&A." She just sat there hiccupping on her breakup sorrow, so I grabbed the proverbial bull of depression by the horns. "Right down the street from Anthroplogie . . ."

Still nothing from her, so I got serious. "Molly. *"There's no crying in baseball'!"* This, I knew she remembered, was Tom Hanks's philosophy from *A League of Their Own*.

"Get your jacket."

# Nineteen

Kevin Bacon has been in a lot of movies. But early Bacon is best, as in *The Big Picture,* when he is an ambitious student filmmaker navigating his way up the Hollywood escalator. He scrapes and scrambles to get his first directing gig, losing his loyal girlfriend and alienating his best friend in the process. He outgrows his britches very quickly, and soon enough, Hollywood's courtship of him completely evaporates, along with Teri Hatcher's sexual invitations. Just as fast as he rocketed up the Hot list, he's stone cold and hits rock bottom. He imagines the increasingly depressing events of his life in cinematic fantasy, including calling on his ex-girlfriend, whom he now, of course, wants back. She's in black and white, Dietrich style, sporting riding jodhpurs and a crop. In his perverted vision she is wealthy, powerful, gorgeous and totally disinterested in him. She has, to his despair, moved on.

When David got back from the cruise, he called me at the office. Adriane knew how irritatingly awful it was for me to see **David** on the Amtel, and I could hear her typing softly, apologetically. I was going through the proofs from Kirk and Danni's shoot. In more than one, the Neanderthal Danni was making obscene gestures—flipping the bird, grabbing her crotch, sticking her tongue out, and my favorite, liquorice sticks suspended from each nostril. Where had those come from? Not the caterer? Why had I not seen/prevented that happening? Oh yes, I had been with Vet Man outside in the rain. I put the proofs down and picked up the phone. David didn't even ask me how I was, how Molly was, how the six-hour trip driving the huge U-Haul van on I-5 was, how I was coping at work; he just said (can you guess?):

"How's Harve?"

Later that night, he came over to get some of his stuff. I shouldn't have been home between 9:00 and 9:30 like we agreed, and I hadn't asked him how he planned to get any moving accomplished in half an hour, or why he couldn't possibly do some packing during one of the nine hours during the day I was *not* at the house, but at 9:15 I was in bed with cramps, devouring *Four Weddings and a Funeral (Hugh, tell her, tell her you love her now, before she gets engaged to that pompous Scot)* on Comedy Central, wearing my glasses, a menstrual zit blossoming on my chin, and a stale, half-eaten blueberry muffin balanced on my chest. Molly was at Aunt Kris's until the weekend. He knocked on the bedroom door and came in without waiting for an answer.

"Hey . . ." I stiffened in the bed, crumbs toppling from my breasts. Maddeningly, he was cheerful, upbeat, and looked amazing. Newly tanned, rested, with a few healthy pounds of Princess Cruise food filling in his hollowed actor cheeks. I was PMS-alert ugly with flat, straight hair and greasy white flesh under crumb-filled sheets. "So," I choked, pulling the blankets up further, "the cruise was fun?" Why was this happening?

"Oh, we had a great time! Those ships are amazing!" His tone was positive, friendly, borderline bored—he talked at me as if I were an old aunt. He did not ask one question about how I was. Or Molly. Or Little. Dick. Then he launched into a detailed description of the cruise and how fun it was and how my family should go on one and how you were never bored, there was so much to do! I volleyed with my tales of driving Harve for his shots, picking him up from Victor's in the pouring rain in a truck with no gas that Little had vomited in and the marathon of flying up and driving back from San Francisco with Molly, unloading the truck by ourselves in the pouring rain . . .

"Oh, is that what happened in the driveway? Are the skid marks from your rental truck?" he inquired politely, focusing on my blimple.

"I was trying to keep it from backing into Harve, because we had no one to help us," I replied sharply, instinctively crossing my legs to make them look thinner and longer.

"I hope Agotha doesn't try to charge you for that," he said casually, either choosing to ignore my sarcasm or missing it altogether, I'm not sure which. Goddammit. I scrunched into the bed. "You're going to have to go buy nice pillows now when I take mine," he laughed. It was true that until I'd met him I'd preferred big fat synthetic pillows. Man-made slabs that made your head bounce instead of sink. A faint smile escaped from my lips. He sensed the break, saw the opening. Those little memories of our secret familiarity, those were the Trojan horses in our battle to be understood.

"You'll be out shopping for four-hundred-thread-count sheets once I pack mine up," he said in a voice meant to be friendly. *The four-hundred-count sheets that your mother bought for you.* I didn't say. He seemed to be doing just fine. I wanted him to leave me alone, and the mean part of me hoped he never got that soap job *(Winston Edward is a tough, brutally handsome man whose whiskers weaken most women's knees)*. I wanted him to see what it was like finding an apartment on his own. More than anything, though, I wanted him to be pale and fat.

The following week, when Molly was back from Orange County, David and Harve finally moved out of the apartment, with much fanfare. So that Little would not freak out, run away or die during the transfer, I had installed her with Kikki for the day, free of charge as promised. I went to work thinking, *When I get home, the house will be emptied of him for good.*

| DATE/TIME | CONTACT | NUMBER | MESSAGE |
|---|---|---|---|
| 3/8/00<br>9:04 a.m. | Eugene R. | No number—<br>think it was<br>that # pay<br>phone | WHY aren't we in the *USA TODAY* summer preview! Needs to add a few people to the premiere list; are Kirk & Danni invited? Letterman? Giulian? The Hilton sisters? Let's talk. |
| 3/8/00<br>9:30 a.m. | Sara-Anne | Cell | Is he gone? Has a bottle of 1990 Beaumont Crayeres Nostalgie for you; call her. |
| 3/8/00<br>9:45 a.m. | Kikki | Home | "Wittle" isn't eating. She misses you. (?) |
| 3/8/00<br>10:01 a.m. | Sassa/NY<br>Party Promoter | 212-be-cool | Needs final list for *Shades of Gray* premiere party; is getting calls about Mike Tyson & Robert Downey Jr., are they coming? Security plans?! Plse call. |

| DATE/TIME | CONTACT | NUMBER | MESSAGE |
|-----------|---------|--------|---------|
| 3/8/00 10:05 a.m. | Kirk | Home | Wants to talk about what he should wear to BET appearance. Which clip are you showing; thinks it should be overdose scene. Plse call. |
| 3/8/00 10:12 a.m. | Marcos | Cell | Is David moved out? Is giving his friend Martin your phone number. Also, *Flatliners* is on tonight on AMC. |
| 3/8/00 10:20 a.m. | Jean-Paul Du Monteay Cannes Registration | 011-33-1-46-58-99-79 | Need your photo & registration; needs to discuss venues for *Portland Girls* event. Also there are dress codes you must respect. |
| 3/8/00 10:34 a.m. | Bridget/ *Entertainment Tonight* | 323-956-7812 | What is happening with Robert Downey Jr.; is hearing he's getting out of jail? Plse call. |
| 3/8/00 10:35 a.m. | Dan/*Details* | 212-286-2860 | Needs materials and comments on *Portland Girls*/Danni story. On deadline. |

| DATE/TIME | CONTACT | NUMBER | MESSAGE |
|---|---|---|---|
| 3/8/00 10:39 a.m. | Sam/BET/ *Live from L.A.* | 310-388-4559 | Danni on the show; need clips for her appearance (not the overdose scene, plse). p.s. fyi we only have candy in green room; no real food (so eat dinner first). |
| 3/8/00 10:42 a.m. | Mom and Dad | Home | They found a cheap fare and would like to come out to see you for a few days . . . |
| 3/8/00 10:59 a.m. | Molly | Aunt Kris's/ 970-322-6878 | Is he gone yet? I'll be back from Aunt Kris's on Friday. |
| 3/8/00 11:05 a.m. | Frank and Anne (on conference) | Anne's office 310-233-8879 | Heard you are going out with Martin? Plse call; we want details. |
| 3/8/00 11:10 a.m. | David— URGENT | On his cell or at the apartment | Harve got hit by a car! He's at the Pet Vet Clinic for the rest of the day/Can't finish moving. |

With such an investment in this dog you'd think it insane of David to let Harve roam freely in the yard and street as he was finally moving his life out of mine. You'd think it even more unbelievable that Harve actually got hit by a car as David was wresting his futon from the front door. But, having put it off for so long, David and Harve were in a hurry to escape their old life, and that is what happened. So the move was delayed and Harve was hospitalized. At least David had taken away the futon (and the down pillows and 400-thread-count sheets), so Molly had somewhere to put the one piece of furniture she'd brought—a bed.

Little returned from Kikki thinner than ever. "We need a second opinion," said Molly authoritatively on Saturday morning as she shoved her bed across the study's hardwood floor and against the wall. Since she'd moved in, we had become a *we*.

"You mean a third opinion. David's vet didn't know what was wrong either," I replied, noticing all the scratch marks Harve had contributed to the floors in the last year.

"Why would you even bring her to that place?" demanded Molly accusingly. "Look what they did to Harve! What's wrong with her old vet?" It was a good question.

I called Dr. Niblack, whom I'd trusted all along, and who'd known Little since kittenhood. He wasn't snotty or scolding, didn't ask me what vet clinic we'd been to, and told me I didn't need an appointment. "Alexis, you know you can bring her in anytime. We've missed her." Sometimes, it's OK to go back to the well.

Ironically, the day Little returned to Dr. Niblack was also the day I decided to return to therapy with Loren Fisk. Our appointments were closely scheduled. Maybe it was a sign, I thought. I was over the breakup, and on to figuring out how to define what I wanted out of life. Maybe that way I could learn to appreciate what I had and stop trying to make things different. Or maybe it would just be a waste of a hundred and fifty dollars.

The plan was for Molly and Little to take me to work (with my car), drop Little at Dr. Niblack's and then pick me up for my appointment. I'd go back to work after therapy, and hopefully Little and I would be fully cured and content, once and for all. Molly had only just arrived and already had an entire day's activity being my wife. She was grateful for the distraction, I knew. "Can you pick up the dry cleaning and water the plants?" I asked her when she called me from Dr. Niblack's office. I pictured her with a fresh martini and a roast waiting when I got home.

Loren Fisk wondered where I'd been. I had to recount the entire breakup story for her, adding the details of the fights, the cruise, and Molly moving in, supplementing the whole with a bit of the trip home, the boat purchase, Andrew Sullivan nostalgia and Kirk Olmstead longing. She glanced into my file and leaned forward with her crinkly eyes and patient smile full of whitened teeth. "Are you interested in this Kirk person?"

"I guess so," I said, thinking how odd "Kirk person" sounded. "I mean, he has almost everything I'd be attracted to in a man. He reminds me of a grown-up version of Andrew . . ."

"Are you still in love with Andrew?"

"That's irrelevant," I answered tightly. This was my standard response to anything involving Andrew Sullivan.

"Oh," she said knowingly, leaning slightly away from me as though she feared I might hit her.

"I know it's not a good idea to get involved with someone I have a professional relationship with, but I can't stop thinking about Kirk," I said in a rush.

"It sounds like you're confused," she offered helpfully. Duh. *In Style* was on her coffee table, the stars spilling out of their Golden Globes outfits. There was Jenna Wilson in the red number again. It seemed a lifetime ago that Molly and I had gone to that party, seen Kirk there in his Banana Republic outfit. . . .

Loren Fisk drew a careful breath and spoke with a frankness that was both friendly and upsetting. "You seem to be drawn to men who aren't available or who are not right for you. Maybe you need to spend a little time on your own, Alexis. Alone. *Alone.*"She repeated the word clearly and slowly, as though I were autistic or blonde. "Have you ever given any thought to that?"

The dull hum of logic filtering into a bland office in a bland building in the morning haze of Pico Boulevard: *This is the L.A. no one reads about,* I thought absurdly. The one no one photographs. I searched. Finally I admitted, "I feel like there's something wrong with me."

"Why?" She leaned in and offered a box of tissues, but I wasn't biting. "Because . . . I feel like there are so many thing in my life that I should be grateful for, but the truth is . . . I seem to never be satisfied. Nothing is ever the way I want it to be." I realized with some shock that I'd never admitted this to anyone, including myself.

She gently prodded, "And how do you want things to be?" *The way things are in the movies. A lesson learned, a conflict resolved, a villain vanquished, a lover hard won. A happy ending, the perfect song to accompany the credits . . .*

"I don't know," I lied. Loren seemed satisfied. She grabbed my knee supportively. "The deal is, you have to do some *work.*"

"What do you mean?" I asked in a withered tone. Wasn't the work over? David was gone, I didn't want him anymore, Harve was gone, Molly was here, presto. New life. Why wasn't everything great?

Loren Fisk almost laughed. "Honey," she exclaimed in the caring but exasperated voice of a flaming hairdresser, "you've been through a *major* transition. Working on our issues takes time! You're never *done.* What time is good next week?"

When I exited the building, Molly appeared with my car, which now had a new window permanently stuck open and no gas, and smelled of wet clutch and fresh cat pee. It rained harder.

"How do you take a left in this stupid city?!" she cried as I hauled myself into the seat.

"Like everything else, practice," I replied, adding carefully, "you have to be careful with the windows. Sometimes they get stuck open."

"Really, Einstein," she said, irritably flicking on the wipers.

"What happened at the clinic?" I asked, shaking the rain from my hair. Molly focused on the road.

"He's doing more tests and X-rays. She'll be ready in an hour." She fiddled with the wipers, and we drove in silence toward the studio. She pulled up to the gates and waited at the security check-point.

"OK, so you'll go wait for her and call me when you know something, and pick me up at six?"

"Yes, Darren, and by four o'clock I'll have a new slogan for your latest campaign," she deadpanned as she stopped the VW in front of the marketing building. Then she got that sad look again and rubbed her forehead.

"Hey," I barked at her. "There's no crying in baseball."

"I know," she said, and drove away.

Later that afternoon, as I reviewed my travel itinerary for Cannes (business class! To Europe!), fended off rumors about Robert Downey, Jr. (no, he wasn't getting out of prison for the premiere but think of the press line we'd have if I pretended not to know that!), pulled a few select clips of Danni for BET, lunch-called Dan from *Details* so as to avoid him, and manhandled the *Shades of Gray* premiere guest list, Adriane Amtel-flashed **Molly— Mobil.** A teacher from San Francisco, Molly did not have a cell phone. She was calling from a gas station, bless her heart.

"Well, get ready for bad news," she said, against the sound of a muffler being tested in the background. Little's bill was $300. It would have been $700 if she'd spent the night for "observation," which is what Dr. Niblack had recommended, but Molly hadn't wanted to make any decisions without talking to me first. Molly had then unjustly incurred the guilt of the frosty clinic receptionist, who had responded with an incensed *"You're going to do nothing for her?!"* when Molly had informed them Little would be returning home for the evening.

"God," I said, feeling helpless and broke.

"Full blood work is the 'absolute minimum' her doctor feels comfortable with, and the results will be ready in a few days," continued Molly. "That guy has weird shoes."

"How much is the blood work?" I asked, instantly hating myself for it.

"A hundred and fifty dollars," said Molly apologetically. It didn't seem like a minimum of any kind, but I told her to do it so they wouldn't think I was a bad pet owner. I thought about what $150 could buy . . .

"Lex," Molly interrupted my thoughts. "Dr. Niblack wants you to call him, and I need directions on how to get back to the studio. I have no idea where I am."

Later that night at home, incredibly, Little seemed fine. She lay on the couch watching *Jeopardy!* (Famous Phrases) and purring. Molly scooped some Tuna for Cats! into her dish, and she scampered over to eat it. *That is correct, What is A Stitch in Time Saves Nine?*

"Maybe she's glad I'm here," said Molly, and I wondered if sometimes, like people, cats just needed a change in their environment, a new person to pay attention to them, even though they pretended they didn't need anything.

Molly and I established a comforting pattern during the week of making dinner, watching *Jeopardy!* and going to bed in my bed so we could read together at night. This was not as creepy as it sounds.

After Harve left ICU, David removed the remainder of his things from the apartment. Molly and I agreed to be out all day, wandering from Runyan Canyon to the movies (Michael Moore's latest documentary) with Sara-Anne and then to Bed Bath and Beyond to spend $600 we didn't have on bed dressings and linens we didn't need, but which made us feel grown up. "It's a better idea than going to Burger King," I said, and she just smiled. When we got back to the apartment, we would put our new linens on, put away all her new things and stoke the fires of domestic sisterhood.

I was pulling tags off some new yellow towels when I heard Molly yelp.

"Oh my . . . God," she cried, *"what is that?"* I turned to see Little sitting beside one of the shopping bags . . . with a . . . *hump.* Somehow, while we'd been out, a hump had appeared in the middle of Little's back, a hump so distinct it took only a few seconds for me to admit that it was not just the shape of her fur after she'd slept on it. What fresh hell was this? She got up and yawned, and the hump seemed to . . . expand. It was horrifying. She was a hunchcat. I left an emergency message for Dr. Niblack, immediately sorry I had late-called him the day before.

"Hi, um, it's Alexis Manning, with Little? I was supposed to call you earlier . . . but, um, I hope you can call me back, I think it's really bad now . . . she's gone from a hole to a hump," I rambled into the phone, hoping he'd understand.

Molly and I followed Little into my bedroom, where she flopped comfortably onto the bed, purring, and the hump moved with her. The odd thing was, she seemed fine, like she didn't notice this morbid new part of her at all. "I think," said Molly slowly, "it's a tumor."

"No, it isn't," I protested, the fear rising. "A tumor can't grow that fast. It's the last stage of whatever thing she had. This must mean she's getting better." Molly looked doubtful. I hoped I was right.

# *Twenty*

In *The Usual Suspects*, Kevin Spacey plays the mild-mannered, disabled, quiet and unthreatening character Roger "Verbal" Kint, who is secretly Keiser Sose, the feared kingpin of a hugely complex criminal operation. No one would ever guess that Verbal is the brains behind the job. By quietly staying in the background of a cast of characters larger than life, Verbal travels unnoticed. He fools just about everyone, including slick U.S. Customs agent Dave Kujan (a brilliant Chazz Palminteri) until the end, when, of course, it's too late, his cripple's limp fading as he dons ultra cool sunglasses and slips into a waiting vehicle outside police headquarters. Edward Norton plays a similar character in *The Heist* with Robert DeNiro; no one suspects the mildly retarded janitor is the heist's cold-blooded mastermind. These characters remind us that no matter how well you think you know someone, you don't know him at all. Everyone has a hidden side. Or two. And people will, almost always, surprise you.

Dr. Niblack called at 7:30 a.m. on Monday. "Good morning, Miss . . . Manning," he began. "We have Little's test results."

"And? . . ." I asked fearfully.

"I'm afraid she has an internal infection." He was calm and matter-of-fact.

"What about the hump—ah, swelling?" I asked nervously. Hadn't he gotten my message?

"Alexis," he sighed patiently, "I'm afraid you might have to bring her in for a procedure. But leave her here this time. You have to trust me, OK? I'll see you soon." He hung up. A newfound assertiveness trickled through the line—meek Dr. Niblack was not to be argued with.

Molly helped me force Little into the Mobile Kitty Carrier. *"RRAUUULLLL!"* she snarled. We plopped her on the counter, and she glared through the plastic slats. "What time do you have to be at work?" asked Molly, closing the locks on the carrier.

"Whenever I get there," I answered absently.

"You know, you're pretty lucky to have that freedom in such a high-powered job. I'd have to take a personal day to go to the vet," she said.

"Yeah, I guess you're right," I replied, grabbing the keys.

"You shouldn't take that for granted," she warned.

I turned to her, struggling under the weight of Little in her carrier. "I know, OK? What are you, my conscience?" I liked having her around, but sometimes it felt like Mom had moved in.

"I'm just trying to help you see the positive, like your therapist said." She had me there.

"Remind me not to tell you about my sessions anymore," I growled as we packed into the VW.

At the clinic, Dr. Niblack's new partner, a perky blonde woman, short and athletic, cheerful but businesslike, appeared in our examining room (which had the same Cat Breeds from Around the World poster as all the other feline examining rooms). Dr. Niblack had an emergency surgery to attend to. The new vet took one look at Little and her hump and poked it.

"So this is the famous Little!" her voice sounded like she had inhaled helium. Little swiped at her, barely missing.

"Where is Dr. Niblack?" I inquired.

"This little girl is in bad shape, all right," the blonde vet said in a singsong voice, reading Little's chart with the new blood work results. How could she say it in that tone? Dr. Perky. Ron the Vet Man, formerly a river guide. Dr. Salome, aka Andy Garcia. I was sick of them all, and I wanted to deal only with Dr. Niblack again. A white-smocked attendant took Little away. I thought of *One Flew Over the Cuckoo's Nest,* suddenly feeling like there was no escape. *The Tabby is the classic American family pet . . .*

"Dr. Niblack said he would meet with me . . . he said he had the test results," I said sharply.

Perky gave me an aggressive smile. *"You* need to leave her here so we can drain the affected area. Dr. Niblack is very busy. He'll call you," she said sternly, smiled and left the room. So that was it. They thought I was neglecting her and were running an intervention. I'd come back to find an ASPCA officer and the local news crew. Hours later, at work, Adriane Amtelled me:

**Line 1: Dr. Niblack's office / Little Line 2: Jermaine Jackson's agent re: Shades of Gray premiere list; Line 3: Dan from Details magazine—urgent**

Jermaine Jackson was not coming to our premiere if I had anything to do with it, and Dan from *Details,* was running a story on Kirk and Danni that I had not orchestrated. I pushed line one. It was not Dr. Niblack; it was Perky Blonde Vet. "It was an abscess, and it was really bad," she began. "We drained about a cup of pus from your little cat," she explained as I savored the visual.

"What?!"

"Anyway, I think she'll be fine. I recommend making her an indoor cat from now on, OK?!" she said perkily but sternly. "We can hold her here until five p.m. but after that it's twenty dollars for each additional half hour."

I clenched the phone. "So it *was* an abscess this whole time?" My Amtel beeped: **Line 3 / Agotha**

"Yes, but there was an internal infection, and we still don't know what caused it," she confessed. I hit the **Take a Message** button on the Amtel. "We close at 6:30. After that, an overnight stay is one hundred and twenty-five dollars," Dr. Perky warned, and hung up.

I blew off the Cannes logistics meeting and raced out of the office to arrive at the clinic by 6:30. I found Little shaved and dazed, with two rubber tubes protruding from the top and bottom of her middle (her thorax, her chart said) and the giant satellite dish/Elizabethan Poet collar balanced around her tiny head. Little looked like a bizarre novelty hot water bottle, and I began to sob. "Your total is five hundred fifty dollars and sixty-two cents," the receptionist said cheerfully. I choked back the tears.

"Five hundred dollars?!" I managed to say.

"Noooo," she said patiently, "five hundred fifty dollars and sixty-two cents."

Dr. Perky handed me the latest X-rays. "I don't like this shadow here," she said, frowning at the shadow only she could see. Being a movie publicist and not a vet, I couldn't see a thing other than the vague indication of a rib cage. "It leads us to believe there's a foreign body in her lung, which could be the cause of all this," she continued, holding the X-ray to the window. An engagement ring clamored for light on her left hand. Pear shaped.

"I thought you just removed the cause of all this," I ventured. Over a carat, maybe two.

"We removed the pus, the *symptom* of the infection. The tubes will act as a drain, but that shadow could be any number of things."

The door opened, and Dr. Niblack appeared and jumped into

the conversation as if he'd been rehearsing it. ". . . and the pus could come back," he announced boldly. "Then we know there's something else in there." He was wearing his weird shoes and calm expression. He glanced at Dr. Perky with unchecked affection, and she returned his look with an added nuance that said, *She's not listening to me.* He smiled ever so slightly as she left the room, the tiniest gesture of united coconspiracy, and I knew then that they were engaged. Christ. Even Dr. Niblack had found his other half. Suddenly he wasn't so weird.

He told me to keep an eye on her and monitor the "drain." He turned to go, and I stepped on the scale presumably reserved for large dogs. I'd lost weight! At last! *The Bobcat is lean and graceful, rarely spotted by its prey before attack . . .*

"That's, ahh, really not for people . . . ," said Dr. Niblack quietly. He was standing in the doorway, holding a complimentary bag of kitty breath fresheners. Our eyes met, and I laughed. He looked relieved. "You *will* keep Little inside now, yes, Alexis? At least until she heals this time?" His freckles seemed to gather upon him, staking claims on every inch of pale Irish real estate.

"Yes, I will. Hey, congratulations," I said, pointing to his freshly bound left ring finger. He smiled, a gaseous explosion of goofy happiness that started at one end of his face and spread infinitely into every freckle. Then I lifted Little's carrier and left.

When we got home, a groggy Little stumbled from room to room to make sure she was indeed home. With each step her tubes wiggled, shaking like two thick worms searching for light as they emerged from either side of her torso.

"That," said Molly, while carrying a grilled cheese sandwich and turning on *Jeopardy!* "is the most disgusting thing I've ever seen." *American Poets for $200.* The doorbell rang, and Sara-Anne, Frank and Sue burst into the apartment using Sara-Anne's key.

"Sweetie," said Frank, bounding up the stairs, "we came over as soon as we heard the news. "Where is she?" Sue put down a ridiculously overpriced and fancily packaged bag of cat treats as she knelt down by Little. She took in the full horror of her appearance, taking a slight step back. "Jesus, they really cut her up, didn't they? Poor Little."

"Stupid feline bitch, how much that set you back, Lex?" chirped Sara-Anne, opening a Corona from the six-pack she'd brought over as a condolence.

"That doesn't matter," I bristled, adding, "How's Richard?"

"He's an asshole. How's David?" she countered.

"Gone."

Sara-Anne held up her beer. "Cheers, sugar. I'm proud of you. You ready to go bird-doggin' again?"

"We heard you're going on a blind date with that Martin guy? . . ." teased Sue, settling into the couch next to Molly. "I love *Jeopardy!*" she said to her. "It's like religion in my family."

"Who's Martin?" asked Molly.

Frank opened a beer and set up camp on the couch. "Just some fancy friend of Marcos's that would be a perfect transitional lay for Lex," he said smugly.

"Frank!" I gulped.

"Hey, there's nothing wrong with that, sweetie! You need a decent lay for Christ's sake, it would do us all good."

"How kind of you to point that out. But we're not here to talk about me getting laid. We're here to comfort Little. She's been through a very traumatic experience."

"Damn cat could use a good lay too," mumbled Sara-Anne under her breath, and Molly shot her an empathetic smile. "What about that hot new director of yours, Lex?" she asked. "He's a juicy distraction . . . aren't you going to Cannes with him?"

"Oohh, yeah, we saw him on *Hollywood Access!*" chirped Sue, sucking on a Corona.

"*Access Hollywood,*" corrected Molly politely, adding, "Lex doesn't want to get involved with anyone she works with."

"Remind me why I invited you guys over," I said. They all looked at me, then over at Little, who was slumped in the corner wearing her oversized satellite dish and a drunken expression.

"What a horrible sight that poor cat is," commented Frank.

"Well, at least she'll get better now," I protested.

"If she doesn't get worse first," countered Molly. "Things always get worse before they get better, like Grandma said."

"Ain't that the truth," sighed Sara-Anne.

We all focused on the TV. Frank rubbed Sue's back, and I saw Molly stiffen uncomfortably. "Poets for one hundred," she said to the TV. "Oh, Mom and Dad called, Lex. They get in next Friday."

"Your folks are coming to town?" asked Frank. "That's cool."

*This poet wrote of two paths that diverged in a wood . . .*

"I'll bring over some pinot, Lex, they drink red?" offered Sara-Anne, adding, "Who is Robert Frost, *duh.*"

Finally realizing that I wasn't taking her calls at the office, Agotha nailed me at home before work. I recognized her stale voice instantly. "Alezxissssss, I have been trying to reach you."

"I'm sorry, but it's been crazy," I apologized. It occurred to me that I had good news for her. "Agotha, David moved out. The dog is gone and my sister is here," I offered cheerfully.

She was unmoved. "I haf new tenants coming for downstairs, they move in this week." She inhaled. I waited. "I expect no problems with ze dogs or ze cats or ze gates . . ."

"No more problems, I promise. In fact, my parents are coming for a visit next week, just to let you know. Everything will be fine . . . ," I assured her.

She drew a raspy breath. "Ze woman hass a child, a little girl. Ze cat cannot aggravate ze child."

"Of course. I understand," I said submissively. Then I remembered her hospital visit. "Are you all right, Agotha? Didn't you have some tests done?" Maybe if I treated her like a human being she'd return the favor.

Her tone dropped an octave. "No. I am not all right. Zat is why I need less stress in my life. Your sister should sign ze lease. She has no pets, yah?"

"That's right," I confirmed pleasantly. "We just have the one cat now."

"And ze cat—it is well?" Her voice cracked a little, and suddenly sounded . . . tender?

"Yes," I answered quickly. Little wobbled through the kitchen, shaved torso and tubes flapping. "All better."

Agotha sighed, a powerful sound. "Das good. Being sick iz no fun." And she hung up, offering no further details on her own health.

Angry at being locked in the house, Little began the determined project of clawing the wood molding in the apartment. In the evening she would howl from the confines of my bedroom and leak bloody pus on my new four-hundred-thread-count sheets. Then Molly announced at breakfast one day that she had found temporary work, and would be starting the next morning.

"A job, already?" I asked, coffee in midair.

"Yeah, I thought you'd be happy! I've got to get out there." She smiled with the strength of a new person.

"How are you going to get to work? What is work?" I liked knowing she would be there when I got home.

"It's just temping at UCLA, just filing and stuff. I'll take the bus," she said simply. She spread peanut butter on her English muffin. I now lived with someone who was going to get up in the morning and go to work. I would have to fight for the shower now. I might have to hire a cat sitter. It occurred to me that I'd been taking her for granted.

"This is L.A. No one takes the bus," I said in a haughtier tone than I'd meant.

She raised an eyebrow. "Well, maybe *you* and *your* friends don't take the bus, but I don't have a choice. Unless *you* want to drive me there at eight-thirty every day, that is."

"But . . . Little needs to be watched!" I cried, knowing with each departing syllable how ridiculous it was for me to presume my sister would stay home and keep an eye on the hole in my cat rather than get a job.

"Lex," Molly breathed patiently, "it's been three weeks. I can't sit around here being your housewife forever, you know."

The phone rang, slicing through the moment. We all looked at it and waited for the machine to pick up. A male voice cracked to life. "Hi, Alexis, it's Kirk . . . are you there? I um, I'm just wondering if we can have another meeting about the Cannes schedule. I'm looking at all this stuff we're doing, and I uh, I'm kind of freaking out. . . ."

I felt my face get hot. "He has your *home* number?" teased Molly.

"All the talent has my home number," I shot back.

Kirk continued his one-sided conversation. "Like, do I really have to talk to *Time* magazine? Hey, are you there, Manning? I really feel like an ass talking to you this way. Are you at a screening? Where else would you be this early? Pick up . . . hello . . . helooo, hello! HELLO!" Kirk did a perfect impression of the Three Stooges' trademark opener, and a giggle escaped my lips.

"God, he even has Andrew's stupid sense of humor. I can't believe you're not picking up," said Molly, smiling knowingly and finishing her coffee.

"Are you driving me to work today or not?" I huffed.

Adjusting to Molly's new job was difficult for everyone except Molly, who had found a new purpose for her energy. Little was improving but still not eating much. Furious at being confined to the house, alone all day, she had taken to pooping on the plants Molly had brought from San Francisco. Molly told me for the fifth time, "If she keeps doing that, my plants will die," and I lashed out, "Then tape her ass shut!" That's what Molly got for getting a job.

I also had to make sure Little was quiet during the day, in case the new neighbors moved in while I was at work. I couldn't have them calling Agotha about a yowling cat. I also had to try to convince her not to pull her tubes out with her hind legs. No one at work understood why I rushed home for lunch and had to leave the office by six. Viv would catch me sneaking out. "Lex—Kirk wants to see the press list for Cannes. And how's the *Shades of Gray* premiere list coming? And you really have to get both him and Danni some decent media training . . ."

"I know, Viv, I know, I'm on it," I lied.

When I got home I tried to force one of the tubes, which had become unlodged, back into Little's hole, and she attacked me with her hind feet, understandably confused at this new method of torture. I tried to administer her pills, huge and chalky, by shoving them down her throat through the confines of the Poet Satellite collar. She gasped for air, pretended to swallow them, then projectiled them across the floor the instant I released her head. As her guardian I felt like Ellen Burstyn in *The Exorcist,* rendered powerless and bewildered by the situation controlling her daughter, which worsened daily. Soon I would don a kerchief and wide, Jackie O. style sunglasses and sit staring from an ancient bridge, tendrils of cigarette smoke curling up around me like unheard messages to God as I waited for a priest to guide me through my troubles.

Little spent the night under my bed, testing every variation of *Meow* (I have learned there are many) throughout the night. Meow. *Meeaoooww!* Murrlow. Mow. Moe. Miauwuuuawa. I imagined the translation: *Why are you doing this to me? I hate you! Get this goddamn thing off my head. I'll call PETA!*

I dreamed of high school. Andrew Sullivan and I were dissecting cats in Mr. Tingley's biology class and watching the Academy Awards. Kirk was a presenter, partnered with Cameron Diaz. They were eating Kentucky Fried Chicken and whispering about me backstage. For some reason, a minute later Andrew and I were in a rain forest that smelled of poop, and the transition did not seem odd to either of us. I asked Andrew if he liked building houses, and I woke up before he could answer.

# *Twenty-One*

In *Looking for Mr. Goodbar,* a film you should run, not walk, to rent if you've never seen it, Diane Keaton is so young and fresh she's dewy. She's a single gal in New York City, enjoying her freedom and discovering her sexuality. By day she works with deaf mute kids, and by night she cruises the disco scene, experiments with the drugs du jour and searches for the thrill of the unknown. You think it's all sexy and fun until she meets Richard Gere, whom you never imagined was ever as young as he is in this film (pre *American Gigolo*). Diane begins a dangerous dance with Richard and, much to her parents' shame and dismay, lets loose in a manner that leaves her dead. And he wasn't even a blind date. The movie teaches us that in matters of sex and discovery, you must never let your guard down. Here in the new millennium it's difficult to imagine a time when people went out nightly, high, drunk and stoned, for the explicit purpose of taking home a stranger for sex. America used to be different, back in her naïve, sexual development years. Now people meet electronically after screening each other through a series of pragmatic questions about whether they want children, own real estate or practice yoga. And while it's less fun, it's really no safer.

Mom and Dad arrived, parentally summoned by the fact that their daughters had gotten simultaneously disengaged and were on the road to Spinsterhood together. They were worried about us, but they could also use the trip to see my aunt Kris in orange county while they were here. We spent the first day showing them the La Brea Tar Pits a few blocks away. There's a huge famous pool of tar there, evidence that L.A. does have a sense of history, albeit a prehistoric one. We walked along Wilshire Boulevard, on the block known as Museum Mile, and they marveled at all the cars, wondered at the thinness of people and complained about the sun.

"It's a cute neighborhood," allowed my mother, instead of talking about what had brought them here. Just having her tiny feet walking next to mine was comfort enough.

"Are those woolly mammoths?" asked Dad as we approached the park, noticing the huge sculptures of the alien beasts hulking in the burbling tar lake.

"Yeah, aren't they great?" I was proud of the one cultural attraction in our neighborhood we could all agree on visiting, having argued already over the L.A. County Museum of Art, The Museum of Miniatures and the Petersen Museum of the Automobile.

On our walk through the park I saw them again. The Asian couple. Step by step they made their way around the exhibit path, and I wondered what they would do when they got home. Would he have coffee, read the obituaries? Would she retire to her needlepoint, would he head off to the track? Did they have children? They disappeared around the corner behind the saber-toothed cats. We arrived at the lake display. There were two life-size model mammoths on the banks and a smaller one waist deep in the tar, its eyes wide and its trunk raised in pachyderm panic. Nearby there was a placard detailing what had befallen the unsuspecting mammoth family.

On a family outing this curious youngster waded too far into the pit. Now its parents watch help-lessly from the bank as it struggles to avoid the inevitable—a slow and agonizing death as it is sucked into the tar, deeper and deeper with each attempt it makes to escape.

"I bet the father mammoth tried to *tell* it not to go into the tar," sighed Dad, and Molly and I rolled our eyes. "I bet the father mammoth *warned* that this would happen . . ." His tone was like a doomsday prophet.

"*George,*" said my mother in the tone reserved for such occasions, but it had worked. Molly and I were laughing. Later we sat in a trendy bistro on Beverly Boulevard, drinking coffee and citrus sodas with limes and perusing the menu of strange salads and fancy sandwiches, which were being eaten nearby by skinny hipsters with dutifully tousled hair, Adidas flip-flops and expensive sunglasses. Local artwork and public radio completed the atmosphere.

"A watercress sandwich?" marveled my father, settling into the uncomfortable antique chair with a tired orange velour cushion.

"Try to be nice, George. We're here for three days," sighed my mother. They put their menus down, and my father glanced at my mother, and Molly and I recognized the asking-permission-to-start-The-Conversation-glance. Mom leaned in and removed her glasses, a sign that permission had been granted.

"Lex. What are your plans now?" Dad asked in the Concerned-But-Stern Father voice.

"What do you mean?" I would try not to be defensive or snippy throughout this conversation, wherever it might lead. Molly played with the sugar packets. Dad was undeterred. "Have you thought much more about your real estate plan?" he pressed.

"You mean since you bought a boat with my down payment?" I replied.

He frowned, then stopped himself and reloaded. "I mean," he said patiently, "have you actually researched mortgage rates, found any affordable properties, talked to any brokers?"

I gripped my coffee mug. "No. I've been kind of busy with work, Dad," I admitted.

My mother, ever the family buffer, jumped in. "Honey, how long do you think you'll be living here?" she asked softly, leaning back so the gloriously emaciated waitress could put a Diet Coke in front of her. My mother smiled kindly at the girl.

"I dunno, Mom. My job is sort of the one thing that's, um . . . stable." I glanced at Molly. "Besides, Mol just got here, and I think we'll be here at least a year, until she decides if she wants to stay or not. She just found a job!"

Molly stiffened at her responsibility in the conversation. "It's just temping . . . ," she said.

Dad brightened at this. "Hey it's UCLA, a great school. It's an in," he said encouragingly. "I bet the benefits are great!" Molly shrugged, noncommittal to her job and to whatever point was being made. My father sighed and leaned in closer, suddenly looking older, from another time, a different world where jobs and investments and benefits mattered. Where engagements were kept and marriages endured. He scowled at his grapefruit soda.

"The thing is, Lex, I was thinking about what you said a while ago. And we want to help you." I looked at him and waited. Help me what? Was he going to offer to pay for my therapy?

"If you're still interested, and you're serious about being here for a while, Mom and I would like to help you with a down payment for an apartment . . . there's also the option of an income property, a dual family, like the one you live in now. That way Molly can benefit as well." He was speaking quickly, not waiting for me to interrupt.

"It's a no-brainer," added Mom, keeping the momentum. "You can live in one unit and rent the other. So your monthly payment would probably be even less than rent is now." They looked at us expectantly, waiting for an answer, probably thinking, *If only our parents had offered to help us buy an income property at your age.* I had a little money saved, and a bonus coming, but in L.A., a down payment in a decent neighborhood was the cost of an entire house back home, and I knew Molly couldn't even afford a fat-free latte.

"What about the boat?" I asked.

"Your father and I have been saving for a long time—the boat wasn't much," explained Mom.

Dad gave her a funny look, then said apologetically, "Well, we'll definitely have to sell it if either of you ever make it to the altar!"

Molly began to sniffle and grow watery. "I'm glad you think it's a joke," she said stiffly. The wastetress clanked our orders onto the table and stood back to observe her work. My mother nodded politely, and she left.

"Mol, he's just kidding," I soothed. "Come on. Don't be so sensitive, he's just being Dad."

My father bit into his Black Forest ham and Gruyère sandwich with radicchio. He chewed slowly and spoke. "Well, girls, think about it. You can't go wrong in real estate. You'll thank me twenty years from now." Molly sniffled silently through her turkey on focaccia. My mother put a hand on Molly's back, which only made her cry more. A bit of moist Gruyère hung on my father's chin.

"I'll start researching properties this week," I told him. I took my eyes off the cheese on his chin and met his gaze. I was lucky. Having good parents makes the ugliness of the world easier to bear. "Thanks, Dad. Thanks, Mom."

My parents didn't understand why I had to be at the taping of BET's *Live From L.A.* until ten o'clock at night and not out for

Mexican food at El Coyote after a day at the Getty with them, and Danni Jones didn't understand why a friend she'd brought along to the taping couldn't also be on the stage with her.

"That's wack," she protested when I explained that her friend Cheryl, while certainly interesting (blue hair, neck tattoos and a supposed tantric sex counselor), was not in the movie and did not act or play an instrument and so her presence on the show may be confusing for viewers and upsetting for the producers, who had no idea who Cheryl was or why she might deserve a place on the stage promoting *Portland Girls*. Danni made that sad face that reflected disappointment in me, until I agreed to buy her sushi afterward.

"You rock, woman!" she crowed as she slapped my back and skipped off to makeup with her motorcycle boots and her skull bracelet. I thought briefly of the *Vogue* cover I was negotiating for her. Starving, desperate Russian models would kill for a *Vogue* cover, and this delinquent hadn't even tried and she had the summer movie preview cover. How the hell was I going to dress her?

"Why can't you control her?" I said irritably to Kirk, who had been amused by the whole episode from the safety of the dusty, smallish and yellow greenroom.

"I thought that was your job," he laughed at me, devouring a handful of M&M's. Why was he always laughing at me? I tossed my company credit card at him, and he caught it midair.

"Take her out to dinner after the show, I have to go home."

"Come with us," he suggested, tossing a green M&M at my head.

"My parents are in town," I pleaded, slumping into a Shabby Chic chair next to the TV in the corner of the room. Mini Baby Ruths sat in a pile in a coffee can. A poster of half-naked Lil' Kim glared down at us.

"Your parents? From where?" Kirk asked eagerly, smiling, and there it was, that flicker of a person who knew me and wanted to know more. In these rare and tiny moments, Kirk was like the best of David and Andrew Sullivan and Johnny Depp and Viggo Mortensen wrapped into one. "Where'd you grow up?" he persisted.

"Not here," I sighed, adding, "excuse me, I have to check on something." I left the room. I didn't like sitting so close to Kirk with Danni in the same building, and I wanted desperately to go home, but Danni had borrowed my leather jacket for her interview segment and I couldn't leave until she did because if she took the jacket off it would cause "continuity problems."

I wandered into Danni's freezing dressing room to wait it out with Cheryl. There were lots of gummy bears in a jar, far too many to count, but I began counting them anyway. I watched Cheryl watch Danni on the TV screen. She was clearly in love with her. Poor girl.

When I finally got my jacket back and delivered the clip reel to the producer, it was midnight. I sauntered down the hallway toward the parking lot. We were in the BFE area of Burbank. I opened the door to the brightness of floodlights on the pavement, the false midnight blue filling up the Western sky.

"What are you so angry about?" asked a voice behind me. I turned. Kirk. Under the parking lot lights, I noticed his outfit. He was dressed in casual chic slacks and a two-hundred-dollar T-shirt. His hair was evolved. But his eyes were the same. Open. Kind. Curious.

"I'm sorry, it's just . . . I'm tired, Kirk," I whined. "My parents are here, my sister just moved in, there's a lot of pressure at work, my landlord's all over me, my cat has a health problem that won't go away . . . why am I telling you this?" I laughed nervously. Surely the talent did not want to hear about my first world problems.

"Where are you from, Manning?" he asked, leaning on the backstage door. Above him a spinning red light indicated they were taping something again.

## SHOW IN PROGRESS-DO NOT ENTER.

"East Coast. My parents are on the Cape now . . ." I drifted into his eyes. He looked tired, too. There was that odd pause, full of nothing and everything, so I said, "Aren't you taking our star out for sushi?" He ignored my question.

"That's cool that your folks come to see you," he said, shifting his glance away. He reddened, then looked straight at me. "Manning, your eyes are the bluest fucking things I've ever seen." My mouth opened but nothing came out. "Are they that blue when you're happy, too?" He was smiling, offering a connection. It was tempting. Where was Danni?

"I . . . *am* happy . . . ," I said strangely, not recognizing my own voice. I stared at him, a dangerous decision.

"Yeah, and I'm a talented young director on the verge of super-stardom," he deadpanned, and for a moment I couldn't read his tone. "You need someone to walk you to your car?" he offered.

"No, I'm fine," I decided. He studied me. "Good night, Kirk," I said quickly. "I'll see you later." I walked to my car and, resisting every movie-loving fiber in my body, I did not turn back to see if he was still watching me. I got home at 1:00 a.m. and my father had left a note:

> **Maybe on our next visit you can spend more time with your aging father.**

He signed it, "Cats in the Cradle" He thought this was funny, an inside joke. In the seventies when we were kids he would blare Cat Stevens until we stormed from our bedrooms, yelling, "Dad! Stop playing the Cat song!" But now I was at the age where lyrics I'd mindlessly sung for years suddenly had a terrible, immediate clarity. I saw the poignancy of the words, realized that I had no time for my parents because I had not kids with the flu but a movie to promote. *Well the new star's a hassle and the cat has a hole, but it's sure nice talkin' to you, Dad, it's sure been nice talking to you* . . .

In addition to offering me help on a down payment, they bought us a computer (David had taken his, leaving only a Gatorade-stained L.A. Sports Club mouse pad in its place). They also took us out to dinner and went for a walk on Venice Beach with us, but other than that they could not understand us or why we would want to live in L.A. And so, after three days, they left to spend a few days with my aunt and uncle, people like them—older, wiser and married. People who belonged to car pools and did yard work and cooked meals.

"What's he like, and be honest," I said to Marcos as we sat in front of Peter O'Toole on a camel. LACMA (Los Angeles County Museum of Art) was featuring a David Lean festival, and we were in our usual seats.

"Lex, I'm not taking responsibility beyond giving him your number. I just thought it would be fun for you to go out with someone who"—he searched for an inoffensive term—"who's as successful as you are."

"Is he expecting me to be really smart and attractive?" I snorted.

"Why can't you just accept it for what it is and not attach any expectations?" he said flatly to the screen.

"Well, are you and Lisa going to double with me at least?" Peter O'Toole's eyes were like the Caribbean. His skin was live rawhide.

"No, we're going out of town," he said, shoveling Junior Mints into his mouth and not taking his eyes off the screen. "But Frank and Sue are around. Anne and Martin went to school together, they both know him."

"But—"

"SSHHHH!" a voice insisted. I searched the theater, but Kirk wasn't there. So Marcos and I went to the desert for a couple of hours, lost in the sand and wind, the mountains and valleys of someone else's life.

When I got to Frank and Sue's for the date, Sue informed me that Martin was a "friend from Oxford." Two approval points: "a friend" (safe) "from Oxford" (smart). Friday night. Dinner with Sue's Friend from Oxford. Group situation. It sounded harmless at worst and promising at best, right? Frank cheered me on before Martin arrived. "Even if it doesn't work out, it's batting practice, right? You need to get back out there." He poured macadamia nuts into a glass bowl instead of just ripping the top off the jar, losing it and setting the tin on the table for six weeks. Sue had moved in a month earlier.

She sidled up beside him and put her arm around his waist. She had done wonders with the apartment. His animal skeleton collection, instead of just being creepy when he'd lived alone, was now looking like some cool element of a Santa Fe theme. Moreover, the magazines and empty cigarette boxes had disappeared from his bathroom, and he finally had a garlic press. What would men do without women?

Martin, it turned out, was not only an American who held an international law degree from Oxford, spoke four languages and had just started his own Internet music company (legal filesharing), but he also looked like a young Robert DeNiro from *Mean Streets*. As in, *hot*. I stepped into the kitchen and noticed that he extended his hand (one point), offered me a drink (two points) and was wearing great threads perfectly suited for him—Jil Sander moss-green short-sleeved sweater, sleek black DKNY trousers and very cool black shoes (ten points). He looked so good and was so polite that I thought he might be gay. But then we started talking, and if he looked like a young Robert DeNiro, well, he sounded like a young Vinnie Barbarino.

"So you and Marcos knoweachudda long?"

"Ah, yeah, a few years. Are you from Brooklyn?" I asked, smiling coyly, because I'd lived in New York and dug the accent, though its coming by way of Oxford and Arizona, I had to admit, was odd. Because he was already scoring so many points with being (a) polite, (b) interesting and (c) well-dressed, it was a thrilling contradiction turn-on, like the one guys have about the girl next door being the hellcat dominatrix in the bedroom. Here I was on a date with the mind of Hugh Grant in *Notting Hill* (British educated), the body of Omar Epps in *Juice* (delicious, mildly dangerous) and the soul of John Travolta from *Saturday Night Fever* (from Brooklyn). It seemed too good to be true.

It was. Throughout the course of the evening, my humble Robert De Niro from *A Bronx Tale* morphed slowly but surely into Travis Bickle of *Taxi Driver*. The first clue was at dinner when he demanded the busboy bring us more drinks. "Hey. Can we gedanudda-round? Danks, kid." He loosened a sweater button and winked at me. Then when the waitress inquired whether he wanted a salad or starter, he responded, "Does it cumwiddit?" Something my grandmother never failed to ask. (Would you like dessert tonight? "Does it come with it?" No. "Then I'm full. I couldn't possibly.") He overcame these setbacks when we walked over to the Sky Bar.

"We'll never get in there, we're not on the list," I said apologetically, having once been on all the lists when I dated the hottest bartender in town. In L.A., that title is like being the current White House press secretary in Washington. You're not that important in the grand scheme of things, but you know *everyone,* and they make a point of knowing you. Martin was resolute. "Just come wid me," he said firmly and grasped me by the waist as he strode purposefully down Sunset Blvd. Oooh. "It's impossible— they have a really strict door policy. Stupid, but in L.A. that's how it is," I explained. Martin was originally from Phoenix, where a bar was a place to drink, not to get into. We approached the door, the velvet rope and the line. Frank and Sue were behind us. With one glance Martin opened the rope, the crowd, and the door. The doorman shooed everyone aside to let us through. It was incredible. A primal male communication technique—I'd never seen anything quite like it, and, I'm embarrassed to say, it ignited me.

"Do you know him?" I asked my date.

"I've been gettin inta clubs like dat since I was seventeen," he said. "It's all in de eye contact," he winked at me. Confidence, one point, sense of humor, two points. Street sense, priceless. Then a thought. Had he ever killed anyone, stuffed them into the trunk of a Cadillac and then driven to a deserted spot on the Hudson where a colleague had premixed a tub of cement? And wasn't Phoenix the place they sent the Gotti family members who ratted and went in the Witness Protection Program? Still, I couldn't look a gift horse in the mouth. It was a date. Focus, focus.

After several glasses of champagne, our playful pats on the arm turned to squeezes and gropes. I was into it, he was into it, and soon we were searching the crowded bar for a quiet corner. Note to Sky Bar lovers: there are none . . . which drove us to desperate measures. After we contemplated the restroom (too obvious), the elevator (too much security) and the restaurant stockroom (no access), we suddenly found the door of the hotel gym, adjacent to the patio bar. I pushed it and said, "Imagine if this were un—*it swung open*—locked . . ."

Oh my God, I was going to end up in a *Penthouse* "Forum" letter. In an instant we made our way past the treadmills and stationary bikes, sitting like quiet ghosts in the dark, to the rear of the abandoned Ladies Locker Room. Even here in Hollywood no one was working out now, at midnight on Friday. We sat down on a bench and started playfully kissing, which was fun. *I'm kissing a boy again! And it's not some twisted dream with the studio mailroom guy—and he's kissing me back!* Suddenly and without warning he shoved his tongue down my throat, bit my lip and ripped one terrified breast out of my bra. "Ouch," I said, giggling, thinking he was kidding. Ha.

He bit my lip harder, then tugged so hard at my shirt that I heard myself say, "Hey, you're going to rip that and I really like this shirt. Take it easy." This was his cue to lunge at my chest and attempt to inhale my entire breast through my shirt in a manner that can only be described as the violent suction kiss. It was the kind of rough play that looks really hot in movies, but in real life hurts like hell. It wasn't fun, and now there was a big wet lip ring on the left side of my shirt. What to do? This scenario wasn't covered in The Rules.

I tried to be game (*Remember Demi in* Disclosure, *Madonna in* Body of Evidence, *Heather in* Boogie Nights) I thought to myself, but all I could picture was young and helpless about-to-be-raped Geena Davis in *Thelma and Louise.* I found myself pressed up against the lockers, facing my reflection in the workout mirror as he dry humped my leg and whispered, *"Uuuhhhh, can ya feel me? Can ya feeeell me?* into my now sopping-wet ear. If I wasn't so scared I would have peed myself laughing. System failure. Full stop. Do not pass go, do not collect $200. It was the turnoff of the century from a man I'd planned to bed before we even got to dinner. Sometimes men are such an unsophisticated species you pity them. I wondered, not for the first time, if I could learn to like women. I clasped myself back together and said, "Hang on. This isn't working for me. Sorry, but let's go back out to the bar." I straightened up.

He protested. "Whattsa matta?" The universal cry of the misunderstood male facing sexual defeat. Oh God. I had given Travis Bickle blue balls, and I was not going to get off easy. I fled to the bar, but Frank and Sue were nowhere to be found. Martin sidled up next to me and began the process of regroping, but it was all over. I was stone cold. He scared me in there. "Look," I said evenly.

"I'm not going to give you what you want tonight. It was cool meeting you, but I'm going home now. Sorry it didn't work out." I backed away. He was stunned. *The batter swings, misses, it's all over folks, that's the ball game!*

> *Him* (friendly; reassuring) We can just hang out an' go-da-sleep if yuh want.
>
> *Me* (resolute) Nope. I'm going home alone. You should stay here, there's plenty of action. You'll have no trouble scoring tonight.
>
> *Him* Who do ya live wid?
>
> *Me* My sister.
>
> *Him* (getting an idea) But d'ya have yarown room?
>
> *Me* (wondering now how to escape) I'm going home alone *to sleep.*
>
> *Him* (desperate and edgy) Wanna take me to de airport to-morra?

*I'd rather give birth to a barcalounger,* I thought. I escaped, walked myself past the bouncers, down Sunset to my car and drove home at record speed. Molly was asleep when I got home. Little looked up accusingly from the bed when I turned the light on.

I dreamed that Christopher Walken was my boyfriend and I was simultaneously proud (because he was a famous, successful actor) and repulsed (because he was, after all, Christopher Walken). Then I had to issue a press release announcing that he was, in fact, going to turn into Godzilla. "But how, how will you do that?" I kept asking him, and his stony silence told me everything I already knew about our relationship and why it would never work. Actors.

My little sister had been right, again. I wasn't ready to date.

# Twenty-Two

| DATE/TIME | CONTACT | NUMBER | MESSAGE |
|---|---|---|---|
| 4/15/00 3:01 a.m. | Jean-Paul/ Cannes registration | 011-33-1-46-58-99-79 | Plse call to confirm "le menu" for *Portland Girls* "soiree." Do you want "prawns?" (shrimp?) (Time diff. is 9 hrs; he early-called you.) |
| 4/15/00 9:37 a.m. | Sara-Anne | Cell | What are you doing tonight? Has a '73 Rothschild and Spanish winemaker in town— Richard's in NY. |
| 4/15/00 10:03 a.m. | Glenn/ Travel | X4566 | Danni Jones needs a passport for Cannes (she has no driver's license or credit cards). Are we handling? |

| DATE/TIME | CONTACT | NUMBER | MESSAGE |
|---|---|---|---|
| 4/15/00 10:45 a.m. | Viv | Office | Let's go to the movies tonight. |
| 4/15/00 10:48 a.m. | Mom | Home | Andrew Sullivan is building another house on our street. |
| 4/15/00 10:55 a.m. | Rhonda Wallace/ CAA (Danni's agent) | 310-338-4944 | What is the plan for Cannes? Parties, cars, travel, tickets, etc. Need to hear from you ASAP. |
| 4/15/00 11:01 a.m. | Frank & Sue | Home (conference) | What the hell happened to you the other night? Pls call. |
| 4/15/00 11:09 a.m. | Agotha | Home | New tenants are in. Your sister should sign lease. Has other news (?)—Please call. |
| 4/15/00 1:20 p.m. | Julie/Ink, inc. PR (Robert Downey's publicist) | 310-248-6106 | Robert is not attending NY premiere; please clarify to press. (Was told you're telling people he'll be there. Stop telling them that.) |

| DATE/TIME | CONTACT | NUMBER | MESSAGE |
|---|---|---|---|
| 4/15/00 1:45 p.m. | Jo Jo Free/ PETA website | No need to call | Is congratulating our studio on their website for removing the cow tipping scene from *Portland Girls*-needs art & release date info. (I sent.) |
| 4/15/00 2:17 p.m. | Marcos | Cell | Want to go to Passover dinner w/ us on Thurs? |
| 4/15/00 3:45 p.m. | Claudia/ *USA Today* | 703-535-0999 | Re: Summer preview; need photos of all releases (I sent). Doing mostly Blockbusters with one paragraph for "smaller films"; no guarantees. |
| 4/15/00 3:56 p.m. | Rob/Photo Editor, *Entertainment Weekly* | 212-522-9475 | Re: *Shades of Gray* photo shoot; need to know who is coming. Need sizes. Do I need security? |

Viv, Sara-Anne, Molly and I went to see *Keeping the Faith*. Ben Stiller and Ed Norton are best friends and happen to be a rabbi and a priest. Ben Stiller, the rabbi, not only falls in love with the blonde shiksa, he gets his mother's blessing, confesses his crime (loving a shiksa and *lying* about it, *oy*) to the entire congregation, who is extremely understanding, and by the end Jenna Elfman is taking classes to convert and the boys have opened their interfaith youth center (complete with nondenominational karaoke). Of course Ed and Ben have forgiven each other for drunkenly crashing Sabbath services and furtively frolicking around Manhattan with Jenna, respectively. And there is the inevitable scene of Ben running through New York City to stop Jenna from going back to the West Coast for her Superjob, which had no details except a fancy office, a cute assistant and a big salary.

If just once in my life a man—make that anyone, really—runs through rain, snow, or the traffic of the 405 or lower Broadway or the subway platform in Times Square or the ferry line in Hyannis or through Heathrow airport or past the Champs-Elysées or over the Great Wall or under a departing Concorde or across an aircraft carrier to stop me from getting on a plane—then, I will have lived.

Passover. It was oddly sad that I would not have a seder this year, and I was missing the stories and the matzos. So, I decided to go to a Passover dinner with Marcos and Lisa and two of their Jewish friends, Steve and Lara, who weren't very Jewish; we went to Nate & Al's deli and ordered pastrami and cheese sandwiches. Over dinner I learned that Steve's wife, Lara, was a practicing Catholic (Steve was Jewish) and they went to church together on Sundays but synagogue only on the High Holy Days. And when I asked them what their kids would be, they gazed lovingly at each other, and she said, "Catholic" as he said, "Jewish" at exactly the same time. Then they laughed, kissed and held hands—and I was happy for them. *Love at work,* I thought mildly as I put away another giant sheet of matzo.

Meanwhile Molly had finally gotten the knack of how to force-feed Little her pills. Molly spent her days temping, job hunting and car shopping, taking the bus, picking me up or dropping me off at work, and taking care of Little. Occasionally we'd tip our toes into the lake of social interaction, but mostly we kept to ourselves. We were settling into this new life together, and it felt right.

Spinster, Spinster. Maybe we would become foster parents. Who needed boyfriends?

When I got home from Nate & Al's I immediately wished I'd returned Agotha the Hun's call. There was a shiny new Coldwell Banker For Sale sign in front of our duplex. I ran into the house, heart pounding, mouth dry.

"Did you see the sign!? She's selling the house! She's fucking *selling* the house!" I wailed. Now I knew why she had had the toilets fixed. Molly and Little had already composed themselves and were on the couch watching Alex Trebeck pepper someone about Historical Heroes with an H. They both seemed relatively calm.

"I know," Molly sighed. "I saw it. I can't believe it. I finally move in, get settled and now we'll have to move again."

"No, we won't! We're not going anywhere! I have a lease," I said triumphantly.

"Hey . . . ," said Molly slowly, half closing her eyes, which was her way of thinking hard. "How much is she asking? What if you bought it? Maybe you could call Dad, he said he'd help."

"No way, Agotha would never sell it to me, even if we could afford it. She hates me."

"How do you know that?" Molly asked.

"Trust me on this one," I said.

"I think," Molly said slowly in her Sensible Mollyspeak, finally looking up from Alex, "we should call a lawyer." The next morning, our new downstairs neighbor, Jody, told me that she also had no idea her new home was being sold, but that Agotha told her this morning there was already a buyer. She was planting something out back in a neat and wholesome manner. Jody was in her midthirties, thin, gorgeous and Asian. As far as neighbors went, Jody was perfectly nice, and so was her little daughter, Ashley, who, at four, was both in love with Little and oblivious to the fact that the poor cat was terrified of her. Jody went out with Tim, a hotshot TV agent at William Morris. Tim and Jody were in love, and Tim got along well with Ashley, who was Jody's child from a previous marriage. A few times that first week I'd come home to find Tim on his cell phone, pacing the driveway around his Porsche, angrily closing a deal, as he stormed by the cat toys in the yard, in his expensive, chunky, black agent shoes. "No, you TELL her we want the back nine episodes confirmed for that price, *that's* how it is." That had been weird. But for the most part they were perfect neighbors—quiet and uncomplaining. They were in love; they cooked together, went to Santa Barbara on weekends and had friends over on Friday nights for Pictionary. Molly and I avoided them and did our best to keep Little away from them.

"What happens to our lease? Will we have to move, or do we get to stay under the new owners?" I asked Jody, trying to make my voice sound casual.

Jody tossed her long black hair and squinted in the sunlight. "I'm not sure. I guess we stay—unless the buyer wants to move into one of the units right away . . . ," she said, thinking. Her long legs looked perfect in her khaki gardening shorts. She didn't have to go to work.

"But I have a lease. So do you, right?"

"Yes, I'm sure it'll be fine," she said reassuringly, carefully removing her gardening gloves and glancing at the scratch marks in the molding of our open door. Uh-oh. If the new landlord had to choose which tenant was to go and which was to stay, would it be the neurotic spinster sisters with the sick cat who destroyed the antique moldings, or the soft-spoken, beautiful Asian woman with sensible gardening habits, an adorably silent child and a Porsche-driving boyfriend?

Molly and I decided against going home to see our parents and our happily married brother and pregnant-with-their-third-child-wife for Easter, and had a barbecue at our house instead. Everyone who came said two things: "Your place is for sale?" and "What's wrong with your cat?" Little's tubes were gone, but she was still half-bald, thin and scarred. She meandered from room to room trying to cajole the guests in the kitchen to let her outside. She was wearing the satellite collar again, which severely impaired her attempts to escape, her latest strategy being trying to claw through window screens.

The Easter Barbecue was a moderate success. Trying to get people to actually show up for a gathering in L.A. is like trying to guess how many condoms are in the jar at the gynecologist's office. Impossible, and not worth the effort. You always have too much food but are plagued by the suspicion that you won't have enough. People, even your friends, come late, leave early, are obliged to attend other engagements . . . it's depressing. Suddenly I realized that this was sort of what I did for a living—plan events and worry that one of two things was bound to happen: no one at all or the entire world would show up. Once again I found myself wondering what I was doing with my life, besides having fun and making good money—things most people would be more than happy to have.

I came to L.A. four years ago armed with ruthless ambition. But four years, five apartments, three jobs, eight (give or take) pounds and a failed engagement later, I hadn't a clue if I was on the right path. If you had some idea of what you wanted, it was much easier getting there, wasn't it? I thought I knew what I wanted. I sort of knew. Vagueness had little currency in the real world. Yet, in Hollywood, it seemed, other people mastered it as an art form and rode it to a seven-figure, three-picture deal, a Malibu home and a trophy wife.

"What do you *really* want to do? What are you good at?" demanded Viv, licking pink frosting from her fingers. She'd made bunny cupcakes in pastel colors. For a Jewish girl, Viv was oddly obsessed with the secular bells and whistles of Christian holidays. She always had a Christmas tree before I did.

"You're my boss, you tell me what I'm good at," I answered, only half joking. She frowned.

"Hah. I'd be happy to tell you what you're *not* good at, which is returning phone calls to pissed-off journalists and being polite to talent agents. Although you are good at entertaining *certain* unpolished directors." She gave a sly smile.

"Point taken. So what should I be doing then?"

"Lex, it's important to figure that stuff out *yourself.*" She pointed a frosting-encased finger at me. "Think about it. You're good at what you do. You enjoy it . . ." She looked at me as if waiting for me to get it.

"And? . . ." I prompted her.

She sighed. "Why isn't that enough?" she finally said, and the thought stopped me in my tracks.

"Why aren't you a therapist?" I said affectionately, inhaling a lavender cupcake. She was so much better at counseling than my counselors had been.

"Because marketing movies involved less education and more money," she deadpanned. "Be what you want, Lex. It's the only real way to be happy."

I was a vice president of publicity, and I couldn't even manage to get our one summer movie mentioned in the summer preview of *USA Today, Entertainment Tonight* refused to cover our *Shades of Gray* premiere party unless I could personally guarantee that Mike Tyson would be there, which, of course, I could not. The *Wall Street Journal* was annoyed with me for not putting Kirk on the phone to discuss what our financial expectations for *Portland Girls* were, and the photo editor of *Entertainment Weekly* was furious because thirteen people showed up for a photo shoot for the movie *Shades of Gray* and none of them were Mike Tyson or Danni Jones. I tried to explain that Danni was in another movie altogether and that Mike thought he looked too mean on his last mainstream cover and was therefore refusing any future publicity requests. The editor hung up on me.

"Things could be worse," said Viv, who'd been dealt her fair share of unfair pain. "Lex. Enjoy your life, my friend. It's the only one you get," she said, attaching the cardboard rabbit to the door. "Hey, how's MollyWatch?" she asked, looking across the yard at Molly, who had been playing the coy glance game with Billy all afternoon. He'd been playing right back. They were seated on the grass. Sara-Anne, who had dabbled liberally in musicians over the years, kept a watchful eye on her from the picnic table.

"So you guys are coming to the CD release party, right?" Billy asked Molly, positioning the seductive instrument over his shoulder. If he started playing it, she was done. Doomed. "Yeah, I think so. Are you going to play all your own stuff?" she gurgled interest. Batted her eyelashes. Billy had that classic Free Spirit Broke Bohemian Musician Artist Sex Appeal.

"Molly! Can you, um, help me in the kitchen?" I called, heading up the stairs. She did not come. I waited a few minutes, then peered out from behind the kitchen curtains a la Piper Laurie in *Carrie*, and I saw him writing something on a card and handing it to her. I began to clean up the dishes by myself. So what, it was probably harmless, right? It was good for her to be flirting again, who was I to tell her what to do, she was a big girl. Little wandered into the kitchen. I looked down and noticed that the healing slit was sealed and was now a swelling balloon—when had that happened? She looked like a freshly fed snake. And it was growing . . . and it was Sunday, which meant the only vet that was open was the emergency clinic and an automatic $300 just to walk in the door. . . .

After much ruminating on what to do, I concluded that (a) there was pus in the balloon and (b) it would have to come out, and (c) I preferred that it not come out in an unanticipated explosion when I was at work the next day. I made the decision to lance the balloon, but I had no lancet and decided that a needle was just as good if I sterilized it. However, the needle from our old sewing kit didn't seem to really be designed for puncturing cat flesh, so I grabbed one of the Tools of the Trade knives that we (almost) never used. I glanced around and held Little, who was purring and gazing at me curiously, down on the counter with one hand and turned on the faucet with the other. Molly entered the kitchen carrying the plastic relish and mustard containers as I was steaming the knife.

"I think Billy's totally cool, I don't see why you—What," she paused cautiously, "are you doing?"

"I'm draining the pus, and I don't want your opinion about it," I said defensively.

"Why? Lex, what are you doing?" She put down the condiment bottles carefully so as not to spook me, as if I were a deranged person who had to be negotiated with. Anthony Hopkins in *The Silence of the Lambs*, Brittany Murphy in *Don't Say a Word*, Gollum in *The Lord of the Rings*.

"The pus is causing the swelling. And you are not to date, or think about dating, or be interested in dating Billy." The knife went in and Little hardly flinched. As I squeezed the balloon and the horrible liquid oozed forth like water through a dam, she flinched quite a bit and got very, very angry. "Rooowwwwlllllll! RRRRRRRROOOOOOOWWWWWWWW!!"

"I think," said Molly, "you're *hurting* her, and I can date *whoever* I want."

"Well, it hurts her more having all this bad stuff inside her," I responded, having no idea, of course, if this was true because I was not a vet. I was a publicist, and I was a bad sister who was bossy and jealous. And now the hole in my cat was back, bigger than ever, and I had done it. It seemed to be widening.

"Oh my God, I think I'm going to be sick!" said Molly as she ran out of the kitchen. Easter never used to be like this.

"You again," Dr. Perky said as I walked into the VCA clinic to explain, as apologetically as possible, that I had stabbed my cat with a kitchen knife but had only had her best interests at heart. Mrs.-Dr. Niblack looked at me for a moment, then pushed a clipboard with a pen attached toward me. "Maybe you could just write it down on this patient information sheet, so there's no, ah, confusion when Dr. Niblack sees her," she said tightly. So I did.

*Cat was healing until the pus balloon became too painful to bear; owner lanced the balloon Easter Sunday in order to drain it (releasing substantial pressure and pus), resulting in current hole in cat. Appetite normal.*

This seemed reasonable, better certainly than

*stabbed cat with chicken knife, then forced icky gook to come out, resulting in cat screaming in pain for several minutes because was too cheap to have it done professionally.*

Later at work Adrian Amtelled me: **Line 1: Dr. Niblack/Important. Line 2: Kirk re: Cannes.**

"There is still an infection," Dr. Niblack said gravely in the voice of the great Oz himself.

"From the chicken knife?" I stammered.

He looked at me quizzically. "Chicken knife?" he began, but quickly moved on. "Like we said, a foreign body that was visible on the X-ray. That is why this hole, as you call it, won't heal."

"But it *was* healing," I protested. How I hated for him to be disappointed in me. "It only healed superficially," he said patiently. "Inside, there is a deep infection."

"Sooo . . ." I prompted him to give me the bottom line. Kirk was holding on line two, and the California Corrections Facility public affairs person was on three, finally returning my call about possibly freeing Robert Downey Jr. in time for the *Shades of Gray* premiere. Adriane was filling out my paperwork for Cannes with Jean-Paul . . .

Dr. Niblack seemed to ignore my impatience. "We have to operate this time, Alexis. We have to get to the source of the infection," he insisted.

"Fine. Whatever it costs . . . ," I heard myself say. So she was going to be opened up. I couldn't fight it anymore. I had to let the veteran veterinarian handle it, once and for all. Later that afternoon, after lunch, my phone sheet looked like this:

| DATE/TIME | CONTACT | NUMBER | MESSAGE |
|---|---|---|---|
| 4/23/00 12:04 p.m. | Dr. Niblack's office | 310-261-7786 | Per your request, quote for feline anesthesia is $560. |
| 4/23/00 1:10 p.m. | Powerful | Cell | "What up"—Reach out to him. (Call back?) |
| 4/23/00 1:15 p.m. | Eugene R. | No # | Has a woman friend who has a catering company in NY; could do the premiere cheap with food from South Africa (good *Shades of Gray*) controversial theme . . . |
| 4/23/00 1:43 p.m. | Dr. Niblack's office | 310-261-7786 | Little is resting comfortably; can go home at 6 pm; will have a chest tube. |

| DATE/TIME | CONTACT | NUMBER | MESSAGE |
|---|---|---|---|
| 4/23/00 2:03 p.m. | Molly | UCLA office | How did Little do at the vet? |
| 4/23/00 2:07 p.m. | Mom | Home | How is the hole in your cat? |
| 4/23/00 2:34 p.m. | Viv | Office | Cannes screening; let's review list and party venue; make sure you have passport, etc. |
| 4/23/00 2:45 p.m. | Gabby/ Montage Agcy | 310-243-0900 | Claudia Schiffer's makeup for the NY premiere is $5,000; is there a budget, who should she bill? |
| 4/23/00 3:09 p.m. | Dope/Hip Hop Today | 212-435-0987 | Please add him, Lil' Kim + 27 to *Shades of Gray*, premiere. Call if ?'s |
| 4/23/00 3:24 p.m. | Kirk | Cell | Danni wants to wear Comme des Garcons in Cannes—can you get her some outfits (and what should he wear?) |
| 4/23/00 4:06 p.m. | Dan/*Details* | You have it | Going to press with story on Danni. Need studio comments before Cannes. |

| DATE/TIME | CONTACT | NUMBER | MESSAGE |
|-----------|---------|--------|---------|
| 4/23/00 | Robbie/ | 212-210-0200 | Rumor on Danni Jones; |
| 5:00 p.m. | NY Post | | printing tomorrow; plse |
| | "Page Six" | | call tonight. |

A 5:00 p.m. call from the *New York Post*'s "Page Six" is something no publicist *ever* wants to see on her call sheet. But since Danni had returned from Sundance, people had been writing about her, talking about her, and making up rumors about her pretty much on a weekly basis. The good news was that usually the rumors paled in comparison to whatever Danni had actually done or said, and I just considered it added publicity for the movie. So I didn't pay much attention. Robbie from "Page Six" had probably heard that Danni had used the wrong fork at a fancy restaurant, or had flipped someone the bird in traffic on Sunset or had been seen crashing into the valets outside the Chateau Marmont, unable to navigate the new Manolo Blahniks we'd forced her to wear to dinner with the *Los Angeles* magazine editor. Or something.

Instead of calling back "Page Six," I picked up Little. She was shaven again and looked more than ever like Mr. Bigglesworth from *Austin Powers.* A fresh tube in either end of her back, more draining, and stitches. She was truly FrankenCat, with two huge, stitched-up gashes on either side of her thorax, as her chart called it, which was completely shaved. Only her head and legs had hair. She was groggy and smelled vaguely of peanut butter, which was puzzling but I said nothing. I wondered enviously how Harve had managed to beat cancer and the moving day incident with an '89 Toyota Corolla.

"Why does it keep coming back?" I wailed.

In response, Dr. Niblack handed me a plastic container that held several pieces of what looked like brown, rotting . . . weeds. "This," he said triumphantly, "is what I took out of her." He tapped the bottle. "I don't know how this got into her body cavity, but . . . this was definitely the source of the infection." Together we stared at the brown bottled pieces of grass until it became clear that someone should speak. Dr. Niblack tapped the container again. "It's just plant matter, but it's still a foreign body that her system was reacting to." He sighed deeply and let out a little smile. "There should be no more problems, now."

"The old weeds-in-the-soul ailment," I said, trying to build a bridge of some sort, but Dr. Niblack neither got this nor laughed politely. Instead, he left the room. I waited for him to come back . . . *The Burmese, often confused with its cousin, the Siamese, sports blue eyes and a tawny coat* . . . but he didn't.

There were several post-op instructions. She was now on two kinds of antibiotics: two pills twice a day of the first and one and a half pills of the second, twice a day for the first week and once a day the following week. The next week she'd get a new pill—three times a day, or a quarter pill every four hours. And I was expected to "massage the afflicted area with hot compresses twice a day, to encourage draining." "Moderate exercise is also recommended." Soon I would have to quit my job. I felt like Renée Zellweger in *One True Thing.*

"It's like she's never going to get better," said Molly sadly, after walking home from the bus stop. She put her book bag on the table and looked at Little and her tubes. "I know how she feels." I looked up to see a defeated expression on my sister's tired face.

"What's wrong? I thought you said you liked work," I offered, smashing the salsa jar's lid on the counter edge to force it open. I needed chips. It had been a long day.

"It's fine," she breathed, "but, you know, I used to have a real job. Where people depended on me. Where I made decisions that affected kids' lives. Now I feel like a . . . *secretary.*" Her face grew rubbery. Uh-oh.

"You mean an *administrative assistant,*" I said helpfully, switching on our beloved Alex Trebeck on the little TV in the kitchen.

"No. I feel like a *secretary.*" And she began to sob.

"What is it?" I asked.

"What is it? I have no real job, no money, we have to move again and I'm so lonely, I don't know anyone here and you're busy with work, I miss Jack so much . . . I have a master's degree in education from *Harvard* and I'm answering phones for someone named *Deedee . . .*"

*Fashion Faux Pas for $200, Alex.* How I hated to see her cry. I wound up and delivered my best shots: "At least you're working." Nothing. "You have a place to live!" I cried as I offered her a bright red corn chip, heaving with pineapple salsa.

"Not for long," she said dismally. That was true. Agotha the Hun would no doubt pick Jody and Tim over us and would force us out as soon as she sold the place.

"At least you have me!" I said cheerfully, a last-ditch, pathetic Hail Mary pass.

*What is acid wash, that is correct!* Molly's face boiled over like an unwatched pot when the stuff spills down the edges. I tried to think of something positive to say. I stared at the *Jeopardy!* screen:

| Spinster-hood Beckons | Skyrocketing Vet Bills | Existential Doom of Your Early Thirties | Guess What? Life is Expensive! | Revenge of the Landlord | Eating Chips Is No Therapy! |
|---|---|---|---|---|---|
| $100 | $100 | $100 | $100 | $100 | $100 |

"Things will get better!" I told her. "They always do. Right after they get worse, things get better."

"Whose rule is that?" she asked flatly.

"It's a rule of the movies . . . you know, it's always darkest before the dawn." She looked puzzled, so I explained, "In the middle of Act Three, all seems lost. Like, Luke gets his arm cut off by Darth Vader, the boat starts to sink and Quint gets eaten by the shark, Mr. Potter steals the bank deposits . . . but then things always turn around in time for the final scene!"

"You really have a problem," she said. "Lex, life is not like the movies."

"It can be," I argued.

"No," she said in an ancient voice, "life is life, Lex. That's why there *are* movies." She had me there. But movies or not, things usually did get worse before they got better. Little was proof of that. So was my breakup, and hers, and a million other things. It was part of being human, this constantly shedding and growing new skin until finally, someday, usually in the last third of life, we have the right skin and feel comfortable in it, and hopefully get to enjoy that feeling for a spell before we die and the whole things starts over again. I hugged my sister, not letting go throughout the Manning pats, because there was nothing else I could do.

"Let's get out of the city and go somewhere next weekend. Let's go camping, to Joshua Tree or Yosemite," she hiccuped on the words through her receding sobs, gaining strength from the idea of escaping, however briefly, what her life had become.

"I can't, Mol," I said apologetically. She looked up at me with a hurt expression. There was no other time to tell her. "I have to go on a business trip . . . to, um, the Cannes Film Festival. For ten days . . . next week."

It was Kirk's idea, it wasn't my fault I had to go to Cannes. It was my job. (I know, poor me.) Molly went quietly into her room, closed the door and put on Billy's CD, leaving Little and me to field questions about leg warmers and mullets from Alex Trebeck.

# Twenty-Three

Melanie Griffith used to be fun to watch in movies. I still think her peak was *Working Girl,* where she seizes the opportunity (the broken femur of her boss, Sigourney Weaver) to get her own leg up on a world that isn't fair to thirty-year-old secretaries from Staten Island with big hair and bigger dreams. Harrison Ford is instantly smitten by her combination of spunk and chutzpah, particularly when he realizes that she is only a secretary *pretending* to be an executive because that was the only way anyone would listen to her idea that no one with an MBA had thought of. In the end she gets the glory, the guy and the job, but the most satisfying part is watching her humiliate her arrogant and conniving boss by calling her a skinny-assed bitch in front of a group of powerful men, including Harrison Ford, the one she stole from said skinny-assed bitch. It turns out that the leading man prefers the down-to-earth girl with smart instincts and a work ethic, not the politically savvy Cosmo bitch in designer dresses and a corner office.

The *New York Post*'s "Page Six" reported that "Sundance superstar and Cannes-bound Danni Jones was seen at an L.A. hotspot snuggling *thisclose* to a blue-haired tattooed PYT (that's pretty young thing)—of that same sex!" This had to be Cheryl, from the BET taping, which was odd but certainly not unheard-of behavior from someone of Danni's nature. No one paid any attention to the item. Except Kirk.

**LINE ONE: KIRK-Important.**

"Did you see the item?" he gasped into the phone, without saying hello.

"You mean the *Post?* Yeah, so? It's hardly career-ending, Kirk," I said mildly. I flipped through the Cannes Bible, reviewing details for the screening, party, Danni and Kirk's interview and outfit schedule, map of the Croisette, names of evil foreign journalists to avoid.

"But they're saying she's like, a lesbian . . . or something!" He was panicked.

"Kirk. At this stage of her career, ink is ink. We should be glad that the press still cares about her four months after Sundance." I glanced at the photos we'd be using. Danni here, Danni there. A cow here, some heroin there. Kirk framing a shot with his knobby, beer-drinking fingers, another of Danni, flipping the bird. It was a good thing we were having a "talking points" meeting before Cannes.

"I just think you should be on top of the, um, rumors. That's all." I closed the Cannes "bible" (what we called the bulging notebook of publicity details) and took a moment to mentally translate his strange tone. "Kirk, is there something you want to tell me?" An open-ended invitation was safer than a pointed accusation.

"What do you mean? I . . . Alexis, I just want to protect Danni is all. OK?" He sounded annoyed. I took a deep breath. "Kirk, I can't protect anyone from the press, unless I have"—I searched for the appropriate euphemism—"all the relevant information. OK? Remember that." There was a tight silence. "I'll see you at our lunch, OK?" And he hung up without confirming. Very dramatic.

The instructions for Molly while I would be in Cannes ran three pages long, single-spaced. An excerpt:

> Little's medications are on the windowsill, with dosage instructions on each label. Usually with "Tuna for Cats" or a tablespoon of cod liver oil, available at Whole Foods on Hollywood Blvd. (where we saw Kurt Russell shopping that time; be careful about parking). Make sure Little is kept away from the wood moldings and the new tenants. Do not under any circumstances remove Little's head bucket collar or let her outside. During the day she can be locked in my bedroom with food, water and her litter box and evenings and weekends she can have the run of the house as long as you're home. Extra elastics (for tightening head bucket collar) are in top drawer in the kitchen. Do not loop stereo wire around the gate or put the recycling bins against the door, in case Agotha comes. Be nice to Jody. (See next page for Vet, Adriane and Kikki (Cat-sitter woman) phone numbers.)

This would be Molly's first time alone since she moved in. Ten days alone with Little, in our home that Agotha was selling, oblivious to the fact that we were just settling in to our new life.

"I found a carpenter to fix the door molding," I told Molly. She was trying not to be upset that she would be alone for ten days, and she didn't care about the molding, but I nattered on: "I think it's better to get it fixed, so Agotha doesn't start asking questions if she comes by."

"Whatever," she agreed, running out with her English muffin to catch the bus.

I had to leave Steve the L.A. Carpenter several voice mails before he returned my call. "It's really not convenient for me to meet you in the evenings," he told me when I got him on my cell phone in traffic a few days later. Kirk and Danni and I were on our way to lunch at Pane e Vino, to prepare their "talking points" for Cannes. They were in my backseat as I multiasked on the way to the restaurant.

"How about mornings, then, say around eight-thirty?" I asked Steve, swerving across a lane as Kirk continued our conversation.

*Kirk:* It's my movie. I think I know what it's about.
*Me:* Yes, but it's important to position it the right way, especially to the international audience.
*Kirk:* You mean lie.
*Me:* No. I mean help persuade stupid people who wouldn't go see it because there's no star in it.
*Danni:* Harsh, dude.
*Me:* For example, *Portland Girls* is about friendship and sacrifice, love and loss. It's an uplifting coming-of-age drama with a healthy dose of smart comedy, universal truths and everyday heroes—something for everyone.

"How do you do that?" asked Kirk. He was smoking again. It was disgusting, and it turned me on immensely.

"Do what?" I said irritably, driving, balancing the phone and holding my breath.

"Speak in italics," he answered, smiling crookedly. Was he flirting again? No. His girlfriend was sitting right next to him. Or was she?

"Why can't I just say I kick ass in the movie?" complained Danni, picking a scab on her chin. "Dude, did you get that blazin' Commes des Garcons dress for me or what?" She was wearing her skull ring and her chunky bracelets. They made a lot of noise when she talked.

Kirk said sternly, "Dan, she's on the phone." I had never seen him reprimand her before. There was an energy between them that was almost . . . parental.

I turned back to Steve the Carpenter. "Eight-thirty is a little early," he protested politely. Back where I came from, carpenters started the day well before 9:30. Geesh. I bet Andrew Sullivan was up repairing things for women well before then. I stopped the car and told Steve the L.A. Carpenter he had ten seconds to decide if he wanted to repair my moldings or not.

"Hey—this is an intersection," said Kirk from the backseat. He looked very much like a cheerful Johnny Depp, if such a thing is imaginable.

"Dude," warned Danni, "there's a truck coming—"

I glanced in the rearview. "Danni, *please* stop calling me 'dude.' My name is Alexis." I turned my mouth back into the phone, hit the gas and told Steve to meet me the next morning at 8:45 in my driveway.

That's when I discovered that he wasn't just a carpenter. He was an *aspiring actor.* I found this out when he found out where I worked.

"Oh, you work at a studio! Well, maybe I could give you my headshot."

"Maybe you could give me a cheaper estimate," I said, not really joking as I glanced at my watch. I had to get to the office before flying to France. Steve the Carpenter stroked the splintered, chewed molding with callous-free fingers, and I thought of how much he *didn't* remind me of a young Harrison Ford, who'd gotten his start accidentally because he was the carpenter for a guy named Steven Spielberg who was casting a movie called *American Grafitti* . . .

"This is—or was, I should say,—original molding. I have to replace it and, you know, carve it to fit the other side. Not easy . . ." He smiled a tight smile. He was short and extremely fit. I disliked him. I shot him a withering look.

Maybe Andrew Sullivan would fly out here and fix the door and stay with Molly while I was in Cannes. I had a vision of the tree house he built when we were in junior high, where we'd go after school to be bad. I wondered if it was still there. I wondered if he built trophy tree houses for the trophy children of the trophy wives of his clients.

Steve the Carpenter said, "I'll do a great job, Alexis, you'll see," and offered a bogus smile.

"Great," I answered, adding, "Listen, ah, Steve, it's really, really important that you DON'T let the cat out of the house," I added, attaching my cell phone to my ear and striding down the driveway.

"Wait!" shouted Steve the Carpenter. "My headshot! I was thinking you could give it to the director of *Portland Girls!*" He ran to his truck to get it.

Before I left for Cannes I sat Molly down. "Do not call Jack. No matter how bored, depressed or lonely you get. You are independent! You have started a new life! Do not call him." She was sullen. "Mol, please don't be mad," I pleaded. "I have to go on this trip, it's not like I'm going on vacation. Or a *cruise.*" She was silent, ignoring my little attempt at an inside joke. "I think this will be good for both of us," I told her.

"Better for you, it is," she said in her Yoda voice. She smiled a reluctant smile and hugged me. We gave each other the Manning pat and broke free. I handed her my corporate calling card. "Use this to call me if you need to. And here's the Blockbuster card and my Barney's card. And," I said as I grabbed the *Magnolia* sound track from the stereo cabinet, "I'm taking *this.*"

"What if Jack's already met someone else?" she sniffed. "Then you can use the Barney's card," I told her.

"What if Agotha sells the apartment while you're gone?"

"She can't kick you out in ten days. This is California, we have weird rights," I said. Guilt was sneaking up on me like a creepy little monster in the dark, and I didn't like it. I had to beat a hasty retreat to the south of France. "What if Little's hole breaks open again?" she called after me.

"Then I'll come home."

I got to fly business class for the first time. It was exciting hanging out in the British Air Executive Lounge, though I was unsure about business class etiquette. So I sat down and tried to act like all the other business class travelers—calm, confident, full of purpose, like I had very little time to waste. (I was delivered orange juice in a *real* glass, with a "washbag"—I wasn't sure what was in it but decided it was probably best to wait until later to investigate so as not to tip off my fellow travelers to my inexperience.) I was unable to control my urge to have a complimentary drink in the middle of the afternoon. Then another. There was a mini toothbrush, eye mask and moisturizer in the washbag. The snack "crisps" were so delicious and British that I ate all three bags they gave me. They made me terribly thirsty. After one more British Airways gin & tonic I slept for the remainder of the flight.

I called Molly from my French cell phone as soon as I'd checked into the Hotel Majestique, and Little meowed on command into the transcontinental wire. Both of them sounded better, but Little was moping in my absence and had taken to dismembering Steve's newly renovated original molding one panel at a time. "I lost the instructions note," said Molly apologetically.

"Already? It was right on the table," I said, searching for the *New York Times* film critic in the cafés I was passing. Everyone I avoided in Hollywood was here, only now they were all saying hello instead of late-calling or pretending they didn't see each other at Orso's lunch scene. I instructed Molly to lock Little in my bedroom with her food, water, litter box and the first season of *Sex and the City.*

That first night I was feeling sexy and fun (I was in France, at the Cannes Film Festival, after all) when Viv and I went to a party on a yacht and met lots of people from our own studio that we never knew at home. This seems to be one of the purposes of film festivals: Trapped in exotic locations with nothing else to do, agents, producers and executives find, befriend, eat, see movies and get drunk with people whose calls they would not normally take.

I never did find the *New York Times* critic that night, whom I'd planned to drag to see *Portland Girls* if it was the last thing I did. Kirk and Danni weren't arriving until the next day, so I abandoned my duties and began to polish off several rum concoctions with the help of a sexy and fun British producer we met at another party, at a remote château overlooking the Mediterranean. Someone from Canal Plus was running shuttles from the yacht to the château, and Viv and I climbed aboard one with my new friend. The place was a giant, castlelike structure with turrets and bridges and leaded glass windows and giant shrubbery shaped like animals. The French must have made it specifically for Americans while at Cannes; it was not unlike It's a Small World at Disneyland.

I stupidly drank too much and even more stupidly decided it was a good idea to wander into a dark turret with the bloke, whose name seemed to be Jonathan, and soon we were talking a mile a minute, flirting cross culturally at 90 mph. His friends came to find us, and, after two more of the rum drinks (apparently they were called French Prozacs), they told us they were heading back to town and we should grab a ride with them or be stranded forever at the Château Petit Monde, which is what we'd all started calling it. Jonathan had long legs and wispy blond hair and the look of someone who planned to be successful and influential, or at least good at convincing others he was. His first film was an odd story about deaf people who raised ants. He was appealing, in a skinny, British sort of way, but his chin caved in under a tuft of facial hair that wasn't beard, wasn't goatee, was more young caterpillar than anything else.

"Are you sure you're ready for this?" asked Viv, who had a Spanish media mogul waiting at the Hotel du Cap for her. I had one leg in Jonathan's taxi and one on the sidewalk pointed in the direction of my hotel. "No, but how elshe am I gunna find out?" I whispered drunkenly. After the fiasco of Martin and the Sky Bar ladies locker room, I felt confident I could handle whatever a skinny British Film Producer could dish out. "Don't be late tomorrow," she warned, winked, and shoved me into the tiny taxi. As it careened along the coast with too many sloshed entertainment industry executives aboard, the producer began making out with my neck, which, admittedly, I had encouraged.

When we stopped at my hotel, I decided it was a good idea to invite him in to see what my room looked like. He had manners and wasn't overly confident, a typical British person, which was appealing. We passed through the red banquettes in the lobby, ambled by the gift shop and squeezed into the tiny elevator. Jonathan pulled the gate across and pinned me softly against the rear of the car. Giving his face a final once-over, I succumbed. "You American girls smell so good," he said, nuzzling my neck, nibbling my earlobe and running his hands up and down my body. We made it to my room and collapsed in a heap onto the bed. It was very peaceful letting someone else do all the work, I decided, feeling like an observer as Jonathan removed my clothes, peeling off my silk camisole and struggling with my jeans.

"Bit of help, love?" he asked, yanking on my belt loops, and I erupted into a fit of giggles. How fun it was to not care about the person who was about to work very hard to give you an orgasm! Sex. I had sex with a strange man for the first time in three years.

This was a milestone. I was over everything. I had moved on. I celebrated this by postcoitally telling the British producer the whole story of my failed relationship, the Christmas Eve ultimatum, the breakup, David's cruise, Molly moving in, Harve's accident, before an intense headache set in and I grew bored with his presence. Quickly.

"You have to leave now," I heard myself say.

"What . . . do you mean?" He thought I was kidding, that I was testing his loyalty. He pinched my butt cheek. "You've just told me your life story. Now I've got to tell you *mine.*" When he talked, his facial hair moved like a small rodent under his lips.

"Don't. I don't even know you and I can't sleep with a stranger in my bed and I need to sleep, because I have to work tomorrow so . . . you have to leave. Now." I got up and dressed as coldly as Mrs. Robinson in *The Graduate.*

"But . . ."

"Please, Jonathan—it's Jonathan, right? Don't make me feel guilty, just go. And don't forget anything. Here's your phone." I lit a Gauloise for effect. I walked to the corner of the tiny room. "And your keys. And I think I saw your wallet in the shower."

"You're *chucking* me out?!" he cried incredulously in his posh accent. "Let me just sleep! I've a breakfast meeting at this hotel in two hours!" He sat defiantly behind his long skinny legs.

"Then you have just enough time to go home, shower and change clothes," I replied cheerfully, tossing him his pants. He wrestled with the sheets and finally stomped out of the bed and across the room. He frowned in a very European way and said, "American women—Christ alive!" He pulled on his thin black socks, patted his hair down, grabbed his man purse and left. British men. No thank you. I bet he had never caught a fish in his life.

"Look, I'll call you later, OK?" I said, sounding like Charlie Sheen in *Wall Street.* I felt valiant. Sex was still possible, and it was the new millennium, which meant that even though I was a woman, I could have sex like a man. Hunt, gather, climax and move on. A girl could do worse.

I spent most of the next day dodging my new "boyfriend," who had already taken to greeting me with, "Hi, it's *me*" when he called on my cell phone every few hours as I was racing from one end of the Croisette (Canne's main drag) to the other with *Portland Girls* press kits and promotional sweatshirts, while Kirk and Danni endured six straight hours of press interviews while encased in borrowed designer clothes. Jonathan had a chipper British producer phone voice. "What are you doing?"

"I'm *working*," I said, handing a café busboy a *Portland Girls* baseball hat. The busboy scowled. Then he smelled the hat and scowled again. Jonathan persisted, Britishly. "Right. What are you doing later?" His voice had the effect of a chisel, scraping away the veneer of PR pleasantries I usually kept intact for at least the first three days of a film festival.

"I'm busy." My God, it had happened. I had become a man. Later, weary of dodging my new Festival Bur (people who you pick up the first few days of a festival and then can't shake loose,) I decided to go for a drink on one of the boats docked at the other end of the beach. Collect my thoughts, decide what was missing in my life and determine why, despite getting laid by a pompous stranger, I was still thinking about Kirk Olmstead. Maybe moving to the south of France to be a painter was a good idea.

As I was walking down the Croisette among five thousand people from all over the world, I heard someone say, "Lex, is that you?" The words passed through my brain's voice recognition software. I shuddered. It was a voice I knew.

It was David's younger sister, who was in law school in Philadelphia. But somehow, she was standing there on the French Riviera, waving to me not five feet away. "What're you doing here?" she asked. I could not believe my eyes and had to hold onto a French police horse to prevent myself from collapsing. "I'm . . . I'm working, what are, what are you doing here?"

"I just finished school and I'm traveling in Europe. It's so weird to see you here, Alexis . . ." Yes, it was. She was wearing a T-shirt from Paris and a disastrous haircut from . . . Berlin? She was the kindest, sweetest person in David's family, the one I'd gone on walks with and helped buy makeup. I hadn't seen her since before the beginning of the end and could only imagine the terrible things she thought of me since the breakup.

"It's nice to see you, you look great!" she said, and her smile was warm, unburdened, kind.

"It's nice to see you too, Abby," I said, and meant it. We stared at each other. My French cell phone split the silence. "Hi, it's *me.* What are you doing?"

Partly because I remembered distinctly how it felt to be treated like a leftover, and partly to get him off the phone, I invited Jonathan to our *Portland Girls* party, which was held in a restaurant on the water, half under a taut white tent, half in the sand. I regretted this, however, when I saw him across the beach, raising his shirt to display for an intrigued party guest the fresh scratch marks I had accidentally given him the night before. I squinted. A hideous realization. Oh, no. The astonished party guest being entertained by my one-night stand was, of course, Kirk, who was standing there laughing, looking casually delicious and definitely amused. A panicked gas bubble broke free from me and vanished into the party. I headed for the restroom quickly. God was punishing me. Not only was He making a mockery of my one-night stand in front of all my peers but He had also taken control of my bodily functions at the most important event of my first—*pphfffft*—Cannes Film Festival. At least He had a sense of humor.

Kirk hadn't spotted me yet, and Danni was too busy spotting

people spotting her in her Commes des Garcons outfit, which Adriane had donated her left arm to secure. Danni and Kirk were struggling, I could tell. I had been watching them closely, through every appearance, every fashion change, every photo op, every interview gone awry (though I *had* gotten her to stop saying that everyone's dump smelled the same). She was leaving him already. She was on the escalator of fame, and he would not hear from her again until she was en route back to her roots, on the miserable way back down. Perhaps then he would be kind and Travolta-ize her—reinvent her spark by casting her as an older character in an independent, low-budget, critically acclaimed film of Historical Cinematic Importance. For now they smiled and posed for the camera but still deigned to hide their affair, whatever it was, because they had an image to convey, but not, it seemed, because they had something to protect.

When I exited the bathroom *(ppffoot)*, Kirk was standing alone at the bar, alongside rows of giant crab legs and glasses of champagne. The Mediterranean sparkled behind him, the light-bulbs flashed before him, each one taking a little piece of the soul of the girl he'd discovered for the world. The Aaliyah single blared, and Viv held court as the entire studio marketing staff proceeded to get plastered with the London and Paris offices and various influential journalists we would use to force people to love our little movie.

"Pretty surreal, huh?" Kirk commented when I came to collect him for the walk to the screening in the Palais across the street. He was idling by the raw bar, contemplating his place in the world. If he knew about my previous evening's escapades he was not letting on. Good. Maybe it was my imagination. My abdomen convulsed sickeningly. *Pffuut.* The champagne was kicking in, and I couldn't help but think, *Wouldn't it be nice if Kirk knows about the British producer and is, I don't know, jealous?*

"Kirk, it's almost time to—*peewp*—go." Why had I worn a

cinch-waisted dress? Cruel, cruel Calvin Klein; I felt like a wasp with a throbbing thorax. I took a tiny, careful step toward Kirk, who looked at the yachts through his champagne glass.

"Look at this shit! I mean, it's completely wild! Small-town guy from Oregon with a premiere at the Cannes Film Festival . . ." His voice trailed off, waiting for me to pick it up, dust it off, kiss its ass.

I was tired, hungover and jet-lagged, but I found my motivational speaker voice. "But it's everything you've worked for, right? Everything you've dreamed of?" I heard myself say.

Willem Dafoe was talking to Danni. For some reason, she was making a bicep muscle and he was squeezing it. She laughed, squeezed his arm, and glanced discreetly about the party. We noticed. She noticed us notice. Without me to stop them, the flashbulbs went off like a swarm of rabid fireflies. Kirk looked at the scene, at me, and then the water and the night fishermen on the pier. "I don't know anymore," he sighed dramatically. "I thought I just wanted to make films, but this is all a little overwhelming, and I don't know what to feel," he added rather pathetically, shaking his head and downing his champagne. Something like a snort escaped my nose. "What?" he said, smiling.

"Oh, please! If I had a dollar for every time a new director gave me the fucking 'Aw shucks' routine." Uh-oh. Had I said "the Aw Shucks routine"? True, I'd stolen it from Kristin Scott Thomas in *The Horse Whisperer* "Please let's not do the 'Aw, shucks routine,' " she tells a ravishingly rugged Redford in her clipped British), but it felt good saying it to Kirk, the words bouncing off his big head. For God's sake, be professional—*pfweee*—I told myself. PR 101— *Never reveal how you really feel or what you really think.*

Kirk looked at me, puzzled, then smiled. "Tell me, Manning," he smirked, "what is the 'fucking Aw Shucks' routine?"

"Kirk, I'm sorry, I'm tired and I'm not quite myself," I stammered, feeling my face get hot. Why couldn't I ever leave champagne alone? I prayed Viv wasn't witnessing this exchange. *Do not upset the director before he introduces the movie at the Cannes Film Festival—duh.*

*"Au contraire,"* he said laughing. "I think," he paused theatrically, "that this is the *real* Alexis Manning speaking." He grabbed another glass of Veuve Clicquot.

"Why did you want me here?" I demanded suddenly. I suddenly wondered if it was to get me fired.

He opened his eyes wider, as if encouraging this line of questioning. "Because I wanted to meet the real Alexis Manning," he replied. "And I think I just did. Why, aren't you having fun in Cah-hhhnnnnnesssss?" He exaggerated the pretentious pronunciation to annoy me. Despite the new gloss we had shellacked him with, he was still inherently kind, just as some people were inherently smug. It was still there. Andrew. Johnny Depp. David. Jesus Christ. The men of my dreams.

"All right, fine, enough about me. We both know this isn't about *me,"* I huffed, shaking off the tenderness like a wave of nausea. "I want to know *the real* Kirk Olmstead—and what he wants . . ." PR 101—*Dodge the question; change the subject.*

"Do you. Really." He inched into my personal space, daring me to move. I held onto the raw bar for support and felt my panty hose splitting.

"Are you telling me you're not enjoying this?" I said as I made a grand, sweeping gesture across the Palais, the Croisette, the cameras, the boats, the fans, the wannaoes, Willem Dafoe, the crab legs, Danni, my British producer with the scratch marks, just missing Kirk's drink with my arm.

"Well, no, I've always loved crab," he said earnestly, evading the blow that had leveled him in the greenroom of the *Tonight Show.* "Back home, you know, we catch 'em by the dozens, we eat it all the time . . ." He chuckled, then frowned, looking across the beach. "The water smells funny here. Must be the pollution. Back home the water's so clean you can actually eat the fish you catch," he said tiredly.

"Listen, Mr. Pacific Northwest, are you having fun or not? Because it's my job to make sure you are." Kirk looked uncomfortable. I clenched my abdomen shut while he pondered the differences between Portland and the south of France. And then, without warning, he was real, all coyness cast aside.

"At least in Portland I knew what I was doing, I had a goal, I felt sure of myself, I knew what I wanted and who my real friends were . . . this shit here is fucked up, Alexis. I don't know how you stand it," he sputtered, then shut himself up with a crab leg. This, too, I'd heard from many a new talent. In the game of Hollywood Monopoly, we'd moved Kirk from Baltic Avenue to the yellow properties in just the time it takes to get from Sundance to Cannes. He was clinging to his past because he felt guilty about his new sense of entitlement. Ambition was unavoidable, and it had left a sour taste in his mouth. I decided to call him on this.

"So you want me to rebook your ticket coach class, on Sun Airways, back to Portland? You want to go back to maxing out your parents' credit cards so you can make small gritty films that are smart and relevant but that no one will see or pay you for?" He stared at me. Now I'd done it. I gulped the rest of my champagne and prayed for the strength to fend off another gas attack.

"No. I want to get myself a pair of Eurotrash scratch marks before I go back to Portland," he said smugly. My mouth opened, but no sound came out. He grinned accusingly, raising that Andrew Sullivan eyebrow again, and said, "I'm disappointed. You could do so much better than that boob, Alexis!"

A very awkward second passed, and then he took the glass from my hand. And in a perfect, priceless, movie moment, he brushed the hair from my neck, behind my shoulder, and let his eyes rest on that spot by my right clavicle, the cave for David's nose, unused for so long. I thought he might lean in and kiss it, but instead he said, "Hah, thought so. Nice hickie. Here's looking at you, kid," and he winked and turned to go to the screening. I was supposed to be escorting him, but I was anchored in humiliation. "I'll see you over there, right?" he asked, ambling away. "You know I need your support in the wings with all these hostile frogs."

"Do you fish?" I shouted absurdly.

He was getting away. "What?" he yelled. He was in the middle of the Croisette.

"You said the fish in Portland are edible!" I was yelling back. "Do you fish, you know, on the rivers and stuff . . ."

He just looked at me, mopeds and billboards and photographers and publicists and taxis and drag queens and ingénues and executives and hotel concierges and tourists bustling between us on the Croisette. "Of course I fish, I'm a hick from Oregon!" His perplexed smile was the last thing I saw before he was drowned in a sea of black ties and flashbulbs, on his way to introduce his little film to 1,500 people. But most of them would be European and therefore would be contemplative and silent when the movie ended, instead of falling over themselves to blow smoke up his ass. After the experience of Sundance and Los Angeles he would not be prepared for this and would have to be consoled. I headed after him. *Ppfffhhwwuttt.*

The last day of the festival, Kirk was on a directors' panel hosted by Roger Ebert. He was up there with some real heavy hitters and other young guns like himself who had struck with a first feature that was real, relevant, provocative or had a big star in it or big studio behind it. It had been a long week (Danni had been photographed with George Clooney and Vin Diesel, along with Anna Nicole Smith and Willem at our party, and Kirk had almost been forbidden to enter the Palais while wearing his "lucky" sneakers to his own premiere. *Monsieur, les chauseures, absolument non!* He got so drunk at the U.K. Film Commission yacht party that he fell in the water and had to get a tetanus shot after being pulled out by the head of the William Morris Agency, who followed him to the hospital and promptly signed him. I was there through it all to make sure that the press documented every detail. The movie was, after all, opening in a couple of months.

As the festival wore on, Kirk and Danni spent less and less time together. Then Cheryl, the blue-haired Tantric sex advisor from Danni's *Live From LA!* dressing room, mysteriously appeared and set up camp in the hotel. By the last day it seemed that Danni and Kirk were no longer speaking at all. In fact, Kirk ended up spending all of his time with me. But after the romantic comedy climax moment at the party, it was anything but romantic; we trudged from interview to interview, party to party, press conference to screening, and as his fans multiplied I felt like the perverted babysitter/stage parent/road manager, seated in the corner holding his schedule and his phone and palm pilot, puffing pack after pack of Gauloises. Of course, I don't even smoke.

I was so busy and exhausted that the directors' panel was the first time I realized I could sit down, by myself, in several days. As soon as my ass was on the chair, it hit. David. I didn't even know him anymore. It was really over. And just like that, the anger and resentment were gone. But then another thought hit me like a piece of unexpected bird-shit on a nice summer day. I was alone. With my fabulous career. In the blazing Cannes sun, hungover and leftover and going on three hours' sleep in as many days, four pounds of French baguettes and moules frites added to my methane-carrying frame, which was about to turn 32. PMS and jet lag didn't help, so in the last chair of the last row at the Cannes directors' panel, I sobbed. As quietly as I could, under the circumstances. Only the film critic from the *New York Times* noticed, and he discreetly moved several chairs away.

Back at the hotel, struggling to get my enormous suitcase

through the French elevator, I realized that I had forgotten to send any of the postcards I had written. I sat down at a red velour banquette in the lobby and reviewed them. Mom and Dad, Molly, Sara-Anne, Marcos and Lisa, my aunt Kris, Frank and Sue, Adriane at the office—and one blank one. Who had I forgotten? I couldn't send one to David. Or Deke. Could I? Were we at the postcard sending stage yet? No. We would never be there, we would never be friends. I had never been able to remain friendly with any of my ex-boyfriends—it was my own character flaw I was never going to fix. After the third one, I'd stopped blaming it on them.

I walked across the Croisette to where the mailbox was and stared out at the water. Two men were at the end of a dock, baiting hooks and throwing their lines in the water. Then I got a bizarre idea. I would send Andrew Sullivan the last postcard. I wondered what he'd think when he got it. Yes, finally I could send him a postcard from an exotic location. Over the years I had occasionally gotten word of his epic adventures and fishing conquests in a paragraph scrawled hastily on one of the postcards we'd collected on our cross-country trip. Why not return the favor? Why not start reestablishing old ties? Spending all that time with Kirk had gotten me thinking of Andrew again, a man from my past who drank beer, didn't get facials or panic attacks and loved the outdoors.

> Hey Andrew—
> How have you been? Here I am at the fabulous Hotel Majestique in Cannes, where I've been working for a week—some business trip, eh? I'm still in LA working in the film business, what's new? You married off yet. (Thanks to Mom, I knew he wasn't but this was his cue to reveal a girlfriend) or still fishing, globe-trotting and breaking hearts? My mom says you are building some pretty impressive trophy homes on the Cape.

Here's my email if you want to keep in touch: aman@
moviemediacorp.com all the best—
Alexis
p.s. Cannes is glamorous but you can't eat the fish out
of this water!

Outside the hotel I waited for a taxi the size of my shower. Kirk
and Danni were staying for the final evening award ceremony, but
I had to get back to work promoting their film Stateside. I hadn't
seen Danni (or her new roommate Cheryl) all day, but Kirk appeared just as I got to the front of the cab line. "Do you want me to
go wiss you to ze airhhpohht?" he purred in a French accent that
made me laugh. "In case you need help wiss zat . . . behemoth," he
said, referring to the suitcase the tiny man was trying to wedge into
the mini taxi.

"Why would I need your help?" I hadn't meant to sound like a
militant lesbian, but it came out that way.

Kirk raised an eyebrow. "OK, sorry, *working girl.* American
Woman is just *fine* by herself!" he said jokingly in the same accent
as the valet glared at us with cultured French impatience. Suddenly
Kirk grew serious. "Well, then. Thanks for a *splendid* time, then,
*Miss Manning.*"

"Quit that," I clipped.

"Quit what?"

"Speaking in italics," I said. He laughed, and my heart died a
little death.

"You're sure you don't want *my help?*" he asked again teasingly.
He really was cute, standing there on the Cannes sidewalk in his
expensive shoes and fancy jeans and Portland's Best Brews! hat.
The paparazzi all knew who he was by then, and they snapped
away at us. We stared at each other for an awkward moment, and
my question, unasked for so long, escaped from my heart into my
mouth and headed for his ears.

"Kirk, what's the deal with you and Danni—how can you be with her?" There it was, and I couldn't take it back.

But Kirk seemed neither offended nor surprised. He just looked at me, something like relief washing over his face. "Can I trust you?" he asked. An ocean breeze fluttered his hair. The valet had moved on to the next annoying Americans waiting for the next minuscule taxi.

"Of course," I said evenly.

He spoke in a whisper. "Danni and I are not together. We . . . never have been. We just *pretend* to be." His face suddenly displayed a sheepish look. He looked at the pavement under his feet. Then into my eyes with an intensity that was unexpected.

"What?!" I demanded, a little too loudly. The air gushed into me. Some of the photographers stopped shooting and stared at us.

"For her protection," Kirk said obviously. I stared at him, not understanding, an expression of dog befuddlement overtaking my features. "Lex," he said exhaling slowly, "Danni's my stepsister. Technically. Besides, I'm not even sure she's into guys, if you know what I mean . . ." He looked at me, but I just stared. *Danni's his stepsister?* "Her dad remarried my mom years ago. Then they separated. I took care of her through it—it was a long time ago. She's like my kid sister." I stared at him, wanting more. "It's safer for her to pretend she's with me than have to answer questions about her personal life. She's just a kid, Alexis. She's scared to death. Give her a break."

Oh. I felt like such an insensitive, self-centered jerk. "I didn't know," I said quietly. Suddenly and with great horror I realized what the *Details* article was about. I'd been blowing off the editor and he was probably looking for a comment, something, to counter the *National Enquirer*-ish story he was going to break: *Sizzling Sundance Sexpot Prefers the Ladies! Studio Representatives Did Not Return Calls.* You might as well publish your guilt on the front page of the *New York Times*. I should have called him back. "Kirk, it's the year 2000. It's not a crime to be gay or young and naïve! No one cares!" I sputtered defensively, guilt creeping up.

"Alexis," he said patiently, "Danni doesn't have a degree. Christ, she doesn't have a high school diploma! This is her chance to have a life, to take care of herself. I'm not going to blow it for her."

"OK," I said soberly, mentally listing all the phone calls I had to make, starting with Viv. "But Jeez, Kirk, when the press finds out they'll eat you both alive! They'll say she slept with her brother, which I'm pretty sure is worse than being gay . . ." I was starting to panic, but I felt the adrenaline of a PR crisis kick in, and my brain started working. I could do this. I could handle it. "I'll take care of it. Don't worry," I told my director.

"Why would I worry when my publicist is handling everything?" he said, stepping closer to me.

I shot him a look and said, "I'm not your—"

And without warning, he grabbed me and kissed me. A huge, meaningful, tender, exploratory, explosive kiss. I fell into it, surrender washing over me, all the tension in my shoulders, neck and back gone in an instant. He squeezed my shoulder blades together, forcing my head back in the biggest, most dramatic screen kiss you can imagine, my head at a ninety-degree angle. All I could think about was *Cinema Paradiso,* when the director finally watches the reel his old friend assembled for him—every censored kiss from every film he'd loved as a boy. Kirk pushed my hair away from my face like Ryan O'Neil would have done to Ali McGraw. Then he took a step backward and winked at me.

*"Madame?!"* The taxi man was irate. *"Alors?"* he spat, meaning, *are you going to get the fuck in this taxi and back to L.A. where you belong, or not?*

"Oui," I said woozily. "Oui, j'y vais."

# Twenty-Four

| DATE/TIME | CONTACT | NUMBER | MESSAGE |
|---|---|---|---|
| 5/27/00<br>8:00 a.m. | Dan /<br>*Details* | Said you "have<br>his number by<br>now" | "Thanks for returning<br>my calls. Unfortunately<br>it's too late to add the<br>studio comments to the<br>story, which, as I told<br>you, went to bed last<br>week. It is what it is." |
| 5/27/00<br>8:30 a.m. | Rhonda<br>Wallace | 310-255-3838 | Plse call. Re: Danni's<br>situation. |
| 5/27/00<br>8:40 a.m. | Jo Ellen /<br>Legal | X8905 | Plse call re: Danni<br>Jones. |
| 5/27/00<br>9:03 a.m. | Julie / Ink,<br>inc. PR (Robert<br>Downey's<br>publicist) | 310-248-6106 | Re: Danni Jones—does<br>she have a personal<br>publicist? Does she<br>need one (now)? |

| DATE/TIME | CONTACT | NUMBER | MESSAGE |
|---|---|---|---|
| 5/27/00 9:43 a.m. | Babette (D.H.'s agent) | Cell: 323-399-3947 | Remember me from D.L. & Sundance? Wants to talk to you about repping Danni Jones. |
| 5/27/00 10:05 a.m. | Mom | Home | Is it true your actress is gay and sleeping with her brother? Happy Birthday. |
| 5/27/00 10:30 a.m. | Molly | Office | Your birthday plans. Email me. ☺ Is it true about Danni? |
| 5/27/00 10:45 a.m. | Beth / Corporate Communications | X4533 | Re: *Vanity Fair* story; plse call. |
| 5/27/00 10:50 a.m. | Agotha | Office | Re: Your lease. You need it for the new buyer. (She is going to Austria for a few months.) |
| 5/27/00 10:53 a.m. | Marcos | Cell | Did you orchestrate the whole story? Congrats. *What's Up Doc* on tonight on AMC at 11. |

| DATE/TIME | CONTACT | NUMBER | MESSAGE |
| --- | --- | --- | --- |
| 5/27/00<br>11:00 a.m. | Eugene R. | No # | Has a great part for Danni Jones in his next film. Will she be at his premiere? Will she do nudity? A 3 way? |
| 5/27/00<br>11:23 a.m. | Sara-Anne | Cell | Happy Birthday (which day is it?) Congrats on all the ink for your actress. Do you want red or white? |
| 5/27/00<br>11:30 a.m. | Powerful<br>& Herb | No # | Yo, is the hot gay chick coming to our premiere? |

The month of May always brought three things. The Cannes Film Festival, my birthday, and Memorial Day, the official launch of a new season. I was hoping that this year it wouldn't also mean the end of both my job and my apartment. Molly had arranged a birthday/Memorial Day cookout for some friends and Aunt Kris the weekend after I returned from France. I was jet-lagged and dazed but grateful for the distraction. I had to get that kiss off my mind.

Viv, Adriane and I were doing our best to provide damage control for Danni, but the story about her presumed sexual preferences and rumor-laden history with her "brother" was breaking in *Details'* July issue, right on time for our release. The *Details* PR person had, as her job demanded, leaked the story to all of the New York gossip columns, which cover the publishing world like the Hollywood gossip columns cover the movie business—like it is Very Important. Viv and I had an emergency meeting with

Rhonda Wallace, Danni's agent, several potential publicists, Beth from Corporate Communications and the rest of the marketing team, and we came up with a blanket response: "Danni Jones has delivered a breathtaking, award-worthy (never too early to start campaigning for an Oscar) debut performance in *Portland Girls*, and the studio is proud to introduce this new star to audiences everywhere. It is the studio's policy to respect the rights and privacy of all individuals. This 'story' is of no concern to the *Portland Girls* campaign or Danni Jones's career, which, we are confident, will be long and prosperous."

It remained to be seen whether audiences between New York and L.A. would let a little thing like Danni's sexuality or alleged incest with her director stop them from seeing a well-reviewed movie that had some buzz, on top of several top festival awards. Of course Viv and I secretly hoped the controversy would put butts in theater seats and Danni on magazine covers—*Is she or isn't she? Did she or didn't she?* Indeed, that was our planned phase II of the release publicity campaign.

Little's drain had been removed (for the second time), and Molly had carefully saved it in wax paper in case I wanted to see it. I didn't really, but it was sweet of her. Little still had her stitches in but seemed much better and was meowing again, and she could leap onto furniture in a single bound and poop in the plants unassisted.

The morning of the Birthday-Memorial Day barbecue, Marcos called to tell me two things. One, he couldn't make it because he and Lisa were buying a house together and were meeting the seller that afternoon, and two, he'd played soccer with David and found out he was seeing someone.

"I wasn't sure if you wanted to know," he explained.

"I didn't."

"Oh. Well, I didn't want you to find out that I knew and didn't tell you. You know?"

"No."

"Oh. Sorry. Happy birthday."

At the barbecue, over the gas grill, I recounted the story to Billy, who was unwrapping Veggie Burgers. "Yeah. I guess I sort of knew too," he said.

"How?" I demanded, not really wanting the answer. I didn't care, but I did. I wasn't jealous, but I was. It was an odd matrix to be in.

Billy hesitated. "He's, um, bringing her to my CD release party."

"Billy, you're MY friend!" I said, in a tone I hadn't used since junior high. I was over David, but I had to admit I wasn't ready to meet his new girlfriend. How had he gotten one so soon? I had buried the Kirk kiss deep into my heels. I hadn't talked to him since we'd returned, and I wasn't sure how I was going to handle the aftermath of what I was secretly calling the Cannes Kiss.

"I'm not taking sides," Billy said carefully, scattering my Kirk thoughts.

"There are no *sides,* you're MY friend. If he's going to your show with his new *girlfriend,* I'm not going!" I couldn't stop myself, even though I knew I sounded ridiculous.

"Well, OK, I understand but . . . Molly's still coming, right?" Billy asked hopefully.

"I'm still coming!" Molly gushed, appearing with a dish of potato salad, and I glared at them.

"Lex, why d'you care if David's dating? You broke up with him, sugar, *remember?*" asked Sara-Anne, who was, naturally, broken up with but still sex-dating Richard.

"I don't," I said quickly. I hadn't told her or anyone about the Cannes Kiss. So far it was still my treasured little secret.

"David's been dating a lot," added Billy for no apparent reason.

"I *don't* care," I shot back as I stormed up the stairs and then turned, barbecue fork in hand, and suddenly the words came spilling ridiculously out of my mouth. *"I got laid in France!"*

"So that's what you were doing while *Details* was plotting the ruinous story about our new star?" Viv said, unable to resist the dig. Fair enough, I'd earned it. Sara-Anne, Viv and Frank and Sue all began applauding. Molly looked horrified, then hurt she hadn't known, and Jody from downstairs looked chaste. My aunt Kris nestled into her pasta salad, embarrassed.

Distracted by my own drama, I left the door open, and Little shot outside and escaped into the dark zone underneath the house, where the whole business of ingesting rotting weeds had started. The birthday barbecue turned into a search-and-rescue mission to find and apprehend Little before she could rip open her stitches or encounter some other terribly expensive misfortune.

"She can't-a-gone far," said Sara-Anne, bringing her Pinot to the back of the garage to have a halfhearted look around. "I don't know why you keep that damn cat around anyway, stupid-ass feline bitch seems like more trouble than it's worth."

"Kind of like Richard," I said testily.

"I'm sorry, honey, but does the cat take you to Matsuhisa and Fred Segal?" she said, and I had to laugh. She gave me a hug. "Do tell your Cannes story, sugar, I'm all ears . . ."

"We have to find Little first," I said worriedly. "If she cuts open her hole again it will cost me another grand."

Viv stepped in. "How much have you spent on that cat, Lex? How much are you going to spend?" The words were eerily familiar.

"Just run the can opener," said Frank, "all cats come running to that sound." Billy sat down serenely beside the opening to the dark zone underneath the house and began to play "Edelweiss" from *The Sound of Music.* Molly got the flashlight from the garage and kneeled next to him, peering into the blackness. I wandered to the front of the house with my hot dog and sat on the front steps, suddenly realizing how very jet-lagged I was. My head was full of cotton and sand, my legs made of rubber. I rubbed my eyes wearily, like a character who's faced one too many obstacles without sleep or food or hope. Ralph Fiennes in *The English Patient,* Nicolas Cage in *Honeymoon in Vegas.*

The Asian couple passed. It was the closest we'd ever been; they were steps away, and our eyes met. Suddenly he made a gracious but tiny bow, disarming in its unexpected courteousness. I felt that a certain spell had been broken, now that they had noticed me and taken in my presence. They smiled, as if they'd been waiting all this time for a friendly exchange, as if they had noticed me all along. I could no longer wonder about them with the same detachment. Something was gone, the element of mystery. But it was nice knowing they were friendly. They were just neighborly, normal people out for a walk, and it had nothing to do with me.

"We've got her," called Billy. I turned to see him holding his locked guitar case like a tray. It was moving. "Molly said your kitty carrier was broken? Something about overuse, I believe." He goofily blew a leaf from his forelock of thick black hair. It was hard to stay mad at him.

"She's in the case. Billy played 'Hey Jude' and she came right out," Molly confirmed proudly. She was frosted with leaves and cobwebs and was, I noticed, beaming at Billy with girlish glee. She was—uh-oh—*smiling.* Never leave your little sister alone with a man with a guitar.

That night, the message light was blinking. It was from Bryce at Coldwell Banker. He was one of those L.A. real estate agents who had his picture not only on his business cards but also on the For Sale signs of homes that he was selling. As if once people saw how good-looking he was, they'd feel more comfortable shelling out $800,000 for a 2BR 1BA in a neighborhood that boasted only occasional helicopter flybys. He had what I'd call an aggressively hospitable tone.

"HI! The new buyers have been approved, and we'll be coming to show the unit tomorrow afternoon at 2:15. Thanks for your cooperation! It is very HELPFUL!"

This presented a problem. They couldn't enter the house with Little inside, in her condition. It was too late to call Kikki the Cat Sitter, not to mention Steve the Carpenter, whom I had had to hire again to repair the molding work he'd just done that Little had un-done while I was in Cannes. So I left a rather tense message on Bryce's voice mail, stating that 'tomorrow didn't work for me and that I did not want him showing the 'unit" when I was not at home. Period. It was still my home. The next day at work, my call sheet looked like this:

| DATE/TIME | CONTACT | NUMBER | MESSAGE |
|---|---|---|---|
| 5/29/00 8:45 a.m. | Dr. Niblack | 310-239-3838 | Re: Little's stitches removal? |
| 5/29/00 8:59 a.m. | Gwen / Animal Physical Therapy | 310-233-0945 | Recommended by Dr. Niblack; give her a call; 10% off for new clients. |
| 5/29/00 9:46 a.m. | Bryce / Coldwell Banker Real Estate | 323-312-2233 | There is a clause in your lease stating we may enter the unit at any time with 24 hrs notice. If you'd like me to call the current owner in Austria on her vacation and have her call you to clarify, I will do so. |

| DATE/TIME | CONTACT | NUMBER | MESSAGE |
|---|---|---|---|
| 5/29/00 11:30 a.m. | Powerful & Herb | Cell | "Holler back" about premiere. We have more names for the list. |
| 5/29/00 11:32 a.m. | Bonnie / *Playboy* | 310-766-0900 | Re: Danni Jones; plse call. |
| 5/29/00 12:12 p.m. | Steve the Carpenter | Cell | Can come fix the molding again after 11 a.m. Has to be done by 2 for breathing class. Plse call. |
| 5/29/00 12:13 p.m. | Eugene R. | No # | Is Danni Jones coming to my premiere or not? Thinks they should be photographed together. Plse call. |
| 5/29/00 12:35 p.m. | Tammy / *Larry King Live* | 404-233-0988 | Re: Danni Jones? Is she a good interview? Plse call. |
| 5/29/00 12:41 p.m. | Marcos | Home office | *Scarface* is on TNT tonight at 10 pm. |
| 5/29/00 12:49 p.m. | Bruce Martin / *Inside Edition* | 212-398-4848 | Re: Danni Jones. Plse call. |
| 5/29/00 12:49 p.m. | Bryce / Coldwell Banker | 323-312-2233 | There is an angry, sick cat in the house. |

| DATE/TIME | CONTACT | NUMBER | MESSAGE |
|-----------|---------|--------|---------|
| 5/29/00 1:09 p.m. | John Buttle / Court TV | 818-961-9000 | New show, *Celebrity Justice*. Re: Danni Jones interview? |
| 5/29/00 1:13 p.m. | Frank | Work | Want to come over for *Scarface*? |
| 5/29/00 1:23 p.m. | Joey Z. / Access Hollywood | 818-433-3948 | Re: Danni Jones—is she going to the *Shades of Gray* NY premiere? |

We arrived home that evening to find a cheery voice-mail message from Bryce that he and "Kitty" got along fine and that Bryce had "found the kitty kibble—boy she sure likes that!" (Which was strange, as the kibble was hidden in a bathroom cabinet.) Bryce's real-estate-agent-friendly voice added, "The appraisal is tomorrow and the inspection is Monday from two to six, so you should plan to be out of the house. Thanks!"

"How can they do this?" Molly cried. We were watching *Scarface* on TNT and eating dinner. It was the usual: hunks of Cabot cheese, sliced turkey breast, grapes and popcorn. But no bread, of course. Al Pacino and Michelle Pfeiffer had just made an awful scene in a fancy restaurant. He had pursued her relentlessly, killed her husband, and finally won her over and given her a tiger for a wedding gift. Now, years of cocaine-saturated marriage and millions later, they loathed each other. "They can't force us to be out of the house, can they?" Molly said despairingly.

"Well, I think they can strongly suggest we be out of the house. I'm going to be gone anyway, remember? I . . . have to go to New York."

I knew she did not remember and braced myself for the cold

front. "Why?" she demanded, watching Al Pacino get angrier and angrier.

"For the premiere of *Shades of Gray,* our other movie," I said evenly. "I told you I was going."

"Is this the one with Mike Tyson and Claudia Schiffer?" she asked nonchalantly.

"Yeah."

"Sounds like a winner," she huffed. On screen, the youthful, glamorous junkie Michelle left Al in the restaurant, hissing, "I'm leaving you!" as she stormed out.

"Hey. I don't make fun of your job." At UCLA Molly had to give blood to get comp time—four hours for a pint. Which seemed a morbid and fascist way to earn vacation days, but I didn't say that the day she came home faint and excited with purple gauze on her arm. I remembered to feel grateful for my job and its accompanying benefits.

"When are you coming back this time?" She was getting better at it, being alone. Maybe she wasn't even mad.

"Just a couple days," I said. I felt like getting on a plane about as much as I felt like moving out of the apartment. I turned back to the TV. Molly was watching but not hearing the movie. I sensed this. There was a thought waiting in her mouth, like a pregnant drop of water ready to leap from the faucet lip.

"Maybe I'll call Billy while you're away," she tested, eyes on Al and not me. We knew each other so well by now it was scary.

"I don't think he's right for you," I replied diplomatically as Al stumbled out of the restaurant with his henchmen.

"Lex, I'm finally making friends here and you're trying to tell me not to hang out with them!"

I took a deep breath. "Mol, Billy's great, but I just think you need to be careful about dating people who *(how to put it?)* don't have real jobs and want to be famous. It only leads to misery, believe me." She stiffened but said nothing. Now Al was on his own, and it was only a matter of time before he was gunned down in his own home, surrounded by the trappings of wealth, power, drugs, crime and the dead body of his little sister.

"Oh, it's OK for you to go out with Goombas who try to rape you in a locker room or creepy British men who *weigh* less than you, but I can't hang out with a nice guy who's a *friend* of yours?" she said angrily. The unhappy drawbacks of sharing details with your sister is that too often, it comes back to haunt you, usually in your own words.

"Fine. Do what you want," I said tiredly. "I'm not trying to tell you what to do, Molly, I just don't want to see you get hurt." This was true. She put down her glass forcefully.

"Well, what am I supposed to do while you're off jet-setting? Sit around here and be your caretaker?! You're not my mother! I have to have a life too, you know!" She got up and left the room. Little followed her. There was an empty moment that began to fill up with guilt, then she came back—to get the popcorn. Walked out again. Slammed her door. I was hurt and ashamed and knew she was right, but naturally, I wouldn't dream of following her to apologize.

The next morning I got home to find a brand-new molding on the door frame (again), an empty Evian bottle and a handwritten note from Steve the Carpenter.

Dear Alexis,
Thank you once again for the business, or maybe I should thank Little! 😊☺
Anyway, I think you're a nice person and maybe we can hang out sometime, that is of course if you don't have a boyfriend. If you do, keep my number in case he turns out to be a loser . . . just kidding. By the way, let me know if you need help moving. Thanks,
Steve

p.s. this time I gave you a discount!
p.p.s. I helped myself to your coffee! I hope you don't
mind.☺

Which was weird, as the only coffee I had was in the freezer, and he
would have had to grind the beans, take the coffeemaker from underneath the sink (had he searched for it?) and make himself a pot.
Unless he had just helped himself to some of the beans and left.
L.A. was so weird. But I had been asked out, and that felt nice.

Thanks to a fabulous party promoter named Sassa, there were
650 RSVPs for the New York premiere of *Shades of Gray,* which
was at a hot downtown club called The Place, which held 300
people. I got there early, after the movie started and before an un-
pleasant encounter with Farrah Fawcett not getting her seat and
Rudy Giuliani giving her his. Viv handled it. The very first person I saw when I entered The Place was not the owner, the head
bartender, or even Farrah Fawcett but David's brother, the older,
successful stockbroker. I was the head of publicity, I controlled
the guest list and the invites, even the RSVPs, and I could not
fathom how his name had possibly escaped me. But there he was,
ordering a dry martini at my bar at my party. I turned and decided
to wait for some of the 650 guests who did RSVP to come between
us. I was done with the relationship at last, but David's family
seemed to be stalking me. *Must be some sort of test,* I thought to myself. *I will not let this bother me. I am a professional, and this is my
event.*

Literally eighteen minutes into the party I was summoned to
the back by the New York City fire marshal, not the party's favorite
person. He was tough, cranky and professional. He wore a
starched white shirt with his badge pinned to his left breast, and
his face was like the road map to a forgotten cave somewhere in
Utah, his eyes pinions of steel.

"You. This is your party, right?" He reeked of stale tobacco and New York seen-it-all weariness.

"What seems to be the problem?" I asked crisply, knowing full well what the problem was.

He pointed to the front door, where Powerful's manager, Herb, was looking flustered and upset with three New York cops who must have been telling him the party was at capacity. Trouble seemed to be brewing, and I headed over. Herb saw me and launched "Lex, my people are out here on the *street!* They *need* to be inside! This shit ain't right!" All six-feet-seven of him was yelling, and it was still hard to hear him.

"Herb, calm down, we'll get them in," I said diplomatically, striding over to the side door, where Eugene R. was sizing up the coat check girl.

"Who *are* these *trendy motherfuckers* fillin' this place up when my people *is out there in the street* trying to get in like, like some, some smelly fucking immigrants *off the boat!* Lex!"

"I know. Herb, I feel you, but there are forty-three of them."

*I feel you?* I opened the door to peek out a crack and saw an angry mob of faces: black, white, hip, fat, fabulous, impatient, determined, incredulous, incensed. This was the worst thing to do in a situation like this (an overcrowded premiere at the hot club o the moment) because when the faces saw you they knew you had the authority to get them inside (if you really wanted to). The mob roared when it saw my staff badge, and I felt like Madonna's Evit on the balcony. Herb then threatened, "Lex, if my people can't get inside, we gonna storm the door."

*Brilliant idea, Herb, that will solve everything!* I didn't say. Instead I said, "Now hold on, Herb, calm down."

Eugene R. slithered over. "What seems to be the problem Herb? This lady giving you trouble?"

"My people are ON THE STREET!" His black face was getting red. It was true, his people were on the street, but they *shou have* gotten there on time. What I did not say was that the club's manager and Sassa—the promoter who was being paid by me—shouldn't have let all their stupid, sashaying Soho friends and models in before the people who were actually paying for the party got in. But the thing was, this was the hottest premiere we'd ever thrown. The photographers and crews were inside, which, sadly for Herb, was my chief concern. Oh, well. First world problems. The fire marshal headed right for us, toppling Brooke Shields's makeup artist's martini on the way.

I touched Herb's shoulder, trying to soothe him. "Everyone will get in, we just have to chill for a few minutes. If the fire marshal shuts us down, Herb, you and I and everyone in here will be out on the street. We have to just chill for a minute, OK?" I stared him directly in the eyes until he had no choice but to admit I was right.

"Don't make me play the race card, Blue Eyes, this shit ain't right," he warned.

"What're you gonna do, call Al Sharpton on me?" Perhaps that was overstepping. I thought of Kirk and decided that he must be responsible for my newfound boldness in dealing with temperamental talent. I suddenly wished Kirk was there. As it was, the press were all searching for Danni, who was also not there but hiding out quietly to ride out the media storm in Laurel Canyon with the safety of her skull bracelets, comic books, video games and some kind bud sent from a cousin in Vancouver.

Herb thought a moment. "Tell me how you gonna fix this and I will not tweak on you, Lex. You got thirty seconds."

"Let me go talk to the manager of the club; she probably has some pull with the cops." I retreated into the party depths, found the manager and the fire door, and let twenty of Herb's people in as I kicked twenty of the manager's friends out. Herb seemed grateful, so I handed him a bottle of Chivas and an empty table, and he kissed the top of my head.

"Thank you, Lex. It's nice to be treated like the talent."

Police and fire reinforcements showed up, and so, finally, did Ben Stiller, whom I was angry with. I had ordered a car for him to attend the screening—so he could work the press line, talk to *Entertainment Tonight* about Robert Downey Jr. being in jail, and participate in the photo op—and he hadn't shown up at the red carpet. He had chosen instead to just hit the party. For all I didn't know, he could have been at the hospital checking on a relative or doing charity work, but I didn't care because he hadn't worked the press line. It was my job to ensure that the stars in the movie worked the press line, and he hadn't done it. The limo and the $1,500 charge for his groomer had been a waste, a soil on my budget. Viv approached me in the back, sliding up in tight red leather pants. "Hey, you're really working the room tonight. What are you doing?"

"I'm sending every annoying, pushy photographer and camera crew here to Ben Stiller's table to invade his privacy. You?"

"Kicking the Hilton sisters out of the studio president's table. Then I was going to yell at the club owner for letting all her friends in before our executives, then there's the fire marshal and Powerful's angry cousin to deal with, and Eugene's hitting on all the waitresses, and after that the crab dip looked pretty inviting."

"I'll meet you there in five. David's fucking brother is here."

"What?" she whipped around. "Christ, his family gets around! You OK?" I nodded. "How did he get in?" she asked, dipping a finger into her apple martini.

"Probably the same way everyone did—stupid bimbo at the door." Wait, I was supposed to be in charge of the door.

"Don't worry about it," she said casually, reading my mind. "It's the hottest party in town, good job. Everyone's already forgotten that our other movies star is a potential lesbian who might have had sex with her stepbrother." She held up her martini and flipped her luscious, chemically straightened hair. We toasted. "Congrats, Lex. Like it or not, you are very good at what you do, my friend."

"Thanks, Viv. I know I am. And you know what?" She waited, taking another sugary apple sip as Eugene R. made his horny way toward us with an embarrassed-looking Tony Danza in tow. "That's all I want. It feels good. It really does. I love movies, and this . . ."—I looked around the room—"this job is what I want. At least for now."

She held up her glass again, the green liquid swilling about like a superhero's potion. "To having cool jobs," she laughed. "Speaking of which, do you want to come to Tim Gordon's MTV party on Thursday?"

"Who's Tim Gordon?" I asked, licking the rim of my toxic pear martini. Vodka in my veins felt good, warm, wholesome even, a sweet release.

"A Very Rich Man who's actually single, come to think of it. Producer. Did the Emmys and MTV Awards for the past three years," she said, glaring at Sassa, who was across the room getting Sarah Jessica Parker's digits. "He's a nice guy but he doesn't know anyone," she added.

"Always glad to help out a rich, single man in need," I quipped. "Speaking of which, there's P. Diddy. Didn't see him on the list either." I downed my drink, chewing on the pulpy fruit.

"He's a friend of Eugene's. They did some real estate deal together and now Eugene has somehow convinced him to finance his next movie . . . starring Danni," Viv said, squinting at them. Viv never wore her glasses to parties. "In fact . . . I think I'll go over and say hello." She vanished into a glittering black sea. I ordered another drink and decided that I should be happy. I had friends, I had interesting experiences, and I almost had enough money for a down payment on an apartment and all my vet bills. Almost.

When I was a kid in the seventies my parents used to have parties, back when all their friends were still alive and married and smoked. There were clambakes, neighborhood block parties, live bands, friends who sang Carole King tunes. I remember lying in bed, Molly in her crib next to me as the voices and the smoke and the Eagles and Chicago and the scent of Charlie drifted down the hall and into my room. I remember hearing laughing, whispers, hooting, talking, teasing . . . and I wondered, what are they talking about? What are they laughing about? What are they doing? Why do they gather like this? I knew it was some secret world for adults that I was not part of and could not understand. I wanted to run out and talk to them, see them, show them my stuffed animals, yet something told me this would be a violation of sorts. I sensed I might see something I shouldn't. Then I'd hear them go outside, bodies huddled in the bushes or on the front steps and other, stranger, smokier, tangier smells would drift up into my window. This talk was more hushed, more sensual, and I could feel then the quiet urgency of humans needing each other, and it scared me.

My cell phone buzzed. *Kirk.* I let it go to voice mail, savoring the taste of pear-flavored vodka and realizing I wasn't sure how I was going to handle whatever it was Kirk Olmstead had to say.

When I got home Molly had made signs from her and Little that said Welcome Home! and We Love You! and she'd hung them on the Coldwell Banker For Sale sign out front. There was a new CD by Billy on the living room table. Had she left it in such a conspicuous spot on purpose? Little was now through with all her medication, and the Poet Satellite collar had been retired. Even her fur was growing back, and she was eating like a pig. Other than a few new claw marks in the front door, she had behaved herself while I was away.

"How was Billy's CD party?" I asked Molly while dragging my behemoth suitcase down the hall.

"It was fun. I met a few people, and Frank and Sue were there. Sara-Anne and Richard broke up again, and I think Marcos is going to direct Billy's video."

"Billy's doing a video now?" I asked, surprised. Good for him. Maybe he would be a star, who knew.

I caught a thought in my throat, and Molly spotted it. "David wasn't there," she answered without my asking. I reached my room, grateful to be home. "How was the premiere?"

"Great. It was a huge success, actually. I mean, no one cured cancer or anything," I said, a little sheepishly.

"That's good. Did you get laid again?"

"Molly!"

"Sorry . . . resist, I could not . . . ," she admitted, laughing. "Anyway, Billy's party was great too. It was fun to be out again," she added, plopping on my bed. "I think I'm finally ready to socialize regularly."

"Well, good, because Viv got us invited to an MTV party!" I told her. "Next week is the Movie Awards, and the producer of the show is really cute. He's an old friend of Viv's from Orange County, and he's smart and funny and single, and he's having a viewing party . . ." I improvised quickly, wanting to capitalize on her social enthusiasm in case it was fleeting. No way was I going to this party alone.

"I don't have anything to wear to an MTV party!" she said excitedly.

"That doesn't matter. We're going. We need to start going out again. We haven't really gone out on the town together since the Golden Globes party!"

"Wow, you're right," she said slowly, almost nostalgically. "Remember that time we saw Steve Martin? Remember that red thing Elizabeth Hurley was wearing? Remember—"

"This one time, at band camp . . ." I recited the tired line from *American Pie* that was somehow still funny, and she laughed deeply, heartily. "The women in this house are going to start getting out! We're single and proud, *goddamit,*" I declared dramatically, zipping open my toilet kit, which was exploding with free soap, bath gel and shampoo from the New York hotel. Molly instantly began sorting the bath products. As if on cue, Little leaped onto the bed and sniffed the soap delicately before recoiling at the strong scent. "I think Little's finally better," I said proudly. She had her energy back, and her fur was on its way.

"She does look a lot better," agreed Molly. "Maybe she can go out again, too." I thought about this. Maybe Little's crisis was finally over. I picked her up, examining her wounds. Molly was encouraged. "Let's let her outside! Come on, she's been cooped up for so long!"

I ambled off the bed and walked to the kitchen. Molly followed, and Little was right behind. With great ceremony we opened the back door and Little to wander down the stairs, unsupervised, and enjoy the privileges of regular cat behavior. She looked at us disbelievingly and finally, after a few moments of deliberating, padded one step at a time onto the lawn, where she disappeared into the dark. We left the door open for her in case she had second thoughts.

# Twenty-Five

In the last scene of *The Way We Were,* the ever-politically active Katie (Barbra Streisand) is passing out flyers in front of the Plaza Hotel in New York. Then she sees him, exiting a limo—her Hubble (Robert Redford). Only he's not hers anymore, because everything came undone after their stint in L.A. and his tryst with a winsome goyenne who'd wanted him for years. But that's all in the past. "Your girl is lovely, Hubble," Barbra says of the replacement waiting by the car, and then she summons all her Yentyl courage to extend a social invitation . . . but he declines. He won't be *coming by later for a drink.* Whatever they had is gone, slipped into another dimension, farther than memory and deeper than pain, and the faintest reminder is unwelcome in the face of progress. You didn't think it would end that way, and that's what makes the movie great. The way they were has nothing to do with the way they are.

I got to my office, and Adriane mouthed the words "Conference Call" and pointed to the phone. The weekly PR conference call is a tradition in which all the VPs of Publicity for each Studio

Division spend a few moments justifying their jobs to other people at the studio who have no idea what they do all day, and the head of Corporate PR says things like "We need to be sure our ducks are in a row" and "Let's be sure we're not comparing apples and oranges" and "Let's leverage our key relationships" and "How can we optimize that effort?"

When it was my turn, I recounted our tales of success in Cannes and New York, and how *Portland Girls* would probably win a lot of awards next year, how Danni was on the "It" list despite our "Significant PR Obstacles," and Kirk was on the Hot list despite the muckraking about Danni's dating habits, and *Shades of Gray* was on the premiere party list of the week and both movies were on the Fall Preview list and our division finally made the Power list. As I was basking in all my PR glory, Adriane popped her stunning head into my office and held up a big Post-it.

### Dr. Niblack on line one

Adriane stood proxy for me on the conference call as I picked up the other phone in my office and pushed a button. "Dr. Niblack?"

"Well hello, Alexis," he said in a friendly but professional voice. "I don't mean to bother you at work, but we wanted to make sure you're bringing Little in for her suture removal and post-op exam?" I glanced under my desk, where Little was napping peacefully in a brand-new carrier.

"Yes, we'll be there. Noon, right?"

"Yes," he replied. I felt a strange hesitation on the line. "There's just one other thing . . ." My heart sank. Oh, no. Was he going to tell me he found something in her blood work? A shadow in her X-rays? Cancerous cells in the weed autopsy? Had my check bounced?

"There's something I'd like to discuss with you. For Little's benefit. Will you have a few extra minutes?" he asked and I didn't say anything, trying desperately to translate the meaning of his vague request. My throat went dry. "I know how busy you are, but I think you might be interested in this—"

"Sure," I answered quickly. "We'll see you at noon."

Dr. Niblack gave away nothing as he removed Little's stitches, took her temperature and refilled her antibiotics prescriptions. He went through all her vitals, mumbling, "Good . . . OK . . . excellent . . . normal . . ." as I studied the Cat Breeds from Around the World. He removed his stethoscope, folded it with a snap, and smiled a toothy, nerdy grin.

"Little's recovering nicely. Just keep her on her meds and make sure her wounds stay clean while they heal. I'll be right back," he said eagerly, adding, "I'd like you to meet someone." He disappeared through the examining room door. I braced myself for the appearance of an ASPCA officer as I read, *The Abyssinian is one of the oldest short-haired breeds . . .*

The door opened and Dr. Niblack appeared, holding a tiny ball of happy fur. Little stood at attention, and Dr. Niblack smiled warmly, extending his hand. In it was a tiny orange kitten. *"Mew!"*

"This is Edward, and he needs a home," Dr. Niblack explained. "And it seems to me," he continued without waiting for a response, "that if Little had some company, she might get into less trouble." The tiny ball of fur hurled itself at Little with joy and ricocheted off her leg, rolling on the table. Little swatted at it playfully, then began licking its head.

"Look at that, they get along already!" exclaimed Dr. Niblack.

I looked at the little kitten, and my heart melted. "Oh, I wish I could take him, but I can't have another cat, Dr. Niblack," I said sadly.

He looked hurt. "Why not? What's one more?"

"It's my building. They're selling it and, well, I'm not supposed to have any more pets. In fact, I probably have to move," I told him. Edward climbed on my arm, mewing excitedly while Little licked his back.

"Well," began Dr. Niblack, "if you have to move anyway, you need a place that accepts at least one cat, right?" he prodded. When had he learned to be charming, my weird vet? "I'd take him, but Paula and I have four between us as it is," he explained.

"I don't know," I said warily, but I was thinking about his line of reasoning, and he was right. Molly and I were probably moving anyway, and I certainly wasn't giving up Little after everything we'd been through. And she did need company, with Molly and me gone all day. Dr. Niblack sensed victory.

"Who named him Edward?" I asked.

"I did," he replied. *Edward Scissorhands* is one of my favorite movies," he admitted.

"Me too," I replied.

"Just be sure to bring him back in a couple weeks to be neutered, OK?" he asked, smiling.

I smiled back. "Will do," I promised. "Mew!" said Edward.

On the way home with Edward and Little sharing the new carrier, my cell phone exploded. I looked at the display: KIK. I didn't want to be coy or flirty anymore, but I could not avoid Kirk forever. "Hello?"

"Hi it's *me,* "he said.

"Very funny." I tried to control my stomach, which was doing somersaults at the sound of his voice.

"Where've you been hiding, Alexis? I feel like a skinny British producer the way you've been avoiding me—"

I took a deep breath. "Where are you now? Can you meet for a late lunch?"

Kirk was waiting at a table at Chin Chin when I walked in. I'd dropped Little and Edward off at home first. "I'm . . . just coming from an appointment. My cat was at the vet," I told him, sitting down. *Keep it professional,* I told myself. He looked great as usual, but he had returned to his roots. Old jeans, plain white shirt, work boots.

"I ordered a couple salads, I figured you were in a hurry," he said. "Thanks," I replied stiffly.

"What's wrong with your cat?" His compassionate, earnest tone invited the truth in everything.

I sighed, realizing I felt very tired. "She's had this terrible infection and had to have surgery, and it just kept coming back, but now she's OK. I think she is, anyway." I sipped my water.

"Well I'm sure you're doing everything you can for her, Manning. You take care of everyone except yourself better than anyone I know!"

I answered his pause for laughter by suddenly erupting into sobs. Where was this coming from? Something he'd said had hit a nerve, and now I couldn't stop. I felt helpless and pathetic. Other diners turned toward our table.

"Hey, sorry—hey, Alexis, what's going on?" he asked, concerned, but I just put my face in my hands and shook my head, battling for control. "Ahhh. This is about more than your cat—isn't it?" He touched my arm. "Alexis?" I tried to control myself, wondering absurdly why I was upset at all. Sometimes in the movies people cry without warning or explanation. Holly Hunter in *Broadcast News.* I'm sure there are tons more examples, but to be honest, I was done comparing my life to the movies. I was emotional and didn't need a reason. "You feel like talking? I'm an unemployed director, I got all day," Kirk said sweetly, sipping his iced tea in a calm manner that comforted me. So there at Chin Chin I told him the whole story, about David, about how I'd gotten engaged when I'd known I shouldn't have, about how I'd blamed him even though I'd known we hadn't been right for each other, about how I'd nagged David for spending so much money on Harve's treatment, about how I hadn't taken care of Little properly because I'd been so caught up in myself, how Molly had moved here and depended on me but I hadn't been there for her, how rudely I'd behaved in Cannes, how Molly and I were getting kicked out of our apartment and how I was a horrible, self-centered person, right down to the way I'd been avoiding him for the past two weeks. "And now I have a new kitten to take care of!" I exploded again.

"Hey, Manning, take it easy on yourself," he said sweetly. "I don't think you're a horrible person."

"You don't?" My voice was meek and pathetic, Meg Ryan in *When Harry Met Sally.* Meg Ryan in anything before she started playing crazy sluts.

"You may be a horrible one-night stand, but there are worse crimes," he chuckled, an infectious, cheerful sound, and I started giggling. Then I was giggling as hard as I'd been crying. "You OK?" he asked me, brushing the hair from my face. I collected my breath and nodded. Then Kirk said slowly, "Look Blue Eyes, things are not so bad. We haven't talked about our movie moment in Cannes."

"No, we haven't," I admitted, feeling my face get hot again.

Then he said slowly, "You want to go out to dinner with me? Just the two of us, a proper dinner date?"

The truth was that I did want to. When I thought about it, it occurred to me that I'd wanted that for months, since the first time I laid eyes on him at Sundance, since the first time he'd reminded me of . . . Andrew. But I needed time. I needed to be on my own for a while, relying on me and not a relationship. And there was something else I needed to do. . . .

"I'm, ah, waiting for you to answer, here. Just, uh, waiting like the shmuck in the date movie . . . Alexis." When I smiled but said nothing, he continued. "Um, so this is the part where the music swells and we cut to a montage of us on a date having, um, a really good time."

I collected myself before speaking. I knew what I had to say, hard as it was. I really liked him—but I had to spend some time dating casually. "I can't right now. I'm sorry, but I can't." I swallowed and told myself the truth. I wanted to be in control of my emotions and my life. I wanted to be responsible. I wanted to be a good pet owner and a good sister and, someday, a good girlfriend. That last one was down the road, after lots of rest stops and fresh fuel.

"Go ahead," he coaxed.

"I have a lot of things to take care of in my life and . . . I hope you can understand that I'd like to, but I can't right now. Maybe someday." I looked him in the eye and gave a courageous smile.

"I understand," he said after a while, and I could tell he meant it. There was a pause. "Well how about we go fishing sometime, then?" he asked, and I laughed.

"That would be great, I'd really like that," I admitted. There was an awkward silence as we each weighed whether to start a new conversation. "Sometimes, timing is everything," I finally said.

"Is that the new tagline for *Portland Girls?*" he asked. I thought about it. It actually wasn't bad. "Manning," Kirk said abruptly as the waitress brought our Chinese Chicken Salads.

"What?"

"I wanted to thank you."

"For what?" I asked.

"For everything, dumbass," he said. "For helping me, for Danni, for dealing with us and our little ah, secret, for tirelessly promoting the movie. I wanted you to know . . . that no matter what happens when the movie opens, I'm . . . grateful. You're a good person, and that's kind of rare in these parts." There was a pause as mutual gratitude filled the air.

"So are you," I said and mean it. "And I hope we'll be friends for a long time." And I kissed him on the cheek, which felt nice, and more importantly, sufficient.

\*    \*    \*

I sweated out Little and Edward's first full day alone together, which was also the first marketing meeting with the producers and director of our new movie, *Hub Caps,* which meant I was away from my desk for most of it. Ben Stiller was in the movie. So was Steve Martin. I returned to the office, and the phone sheet looked like this:

| DATE/TIME | CONTACT | NUMBER | MESSAGE |
|---|---|---|---|
| 6/04/00<br>1:30 p.m. | Molly | Work | Went home at lunch to check on Edward and Little—everything fine. |
| 6/04/00<br>2:01 p.m. | Bridget /<br>*Entertainment<br>Tonight* | 323-456-8909 | Wants Steve Martin for *Hub Caps;* what is release date? |
| 6/04/00<br>2:08 p.m. | Tracie<br>Johnson /<br>*Tonight Show* | 818-840-2000 | Need to review questions for Danni Jones appearance; review her outfit. Clip reel—do you have funny B-roll of her in Cannes? Will she talk about "It"? Also, let's talk about Ben Stiller and Steve Martin dates. |
| 6/04/00<br>3:20 p.m. | Dr. Niblack /<br>VCA Animal<br>Hospital | 310-234-9090 | Re: Appointment for Edward to be neutered. Please call. |

| DATE/TIME | CONTACT | NUMBER | MESSAGE |
|---|---|---|---|
| 6/04/00<br>3:30 p.m. | Mom | Home | How is Little? Are you coming for July 4? There are cheap flights. |
| 6/04/00<br>3:41 p.m. | Viv | Office | How did it go w/ *Hub Caps* team? Want to talk about revised release plan for *Shades of Gray* (we're limiting theaters). How's the cat? |
| 6/04/00<br><br><br><br>3:45 p.m. | Stu / *US Weekly* Photo Dept. | 212-484-1600 | Really want to use the shot of Danni kissing<br><br><br>Willem Dafoe in Cannes; heard you have it; can he get it? Is it approved? |
| 6/04/00<br>4:10 p.m. | Jon / British Producer (You met in Cannes?) | 011-44-207-324-7675 | Hello. Have a script for you to read; think it's right up your (division's) alley. May I send? |
| 6/04/00<br>4:11 p.m. | Marcos | Cell | Martin's in town. Do you want a 2nd chance tonight? (Ha Ha). If not, *Airplane* is on Comedy Central at 8. |

| DATE/TIME | CONTACT | NUMBER | MESSAGE |
|---|---|---|---|
| 6/04/00 4:15 p.m. | Sara-Anne | Home | How's the cat farm? Hope all's a-ok. Call when u get a chance. Spanish winemaker in town. Has a Mas Igneus Costers de Poboleda. |
| 6/04/00 4:28 p.m. | Dad | Home | Heard your cat is ok finally? Call back re: loan pre-approval process. Has some figures for you. |
| 6/04/00 5:08 p.m. | Lance / Commes Des Garcons | 212-767-0987 | We need the dress back. We've called 3x and if it's not here tomorrow you will be billed $4800. |

I was reviewing this call sheet, formulating a plan of attack for re-turning ALL my calls, when Adrienne Amtelled me: **Line 1: Bryce / Coldwell Banker.**

The young couple was coming to look at the house for the sec-ond time. They were serious. They wanted to know if we would terminate our lease early so they could move in if they gave us money. How soon could we be out? They wanted to live in the upper unit and rent out the lower unit. And they were wondering if the gate would be repaired. And the window screens? What time could they come? Would the cat with the tubes in it be there? Was there any way to arrange to have the mutilated cat absent for their next visit? I casually reminded Bryce that my lease was valid through June of next year. In my mind's eye I saw Jody replanting pansies and sweeping up after herself. I could not compete. We were going to have to move.

"You know, we'd really rather not move, we just got settled in," I said tightly to Bryce, as nicely as possible. Sensing my vulnerability, he countered with aggressive professionalism.

"Well! I guess *you'll* have to discuss that with the *new owners*, won't you! And now that you mention it, and I'm looking at your lease here, well, your sister is *not* on the lease," he huffed triumphantly, "which means you are in *violation* of said lease." The sentence snapped shut with an ominous air of insinuation. The eviction police couldn't be far behind.

"I had an arrangement with Agotha about my sister moving in!" I argued.

"Well, *unfortunately*, she's still *not* on the lease. Neither," he added joyfully, "is your *cat.*" Technically, this was true. David and Harve were still on the lease, because I hadn't bothered to take them off it when they finally left. Little and Molly were illegal squatters as far as Coldwell Banker was concerned. Forget about Edward. I couldn't believe we had to leave, and soon—all because I'd forgotten to revise the lease. If only there was some way Molly and I could seem like ideal tenants. If only I had Agotha's summer number in Austria. Fine, we'd move. We'd survived worse. It would be annoying and expensive, but no matter! Little had a new friend, and Molly and I had an MTV party to go to. Onward!

Tim Gordon was the cute producer of the MTV movie award show (Ben Stiller and Claudia Schiffer were both featured), and Molly and I had finally chosen outfits and strategically stuffed ourselves into my best leather and/or silk numbers to attend the afterparty at his house in Benedict Canyon. We stopped on the way for a bottle of champagne. We were grown-ups, going to a grown-up party. To flirt and be flirted with.

We pulled up and around and around the canyon, finally stopping at the house. Molly, speaking for both of us, just said, "Wow." It was a nice spread, a large, modern, box-type structure with huge windows, in a leafy neighborhood that was one big hill. A valet attendant took the VW away. We freshened our MAC lipstick and pushed up our Robinsons May push-up bras. Showtime for *Spinster, Spinster!*

Tim answered the door, and we both took a breath. He was a vision of American-middle-class-hit-the-Hollywood-Big-Time. A J.Crew model with a *Sports Illustrated* body with a big smile, successful career and tasteful interior design sense. He was tall and muscular and had great skin without being married *or* gay. His wavy black hair and green eyes were perfectly at home within his softly oval eyes and square jaw. Daniel Day Lewis meets Pete Sampras. He gave us each a friendly Hollywood kiss, cheek-aimed.

"Alexis, right? I heard about those blue eyes. And you must be Molly? Viv just called, she's coming later. Come in, come in, welcome!" he said invitingly, taking the champagne and directing us toward a huge outdoor patio and pool, which had two bars, staffed by about twenty professional caterers. There was enough food for all of the 310 area code. When would I learn? You don't bring food or alcohol to Hollywood parties. David and I had once gone to a party at his famous acting coach's house for the Tyson fight (the ear-biting one), and I'd brought a sourdough baguette and block of Brie, which had sat untouched in the corner as tray after tray of hot piping soul food had been delivered by the fanciest black-owned restaurant in town. *Your roots are showing*, Sara-Anne had teased me.

We walked through the spacious den and onto Tim's gorgeous patio and took in the view. Palms, eucalyptus trees, leafy shrubs, bougainvilleas, expansive pool with hand-cut rock wall fountain, etc. "I love your place, and for a straight man, you've done a great job decorating," I gushed as Tim handed me a Vodka Something from a passing tray. The help wore white jackets. Tim chuckled. Molly was strangely silent.

"Well, thanks, but it's my decorator, she did everything. I just told her what I like!" He smiled and didn't look around to see who else was there. His perfect teeth gleamed. Molly stepped on my toe.

I ignored this and kept smiling through my vodka. "So you must be quite relieved the show is over at last," I said, knowing how taxing awards shows could be. If only he would stand here all night. We didn't know anyone, and now that Viv was going to be late, we knew even fewer people. Molly cleared her throat in a supremely obvious way, trying to catch my eye.

"It is a lot of work, but I have a great team," Tim said modestly. Other women were arriving and seeking him. I searched for a line to keep the trite conversation afloat. "Geesh, the MTV Awards must be like, a regular movie premiere times fifty!" I agreed enthusiastically.

"Boy, you're not kidding," he chuckled. "I think we counted this morning, and between the whole staff we averaged four hours of sleep a night for the last three weeks!" He laughed and rubbed his eyes and touched his glass to mine. Molly jiggled my other elbow—what the hell was she doing? Someone called Tim from the kitchen. "Excuse me—I have to play host. Make yourselves at home," Tim said warmly, kindly, touching my shoulder and departing in a cloud of sexy-host maturity. Molly's tapping grew urgent.

"*What?*" I demanded, a little too loudly, turning to her.

"Don't look now, and don't get upset, but . . . David is here," she said quietly, not looking anywhere. I froze and tried to look absorbed.

"Where?" I whispered urgently, the color draining from my face.

"He's tending bar."

I raised my drink to my lips and peered through the top of the glass. There he was, by the potted palm with the twinkly pink lights at the corner of the waterfall by the pool, getting somebody a Perrier. Black T-shirt, muscular arms, that hair . . . those eyes of chocolate . . . he looked the same. I waited to see what I'd feel, allowing my emotional grid to process the connections. Curiosity . . . I was curious. That was all. It was weird.

"What do you want to do?" Molly asked. "Whatever you want to do, just let me know and I'll do it." We both decided to chug our drinks before deciding anything. Good-looking, accomplished, thin, well-dressed guests continued to arrive, not bringing anything.

As we saw it, there were three options. One: Leave. This was both immature and rude and, not to mention, cowardly—and it had the added unfortunate result of blowing anything with cute host Tim. Two: Stay and pretend not to see him. This was more immature and would be difficult and awkward. I was self-conscious enough as it was. Plus it would mean we couldn't drink anything all night, as he was the head bartender. Definitely out of the question. Three: Stay, walk over and say hello. After much ruminating and two more drinks (Tim got them), which had no effect, we approached the pool bar like Mel Gibson advancing toward the British general in *The Patriot*. Mature, civil, determined and confident. Resolute.

David saw me and assumed the expression of someone whose elevator cable had just snapped. "Hi," I said evenly.

He put down a lime wedge and stood up straight. Wiped his hands on his pants. Took a breath. "Hi," he said, in the voice of someone I used to know.

"How are you?" I could feel every fiber of my body shaking. It was like facing a ghost.

"I'm good, I'm good," he said, shifting his weight from one foot to the other and folding and unfolding a cocktail napkin over and over again, in the same way my grandfather did at the end of his life in the bleak light of his room in the nursing home, the simple repetition of something, the ability to control anything, even a paper napkin, preferable to the helplessness of that moment controlling you.

"So . . . how do you know Tim?" I asked. The Hollywood party opener line was lame, but the truth was I had nothing else to say. The truth was I didn't care how he was, or how he knew Tim. He was standing right there in front of me, and though I was shaking physically, I felt nothing emotionally. Actually, that is not totally accurate. I felt pity. Molly was by my side. We were guests. And he was a bartender.

"I got hooked up through my friend Jen," he said, nodding to another bartender. Jen was skinny, tattooed, blonde and cute. So what. She was a bartender. He'd met his match. "So, um, do you want a drink?" he shrugged and let out a yelp of a laugh. I couldn't tell if he was on the verge of laughter, tears, confession or something else.

Molly and I ordered water. I asked him about Harve and told him about Little's surgery and about adopting Edward. We couldn't really have a conversation, though, since he had to keep getting people drinks. Finally, we moved away and sat at the other end of the patio. Guests milled and stood between us and the bar, he poured drinks and we drank them, until we forgot he was there. We stayed at the party until Best Screen Kiss, and on the way out we took back our champagne bottle, went home, put on sweatpants and ordered a pizza. I didn't even mind when she called Billy and invited him over. He was at a fancy party too and just wanted to relax.

Standing on the front steps paying the pizza delivery man, I saw them. The Asian couple. They glanced up from their spousal shuffle, looked at the pizza box, and smiled warmly, silently. I thought of David, our years together, the breakup in Vermont, the struggles between our families, the bitterness, the pain, the denial and the healing. A stark and foreign feeling spread through me like a drug releasing a tightly wound affliction. Forgiveness.

And that was the end of the end.

"Do you want to go to the Cape for July 4?" called Molly from the computer room. She was getting her e-mail. The computer Mom and Dad had bought us was nice to have. I turned on the TV and plopped to the couch for Alex. The category was *It Came from the 80s.* "Mom wants to know if we're coming. John and the kids will be there. They're planning on, ah, christening the boat."

"Sure, why not?" I yelled. We were ready to face our family again; besides, it was the launch of a new season. I'd paid dearly for that stupid boat, and I was going to use it.

*"This 80s hit song warned 'don't turn around' because he was in town."*

"Do you want to check your e-mail?" she yelled. *"Who is der Kommisar?"* I said.

"What?"

"Yeah, I'll be right there." We traded places, Molly seated loyally in front of Alex and me in front of the computer our parents had bought us. The New Mail button was lit, but I no longer grew excited about that. Most likely it was another one of the many spams I received daily from veterinary clinics, animal hospitals, online pet stores, any number of animal organizations that now had my name and e-mail address, thanks to Little's escapades and adopting Edward. I was officially part of a new cat demo. I had two e-mails. The first one was from Agotha.

> Dear Alexsis-
> I am sorry to not be ableto return your calls as I am in the hospital. You see I am very ill and won't be coming back to the United States. I wanted to thank you for re-

pairing the molding in the apartment. My father put that molding on years ago when we came to the US and it was thoughtful of you to fix it so nice. I will try to help you stay in the apartment if I can. No one has this email address but you. But I want to tell you: This new buyer has a problem with financing, so you see the apartment is available again. You said you were look-ing to buy—are you pre-approved? That is what we need. Here is the name of my agent. He knows to wait to hear from you. Good luck. You were a good tenant, despite the rude man and the big dog and the sick cat. I am glad for you.
Kind regards
Agotha

Relief! The buyer's financing had fallen through. According to Dad, this was not uncommon. I had to act fast. I'd already begun the preapproval process, thanks to Dad's nagging, and tomorrow I'd call the agent. I typed a grateful thank-you to Agotha, realizing that I had misjudged her. She wasn't a horrible person. Turns out, nobody was. Except Joan Crawford.

I scrolled down to the next envelope. Who was sully@inter-link.net? I opened the e-mail. My heart shot up through my throat. It was Andrew. Andrew-high-school-heartbreaker-turned-trophy-home builder. He was finally answering my postcard from Cannes! What would he have to say?

hey lexy-
what a surprise to hear from you, glad your career is everything you dreamed it would be when you left town all those years ago! Saw your folks and they seem to be doing well. Yes I am quite busy building houses, I wouldn't call them trophy but they pay my

bills. Have been doing plenty of fishing; hiking, camping etc. but less and less traveling as work gets busy and clients get demanding. You wouldn't believe the aggravation one solar panel causes. speaking of travelling, any chance you'll be out here this summer? I just got a boat and it's getting sunny already. Guess you don't need sun though, eh? You live in California now, keep in touch. andrew

p.s. no I'm not married

"Mol!! Come here, quick!"

"Oh my God!" she said, reading. "He's so . . ."—she searched for a word—"honest."

"I know, I can't believe he wrote back!" I said. It was a great e-mail, full of information yet short and sweet, no pretensions, no competition, calm, confident, no-nonsense, no veiled irony. Pure Andrew.

"And," teased Molly, "he appears to be single. Hey, you can see him over July 4!"

*It Came from the 80's for $400 Alex . . .*

"You can do the 'meet for coffee' thing! That's safe! Or go out on his boat. Or *your* boat! Bet he'll be impressed you have a boat! That's platonic enough," Molly calculated quickly, sounding like an L.A. veteran of stealth dating.

"I don't know . . . ," I pondered. "It'd be weird to see him after all this time." Still, it was enticing. What had happened to Andrew Sullivan in the past ten years? What had he learned? What shape was his optimism in? I had to know what it would be like to see him again.

*This "colorful" performer claimed that girls just wanted to have fun . . .*

Molly, Little and Edward went back to *Jeopardy!* and I stared at the computer screen, searching for hidden meaning, clues, rereading every line until I was so exhausted I had to go to bed. I dreamed of Andrew and fishing. We were on a charter boat with Danni, Ben Stiller and Tim from the MTV party. Nobody caught anything.

Edward came home from being neutered on a Saturday. We drove to the hospital to get him, and I noticed the clinic had a new huge neon sign out front, like the Times Square billboard, only it was flashing messages about pet care and products they provided. *"Have your dog's teeth been cleaned lately?"* There was something wrong with this. They clearly made too much money.

As soon as we got him home he began frantically licking himself all over, meticulously self-cleansing, as if he couldn't escape the stench of the hospital fast enough. Little rushed over to him and began grooming him in earnest. I didn't have the heart to make things more difficult for both of them by administering the Poet Satellite collar.

We checked the messages, and Steve Martin's agent was trying to reach me. I erased the message dismissively and plopped on the couch. "Aren't you going to call that guy back?" asked Molly, flipping on *Entertainment Tonight* in time to catch Kirk and Danni's segment on making it in Hollywood. *Us Weekly* had just christened them both "Top 2000 Talent."

"I'm sure it can wait," I said absently. Things were back to the way they should be. We had a life together, my sister and me and Little and Edward.

"You should return his call at least . . ." Her tone was ominous.

"I will, Mol, eventually."

"You know, Lex, when you take care of things early on, they don't have a chance to snowball into larger problems," Molly said, like an older sister, or someone in successful therapy.

The phone rang before I could argue with her. It was Dr. Niblack calling to check on the cats. He assured me that Edward's frantic licking was normal and that there were no more foreign objects in Little's body cavity. I pictured Dr. Niblack as the tiny, odd Southern clairvoyant woman who emptied the house of ghosts in *Poltergiest. This cat . . . is clean.*

"I don't know how to thank you," I said, thinking, *Other than by giving you over two thousand dollars, I mean.*

"There's no need to thank me," he said humbly.

"You must get such satisfaction out of what you do," I told him.

He paused a moment, like he wasn't used to people being grateful on a post-op instruction call, then said thoughtfully, "Sometimes."

"You save people's pets!" I said, a little too loudly.

He laughed, a merry little sound of surprise. "She's a feisty one, your little cat. She's going to be just fine. It's always hard in the beginning with a complicated wound like that."

"Yes," I said. "It is."

# *epilogue*

## Independence Day, 2000

| DATE/TIME | CONTACT | NUMBER | MESSAGE |
|---|---|---|---|
| 70/04/00<br>3:15 a.m. | Eugene R. | No # | What can we do to make noise about the DVD release of *Shades of Gray*—great uncensored scenes of Robert Downey Jr., Brooke, etc. Plse call. |
| 7/04/00<br>9:09 a.m. | Viv | Office | Congrats on *Tonight Show*—Danni did GREAT—Keep fingers crossed for weekend numbers. Call when you can. Enjoy home. |

| DATE/TIME | CONTACT | NUMBER | MESSAGE |
| --- | --- | --- | --- |
| 7/04/00 9:13 a.m. | JoBeth / Letterman | 212-987-4433 | WHY can't we get Danni Jones?! Plse call. Dave is upset. Isn't she from NY? |
| 7/04/00 11:15 p.m. | Kirk | (on machine) | Come back—we miss you. Grosses for Friday so far are great. Have champagne on me! Bring back some fresh bluefish. |
| 7/06/00 9:45 a.m. | Beth / Corp. Comm. | x4533 | Need your approval on grosses and statement from studio re: success of *Portland Girls*—(gave o Viv). |
| 7/06/00 10:13 a.m. | Bridget / ET | 323-456-7812 | Is running top 5 movies this weekend—any new clips of Danni? (I sent). |
| 7/06/00 12:09 p.m. | Billy | At home | Is fixing boiler. Where is the gas valve? Also, Little has killed a mouse. What should he do with it? |

| DATE/TIME | CONTACT | NUMBER | MESSAGE |
|---|---|---|---|
| 7/06/00 12:30 p.m. | Marcos | Home | Need your address for the wedding invite—do you have a new address? Congrats on *Portland Girls*—can you get me a meeting w/ Danni Jones? (Just kidding) |
| 7/06/00 3:29 p.m. | Tom Striker / FKU PR Steve Martin's publicist | 310-976-1231 | Need to discuss tickets, travel, schedule for Toronto festival; Steve's groomer is faxing you an estimate; he travels w/ 5 people, plus me. |
| 7/06/00 4:00 p.m. | Danni | Home | Found the Commes des Garcons dress in her trunk—very sorry. It's dirty. She'll get it cleaned. |
| 7/06/00 4:40 p.m. | Leslie / Sunset Mortgage Co. | Office | Sending your tax documentation; no rush. Sign and send back when you return. Congrats. |
| 7/06/00 5:09 p.m. | Frank & Sue | | Saw *Portland Girls*—it's great. Congrats. |

| DATE/TIME | CONTACT | NUMBER | MESSAGE |
|-----------|---------|--------|---------|
| 7/07/00 8:08 a.m. | Sara-Anne | Home | Tell me about your fishing trip! Call when you can. p.s. broke up w/ Richard—he moved to NY. When are you having a house warming? Saving a '96 Altamura Cabernet Magnum for you. |

Adriane has, as always, faxed me my most recent call sheet, this time to my father's Paleolithic Age fax machine, which sits in my parents' attic. The New England weather is hot but not overly humid for the July 4 cookout at my parents' house on Cape Cod. For some reason, on the East Coast it is a cookout, not a barbecue, and everyone you invite not only shows up but also brings food involving mayonnaise, and no one is on their way somewhere else to be with other people who are better than you.

This is the first time the whole family has been together for a holiday since the disaster that was Christmas, and my parents, brother, and sister-in-law approach us with tentative encouragement. They cautiously broach conversation topics and personal borders, as if we have both recently survived quadruple bypass surgery. Even though this is not necessary anymore, we let them. Everyone congratulates me on the purchase of my new duplex in Miracle Mile, the result of my parents' help, an unexpectedly generous bonus from the studio for all my hard work over the last year, and having better credit rating than the original buyers. And on scoring our first tenant, the hot young musician Billy Brady, whose CD is climbing the charts while he lives underneath us and courts Molly. No one here knows that *Portland Girls* is the number one limited release movie for the weekend, outperforming *Accelerator*

*III, James Bond's Blonde Diaries* and *Mr. Toad's Princess* in its per screen average.

We brave the jetty beach, with its hot sand, crushed shells and piles of black seaweed, and sit staring out at the flat water. We return to fire up the grill, welcoming the peak of summer and christening a weekend of family togetherness that is bound to become annoying once the initial novelty wears off and everyone has eaten and drunk too much. My dad begs me to tell him "an exciting story from Cannes." I have none, except of course the one about the British producer I screwed and then kicked out of my hotel room, or about farting uncontrollably at our premiere, or crying in front of the *New York Times* film critic, so instead I try to re-create the scale and significance of the famed Hotel du Cap. He seems unmoved, so I attempt to describe how rude the French are and how impossible it is to get to dinner reservations before 10:00 p.m. and how none of the limo drivers know their way around and they wouldn't let our director wear sneakers to his screening. . . . He stares at me like I am speaking Japanese and so I hand him my photos, hoping he can work out a clearer picture for himself.

I settle quietly and comfortably into the hammock in the front yard of my parents' house on Shore Road, a haven from the world, a dreamy realm where no one knows quite yet who Danni Jones is or what the point of a groomer or a clip reel could be. *Portland Girls* opened well, and Danni kicked ass on the *Tonight Show*. She did not tell Jay Leno that everyone's dump smells the same, and he did not ask her if she was gay or sleeping with her brother—but I don't care because I am waiting to be picked up to go fishing. In my new boat.

"LEXY! Hey, Manning, are you coming or what?" The rough, sexy, maple-sugar voice is one I used to know. Andrew Sullivan is standing there outside his truck, fishing poles in his hands, straw hat on his head, guarded invitation in his eyes. It is like five days, and not ten years, have passed. In fact, I bet there are cold beers and cheese sandwiches and a map of the shoreline in the truck. He looks the same, mischief and irresistible charm lurking behind every inviting feature. Dirty blonde hair that's always a little too long, gray eyes that drown you. He's a grown-up now. A man. I struggle to remember why it had never worked out. Oh yes. We were younger. A lot younger than even the years between us would suggest.

"You're late, Sullivan," I say, hoisting myself from the hammock and giving my hair a toss.

"Where's your dad's boat?"

"The Sea Devil is *my* boat, and it's in the water. Isn't that where they keep boats these days?" He arches his eyebrow and gives it a twist, that old gesture that made me laugh so many times. "It's at the marina down the street," I admit as I fish the keys from my pocket and toss them to Andrew. He catches them without missing a beat, giving the studio logo key chain a glance. Then he looks back at me.

"You're not wearing those shoes, I'm assuming." He smiles that crooked smile, which hasn't changed a bit. Direct, uncomplicated, real. He tosses one of the rods at me. I catch it without hooking myself, but not without looking like I haven't handled a fishing rod in a long, long time.

"Nice catch. For a Hollywood chick," he flirts.

"Sometimes," I say, "timing is everything."

# Try these Downtown Press bestsellers on for size!

## American Girls About Town
Jennifer Weiner, Adriana Trigiani, Lauren Weisberger, and more!

Get ready to paint the town red, white, and blue!

## Luscious Lemon
Heather Swain

In life, there's always a twist!

## Why Not?
Shari Low

She should have looked before she leapt.

## Don't Even Think About It
Lauren Henderson

Three's company…Four's a crowd.

## Too Good to Be True
Sheila O'Flanagan

Sometimes all love needs is a wing and a prayer.

## In One Year and Out the Other
Cara Lockwood, Pamela Satran, and more

Out with the old, in with the new, and on with the party!

## Do You Come Here Often?
Alexandra Potter

Welcome back to Singleville: Population 1.

## The Velvet Rope
Brenda L. Thomas

Life is a party. But be careful who you invite…

## Hit Reply
Rocki St. Claire

What's worse than spam and scarier than getting a computer virus?
An Instant Message from the guy who got away…

Great storytelling just got a new address.

Look for them wherever books are sold or visit us online at www.downtownpress.com.